WHAT PEOPLE ARE SAYING ABOUT

the Promise Remains

*"A tender romance about unrequited love and second chances.
This story is fresh and full of surprises."*
ROMANTIC TIMES BOOKreviews MAGAZINE

*"Suspenseful and romantic . . . Readers encounter surprises
and heartache as the story moves through 12 years."*
CBA MARKETPLACE

*"A sweet love story of uncompromising faith, a rebellious heart,
and God who hears and answers prayers."*
FRANCINE RIVERS

*"Tender and touching, this aching love story is undergirded with characters
whose reliance on Christ is an inspiration. Heart-catching surprises and tearful
reunions will leave the reader filled with both hope and comfort.
An enchanting debut for Travis Thrasher."*
CATHERINE PALMER

WHAT PEOPLE ARE SAYING ABOUT

the Watermark

*"A beautiful, sometimes whimsical journey to faith as a man grapples
with feelings of unworthiness while learning that God has been there all along.
A highly recommended work from the author of* The Promise Remains.*"*
LIBRARY JOURNAL

"Don't start reading The Watermark *until you have a block of uninterrupted time
so you can savor each word of this finely crafted contemporary novel."*
MOODY MAGAZINE

*"Thrasher's novel is . . . told with intensity and passion.
This is good fiction that should find a wide readership."*
CBA MARKETPLACE

the *Promise Remains*

A COLLECTION OF LOVE STORIES

the *Watermark*

TRAVIS THRASHER

TYNDALE HOUSE PUBLISHERS, INC.
CAROL STREAM, ILLINOIS

Visit Tyndale's exciting Web site at www.tyndale.com

TYNDALE and Tyndale's quill logo are registered trademarks of Tyndale House Publishers, Inc.

The Promise Remains & The Watermark: A Collection of Love Stories

Designed by Jessie McGrath

This special edition, first printed in 2006, includes the following titles:

The Promise Remains

Designed by Timothy R. Botts

Edited by Anne Christian Buchanan

Scripture quotations are taken from the Holy Bible, New Living Translation, copyright © 1996. Used by permission of Tyndale House Publishers, Inc., Carol Stream, Illinois 60188. All rights reserved.

The Watermark

Designed by Julie Chen

Edited by Anne Christian Buchanan

Scripture taken from the New King James Version®. Copyright © 1982 by Thomas Nelson, Inc. Used by permission. All rights reserved.

This novel is a work of fiction. Names, characters, places, and incidents either are the product of the author's imagination or are used fictitiously. Any resemblance to actual events, locales, organizations, or persons living or dead is entirely coincidental and beyond the intent of either the author or publisher.

Library of Congress Cataloging-in-Publication Data

Thrasher, Travis, date.
    The promise remains ; & The watermark : a collection of love stories / Travis Thrasher.
       p. cm..
    ISBN-13: 978-1-4143-1506-5 (pbk.)
    ISBN-10: 1-4143-1506-6 (pbk.)
    I. Thrasher, Travis, date. Watermark. II. Title. III. Title: Watermark.
    PS3570.H6925P76 2006
    813′6—dc22   2006026991

Printed in the United States of America

12 11 10 09 08 07 06
7   6   5   4   3   2   1

the Promise Remains

A NOVELLA BY

TRAVIS THRASHER

To the sweet and adorable girl
who asked me to be her partner
in our high school play and who has
remained by my side ever since.
I love you, Sharon.

Acknowledgments

With special thanks:

To my parents, for loving and encouraging me. To my sister, for putting up with me. To Ron Beers, for seeing so much potential not only in a novel but also in a crazy kid he hired. To Anne Goldsmith, for your honesty and encouragement regarding my writing career. To Anne Christian Buchanan, for making this story as good as it could be. To Francine Rivers, for telling me to write the story in my heart. To Jerry Jenkins, for your insight, encouragement, and friendship. To Catherine Palmer, for never once doubting this would happen. To the Macks, Odells, Pehrsons, and Swobodas, for your loving prayers. And finally, to anyone anywhere who ever listened to my dreams from third grade on—well, you're holding one of them in your hands.

Love never gives up, never loses faith, is always hopeful, and endures through every circumstance. 1 CORINTHIANS 13:7

Prologue

THE YOUNG WOMAN stood on the deck of the log cabin, looking into the tear-filled eyes of the man she loved. The normal mixture of mischievous charm and boyish confidence was gone. In its place lay emptiness and defeat.

All because of her.

The pain in his face caused an answering wrench in her heart. Yet she still couldn't utter a single word in response to his question.

He countered her silence by asking again, this time with more urgency, "Will you marry me?"

Words she had waited a lifetime to hear. A question she had prayed would one day come.

Another suffocating moment passed. Finally, she gasped her answer. "I can't."

With the simple utterance of two seemingly insignificant words, all the hope and longing held in her heart vanished. The memories forged by years of dreams meant nothing now. Just like that, it was over.

Snow began to fall, reminding her of where she was.

I can't believe I'm doing this, she thought. *Dear Father, please forgive me for hurting him. You know I don't want to hurt him.*

"There has to be a way," he said. "I don't understand."

"No—"

"I'll give you time to think. Maybe all you need is time."

"I've had time," she replied. "I'm sorry."

"This can't be happening," he said. "Not like this. Not now."

She stopped herself from apologizing again. "I don't know what else to say."

"Say anything except no. Say there's a chance. There has to be, right? Say something. Give me some bit of hope."

"I don't know."

He choked her name out. "There has to be a chance. All these years. You know how I feel, and I know—at least I thought I knew—how you feel."

"You do," she said, afraid of what he would say next.

"Then why? Why are you doing this?"

"I've explained it to you."

"There has to be another reason. Something that makes better sense. Tell me you don't like my sense of humor. Or the way I dress. Or something like that. Give me something that makes sense."

"I just—" And then came her tears.

"Oh, man, I'm sorry," he said, his hands cupping hers. "I didn't mean to say all that. I'm sorry. Please, don't look away."

When she glanced up again, she marveled that his smile looked as warm now as it had when she first met him. Even years later, she could still remember it—the carefree and engaging grin that had captivated her. The smile that could still appear anytime she closed her eyes in the midst of life's little problems.

But this was not one of life's little problems; this was her whole life. Her whole life shattering before her very eyes.

"I'm sorry," he said again. "I shouldn't go on like this—I'm just making it harder for you. I do respect your convictions—that's one of the reasons I love you so much. I just don't know how to . . . well, I know this sounds corny, but I don't know how to let you go."

Her tears began to fall faster now, and she knew she was losing control. She didn't want to cry—not this way, not if they were saying their final good-byes.

"I'm trying to think of something more to say than sorry," she said.

"You don't have to. I just want to hold you and tell you I love you."

How can you? she asked herself. *How can you say those things after what I'm doing to you?*

As she embraced him, she searched for the right thing to say. There were so many words she wanted to utter, so much of her soul she needed to bare. But the words failed her.

"I'm never going to stop loving you," he whispered in her ear. "I promise you with everything I have and everything I am that my love for you will never die."

How can you say that? her mind screamed. *How can you even dare make such a promise?*

She knew if she didn't leave soon, her resolve would weaken. She would retract her words and reaffirm her undying love, only to resume the battle of heart and mind that had brought her to this point in the first place.

"I have to go," she said, pulling away from him. "The storm——"

"I know."

She took a few steps away from him, then turned. "I'm going to make a promise to you, too," she declared. "I'm never giving up on you. Every night I'm going to pray that you find your place in this world, that you find hope."

"I've already found my place," he replied, wiping his eyes. "It's by your side."

I know, she thought as she carefully stepped down the snowcapped steps leading off the deck. *God, why does this have to feel so wrong—when I know I'm doing the right thing?*

The word *promise* seemed to echo off the surrounding snowbanks.

"Don't forget this," he called out behind her. She turned again. He was following her down the steps, holding out something in his hand.

"No, I can't. Seriously . . ."

"Please take it," he said as he wrapped her hand around the small case. "I don't want it. It's yours. You're the only one it can ever belong to."

She walked toward her car, urging her feet and her heart not to turn back. Her fingers still clutched the little box she just couldn't open. She knew it held a ring.

Will I ever be able to look at it? God, will you ever give me the chance to?

"Don't forget me," his voice rose over the howling winds.

With a turbulent heart that mirrored the approaching storm, she believed they would be the last words she would ever hear him say.

THE PROMISE REMAINS

PART ONE

Where can I begin?

Secrets

SARA ANTHONY opened her eyes and wondered where she was. After glancing around the room for a few minutes, she saw a card propped open on the nightstand next to her and then remembered.

It's been a long time since I woke up in my old bed.

Actually, it had been exactly a year since she had last spent the night at her parents' house. Exactly a year since she had taken her mother's suggestion of sleeping over, even though her town home was only twenty minutes away. Mom had asked her again this year, and Sara had found no reason to refuse. In fact, she enjoyed this new tradition of spending the night before her birthday with her parents.

Her birthday . . . *Can I really be thirty years old?* she asked herself. *I don't feel like I'm thirty.*

The date told her otherwise: June 11. Sara rubbed her 8:30 A.M. eyes and read the card.

To Our Beloved Daughter
No matter how old you are,
you'll always be our little girl.
Happy Birthday.

Her mother had signed the bottom of the card.

"Sara: We are so proud of you. You are such a blessing to both of us. We love you. Mom and Dad"

Carrying the card, Sara padded sleepily downstairs, where the scent of Mom's breakfast and Dad's coffee greeted her. Before even asking she knew the flavors of the day: blueberry pancakes, her favorite, and hazelnut-blend coffee. Birthday-morning pancakes and coffee were an Anthony household tradition.

"It's the birthday girl." Her dad sat at the table, smiling over the sports pages of the *Atlanta Constitution*.

"Happy birthday, dear," her mom added, following her greeting with a hug.

"Thanks. And thanks for the card. But I've got to tell you—I'm still in denial about this birthday stuff. So I'm going to try to enjoy some of this beautiful day without being depressed."

Sara poured herself a cup of coffee—she owed her caffeine habit to her father—and sat down at the table.

"There is nothing depressing about having a birthday," Mom stated in her firmest, most optimistic voice.

"Unless you're turning thirty," Sara said, a bit of sharpness in her morning voice.

"What's wrong with thirty?" her father asked.

"Nothing if you're married and have a family. But for us single ladies—"

"Who's single?"

She looked at her dad and smiled. "Okay, not single. But unmarried. Not that I'm rushing to get married or anything, but still . . ."

"Your time will come."

"I know. It probably will. But I always thought I'd have a family by thirty. It was one of those unspoken goals."

"I always wanted to climb Mt. Everest by the time I was thirty."

"I didn't know you were a climber," Sara said to her father.

"Well, I'm not. But you know, that was one of my unspoken goals. Just because you have them doesn't mean you actually have to fulfill them."

Sara glanced at her mother and was surprised at her silence. Sara's unmarried state was one of Lila Anthony's favorite topics of speculation.

But maybe she was deliberately biting her tongue in honor of the day, Sara reflected gratefully.

"Breakfast smells great, Mom."

"It's your favorite—blueberry pancakes. Your father has been nagging me to make them for several weeks now."

"I have not," he said, winking at Sara. "I'm fully content with my usual bagel every morning."

Sara leaned back in her chair and sipped her coffee.

"I'm really tired this morning," she told her parents. "I don't know why."

"You're an old lady now," her father said with a laugh.

"What time did you go to bed last night?" Mom asked in a statement that really meant *What time did Bruce leave?*

"About eleven or so," Sara replied. She did not explain further.

"How's Bruce doing?"

"Good, as always. We just went to a movie." Sara proceeded to describe the film, carefully avoiding any further mention of Bruce, dating, marriage, family . . . or any other subject her mother might pounce on.

Being the only child had many benefits, Sara realized, but sometimes she wished she had a younger brother or sister. Then maybe she wouldn't be so pampered, so cared about, so *scrutinized*. She loved her parents and felt a close bond with each of them. Yet sometimes they still treated her like a little girl instead of a twenty-nine-year-old woman.

Make that thirty-year-old, she thought with a sick feeling. *Thirty years old, and I'm still here being babied and questioned.* She thought of the birthday card: *You'll always be our little girl.*

She sighed. But then she looked over at the large stacks of delicious pancakes and told herself she really couldn't complain.

Her mother served the pancakes, starting off with the stack that held the lit candle.

"Mom," Sara said, rolling her eyes. "Please." But she had to smile.

"Now we all have to sing."

And as the three of them sang the corny tune of "Happy Birthday," Sara felt her morning mood lift. She found herself thanking God—not only for having another birthday, but for having such loving parents.

⚜

Sara shifted to fifth gear as she accelerated five miles above the speed limit
on the highway connecting her parents' neighborhood of Groveton,
Georgia, to her town home in Rex. The white Toyota convertible she
drove was her birthday present—a present from her parents, who had
helped on the down payment—and from herself. It had only two hundred
and twenty miles on it so far, and the new-car smell from the leather seats
filled her with delight. It was the first brand-new car she had ever
owned—an unaccustomed luxury. Sara hardly ever bought herself anything except the basic necessities and an occasional outfit for school. But
outfits that would become stained with paint and chocolate and markers
as she taught kindergarten were necessities, too. The car was a bit extrav-
agant, but she figured she would only turn thirty once. Besides, she was
thinking that it was time she made some changes in her life. She had been
in a holding pattern way too long.

Wind whipped her long bangs across her sunglasses. She listened to a
combination of her favorite CDs as she drove past kudzu-covered walls
edging the freeway. The Atlanta skyline could be seen in the distance on
her left, but today she ignored it entirely. Something about the clear and
beautiful summer day made her unaccountably sad.

Sara had lived in the town of Rex since moving into her town home five
years ago. She liked having a place she could call her own while still being
close enough to visit her parents. She enjoyed her job as a kindergarten
teacher at a public grade school only minutes away from home. She also
loved the summertime break, when she became more involved with min-
istries in her church and with the friends in her small group.

Her father, Daniel Anthony, managed the computer technical-services
division at a business in downtown Atlanta. He had worked there ever
since the move to Georgia during Sara's college years.

The move. The dreaded move. They had lived at the end of Herrington
Lane in Groveton for the last ten years. The move from the small town
of Maryville, Tennessee, had taken place just before Sara's twentieth
birthday. Even after ten years, Sara still did not consider Georgia her
home. Home would always be where she had left a part of her heart. She

understood the opportunity the job had offered her father and their family, but the memories of the Smoky Mountains still brought an ache deep inside her, reminding her of a monumental loss in her life.

A loss her parents would never know about.

Sara thought about her mother and dad. She knew they looked forward to the one day she would walk down the aisle and say "I do" to the man of her dreams. Why wouldn't they eagerly await that moment? Sara certainly did.

I never thought I'd wake up alone on the day I turned thirty.

Sara knew that her sociable, energetic mother was disappointed that her one and only child was still unwed. Lila was one of those dynamic, take-charge women who liked to do things right, and Sara's unmarried state seemed to make her mother feel strangely incomplete. Besides, Lila positively salivated at the prospect of planning a big, beautiful wedding, and she couldn't wait for grandchildren. She had talked more and more about marriage as time passed—especially since Bruce had come on the scene.

But Sara found herself hesitant to think about the M-word. Yes, she did want to get married, but she didn't feel as ready as her mother wanted her to be. And yes, she cared deeply for her boyfriend, Bruce Erickson. But marriage was such a big step. Such an incredible commitment. One Sara had not wanted to face the last couple of years.

In her mother's eyes, Sara and Bruce were more than ready. Sara knew her mother was already collecting brides' magazines and browsing in wedding shops.

Could she ever be like her mother? The two of them certainly looked alike—both small and dark—but her mother carried an air of sophistication and confidence Sara knew she could never carry off. Everything about Lila Anthony was organized, structured, efficient. And while Sara had many of these traits as well, she lacked her mother's energy and drive. When it came to personality, she definitely took after her soft-spoken father.

Both of them loved her so much and only wanted what was best for her. *What is best for me, Lord? Why do I dread getting married like it was some sort of disease?*

She drove on, the late-morning sun bearing down on her and reminding her of past years when she didn't have a care in the world. Those memories

used to encourage her. Now they only served as reminders of just how
much she had failed.

⚜

Sara heard the cordless phone ringing but couldn't find it. It took her five
rings to finally locate it underneath a small sofa cushion in her living room.

"Hello?" Sara asked in a tone that said, *You'd better not be selling anything.*

"Happy birthday, little lady."

"Hi, Bruce," she said, a smile coming over her lips.

"Has it been a good one so far?"

"Well, besides the fact that I'm thirty—yeah, I guess it has been."

"How's the new car?" Bruce asked her.

"Still as nice as it was when I drove you around."

"You want to drive tonight?"

"Sure. Where are we going?"

"It's a surprise. I just wanted to call and tell you I'm heading over—I'll
be there in fifteen minutes. Is that okay?"

"Yeah, sounds great."

"See you soon."

Sara clicked off the phone and carried it to her bedroom. The alarm
clock on her nightstand informed her that it was 6:45 P.M. Sara knew that
meant Bruce would be knocking on her door at exactly 7:00.

Slightly flustered, she rummaged through a dresser drawer for a black
slip. She usually ran a little late whenever she went out. Bruce, on the
other hand, always arrived on time. Always. Sometimes it was scary how
prompt he was. It was as though he sat outside the house waiting to hear
his stopwatch go off.

But that's a silly thing to complain about—promptness, she told herself. *This
birthday just has me in a bad mood. There's nothing wrong with being dependable.
Nothing wrong with Bruce. He's a good guy.*

Bruce Erickson had first asked Sara out two years ago after a Sunday
evening service at church. They had met in the singles' Sunday school
class. But unlike many other women in that group, Sara wasn't looking
for a boyfriend or a husband. She wanted Christian friends, male and
female, and had decided that church would be a good place to find them.

So when Bruce asked her out that first time, Sara told him no. She didn't lie to him or come up with some excuse. She simply told him that at the moment she wasn't ready to date. Bruce never asked her why but simply said okay and tried again two weeks later. Sara said yes that time, figuring it would be no big deal. An actual date with a decent guy might be nice for a change.

After several dates with him, Sara began to enjoy his company. It had been a while since she had gone out with anyone, and Bruce was charming and likable. He was confident and extroverted, never letting the conversation drag or halt, but he was also genuinely interested in Sara. In fact, she could remember him mentioning the L-word on their fourth date. She hadn't said anything in response. It wasn't that she could never love him, but she just wasn't there yet. She wanted to take things slow.

Her mother, of course, had other assumptions. "I just adore him. Don't you?" she asked Sara one day when they met for lunch.

"He's a nice guy," Sara replied with a casual shrug.

"Well, he's certainly handsome, too. Not too tall, nice dark hair— looks perfect alongside you."

"Mom—"

"Honey, you've gone out several times now. Don't you think you should at least have him over for dinner?"

"I probably will. Just not yet."

Mom shook her head. "Why do you have this aversion to fine young men?"

That statement had hurt. Sara had looked at her mother's determined face and had almost begun to cry. Obviously her mother only wanted the best for her, but was Bruce necessarily the best?

"I'll call him, all right? I just don't have time this week."

"I just don't understand you sometimes, Sara." Her mother had walked to the ladies' room and left Sara sitting at the table, wishing she had never introduced her to Bruce.

That was the beginning of it all, the start of The Issue. The dating, marriage, family issue.

Sara could never explain it to her parents—that, as seemingly perfect as Bruce was, something wasn't there. Or more accurately, however perfect Bruce might be, he could never be someone else. That was the real problem.

And yet, for two whole years now she and Bruce had been dating, and they had even become what her mother called "an item." It was almost inevitable, when you thought about it. Dating for two years? Obviously, that was serious. With Sara and Bruce both being thirty? That was serious with a ton of implications to it. But Sara didn't like thinking about those implications—about things like the M-word, meaning marriage. Most of the time she managed to put the possibility completely out of her mind and just enjoy the simple dates and the nice friendship she had with Bruce.

Simple. Nice. Two words she thought about a lot in regard to Bruce. Maybe there's nothing wrong with settling for *simple* and *nice*.

The doorbell rang at exactly 6:59. Perfect timing as usual.

As Sara headed to the front door in her favorite black dress, she got the same feeling she always got before seeing Bruce. She couldn't describe it. It was neither good nor bad. It was . . . something.

The words resonated: *Simple. Nice. Simple. Nice.* Then she chided herself. *Sara, you've got to snap out of this. Bruce is a great guy, and you know it. What's your problem, anyway?*

But she knew what her problem was.

She hesitated before opening the door. Yes, she knew why she hadn't fallen under the spell of Bruce the way so many others had. Others like her mother, who obviously couldn't wait for Sara to walk down the church aisle.

Her nose wrinkled in annoyance. What was the big hurry, anyway? she wondered. Why couldn't anyone be patient and understand?

Nobody understood because nobody knew.

Sara opened the front door to the familiar handsome face. "Hi," was all she managed to say.

Bruce looked at her and grinned. With a flourish he presented her with a single rose. "You look beautiful tonight. Happy birthday."

"Thanks."

Sara could hear her mother saying, "What a marvelous flower, Bruce." Sara found it ironic and even a bit sad that her mother was more impressed with Bruce than she was. Perhaps mothers were just that way. Bruce always said the right things to her mother. Then again, Bruce usually said the right things to everyone, including Sara. And she couldn't help but enjoy the compliments Bruce always gave her.

They went out to their favorite restaurant, an Italian place called Salvatore's. The restaurant was small and exclusive, and Bruce loved going there. Sara did love the food, but she always found the prices ridiculous. They had actually gone to Salvatore's for their first date. Sara had been a little overwhelmed.

"This is really expensive," Sara had said, looking at a simple bowl of pasta that cost more than thirty dollars.

But Bruce had told her she deserved a nice dinner like this. The fact of the matter was that Bruce owned a successful business employing about fifty people. He could afford thirty-five-dollar plates of pasta—and he told her exactly that. Modesty was not one of Bruce's strong points.

They sat at a small booth off to the side of the restaurant. Soft, romantic music floated around them as usual, yet something was different this night. Sara looked around. There didn't seem to be any other diners in the restaurant. She couldn't be certain at first, but after their meals arrived she could see that they were indeed alone, and she commented on it.

"That is odd, huh?" Bruce said, quickly changing the subject.

This was the first moment Sara suspected something was up, and she began to get a queasy feeling in the pit of her stomach. But Bruce said nothing, so she did her best to push her nervousness aside. What was she worried about anyway? Bruce was probably just planning one of his little expensive gestures—a birthday surprise. It couldn't be that bad. It would be nice, she told herself.

It happened after dessert. She ordered her favorite, of course—a slice of rich chocolate cheesecake. She ate it while Bruce drank his coffee. He almost never ate dessert.

"Sara, I've got a surprise for you," Bruce began, scaring Sara even more. "I arranged to have this restaurant all to ourselves."

"You what?" Sara asked with disbelief.

"This was the place we first came two years ago, when I barely knew your name yet was already in love with you. That's why I would like to do this here."

The waitress came out at that time. She presented Bruce with the bill and Sara with a gray suede box on a porcelain platter. Now Sara knew where this was headed, and all she could think about was escape. *Run,* Sara thought. *Run now, and don't look back.*

"Sara, would you please open that box?" he was saying as he put a hand on hers.

He really does love me, Sara told herself. *Do I deserve that love?*

She looked at Bruce and he smiled. His smile made her feel a little better. But her hands still shook as she opened the box to find an exquisite diamond solitaire in a platinum setting.

"Sara Anthony, I have been in love with you for the last couple of years. You know I have dreamt of spending the rest of my life with you. I can't wait any longer. Sara, will you marry me?"

Sara looked down at the sparkling stone and began crying uncontrollably. Of course, an elated Bruce came to her side and took her hand.

"It's okay, it's okay, you don't have to cry," he whispered to her. "I understand. I know you're happy."

But Sara continued to cry. Bruce *didn't* understand. How could he? She barely understood herself.

After a few minutes, she finally managed to control her sobs. Through tear-blurred eyes she saw Bruce kneeling on one knee beside her.

"I'm happy too," he said. "I love you, Sara."

She felt like she might faint any second. *I knew this was coming. But I still don't know what to do. What do I say now?*

"Well," he was asking her, "what do you say?" Strange how he could read her thoughts without having a clue as to what was in her heart.

As if you ever really gave him a chance, she reproached herself once more. Sara took a deep breath and looked at the ring again, then at his happy, eager face.

Bruce loved her, she knew he did. And they were a good match, she had to admit. They could have a good life. Maybe it was time to stop holding out for something that would never happen. All those hopes and dreams— it was ridiculous to hang on to them for so many years. Something like this, someone like Bruce, might not come again. She had to face reality. And really, it probably wouldn't be so bad. Surely you could learn to love almost anybody . . . and Bruce was not so hard to love.

So with tears of regret that Bruce could not distinguish from those of joy, Sara nodded and spoke a word she didn't want to say but felt afraid not to: "Yes."

⚜

To Sara, the evening felt unbearably long, as if she were driving through a deep tunnel with her car lights turned off and the headlights from passing vehicles blinding her. After the proposal in Salvatore's, Bruce took Sara by his parents' house, then to her parents' house to make the grand announcements. Everyone gave them big hugs; the mothers cried, and Bruce's younger sisters all cried and jumped for joy. Sara's mom almost broke down in glorious shock. And Sara, caught up in the excitement, had almost convinced herself it was going to work.

When it was all over around midnight, Bruce gave Sara a tender farewell kiss at the door of her town home.

"I love you, Sara," he said. "We're going to be so happy."

Sara smiled up at him. "We *will* be happy," she replied firmly, and almost believed it herself.

But as she walked to her bedroom, Sara didn't believe her own words. Would they be happy? Would she? Could she be happy with Bruce? Could she ever learn to say the word, the L-word, to him and believe it in her heart?

That was when Sara broke down once again. She examined the ring on her shaking hand and started to cry. *Dear God,* she thought. *What have I done?*

Alone in her bedroom, she could hear the late-night sounds of crickets and cars even through the locked windows. *I shouldn't feel sad, Lord. There's no reason I should.*

The diamond glimmered in the dim light. Sara had always believed a ring like that would mean so much. Now, wearing it felt empty and even wrong.

Forgive me, Lord. I don't know what to think anymore.

For a few minutes she continued to weep, crying desperate tears only God above saw. When she regained her composure, Sara rose and went to her closet. She opened the door and began to rummage around. It took her a while to find what she was looking for.

The shoe box was hidden in a larger box of school memorabilia and old childhood toys that was stuck in the corner of the closet. It had been literally years since she had opened it, but tonight she had to.

Inside the shoe box lay the contents of a life nobody knew about except Sara and one other. Contents of a love and a dream she had held in her heart for so many years. Now that love and those dreams could officially be considered over. She had waited so long for something that wasn't meant to be.

Letters, dozens of them, were bound with a crumbling rubber band. Several trinkets lay beside them—a necklace, a small leather band, a ridiculous pink heart. An envelope full of photos lay inside as well. Not many photos, but enough to stir the hope that had never really left her.

And, of course, the small, square case. She couldn't open it. Not yet. Not now. Not ever.

"I have trusted you, Lord," Sara prayed. "I have remained faithful to my word all these years. So why do I feel so horrible now? Why are you allowing these feelings to remain inside me? Why can't I move on and forget about him?"

She began sorting through the envelopes. Already, tears filled her eyes. How long had it been? How many years? How many lifetimes? How many nights had she dreamed for nothing? How many summer evenings had felt so bland because of remembered nights—remembered promises?

How many prayers had there been? So many—too many to count. "Give me peace, Lord," she whispered.

The letters were as she had left them long ago—in the order she had received them. There were so many.

On the night of her thirtieth birthday and her engagement, Sara Anthony felt miserable. Why did she always do this to herself? Why did she feel more lonely now than ever before?

Because you're angry, a voice inside her said. *You're angry at the one whom you've been praying to for years, praying daily for one thing. You're frustrated because those prayers have gone unanswered.*

But why? Why had those prayers seemingly gone unnoticed? Sara had searched her heart and her motives when praying. Perhaps she had fallen away from God's will in her life and didn't know it. She could remember the way she had been in grade school and high school—so sure of her faith, so on fire for the Lord. She had never felt lonely or empty then. Certainly there had been times when growing up hurt, but she had always been able to go to the Lord with her needs and her fears. She had always been able to pray to God for peace and for forgiveness.

How long had it been since her soul felt at rest? How long had it been since she prayed to God and felt his gentle calm cover her?

She knew it had everything to do with this box, with these memories. Perhaps the Lord was telling her to forget about them, to move on and get control over her life.

Maybe her prayers had been answered. Maybe God was telling her no.

But something made her believe that wasn't right. Somewhere, deep inside, she still believed. She still held on to a promise made years ago on a wintry day.

Remembering that promise, Sara took the first letter out of its envelope. Her shaking hands held the unfolded paper as she read. More tears fell.

She needed to do this. More than ever now that she was about to give up all hope for what she really wanted.

She began to read.

And remember.

Every sunrise blossoms
with the memory of you.

Dreams

MANY MILES from Atlanta, a young man meandered through the nighttime crowds at the pier and tried to make sense of his life. As he approached the festive gathering area cluttered with tables, an older woman accidentally knocked into him and slammed her entire cup of beer into his chest.

She cursed and apologized in the same breath. Ethan Ware looked at the heavyset woman and noticed the glazed look in her eyes. "That's okay," he said.

"Then watch where you're going," she snapped as she wandered off.

Lines of beer dripped down his shirt onto his shorts and legs. Ethan shook his head as he watched the lady waggle off into the crowd. He wrung out his shirt as best he could. The smell would turn sour in a few minutes, but few around him would notice or even care.

Just my luck. I go out for a nice walk and get doused by Ms. Friendly there, he thought with wry amusement.

He sat down at a table near the end of Navy Pier. A stone wall separated him from the dark and shifting waters of Lake Michigan. He faced the lit-up Chicago skyline, a sight that had never failed to excite him. Tonight, though, the familiar cityscape seemed strangely alien. As if everything had changed. Actually, when you thought about it, everything *had* changed. It was amazing how life could change so completely and still look so much the same.

What am I still doing here? he asked himself as he glanced down at the wet spot on his lap.

He had been outside walking ever since finishing his three-dollar dinner, a burrito and soda. It was close to nine now. Probably he should be back at his apartment doing something productive—something besides wandering.

But he still didn't have an answer. An answer to one of the most important decisions he would ever make.

He watched the crowd around him. A myriad of people sat at tables, drinking and talking and laughing. Families and couples walked along the pier. Others rode bikes or darted around on Rollerblades. Everyone looked so happy and content in the blinking, colorful lights of the pier.

Vaguely he wondered if he looked happy, too. What he felt was lonely.

"Can I get you anything?" a frantic waitress asked as she passed by.

How about a few answers? he thought. "Thanks. I'm okay," Ethan said.

He thought about the casual words he had uttered and was surprised by them. Was he indeed okay? And if so, why was he worrying so much about the decision that he had to make?

This is why I'm worrying so much. He took out the envelope from his back pocket and opened the letter. When had he received it? Five years ago? Perhaps. He took out the photo that rested inside and gazed at the dark-haired beauty who had sent him the letter. The smile in the photo still warmed him so many years later.

"Happy birthday, Sara."

If only he could talk to her and know how she was doing and tell her how things were with him. If she still cared at all. But she was probably married, maybe even had children. As far as he knew, she could be living in downtown Chicago, walking the same streets he did every day. Or in China. Or in Timbuktu.

Do you ever think of me anymore? he wondered. *Has it been too long for you to still remember everything?*

Confusion seized him now, just like it had again and again during the past week. Why? Why now? Why after all this time? His big chance finally had come, and all he could think about was her.

Ethan wished he could ask his mother for advice. He would ask her every question his heart longed to know. Mom would know what to do. She always knew what to do. But now it was too late to ask Mom anything.

If only he had paid more attention to what she taught him as he was growing up. *I wish you were here, Mom.*

He thought about the last few years—more than a few, really—and about how much of a whirlwind his life had been in that span of time. Actually, it had been more like a tornado, wiping out almost everything in its path.

It had all started with his mother's death, he mused. Not before. He refused to call his father's abandoning their family the start of his downward spiral. He didn't want to give dear Dad that credit. And although their remaining family of two had had their share of problems when he was a teenager, they had also managed to hold each other together somehow. But then his mother's illness had finally taken its toll shortly after his graduation from college, and that was when the craziness had really begun.

He looked down at the photo, the most recent one he owned. It had been sent a few years after his mom died, before he and Sara finally lost touch. Sara's smile was dazzling, unchanging. He had memorized it long ago.

Ethan thought of his desperate proposal to Sara after his mother died, of the ache and emptiness he had felt when she said no. He had wandered around for a long time after that, trying to convince himself that this was what any writer with romantic sensibilities would do after having his heart broken. But hanging around bars and clubs until late hours of the night, sleeping the days away, living with college friends or friends of college friends, and not writing at all were neither romantic nor impressive. His actions were pathetic.

Finally, he had moved back to Chicago from the town where he'd gone to college and managed to get some stability in his otherwise superficial life. It had come in the form of a newspaper job and the friendship of two people.

Now, even those were gone.

Losing his job at the paper had been the first bit of bad news. He hadn't been exactly surprised, though, considering how competitive the journalism business was and how listlessly he'd approached the job. Besides, it barely paid anything, and there didn't seem to be much of a future in it. His dreams of writing a column for the paper had ended a long time ago, his lofty ideals about journalism and writing deteriorating when he realized his heart wasn't in it. He was still finding it hard to simply pick up a pen and jot down simple notes—and it was hard to be a writer for a paper when you could barely write anything. When the dismissal finally came a week earlier, Ethan had almost felt relieved.

Then his roommate and closest friend, Dennis, had decided to move out without any notice. Dennis was a likable and decent enough guy, but he had family difficulties and eventually they had taken their toll. Ethan could understand some of Dennis's problems, but he wished the timing had been a little different. Dennis had been one of the few people in Chicago Ethan spent time with. With Dennis gone, that left only one other tie to the city.

Unemployed and ready to find another place to live, Ethan had made the third big change himself—he had told Britanny he wanted to cool things off for a while. They had been going out for several months, but nothing much had developed in terms of a relationship. This breakup meant they would probably never talk to each other again. For him, it had been primarily a friendship, but Britanny wanted more.

He certainly understood that dilemma.

This all led up to the letter Ethan had received two days ago from one of the only relatives he stayed in touch with, his mother's brother. Uncle Pete in Germany somehow seemed to know how Ethan's life was going, so he had written to give him a proposition.

The letter from Germany was back in his apartment, not in his pocket, but he already knew its words by heart.

Ethan,

Hope Chicago and the city life are treating you well! I wanted to let you know that our offer is still good, even after all this time. Considering the last

few years, the change might be good for you. Think about it and let us know.
We have a plane ticket with your name on it just waiting.
We would love to see you. Our place is your place.
Hope to hear from you soon. Call us anytime.

Uncle Pete

That letter had driven it home for Ethan. He needed to do something, anything, with his life. Chicago and the job and the apartment and Britanny had been okay, but he had grown up knowing life could be so much more than okay. Believing his own life should be more. He needed to move on, and Uncle Pete's offer could be just the chance he needed.

Yet Ethan could still only think of one thing: *Find her.*

This was foolish, of course. It had been years, many years, since he last saw Sara—almost as many years ago as his mother's death. She had her life now, one in which he no longer belonged, one he could hardly imagine. And what if he did find her? What would he say or do? What else could he say that hadn't been said? He had told her everything in the last letter, and her silence had been a clear response. Enough had been said. Obviously her decision had been made.

Now he thought about the decision he had to make. The offer from his uncle and aunt in Germany to come live with them and work in his uncle's business seemed incredibly tempting. He couldn't stop thinking about the offer, about taking advantage of that one-way plane ticket to Germany his uncle had offered and getting away for a long time—at least two or three years. But what did he have to lose, anyway? He had no real ties to anyone here. In fact, he really had very little, especially in the form of inspiration. Perhaps the one-way plane ticket would be good for him. Good for him and his dreams.

He had always dreamed of traveling to Europe.

As he looked around at the never-ending busyness of the pier, Ethan thought back to his younger days—back when his mom had still been alive, when Sara had been a part of his life, when he had known exactly what he wanted—or at least thought he knew. Everyone he ever met heard about his dreams: dreams of traveling around the world, of writing books, of finding the right person to share it all with. He had been convinced that he would achieve all those dreams and more. Now, so many years later, the only thing he could say for certain was that he had found the right person for him. But maybe he wasn't the right one for her. As for the rest of those dreams, they appeared long gone and certainly impossible.

Impossible? he thought in horror. *How can I even dare to think that?*

He looked again at the photo of Sara and realized he needed to see her at least one more time. He needed to know why she had remained silent for so long.

And if she still remembered the promise she had given him so many years ago.

All I have to do to see you
again is close my eyes. . . .

Plans

"IS EVERYTHING OKAY?"

Sara coughed on her steak and waved a hand that said everything was. Bruce looked worried for a second, until she took a breath and managed a reassuring smile.

"Sorry. Wrong pipe."

And she said nothing more. She had said very little for most of the evening, ever since Bruce came to pick her up for another round of "Let's Plan This Marriage!"

She had tried. She really had. But the plans, the preparations, the endless conversations, the ideas and suggestions, and the decisions all worried her. Especially the decisions. Why did a wedding have to involve so many?

Ethan used to tell her she worried too much, that she spent too much time making decisions. And he had been right. She hated this about herself. "Sometimes you have to just let it all go," Ethan had told her once. "Life's too short to be worrying all the time."

Staring at the imploring face of her fiancé, Sara found herself wishing for a bit of Ethan's carefree attitude. She wondered if he still viewed life the same way. "Every day is a new opportunity to do something really crazy and get away with it." That had been Ethan's motto, one he would always state with his fiery and adorable grin.

She had loved that about him. She had loved virtually everything about him.

Well, now I'm about to do something really crazy. I'm about to say good-bye to one of the nicest guys I've ever known. If I could only figure out how to say it. . . .

Now, one week after saying yes to Bruce's proposal, Sara sat at dinner remembering Ethan and trying to figure out a way to tell Bruce no. She had to stop this nonsense before it became worse.

Everybody seemed to have lost their minds. Bruce never stopped talking about Their Future and Their House and Their Picket Fence with Their Dog Toto. It seemed that he couldn't even greet Sara without saying, "And after we get married. . . ." Her father seemed content and passive, as usual, but he would talk to Bruce about the wedding, too. And her mother already seemed headed for a mental hospital at the rate she was going, dealing with all the Wedding Plans.

There were all sorts of things to think about: the date and time of the wedding, where she would buy her dress, what the cake would look like, who the attendants would be, who would be invited (and of course, Aunt Lizzie would have to come, Mom said), where they would go on their honeymoon, what colors the flowers and dresses and shoes would be, whether guests would throw rice or birdseed or flower petals, and on and on.

Things that crowded her mind every time she closed her eyes.

Things that held no real interest to Sara.

In spite of all the excitement, Sara had found it hard to muster up any sort of enthusiasm. And worse than that, she had even more doubts now than she had a week ago. She had assumed that as time went by and the realization of her decision sank in, she would get used to the idea of marrying Bruce. But that wasn't happening.

She had to tell him the truth. She *would* tell him the truth. Right here, over dinner.

"You're quiet tonight. Everything okay?"

Sara smiled and was about to say something, but Bruce spoke again. "Because if you don't like December 26, we can change, you know. I know it's an odd date."

An odd date summed it up, all right. But her parents had married on that date and had always said they wanted Sara to do the same. She simply had to have a Christmas wedding. So Sara, compliant as usual, had agreed and said little.

"The date is fine," Sara said.

The date wasn't the problem. The wedding itself was the problem.

She wished she had the school and her little kindergartners to cheer her up. But with summer here, there was nothing to divert her attention from the wedding. She hadn't even told anyone at first—her friends or her fellow teachers at school—about her engagement. Only after her mother insisted had she called people and made the announcement.

Not exactly the typical, enthusiastic bride-to-be.

"Bruce, I've been thinking . . . ," she began.

"About what?"

"About this, everything. I don't know. I'm . . . uh, sort of nervous."

"I'm nervous, too. But we've still got a while to let things sink in."

"Aren't we . . . aren't we moving a bit fast?"

Bruce fidgeted in his chair and looked at her. "How so?"

"I just think all these decisions and everything—can't we wait on some of them?"

"Like the date?"

Try the whole thing, Sara thought. But she still couldn't bring herself to come right out and say it. "Like lots of things."

"Sara, what's wrong?"

Could she change her mind now? Of course she could. Of course she could give the ring back and explain to Bruce about her reservations. And of course Bruce would be loving and sensitive, and then take himself and his expensive ring and his thoroughly decimated ego and leave her forever. And her mom—well, her mom would perhaps take the convertible out and wave good-bye to Sara and drive off the nearest cliff.

Better now than later, surely. It had only been one week. It couldn't be that bad saying no. Why had she said yes in the first place? But of course she'd had to say yes. What else could she say? How could she turn down a man who was, in her mother's words, "a perfect guy"?

Sara thought of Bruce and the reasons she enjoyed spending so much

time around him. He was great with kids. He spent many evenings helping her grade papers. He always complimented her and encouraged her
and rarely, if ever, got angry. He was stable and responsible and always
seemed to be thinking of the future.

There really was nothing wrong with Bruce. Maybe something was
wrong with her. . . .

But what about love? a voice inside her asked. *What about love?* This was
the same voice that had been haunting her all week. A voice that whispered one thing over and over: *Do you love him?*

And the answer, of course, was yes. Certainly she loved him. He was a
brother in Christ. He was a good friend, a pleasant companion. He was
good to her, and she cared about him. But Sara knew this wasn't the love
that the voice was asking about, wasn't the love that Bruce wanted or
expected or deserved. That kind of love was the kind she had experienced
only once in her life.

She had wondered recently whether feelings that strong could ever
come back to her again.

"Sara, please," Bruce said, his face distressed. "Talk to me."

Tell him now, the voice inside urged. But when she looked into his kind
brown eyes, the corners furrowed in concern, somehow she just
couldn't.

"I-I'm just not feeling good right now. It's just . . . just a bit too
much. . . ."

"Is it me? Did I do anything?"

"Oh, no," she replied. "It has nothing to do with you." And that, of
course, was part of the problem.

She excused herself and walked to the ladies' room.

*Please, Lord, help me to know what to say, to know what to do. Should I marry
Bruce? Is it wrong for me to marry him when I really want someone else? Or am I
just hanging on to something that wasn't right in the first place?*

Did God have one single person picked out for her from the beginning
of time? She used to believe this and had held on to this belief for so many
years. And she had always assumed Ethan Ware was the one. She had
believed that somehow there would be a miracle, that they would be
together. But that belief was starting to fade away.

Where could Ethan be? After all these years, she still desperately missed him. And she had kept her word—she had continued to pray for him, every day in fact, yet she didn't have a clue whether it made any difference.

Maybe she would never find out.

She leaned against the cool, tile wall as pangs of hurt and guilt swept over her again. She believed she had made the right decision years ago, but that didn't lessen the painful memories. She had been the one to say no, to force the good-bye. It had been her decision, all hers.

So why, then, did she find it so difficult to move on?

She had made Ethan a promise, and she had kept it. But she had no reason to believe he had kept his promise to her. And no reason to believe she should let those long-ago promises determine the course of her life.

So where did that leave her? Thirty years old and trying to face the fact that she was about to enter a marriage with quite a lot of doubts and with very little passion.

But maybe that's what marriage should be about, Sara told herself. Stability. Comfort and companionship. And children—Sara certainly wanted children, and Bruce would be a wonderful father.

Maybe her mother was right. This might be one of the only opportunities a great guy like Bruce would come around. She could learn to live with him and maybe even learn to love him. He might not ever be like Ethan, but who could as far as she was concerned?

Her dear, sweet Ethan. Would anyone ever compare to him or to the memory of him?

Why, oh dear God, why did he forget?

I still dream of being with you.

Insights

ETHAN KNOCKED on the apartment door belonging to his land-lord, a crusty and talkative old man named Herb. The door opened to reveal Herb in ankle-high black socks, white shorts, and a worn Chicago Bears T-shirt that said "Super Bowl Champs." The man smiled at Ethan and told him to come in.

"This is the rent money for the rest of the summer," Ethan said, hand-ing Herb an envelope.

"Don't have to pay it all at once, you know." Herb's deep voice sounded scratchy as usual.

"Our lease goes through August. I wanted to make sure you got the money—Dennis gave me his remaining share. He moved out a couple of weeks ago."

"Yeah, he said something about that. You moving too?"

Ethan shook his head. "I don't know, to be honest. I've got an opportu-nity somewhere."

"Somewhere? Where's somewhere? Here, sit down, come on. Want anything to drink?"

"No, thanks." Ethan sat on the edge of a musty sofa. He was used to half-hour conversations with Herb.

"So where's this somewhere?"

"Europe. I've got an uncle in Germany who's been trying for a while to get me to work for him."

"I've never been to Europe. Always wanted to go, you know. So, when do you leave?"

Ethan shrugged. How could he tell Herb, of all people, his dilemma? That's how things worked for him. Most people had relatives, best friends, or even a psychiatrist to give them advice. When Ethan needed advice, he seemed to get it from people like Herb.

"I'm debating about taking a trip before I go."

"A trip, huh? Myself, I haven't been out of Chicago for fifteen years. I keep on saying I'll go, but then I never get the chance, not with this building and all that. Why do you wanna take a trip before you leave? Ain't Germany good enough?"

Ethan looked at Herb, lounging in a La-Z-Boy chair and sipping a cup of coffee. "To see an old friend."

"Ah, a girl, I bet," Herb said, revealing yellow teeth. "You know, I was married once. Long time ago."

Ethan nodded, trying to show an interest.

"Yeah, a long time ago. She passed on. She was my high school sweetheart, you know. They're the best. Doreen. That was her name. Died of cancer."

"I'm sorry," Ethan replied.

Herb waved a hand. "So, what's your girl's name?"

"Well, I don't really—"

"Come on," Herb urged.

"Her name is Sara. But I don't know—I haven't seen her in years. She's probably married and all that. I really don't know."

"What don't you know?"

"It's been too long," Ethan said. "Too many years since I saw her. And the last time I wrote to her, I never heard back."

Herb laughed. "What a sorry sap. You don't know whether to go see her?"

"I don't even know *where* to go."

Herb continued to chuckle. Ethan stared at him, irritated. Here he was telling this goofy man his troubles, and all he was getting were guffaws. That and a strange odor coming from the kitchen.

"Look, Son. Do you love this girl? That's the only question you need to know."

"Well, yeah. Of course. I've always loved her."

"Did you tell her that? Most guys have a hard time with that word."

"Not me. She knows."

"Then what's your problem? Go find her."

"It's not as simple as that."

"No?" Herb asked, stretching over to rub his foot. "Let me tell you the story Doreen used to like telling others. She was religious, my Dorie, and she liked to preach to me all the time. She was a sweetie, but her preaching got a little old. Anyways, I had to wait for years before she'd finally agree to marry a fella like me. We were different, her and me. But everyone's different, right?"

Ethan nodded and thought, *What am I doing here?*

Herb continued. "Dorie always told me that if Jacob from the Bible could wait for seven years just to marry his wife, then I could certainly wait a year or two. Patience, Dorie told me. Of course, I was thinking I just might die if I had to wait seven years, but Dorie finally gave in. She finally said yes."

I wish it was as easy as that, Ethan thought.

"So you gotta be patient. You gotta be like that Jacob fella that worked and waited all those years. How long's it been for you?"

Ethan wasn't even sure. Eight, perhaps nine years? No, it was right after his mother died. . . .

"Eight years, I think," he said.

The man rubbed his foot again and nodded. "Hey, that's okay. You still gotta be patient. What—you wanna marry this girl?"

"Yeah, I do," Ethan said without hesitating.

"Then go, boy. Find her. You're only young once. Find her and ask her. You gotta know."

"There's one problem."

"What's that?" Herb asked.

"I already found her once and asked her to marry me. But she said no."

"Oh. Well, I guess that could be a problem. What, she doesn't love you?"

Ethan smiled. "She did love me. That's what she said. But things were—they were complicated."

Herb finished his cup of coffee and lowered the footrest of his La-Z-Boy. He pushed himself to his feet, scratching the back of his neck. "Sure you don't want anything to drink? Soda? Coors?"

"No." Ethan stood up to leave. "I really should go."

"Where're you going to go?" Herb asked him.

"Like I said, things are complicated."

Herb walked Ethan to the door. The man looked up at Ethan and gave him another yellow-toothed smile. "Y'know, there's not a day goes by that I don't wish I was thirty or forty years younger. I dream about it, sitting around here collecting rent checks. That's why I do this—you know that? So I can see you young people all the time. It keeps me going."

Ethan nodded and stepped out the door.

Herb stood in the doorway, a clump of his sparse hair sticking out from one side of his head. "Look, Son. I never deserved Dorie. I guess us guys never really deserve the women we love. But it's worth it. The waiting, I mean. And the trying. Like that Jacob fella."

Ethan shook Herb's hand. "Take care," he said.

"Listen to your heart, Son," Herb called when Ethan was halfway down the hallway.

⚜

Back in the apartment, Ethan stared at the suitcases near the door. He was ready to go—but where? Was he going to try to find Sara? To risk another round of rejection?

Things are different now, he thought. But apparently that hadn't made any difference. Did she just stop caring? *She knows everything, yet she never said a word. Not a single word.*

Most likely she didn't know what to say. She'd gone on with her life, and he didn't fit in it.

He could see himself knocking on a door to a happy household. Sara would answer and greet him in a polite manner and show him wedding pictures and baby pictures and pictures of her happy, fulfilled life. What would he do then? Make up something about how he just happened to be in the neighborhood, "Just passing by the state of South Dakota, don't you know"? Tell her he was happy for her?

He could be happy for her, he thought. He loved her that much— loved her enough to be glad that she was happy. Or at least he thought he did.

But how could he live without knowing for sure?

He noticed his answering machine still plugged into the wall and saw the blinking message button. His breath stopped as he pressed it. *Please let it be her,* he silently prayed, even as he told himself it couldn't possibly be. *Let it be her, please let it be her.*

"Hey, Ethan, this is Andy again," the electrified voice on the machine told him. "I'm downtown for a couple of days. Man, you're hard to find, you know that? Anyway, give me a call as soon as you can. It'd be great to hang out."

Ethan found a pen and the back of a used envelope and wrote down the number Andy had given.

Not a good sign, Ethan thought. *I pray and it ends up being Andy. Is that some kind of bad joke?* Andy's voice brought back a wave of memories. How many months had it been since he last heard it? Could it have been more than a year ago?

I haven't told Andy about everything that's happened. I thought he was gone for good. Memories of the dark days of college and the darker ones in the following years seemed to belong to another person, yet they also seemed to have only happened yesterday. Recollections of that long period in his life still stung. They hung above him like murky clouds on a sunny day.

"Andy," Ethan said out loud as if to verify he had just heard the message.

Andy had been one of his closest friends during college, during the time in his life when his mother's health had wavered and there had only been a handful of people he could even relate to. On one end of the spectrum had been his beloved Sara, who encouraged him through her letters, who kept a light shining for him. And on the other end had been Andy, who had helped him take his mind off the painful realities of his life.

Perfect timing, Ethan thought. *A couple of nights out with Andy would make me forget about everything else.* He looked around and thought for a moment. He picked up the phone to call.

Don't do it, another voice said. *That's the last thing you need.*

He dialed the numbers anyway and waited. A voice answered at the other end.

Ethan knew exactly what he would say.

. . . with a smile that could
melt the coldest of hearts.

Words

SARA FOLDED the pages of the letter and slipped them back into the worn envelope. She wiped her eyes and wondered if she should keep reading. *This is so foolish,* she told herself. *Why can't I just grow up?*

Letters lay scattered around her on the bed. Though years had passed, Ethan's letters never failed to move her. His words always filled her with a sense of vulnerability, the kind she might blush over. She had never considered herself to be particularly interesting, so when the letters came asking her to describe her life and her feelings, she had been unsure what to say. She'd felt plain, sensible, and ordinary. What could she say that would be of any interest to a spontaneous and carefree person like Ethan?

Everything, he would implore. He had wanted to know anything and everything.

So she had told him about babysitting jobs and her child-development classes and her friends and her church activities. And to her amazement, Ethan had been impressed with her letters. He had always declared his awe at her life, even though his own was one wild and crazy adventure after another. His own letters told her of his excursions to different places, either with friends or by himself. They enthused about his many different interests—soccer, nature, track, drums, art, skiing—while they also detailed his lack of enthusiasm for anything pertaining to growing up or schoolwork or responsibilities.

"I never want to grow up, Sara," he had once written to her. "When I grow up, I want to live like I'm having a midlife crisis."

He had described to her the details of getting in trouble for doing simple and stupid things—like swimming in a neighbor's pool at midnight and driving over the college's soccer field with his car. Episodes like these still made her laugh and shake her head. Ethan would write things like "I guess that really wasn't a good idea" and then draw a smiley face to show his amusement. Her own letters paled in comparison to his. She always felt she had nothing to tell him except for dull details of her ho-hum life. But Ethan had claimed to find her "constant" attitude regarding life remarkable.

"That's what I like about you," he had written once. "You are responsible, and you think through the things you do. I need somebody like that."

And of course, he had never failed to remind her how much he admired her enduring faith. . . .

A lot of good that did us, she thought crossly as she tucked the letter away.

It was her lunch with Elyse that had sent Sara back to the old letters once again. Or rather, it was something Elyse had said during lunch.

Elyse Barry was one of Sara's closest friends—a fellow schoolteacher she had met in the church singles group. The outgoing and attractive blonde had been the one to invite Sara to the women's small group she loved attending on Wednesdays.

Elyse was also one of the only people she had told about Ethan.

So that afternoon, between bites of Caesar salad and crusty French bread, Sara had shared some of her mixed feelings with Elyse. It felt good to tell somebody about what she was going through, to have someone listen and understand.

But Elyse had also said something that stuck with Sara the rest of the day. "There's nothing wrong with remembering someone you once loved," she had said. "You just have to figure out if you still love Ethan—and if you can ever have feelings like that for Bruce."

That comment had sent Sara back once more to Ethan's old letters. She had told herself she wouldn't do this again. But Elyse was right. There was nothing wrong in remembering the past.

But it's wrong to be stuck in the past. And wrong to keep all of this from Bruce.

Strange feelings still plagued her, and she needed to make sense of them. It was odd that, the more time that went by since her engagement, the more she thought of Ethan. Before, she had been able to banish him fairly easily from her everyday thoughts. Now, she was always seeing his mischievous smile, his brilliant blue eyes, his wavy hair falling against his forehead. She could hear his voice as she read his words, some written more than ten years earlier.

Stop this now, Sara told herself.

She opened another letter. Just one more. Just one.

The distinguishing characteristic of Ethan's letters had been the name he put on the front corner of the envelope where return addresses were usually written. He'd called himself everything from James Dean to Han Solo to Your Secret Pen Pal.

The envelope she held now, though, simply said Ethan. *I remember this one,* Sara thought.

She unfolded the page.

My dearest Sara,

Weeks ago I wondered if I could feel any worse about life. Yesterday I discovered I could.

I can't say I agree with you, but I understand. And I want you to know that my promise will never die, that I will always love you. These aren't vain words, either. I mean them, Sara. I mean them with my whole heart.

I never thought things would end up like this. I really thought we could work it all out. I still don't know what to think about all the things you said—I simply find it impossible to believe all of that. But I will say this. Meeting you in Hartside years ago—that wasn't just chance. I don't know who or what put us together, but I know our paths were meant to cross.

And I believe they're meant to cross again. I won't give up hope.

I won't give up loving you, either.

Ethan

Sara cried and remembered receiving that letter years ago. It had been the final one he had sent to her, the final word from Ethan.

Their paths hadn't crossed again.

What had happened? Where had he gone?

She had sent him a letter back, asking him to read the Bible she had once given him. She had heard nothing since then. Perhaps he had finally decided enough was enough.

Sara bundled the letters together once more, tucked them away in the nightstand, and wandered downstairs. On the coffee table was a stack of wedding invitations to be addressed, on the floor a stack of bridal magazines her mom had brought over. The miniature clock on an end table told her it was close to five o'clock. She would be meeting Bruce at her parents' house for dinner at six.

Her parents still knew nothing about her ambivalence. Neither did Bruce, though surely he wondered about her lack of enthusiasm. And everything was escalating—plans, schedules, details. Everything was building, and all Sara could do was dream about Ethan.

These feelings needed to go somewhere. But where?

Sara ended up in her kitchen by the sink, gazing through the lace-trimmed window at the lush green plants on her patio, enjoying the silence. She had been over at her parents' house so much recently; it felt good to be back in her own place. Standing there in the quiet, Sara lifted her thoughts toward God, asking for direction. And then she prayed for Ethan, just as she had done almost daily for the last eight years. She prayed that he would find the truth, that he would find his way to the Lord. He had been on the verge so many times—Sara knew he had been. He had told her. He was so close, and everything in his life seemed to be leading him that way.

But would he ever find his way? Or were all the prayers for nothing?

Sara had never understood how somebody who could believe in her and in a love that seemed so impossible could not believe in a God who had brought the two of them together. Ethan had been blunt about his lack of belief when they first met so many years ago. In some of his letters he had asked questions about what she believed—he had seemed genuinely interested. In others, he had denied everything—God's existence, his love, his control, his Son. There could not be a God, he had blustered—not in a world like this. Sometimes Ethan had seemed defiant in his unbelief, especially after his mother died. Over the years, he had grown more ardent in his feelings for Sara and more passionate about his disregard for his God. And that was why she had told him no.

That was why she could not marry him, why the love Ethan believed in so passionately could not move forward. Oh, she loved him, too; Ethan would never understand just how deeply she loved him. She had told him that.

No, love had never been the problem in their relationship. The problem was one of doing what was right, doing what the Bible taught her, doing what the Lord required of his people.

Of course, she couldn't forget the promise made to a dying woman. "Promises," Sara uttered in frustration. She had made promises years ago, always thinking everything would work out in the end.

She had dared to hope that things would change and that then their life together would be the kind she had dreamed about. He would tell her he had finally said yes to the God who loved him more than she did. Then she would tell him how she had prayed every night for his soul, for his safety, for his life. And they would both marvel at God's goodness and live happily ever after.

In the silence, Sara reflected on God's goodness. She knew she had doubts, plenty of doubts. And she knew that she wasn't a perfect Christian, either. Not while she was carrying these secrets around, deceiving her parents and Bruce and a lot of other people. Then there was the worry. And the guilt. And the love she still carried deep in her heart.

Was she wrong to wonder where Ethan might be?

She waited, but she heard no answers. She knew some questions never get answered.

If only she could see him one more time. If only she could have one more chance to listen to his voice, to hear him say something, anything.

And then as she stood in her kitchen peering out the window, an idea came. In one second it all came to her. It made perfect sense.

The decision was made. Sara knew what she had to do.

THE PROMISE REMAINS

PART TWO

You loved me enough to
never give up on me.

Encounters

IN THE SUMMER between her sophomore and junior years of high school, Sara Anthony had vowed never to date another boy again.

She knew she had high expectations. Yet that hadn't stopped her from going out with several guys from her high school during her first two years there. They were older than she was, they played football and basketball, they always had dozens of girls swooning all over them. She had given them a chance, and each one had let her down.

Yet even more disappointing than that, Sara felt she had let herself down. Her expectations didn't have anything to do with the kind of car her date drove or how high he rated on the popularity scale or how many sports he played. She wanted someone who made her laugh like her father did, someone who really listened when she talked about anything and everything, someone who felt as passionate about the Lord as she did.

She wondered if there were any guys out there like that. After her short and painful attempts at dating, Sara decided she wasn't going to meet any. It seemed simpler to give up on that scene altogether.

On the first day of Hope Springs summer camp outside Hartside, North Carolina, her resolve had been tested, but only briefly, when a good-looking, tanned senior from Georgia asked if she wanted to take a walk after the evening service.

"Where to?" Sara asked in a polite but direct tone.

"Uh, you know, around," the senior replied, obviously surprised by her response.

"No, thanks," she told him. "I've probably already been there."

Her response left the openmouthed senior speechless—and Sara feeling a bit guilty. She hadn't meant to be rude or arrogant, but she didn't want to think about guys—especially not at this camp. She'd broken up with one boyfriend just a month earlier because he had lied to her about dating other girls, and he had justified it by saying he was just a guy. And that was the kind of person Sara seemed to attract: "Sorry, I didn't mean to lie to you, but I'm just a guy." These were the sort of guys she fell for, and they had humiliated her more than once.

No more, she told herself.

This was her first time at the Christian camp, located several hours from her home in Tennessee. Hope Springs camp meant a lot of things to a lot of people, but for Sara, it was a place to get to know other Christians from both her church and the surrounding churches in the South. For one week, campers would enjoy the beauty of the Great Smoky Mountains as they spent the days and evenings in outdoor activities, fun social events, and Bible study and worship. It would be a wonderful break from the otherwise boring summer and would put a lot of good distance between her and Mr. "I'm Just a Guy."

The camp's location was exactly what she'd hoped for—a collection of small log cabins all nestled in the arms of a great wooded mountain. The nearby town of Hartside, located just minutes from the Tennessee border, lay at the foot of the mountain, about ten minutes from their cabins. Hartside was a quaint tourist town with a hotel, several bed-and-breakfasts, a miniature main street with shops and restaurants, and a cluster of homes—perfect for afternoon excursions. Apart from the town, the area consisted of woods and mountains and small vacation cabins similar to the ones the campers were staying in.

Perfect for getting away.

There were probably more than sixty teenagers attending the camp. At least ten were assigned to each cabin, depending on its size. Guys from Tennessee churches might be in one house, girls from Western North

Carolina churches in another, and so on. They alternated meetings between a small church several miles down the road and a campground in the other direction.

After the first evening service, which consisted of singing hymns and reading the Bible and listening to one of the pastors speak, Sara decided to take the tanned, good-looking guy's advice and go for a walk. She did it alone, however, setting out along one of the dirt roads that the camp leader had pointed out as "within bounds" for campers.

As the sun slipped down toward the mountains in the west, Sara walked along the road and became lost in her thoughts. Once again she began thinking of her life and whether or not she would ever meet Mr. Right. She told herself such a person didn't exist, but at the same time she longed for someone who would genuinely love her and care for her. She wanted someone who was passionate about life and the Lord, someone who would inspire her to forget all of life's worries and letdowns.

Will I ever meet a guy like this, Lord? Am I wrong to want someone like this?

God would show her one day. Deep in her heart, she believed it and trusted him. She enjoyed walks like this, where she thought and prayed and conversed with God. A voice never came back, booming down a "YES, DO THAT, SARA" or even whispering in the winds. But Sara almost always felt a peace inside her when she prayed to the Lord. She felt a similar peace now. A sense that everything would truly be all right.

After ten minutes of walking, Sara found herself looking up at an unfamiliar log cabin perched on a hill above her. A steep, winding driveway curled up to the sweet, two-story home with a deck that overlooked the mountains to the west.

Sara stopped and gazed up at the house. *Is this one of the cabins the camp is renting out?* Sara wondered.

For a few minutes, Sara stared up at the cabin and saw nothing. There was no sign of life. One of the camp managers had said that some of the houses around Hartside were owned by Floridians who visited on and off during the year. Perhaps this cabin was one of those.

She stood there for several long minutes, considering, then ventured partway up the winding drive. She didn't see a single car, and the flower boxes on the deck were obviously untended. Pine needles and decaying leaves cluttered the drive. Surely nobody had been home for a while.

Maybe it was being away from home, or the beautiful clear evening sky, or the recent prayer she had lifted up to the heavens. Whatever it was, Sara felt compelled to walk the rest of the way up to the cabin and stand on the deck.

She told herself the view would be worth risking embarrassment if an owner were to find her there.

What a view it was.

The surrounding mountains rolled off into the distance in every direction. The tops of their thick trees looked comfortable enough to lie down on. Distant clouds seemed to hover above the peaks, with shadowy outlines of mountains farther behind them. God wasn't merely evident in this panoramic display before her; he seemed to be living and breathing all around her.

Sara stared at the view in front of her and said another prayer out loud. "Dear Father, thank you for the incredible beauty of your creation. Thank you for all you give to us. And all you've given to me. Thank you for always being there, and for—"

"Hey."

Sara felt her heart roll up into her mouth as she let out a gasp. She turned around and saw a boy about her age standing behind her on the deck, smiling.

"Who are you talking to?" he asked her.

Sara took a deep breath and composed herself. "I was—what are you doing? Did you follow me?"

She was trying to remember if she had seen this boy earlier that day. He didn't look familiar.

"Follow you?" he asked.

"Yes, from camp."

"Yeah, that's exactly what I did. I've been following you. I always follow girls out in the wilderness to spy on them."

From his tone, Sara knew he was kidding. But who was he? She thought she would have remembered him from camp, even if she wasn't making it a point to check out the guys. His wide, slightly crooked smile almost made her laugh, for no reason at all. His blue eyes looked fun loving and luminous, saying as much as his words had. He looked friendly. Whoever he was, she felt comfortable—if a little bit breathless.

"Nice view, huh?" he asked her.

"Yes, it is."

"Who were you talking to?" he asked again.

"Who was I—oh, I was praying."

He nodded and raised his eyebrows but remained quiet.

"I don't think I saw you at camp today. Where are you from?"

"Chicago," he said.

"Chicago? Seriously?"

"No, I'm lying. Not only do I spy on girls in the evening, but I also make a point of lying to them."

Sara laughed. "No, it's just—that's a long way to come for camp."

"Camp?"

"You're here for camp, right?"

The boy laughed. He walked to the edge of the deck and sat on the railing, more than three stories above the drop-off below. "I live here."

Sara felt sick. *This has to be a joke, right? Of course it is. He's joking around.* But his eyes met hers, and she couldn't tell whether he was joking or not.

"You're not from the camp?"

He shook his head. "Nope. Never attended a camp in my life. Well, I think maybe Cub Scouts or something like that, but I got booted out. Can you believe that? Getting kicked out of Cub Scouts. I was scarred for life."

Sara laughed again. "You really live here? In this cabin?"

"Well, for the time being. I really do live in Chicago. My mom and I are—we're taking a vacation of sorts." He locked his legs around the wood railing and leaned out over it. "Ahhhhhhhhh."

"Don't do that. Are you crazy?"

"This wood is hard as a rock. It's not going anywhere."

"I'm sorry I'm—" Sara stopped, unsure what to say. "I'm sorry I just walked up here."

"I don't care. Not like we get many visitors."

Sara still felt embarrassed, but curiosity filled her. "What do you do up here?"

"I'm beginning to learn how to talk to groundhogs. They have a primitive language, but I think I'm finally starting to break through."

Again, Sara laughed. She couldn't recall the last time she had met someone so sarcastic and funny. Who was this guy?

"Actually," he said, "I don't do much of anything except read and write."

"You like writing?"

He hesitated before answering, a reaction that seemed to contradict his outgoing personality. "Yeah," he said, "I do."

Sara looked up and saw his face outlined by the colors of the fading sun behind him. "I should go. It's getting late."

"You don't have to go. Like I said, my conversations with the groundhogs haven't been as fulfilling as I had hoped they would be."

"No, I really have to. We have a curfew. At the camp, I mean."

At first, he didn't say anything as she began to walk away. Then she heard his voice call out to her. "Wait a minute."

"What?" she asked.

"What's your name?"

Sara blushed, thankful the light was fading.

"Sara. Sara Anthony."

"Well, Miss Anthony. I'm Ethan Ware. Feel free to visit our deck anytime. For the view, or to pray, or to do whatever."

She nodded and thanked him. She thought about mentioning the evening services at camp to him, but she felt stupid and decided to not say anything.

That night, on the first night of her Hope Springs camp experience, after vowing not to have anything to do with guys whatsoever, Sara dreamed of Ethan Ware.

I felt totally alone, and I finally realized that nothing or no one could fill that emptiness.

Prayers

ETHAN SLICED his finger on the open can of soup and let loose with a loud curse he had been storing for a while.

His mother, sitting only a foot away at the table, looked at him with disappointment. "Ethan, please. Don't swear."

"Blame the soup can. Besides, I'm getting sick of soup for lunch every day. Can't we go out occasionally? Get a hamburger or something?"

"You know we're on a budget."

He looked at her with frustration in his eyes and shook his head. "So, are we going to be on a budget for the rest of our lives?"

"Ethan, you know how things are."

"Not really, Mom. How are things, really? You never want to talk about what's going on."

"I don't know what to tell you."

"What to tell me? Okay, then, how about this? What's up with Dad? I mean, really. What's going on?"

Marietta Ware looked down at the table and said nothing.

"I hate him," Ethan said.

"Ethan, stop that now. Please stop."

"Well, I do. I can't help it. He never did love us—"

Ethan stopped when he saw his mother break down again, this time with heaving sobs that even he couldn't ignore. He rushed to his mother's side, kneeling before her and holding on to her knees.

"I'm sorry, Mom. I'm sorry. I shouldn't have said anything. I'm just so mad at him. But I didn't mean to hurt you. Mom, please . . ."

"It's okay, honey," Marietta said as she tried to compose herself.

"I can't believe he just left us like that. I still can't. I-I hate him for doing this to us, especially to you."

"Sweetheart, he's just lost."

"No, don't do that," Ethan said, pulling back.

"Honey, it's true."

He shook his head. "Don't give me any of that Christian junk. Not now. I don't want to hear it."

"We can still pray for him, Ethan."

"I'm not praying anymore. I've prayed enough. What does that get us? Huh? We're living in Uncle Pete's cabin in the middle of nowhere, and we don't even have money for a hamburger. That's an answer to prayer?"

"Please, Ethan."

"You know what, Mom? I try to pray. I do, and I don't get any answers—all I get is angry and confused. I'm angry that Dad just walked out on us, just like that. I'm angry that your so-called God let it happen. It just makes me sick."

Marietta Ware looked down at her son and reached for his hand. "But that's what anger does, Ethan. It will make you sick. It made your father sick. I tried to help him, to be a good wife to him. God knows I tried over the years. But he never stopped being angry. He only grew bitter with his hatred toward God. All I can do, all we can do, is pray for him—and try not to let the anger get us, too."

Ethan stood up and headed for the door. "I'm not going to do it. I'm never going to pray for that guy again. As far as I'm concerned, he might as well be dead."

Outside on the deck, away from his mother's gaze, the sixteen-year-old stood and wept bitterly. Tears fell again. Familiar tears. Tears he allowed no one else to see. Except for God, if there was a God.

Are you watching up there? Ethan asked, looking toward the heavens. *Can you see how horrible I feel, how sad Mom feels? Do you even care?* As usual, silence answered his prayers. That was the only answer he ever got: silence.

Leaning his elbows on the deck railing, Ethan struggled to regain control. He didn't want his mother seeing him break down. He needed to be a man now, something his father was incapable of doing. Ethan needed to be strong for his mom. He had no choice.

As he wiped his eyes, though, he thought he heard the voice of an angel. "Hello?" he said, looking up to the heavens. "Anybody there?"

"Down here," the angelic voice replied. It sounded familiar. Ethan looked below toward the road. There stood the petite, dark-haired girl who had showed up on the deck of the cabin yesterday. The same lovely girl he had thought about all night and most of this day so far. Sara Anthony.

"Talked with any groundhogs today?" Sara yelled up to him.

Quickly he swiped at his nose with a sleeve and cleared his throat. "Funny, 'cause you kinda sound like one," he replied, trying to sound as cheery as he had the day before.

"Very funny."

"You lost? Or decided to go trespassing again?"

"I just thought I'd come back this way. It's nice up here."

"You can come up to the deck," Ethan said. "I'm mostly harmless."

"Mostly?" Sara asked.

"Well, you're safe with me."

As Sara walked up to the deck, Ethan wiped his eyes again with the sleeves of his T-shirt. Thank goodness the road was far enough away from the deck that his tears could go unseen.

"Hello again," Sara said as she stepped out on the deck.

"Trespassing again," Ethan said with a smile. "You know, we might be forced to call the police."

"Very funny."

"So you can leave your camp just like that?"

"Well, we had some free time after lunch, and we're allowed to go anywhere between the church and the campground."

"Did you eat lunch? We've got every kind of Campbell's soup known to mankind."

Sara laughed. "Yes, I ate, but thanks. I enjoy the walk up here—the view is beautiful."

So are you, Ethan thought as he nodded.

They spent the next hour together, talking on the deck and walking along the road that wound away from the campsite and Ethan's home. Ethan wasn't sure why Sara had come back to see him, but he didn't think much of it. He only wanted to be with her—and to get away from the cabin, from the pain he had been feeling for a long time. He only briefly introduced his mother to Sara, avoiding any further conversation by telling his mom they were leaving. He would explain things later.

Their conversation was occasionally awkward, since neither knew the other. But Ethan was good at filling in any lapses when the conversation stalled. He kept making jokes, making her laugh every other minute. He enjoyed doing it. It was good to hear some laughter up on this mountain. There hadn't been a lot of it lately.

Around one-thirty, Sara told him she needed to return to camp. They sat on a fallen tree that overlooked the valley below. Ethan had found the tree one day while roaming the mountain. There weren't many things to do in the mountains beside roam.

"Maybe you'd like to come to one of our evening services sometime," Sara suggested. "I think it would be okay if we asked the camp director."

"Could I sit by you, or would they put me in the back row?" Ethan asked, joking as usual.

"Of course you could sit by me. I like sitting near the front so I can hear better."

"I don't know," he replied. "I'm not big into church services."

"It's not what you think. It's pretty casual. We sing and talk and the speakers are all great. You might like it."

"Well, you didn't mention anything about singing before!" Ethan sarcastically exclaimed.

"What, you like singing?"

Ethan laughed. "No."

"You'll still like it. I know you will. Come on."

Ethan doubted it but figured he could endure anything as long as Sara

Anthony was by his side. "I guess I could try it out, see what it's like," he said. "What time is it?"

As Sara recited the time and place for the evening gathering, Ethan found himself lost in her dark, wide eyes. Soft and endearing, they gave her a look of grace he had never seen before. Strands of her shiny, black hair tended to stray into her eyes, and she would occasionally brush them back. He found it hard to breathe when she did that.

"Can I ask you something?"

Sara nodded.

"Why did you come back here today? I mean, I figured I acted like a total idiot yesterday and probably was rude on top of it."

"You weren't rude," she said softly.

"Well, then, just idiotic. Were you just walking by again?"

The corners of her mouth turned up slightly. "Why do you ask?"

Ethan shrugged. "Call me paranoid."

"The groundhogs sent me."

"Oh, they did?" Ethan replied. "Now I see. Are you the special interpreter they were talking about?"

"I am," Sara said with a shining smile.

"Oh, now it all makes sense."

But nothing made sense, Ethan thought. Nothing at all. Not his life, not his parents' marriage, not living on a mountain, nothing.

Looking into this girl's eyes makes sense, though, Ethan told himself. When he gazed into those eyes, for the first time in a long while he began to forget some of the pain he had been carrying around. All the anger and confusion simply seemed to vanish when Sara was around.

"I really do have to go back," Sara was saying as she stood up. "So, maybe I'll see you tonight?"

Ethan smiled. "Well, I will certainly have to check my calendar. I hear there is a big party in the woods tonight."

"Oh, really?"

"Sure. But, you know, I might have to miss it. I haven't been preached to for a long time."

"Nobody's going to be preaching to you," Sara replied.

"I might actually need some preaching to. Who knows?"

They had arrived at the cabin's driveway. Sara looked up at him and gave him another dazzling smile. "Are you ever serious?" she asked.

Ethan pretended to think a minute. "I'm afraid to tell you but . . . I really don't think so."

"Well, you'll have to behave tonight."

"It's a date," he said.

"A date?"

"No, not a 'date' date. You know what I—"

"Gotcha," Sara said, already starting down the bumpy dirt road.

Ethan waved and watched her go. He looked up at the cabin and suddenly noticed something amazing. The sinking feeling he usually got when he glanced at the cabin wasn't there.

Ethan remembered his own words earlier that morning as he had stood on the deck. They had been addressed to his mother's God. *Do you even care?*

Maybe, just maybe, God did care. . . .

Ethan pushed those thoughts away. Sara's appearance wasn't heaven-sent. It was just luck. Pure luck. Destiny. Chance. All those wonderfully curious things.

But a voice still turned over in his head.

Maybe.

There aren't enough words
to describe my love for you.

Good-byes

"I WANT to take you somewhere," Ethan told Sara as they walked holding hands.

The final evening service had ended minutes earlier. It was the third service Ethan had attended in the last week. This one had started much later than the others so everyone could sit around a blazing campfire and listen to the pastor speak. He had held Sara's hand for the first time during the service. She had been hesitant when he first reached for her, but then she relaxed and let her fingers stay entwined with his.

Now Sara looked at her watch and shook her head. "I'll have to go in soon. I shouldn't."

"Come on. Break one rule. What are they going to do? Make you go home tomorrow?"

"Maybe they'll make me stay here," Sara said with a smirk.

"Now wouldn't that be a terrible thing?"

She gave in, so he led her up a hill that veered away from the campgrounds. Shining a flashlight before them to light the path, Ethan walked on through the dark woods. Sara silently clung to his firm grip. Ethan assured her it was safe. "I've been here a bunch of times," he said.

"At night?"

"Sure. That's the best time."

By the time they reached the big rock and climbed it, it was twenty minutes after curfew.

"I really have to go," Sara said in a nervous voice.

"I know, I know. But wait. Please. Just stay here for a minute. You've got to see this."

Ethan led her to the other side of the boulder. At the far edge, the ground dropped away suddenly, so that the giant rock seemed to hang far out over the valley below. In the distance, the silhouettes of hills and mountains stretched on forever. Two owls called back and forth to each other. Stars—millions of wondrous points—speckled the sky, lighting up the evening for them. And the moon smiled back at them from so close and far away.

Sara felt mesmerized by the majestic scene. Suddenly everything—the view, the mountaintop, Ethan—felt like a dream. "It's breathtaking," she uttered, instantly forgetting about the time.

She held on to his hand, and they both sat on the smooth top of the rock, talking quietly and gazing out at the sights below and above.

"I come out here and think about a lot of things," Ethan said. "I could never do that back home in Chicago. There wasn't anywhere to go."

"That's a benefit of living up here, isn't it?"

"Yeah, you're right. It is."

Sara knew about the ugly divorce Ethan's parents had just gone through. She knew he needed someone at this point in his life. And she was glad to be that person, if only for a few days.

"It's certainly peaceful," Sara said.

"I've been thinking about all that stuff they said at the services. I think that if I were to ever believe in a God above, it would have to be because of this."

"Because of what?" Sara asked.

"Because of this—this beauty. It's hard to believe that all of it just accidentally appeared one day."

Sara didn't say anything for a moment. She just stared off into the distance. "Then don't believe it was an accident," she finally stated. "It gives me hope to believe that God is above and that his plan included all of these mountains and stars and everything, including us."

"I think he might have goofed with me," Ethan said, half joking.

"I don't think he goofed. Not at all." Sara squeezed Ethan's hand.

Ethan nodded. "Did I tell you my mom believes in all that stuff?"

"She's a Christian?"

"Yeah, and she's always trying to get me to believe it all, too. It's just—I have a hard time. I mean, how can there be this loving God if life down here can be so horrible? When people are always leaving you, always saying good-bye—"

"God never leaves you," Sara said gently. "I look up above and know he is there, and sometimes he is the only one who keeps me secure and keeps me sane. I know he is with me all the time—like the day you first saw me."

"When you were praying?"

"Yes, when I was trespassing on your deck."

"I just—I don't know. My mom believes in all of that, yet how can she after my father left us on our own? I mean, she works so hard, and we can barely make ends meet."

Sara remained silent, holding his hand and listening. That was all she could do.

"Well, I know one thing I believe in," Ethan said. "I believe in us."

Sara looked at Ethan and smiled. His answering smile seemed as brilliant and as close as the light from the stars and the moon.

"I do too," she whispered.

"Can I ask you something, something serious, Sara? I actually want to be serious."

She nodded.

"I know this was weird luck, us meeting and everything. But I would really like to stay in touch. No commitments or anything, just stay in touch."

"We can," Sara replied with full sincerity in her voice.

"I know how these things go, when you meet someone and then you leave and go your separate ways. But right now I need to know there is someone I can believe in. Tell me you won't forget about me, about us."

"I won't. I won't ever."

Ethan moved toward Sara and gave her a sweet and simple kiss on her cheek. So brief and yet so meaningful, just like the last few days had been. Sara didn't move away; she looked back at him with a subdued smile.

"Sara, I've never met anyone like you. I know I'm young, that we're young, but I think I'm never going to meet anyone else like you. I don't want to."

Sara looked down. "I'm sorry," she said, wiping tears away. "I'm not upset. I just don't want to go. I don't want this to end."

"We'll see each other tomorrow," he said, but he knew they wouldn't have much time.

"Will you write me?" Sara asked.

He chuckled. "Remember? That's all I do around here besides talking with the groundhogs."

Sara smiled and wiped away more tears. "You will, then?"

"Of course I will," Ethan said. "But I want letters back."

She nodded. "It's a deal."

Ethan looked out over the valley below. "Wouldn't it be nice to spend the rest of our lives at a place like this, away from the world and its craziness?"

"I imagine heaven to be this beautiful," Sara said. "Even more."

Ethan looked into the skies and said nothing. Sara wasn't sure, but she thought he had tears in his eyes as well.

Your love gave me a chance.

Letters

Dear Sara,

It's cold, and the holidays are almost here, and before Santa Claus kidnaps you, I wanted to say Merry Christmas. I miss you. Yes, two and a half years after waving good-bye to you in that van headed back to Tennessee, I still miss you. I write to you from the same apartment in Chicago. Snow is falling, and they're predicting something like a foot. I still wonder why so many people endure these Midwestern winters.

I hope your first semester of college went well. Mine—well, the junior college isn't much. I live at home and make the ten-minute drive every day. I work at a local supermarket in their—get this—"farmstand department."

Still writing—all the time, in fact. My social life—well, there isn't much of that. Mom hasn't been doing too well these days. I think it's this weather. She seems so tired and sick all the time. Besides going to a few classes and working and helping take care of the apartment, I write. Still trying to finish that Great American Novel.

Your last letter said you were pretty serious with another guy. Good for him. As for me, well, I still have this dream that at some point in my life,

I'll see you again. I keep meeting girls and then comparing them to this dark-haired beauty I met years ago. I sometimes think nobody will ever measure up to you. I probably shouldn't do that, but I can't help it. You're special. I knew it the first time I saw you on the deck, praying of all things.

Thank you for the early Christmas present. The Bible is beautiful. I will do as you asked——I will read it. I promise.

Thanks for the photo as well. Needless to say, it is on my desk at home and is there in front of me whenever I write to you. The smile sends me off every day. Your sweet smile.

I hope the holidays and next semester will go well for you. Drop me a line when you can. I know you're busy. I'm still thinking about you.

Sincerely,
Ethan

Ethan:
Sorry for not having responded to all your letters. I love receiving them——I really do! The one you sent around Valentine's Day made me cry. Scottie and I broke up, and I felt pretty low, and then, of course, your letter and poem came. Thank you.

Probably the biggest thing in my life now is the news that my parents are moving to the Atlanta area. They'll be closer to me, since Covenant College is only half an hour from Atlanta, but still——I can't believe they'll be moving away from Tennessee. My dad is excited, and my mother's stressed——but she hopes to see me more. Sometimes that thought makes me happy, and sometimes it scares me to death. My mom and I have a, well, sort of a complicated relationship.

Sophomore year has been a lot more difficult. I'm taking a lot of basic courses that I have to take——like chemistry and philosophy. They're a lot of hard work. School's okay, but I think it'll be more fun once I get more into my major. I've decided to call it quits with the guys around here. I seem to do that every few years. Maybe if I meet someone who sends me poems and writes me lovely letters that will change. But I doubt it will.

I would love to see you. It's been so long——it would be hard to know how to act around you. I shouldn't feel that way, but I do. It seems like I know you so well. I mean, I guess I do, with all your letters and everything. They mean more to me than you'll ever know.

I pray for you every day. I still do. I pray for your mom, too. I hope she gets better. I'm sorry for all the stuff you are having to deal with. You have a huge heart, Ethan, and God certainly has plans for you. I know that.

I look forward to hearing from you. Take care of your mom and yourself.

Love,
Sara

I think I can actually begin
to understand that love.

Surprises

SARA HEARD the fifth ring and stood up from her desk to answer it. She had assumed one of her four roommates was around. She roamed the suite to find the cordless phone, finally spotting it on top of the microwave in the kitchen.

"Hello?" Silence for a second. Annoyed, Sara said hello again.

"Sara?"

"Yes, this is she." Sara began to think this was either a sales call or a freshman prank. "Who is this?"

"Sara, it's Ethan."

She couldn't believe it. His voice sounded so different, so much older. For a minute she was unsure what to say.

"I'm sorry to be calling you," Ethan said. "It's just, well, I had to."

"It's okay. It's great to hear from you."

It had been more than a year since Sara had last heard from Ethan. He had called her only a handful of times since their first meeting. Ethan had always made it clear that he wanted to talk to her but didn't want to pressure her in the slightest way. Most of the time, the letters had been enough for both of them—for some reason they cherished the special quality of their written correspondence. But special circumstances, like the news of her family's move to Atlanta, had prompted him to call her. Even then, he always apologized for calling and kept the conversations short—just long enough to make sure she was doing okay.

This time he quickly avoided any pleasantries. "My mom is really sick," Ethan said, his voice serious and direct.

"Is she—is she okay? I mean, what happened?"

Ethan's letters over the years had detailed his mother's declining health. She had a rare disease that had only been diagnosed in the past year. Since then, she had stopped working. Ethan's letters had been optimistic, however. This call came as a surprise.

"I've taken her to get some tests and stuff done."

"Where are you?'

"Well, actually, that's why I'm calling. We're seeing a specialist at Emory University Hospital. My mother got a bunch of information on this doctor off the Web, and we decided to give her a try."

"You're in Atlanta?" Sara asked, surprised that he was only thirty minutes away from her.

"Yeah. I know this is a surprise and all that, but I'm going to be around for a while, and I figured—"

"Ethan, I would love to see you."

"I know I'm sorta intruding. You might have plans and all that—"

"No, of course not. Please. I could come up to the city."

"Or I could come see you."

"Well, if that's what you want," Sara replied.

"To be honest, that's about the only thing I want right now. I've gotta get out of this hospital. My mom will be resting and having more tests. I can get away tonight."

"Well, I was just studying."

"You sure are a party animal."

"Here, let me tell you the directions. We can meet at the college."

As Sara dictated the turns and landmarks, her body felt alive with excitement and worry. How did she look? Oh, she looked horrible. She would have to change her clothes and definitely do something with her hair, and—

"Sara?" Ethan said.

"Yes?"

"Look, don't worry about me coming. I know this is unexpected. I don't want to make your life—or mine—any more complicated. I just need to see you. Right now, I kinda need a friend."

Sara smiled and wished he was already there. "Just hurry and get out here."

⚜

Sara sat at a picnic table in the center of the campus lawn that stood between the campus parking lot and one of her old dorms, Alabaster Hall. The April evening felt cool and still. She looked up through the trees and saw stars and remembered the evening with Ethan on the mountaintop in North Carolina. Her heart raced at the thought of seeing him again.

When the figure came walking toward the dorms, Sara knew it had to be Ethan. He was taller now, but with the same thick hair and bouncy walk. He wore khaki pants and a polo shirt. When he got closer, Sara could make out the serious look on his handsome face.

"Ethan . . . ," she said tentatively as she rose and approached him.

He glanced her way, and his face changed. He smiled and walked toward her. "Is that really you?" he asked, standing before her and continuing to smile.

"It is," she said, unsure what to do.

He looked down at her and took her hand. "I've rehearsed maybe a hundred times what I would do if I saw you again. What I would say." He looked at her hand. "I've missed you so much. I would have missed you more if I had known how beautiful you've become."

"Ethan—," Sara said, embarrassed.

Then Ethan let go of her hand and put his arms around her. She embraced him and buried herself in his open arms and against his chest. They held on to one another for several minutes. Sara realized Ethan was crying.

He pulled away from her and choked out a laugh. "I'm sorry. All that rehearsing, and what do I do? I act like a five-year-old."

"It's okay," she told him. "Things are going to be okay."

"It's so good to be near you again."

They walked over to the picnic table and sat down.

"It's been a while, hasn't it?" Ethan said, once again under control, once again smiling.

"A very long time. Almost six years."

"Sorry to drop in out of the blue."

"I'm sorry to hear about your mother."

They talked for hours, first at the picnic table, then at a coffee shop, then in the living room of her shared apartment—about Ethan's mother, about each other, about their senior year at college, about their prospective careers, and about everything else they could think of. Sara remembered why she had fallen for Ethan. He had this gift of opening up to her and letting her see everything about him, even his insecurities. He talked about his mother, and she winced to see the pain in his eyes. She remembered the last time she had seen him—that summer when they met. The pain had been there then, too, from his parents' divorce.

Why does life have to be so hard for some people? she wondered. She felt almost guilty. Except for the occasional conflict with her mother on the subject of her future, her life was really pretty easy.

Before he left to go back to Atlanta, Ethan made a request of Sara. "My mother asked me to ask you. Would you go see her?"

Sara swallowed and nodded. "Of course. Now?"

"No, in the next day or two. I told her I would ask you, but please, don't feel like you have to. It's just—I know you guys only met the week of camp years ago, but I've talked about you so much, she feels she knows you."

"Ethan, I'd love to see your mother. I feel like I know her, too."

"Tomorrow, then."

A silence drifted over their conversation for the first time since Ethan had approached Sara. She could tell he was lost in something, holding back his thoughts.

"What are you thinking about?" Sara asked.

"I didn't even ask you if you had a boyfriend or anything. I know you said in your last letter you didn't, but . . ."

"I still don't. Ever since sophomore year. And it drives my mother nuts. Every time I talk to her, she asks me if I've gone on any dates recently. And I always tell her no."

"Why haven't you?"

"I don't know. There have been some nice guys around here. I just—I don't know. It seems the only reason I'd be going out with any of those guys would be to please my mom. That's not a very good reason, is it?"

"Probably not."

"And you? What about you?"

Ethan smiled. "I still think of you every day, Sara. Don't say anything, please. I just want you to know that. My letters, the stuff I pour into them, are all true. You probably think I'm an idiot for continuing to write so much to you—"

"But I don't. I love your letters. I just wish I were better at answering."

"Can I ask you one question, then? Just one?"

"You can ask me anything," Sara said, afraid of what he would say.

"Was the thing that happened in the mountains years ago—was that just some high school crush?"

Sara looked at him and shook her head. "No, of course not."

Ethan took her hand and kissed it. "Thank you so much for seeing me tonight. And for going to see my mom tomorrow. I promise, no more questions about us. For now."

⚜

The hospital room where Marietta Ware lay was warm and comfortable. Ethan had brought some things from home to make the stay a little more pleasant—a few framed photographs, a whimsical stuffed bear, and a compact disc player. Sara greeted Ethan's mother with a bouquet of flowers.

The woman lying in bed with a hospital gown on and an IV in her arm smiled as if Sara were bringing her flowers at home. "It's good to see you again, Sara. It's been a long time, hasn't it?"

After a few minutes of small talk, Marietta turned to Ethan. "Now, Ethan, if you don't mind, I'd like to have a few minutes alone with Sara."

Ethan looked at his mother with surprise, his face flushing a bit. "What for? Why do I need to leave?"

"I just have something I'd like to talk to Sara about, if that's all right."

"Mom, come on. There's no reason—"

"It's okay, Ethan," Sara said, touching his arm. "I'd love to talk to your mom. It's fine."

Ethan looked at his mother as if to warn her not to say anything she shouldn't. Marietta only smiled at her son as he left the room and closed the door behind him.

"Sit down, please."

Sara pulled up a chair close to the bed.

"You're all he ever talks about—did you know that? Or thinks about."

This time, it was Sara who blushed. She didn't say anything.

"I see all those letters he sends. I knew it years ago after you left—how much in love he was with you."

Love, Sara thought. He had never said the word *love.* Did he love her? Was that true?

"I don't really know you, Sara, except for the things Ethan has told me about you. But I do know you've been a positive influence on him. He has been reading that Bible you sent to him a few years back."

"Oh, I'm so glad. I thought it might be good, you know, with the questions he has."

Marietta Ware sighed. "I no longer try to tell Ethan what he should or shouldn't believe in. I don't have the energy to try and make him believe anything. Besides, he's an adult now. He's twenty-two, you know? I imagine you are, too. Anyway, he doesn't listen to me. But he listens to you."

Sara nodded, surprised by Marietta's words. She felt afraid of what the woman might say next.

"Can I ask you a question?" Marietta said.

Sara nodded at the gaunt and pale figure in the bed.

"Do you love my son?"

Sara breathed in deeply and felt herself blush again. She hadn't expected any of this. "Well, I-I'm not sure. I—"

Marietta grinned. "I'm asking for my sake, not for his. And trust me, this is just between us. Now, can you see yourself ever loving Ethan?"

"Well, of course. It's just—I've never said that. We've never used that word, but—"

"Ethan loves you, dear. He loves you more than his own life. I see it. I don't need to hear it to know."

"Mrs. Ware, don't misunderstand. I think Ethan is wonderful. I just don't know—"

"Sara, I'd like for you to make me a promise. Just hear me out, okay. Actually, I can't believe I am talking to you like this. If I knew I had another ten years to live, I wouldn't ever bring this up. But I think the Lord is calling my name; calling to bring me home. I don't have much time left."

Sara's heart sank.

"You know about Ethan's father and me, right?"

"Yes. I'm sorry."

"I am too. That's been the most heartbreaking thing I ever had to go through. And to see Ethan hurt. But it was my fault as much as his father's. I married him knowing full well he wasn't a believer and never wanted to be one. I thought I could win him over. But I-I learned that some people in this world will never be won over. They'll never know the truth. Or at least they can't hear it from someone they're married to."

Marietta pointed to the door. "Now, Ethan out there—I pray for him every day. I guess you might be praying for him, too."

"I do. Every day."

The woman smiled. "That's good to hear. We need to pray. Now, like I said, I need you to promise me something."

Sarah nodded. "What is it?"

"Regardless of what happens between Ethan and you, don't ever give up on him. You're my only hope, I feel. Don't stop praying. I'm scared that if I'm no longer around, he will grow even more despondent."

"Don't say things like that," Sara replied.

"Please, Sara, promise me. Promise me you won't give up on him, that you'll keep him in your prayers. He's so close, I feel. So close to knowing the truth. He needs someone to help him find the truth."

"I won't give up on him. I've always hoped that he would come to know the Lord. Then things between us would make more sense. Or at least make more sense to me."

"He has cursed God, Sara. I've heard him do so. The bitterness inside him has grown over the years. And when I'm gone, I'm afraid the bitterness will grow even more."

"I won't stop praying for him. I promise."

Marietta smiled softly and seemed to sink back into her pillows. She was quiet a few seconds, as if gathering her energy again. "There's one more thing I want you to promise," she said.

"What is it?"

"This may be hard," the woman warned.

"Just tell me."

"If he doesn't, if he won't—oh, Sara, this is so difficult. I want you to pray for Ethan. I want you to care about him. But Sara, you need to hear this. Don't let yourself make the same mistake I made. Don't marry a man who doesn't love the Lord—even if it's my Ethan. It'll only cause more heartbreak."

Sara squirmed in her chair. "Mrs. Ware, we're not—I mean, I don't think—"

Marietta looked at a picture of Ethan and herself on the bedside table. "I thought marrying the man of my dreams would make things easier. I thought that all we needed was love. I thought having Ethan would bring us closer. But in the end he left me. In the end, I realized I wasn't what he needed. It was Christ."

"I'm sorry," Sara said.

"I'm saying all of this simply to ask you to be careful. Ethan's the only son I have, and it would be a blessing for him to end up with a woman like you. But you have to be very careful."

"I will."

"I recently realized that the only things that will follow you into heaven are loved ones who trust in Christ. And to think of Ethan not being there—"

The woman stopped and breathed in deeply as she wiped her eyes. Sara held on to her hand and searched for the right words to say.

Marietta smiled and relaxed once more. "I'm sorry to drop all of this on you. Please don't think of me as some overbearing mother."

"You're like any mother—you love your son."

"He's a good kid."

"I know."

"And he really does care about you."

Sara nodded.

"Don't give up on him, Sara. And never give up on our Lord, either. He has a plan for all of us. That includes Ethan and you."

Is there a plan for Ethan and me, Lord? Will we have the chance to be together? Could we ever be together?

"I don't know," Sara said.

"The Lord knows, Sara. Remember that."

There is still so much to comprehend.

Crossroads

ETHAN LOOKED out over the rocky ledge on the mountainside and spoke aloud to the emptiness he tried to convince himself he believed in.

"Will you take her from me, God?" he asked, the echo drifting away with the wind. "She's all I have now. You know that. How could you do that to me?"

He wanted an answer. He felt he had a right to one.

Is it too much to ask for?

The beauty answered him. The serenity of the skies replied to his words.

I need more, Ethan thought.

"God, don't take her."

He knew this was clichéd, his sitting on a hilltop, an unbeliever tossing up a last-minute prayer. But he didn't know anything more to do.

It had been a month since Ethan had brought his mother home to his uncle's cabin in Hartside, North Carolina. Every day he juggled the duties of a nurse, a maid, a cook, and most of all, a friend. He did everything he could for his mother. Yet nothing could stop the progression of her illness. Daily he saw her decline.

A week ago, Sara had driven up to the cabin to visit them. She had spent that week with them, sleeping upstairs in Ethan's loft room while he slept on the couch on the same floor as his mother. And in a way, despite his worry over his mother, it had been the best week of Ethan's life.

For the first time, Ethan was able to spend hours and days around Sara. He saw her messed-up hair and babylike complexion in the morning as he drank coffee; he got to see her eyes drifting closed as midnight approached. The two of them did everything Ethan had wanted them to do for years—watch movies they rented from the little store in town, take walks, talk for hours, read to each other from the various books in the cabin. It was more than romantic. Their time together had filled an emptiness in Ethan that he believed nothing else could.

But now that time was nearly over, and Sara would soon be leaving again. Ethan couldn't believe the week had passed so quickly, that he would have to tell her good-bye. *When I say that good-bye,* Ethan thought, *when will I see her again?*

He opened the spiral-bound notebook he had brought with him and began a short note for Sara to read after she left.

"What are you doing?" a voice asked from the forest behind him.

He smiled and closed the notebook. "Just writing," Ethan replied.

"I would have thought you'd want to see me some before I left."

"Do you have to leave today?"

"I've been here over a week," Sara said, sitting next to him. "I really should be leaving, even though I don't want to."

"Mom tell you where I went?"

"Yep," she replied with a smile.

"Strange how well your parents can know you, isn't it?"

Sara simply nodded and looked into the distance.

"What? What did I say?" Ethan asked.

"Nothing. Just the parent thing."

"What about it?"

"My parents don't know I'm up here."

"What did you tell them?"

"Nothing, actually. They think I'm still at college, tidying up things at the apartment before I go home."

"Will you tell them you came up here?"

Sara shook her head. "I don't know. I don't know what to tell them."

"Do they know about me?"

"A little. But with my parents, or at least with my mom, it's not that simple. She's got these . . . expectations. They expected me to meet some Mr. Wonderful at school and quickly get married."

"I'm not Mr. Wonderful?" Ethan asked, nudging her.

"Not their definition. They have such strong opinions about the guys I should date. My mom does, anyway."

He snorted. "I'll bet. And I bet a guy from Chicago who wants to be a writer just doesn't fit into what they think is right for their baby."

She didn't say anything. She just looked at him.

"But what about your expectations, Sara? You're an adult now. A college graduate. What do you want to do?"

"I just don't know anymore."

"Why not?"

"You're not listening to me. Things would be so much easier if—"

"If I believed the way you do, right? You want me to say there's a God. Okay. There's a God. I was actually just praying to him minutes ago."

"It's not that easy," Sara replied.

"Look, Sara, I know how deeply you believe in your God and all that stuff. And I wish I could believe it, too, but I can't. I'm not saying I don't believe in some of it, but all those rules and regulations, and this business with Jesus and the cross. I just don't know."

"I don't know either."

"What do you mean?" Ethan asked.

"I don't know about us."

"Sara—"

"No, I'm serious. Things are going too fast for me. I will start my first year as a teacher in a couple of months. I'll be living with my parents. There's so much going on right now."

"What about us?"

"This just complicates things, Ethan."

"Why? Tell me why it complicates things."

"Because you live in another state, for starters. And because we're so different. Not just in our beliefs. In everything."

"Just tell me this: Do you love me?"

"Ethan—"

"Do you? Answer me that question. Do you love me?"

"You don't understand. I know this is going to sound hokey, but there's no other way to put it. I love my Lord, the creator of everything in front of us and around us. And I just couldn't be with someone who doesn't share that love."

"Give me time."

"But how much time? Faith isn't something you can buy or something you can earn. You can't wake up one day and decide to have faith."

"So you're giving up on me."

"You know I won't do that."

"It's just, with everything going on with Mom and my life—"

"You need someone more than ever."

"I know I do."

Sara grabbed Ethan's hand. "Don't you see? I can't fill the void in your life. As much as you'd like to believe it, I can't be that person. The person you need is the same one who created this beautiful view in front of us. Remember that conversation we had here years ago?"

Ethan nodded and looked away.

"Can't you see that everything in your life is leading you into God's arms? Not mine, but his?"

Her words seemed to hang in the air. Finally he said, "Listen, let's not talk about this, not on your final day here."

"Ethan, we need to. I can't promise you what will happen when I go back home."

"It sounds like you've already made your decision."

Sara shook her head and stood. "Just keep reading that Bible I sent to you a while ago. Will you do that for me?"

"Sure." Ethan rolled his eyes.

"I'm serious."

"Look, Sara, I know all those stories by heart. Noah and Moses and talking donkeys and all of it. My mom's been telling me about that stuff ever since I was little. . . ."

"Read the book of John," she persisted.

He gave an elaborate shrug. "Okay," he said. "I'll read it. Cross my heart and all that stuff."

"I need to get back to the cabin."

"Sara?"

She turned around and he stood, grabbing her hand.

"I know it takes a lot of guts to be honest with me. I know it's probably not easy."

She looked at him with sad, dark eyes. "And I appreciate your honesty. I know you could have just pretended to believe, and you wouldn't do that. But I just wish you understood what you're missing. The Lord fills you with hope when you're going through rough times. He's always been there for me. I'm not making that up, either. It sounds like a line from a greeting card, but it's the absolute truth. And Ethan—you really need that hope."

Ethan shook his head.

"Keep reading that Bible I gave you," she said again.

He tore a sheet of paper from the spiral notebook he still held in his hand.

"Only if you'll promise to read this after you leave. It's something I wrote for you."

"It's a deal," Sara said.

What about our promises?

Doubts

SARA DROVE for four hours until she couldn't take it anymore. Then she took the next exit off the freeway and pulled into a McDonald's parking lot. In the silence of her car she wept tears that seemed to bleed from her eyes.

Why, God? Why do I have to have feelings like this for someone who doesn't believe in you? Why did this have to happen?

She had hoped that the week's visit with Ethan and his mother would have proven eventful. She had dreamed of Ethan's praying with her and asking for God's grace and salvation. That would have been a dream come true. But instead, Ethan had seemed more defiant than ever. His resistance to God had seemed as strong as his desire for her.

What more could she do?

She unfolded the letter he had given to her.

Dear Sara:
Falling down and masked in silence
I mutter an insignificant farewell as you go
Driving into a sunset and a future
Realizing there's still so much of me you don't know

Seven days having passed so quickly
I still can't believe this good-bye has to come
I cloak my emotions into a chuckle and a farewell
My wisdom fails and the words come undone
But the memories, like the night, will never leave me
A star in the sky will link us together
And years and miles and forgotten moments might pass
But the fact that I love you will last forever

Ethan

He used the L-word. He actually said he loves me.

Sara folded the letter and laid it back on the seat beside her, then put the car in reverse and backed out of her parking slot. She felt weary and confused and unsure what to do anymore.

God, I don't understand why you have allowed me to fall in love with Ethan. I know I shouldn't be, so why does it seem so right? Give me an answer, Lord. Please give me something.

The miles of road stretched out before her. Every time Sara blinked, she could recall Ethan's melancholy smile. With every breath she took, she remembered the lostness of his eyes.

Be with him, Lord. Give him peace. Show him how much you love him, how much you love all of us. Show him the true meaning of the word he used in his letter.

Love.

PART THREE

Have you forgotten?

Miles

ETHAN HAD DONE some stupid things in his life. In fact, he had done a lot of stupid things. He only hoped and prayed this wouldn't go on record as being one of them.

The speedometer in his '86 Honda CRX read seventy-five miles per hour. Ethan realized he was pushing it. One of the many questions he kept asking himself was, would his car endure the trip? He could picture it stalling on the edge of the interstate somewhere in the middle of Indiana.

Three weeks had passed since he had received the letter from Uncle Pete. On five separate occasions, Ethan had almost made the plane reservations for Germany. But ultimately he had decided to go with his gut feeling—to get in the car and drive and try to find Sara. What a hopeless romantic he was. Sara used to tell him that. But he knew it was one of the things she loved about him.

That was also where they differed. Sara would never just get up and go somewhere on a whim. She was so deliberate, so thoughtful and practical about every decision she made.

This certainly was anything but thoughtful—just getting in the car and driving to Georgia. Even though he didn't know where Sara lived, he knew her parents' address. He would spend a few days at his uncle's cabin in North Carolina before heading on to Atlanta. Maybe a little time on the mountain would give him clarity regarding his trip to Europe. Did he really want to go?

Ethan remembered the late-night phone call he had made to Andy, his college roommate and buddy, not long before leaving Chicago. Andy had been delighted to hear from Ethan and asked when they could get together.

"We can't," Ethan had said. "Not now. I've got a dilemma on my hands."

Then he had explained to Andy about the decision he was weighing, about his desire to know for one final time whether or not he and Sara had a future. His old roommate knew the history of Ethan and Sara better than almost anyone; Ethan had told him the whole story many times in the past, over many beers.

"We should get together and talk," Andy urged.

But as much as Ethan wanted to see his friend, something told him that drowning his sorrows in more beer and sympathy was not the way to solve his problem. Not anymore. He turned down Andy's invitations. Several times.

Eventually, Andy told him what he wanted and needed to hear: Go find her then. Andy was a no-nonsense, "put up or shut up" sort of guy. That's what Ethan had always liked about him.

Ethan actually felt a bit of satisfaction at being able to tell his friend he couldn't see him. In the past, anytime there was trouble, Ethan had always tended to lose himself either in his writing or his few friends. Neither had made the problems of life go away.

But things were different now. He was different. Didn't Sara know that?

The old Honda felt unsteady. Anytime he approached speeds over seventy miles an hour, the car shook and threatened to break apart at the seams. And now it was loaded down with all his possessions—several suitcases and a couple of overstuffed boxes.

Taking off on road trips wasn't foreign to Ethan. During his wild college days there had been several weeks when he and his buddies went driving around the country, usually doing nothing worth mentioning.

After college, just after his mother's death, he had taken off on a solo trip, a trip to find the meaning of life and to search for himself.

That had been when the writing stopped. He had driven the same Honda and filled the backseat with journals and books, planning to write down thoughts and poems and impressions and perhaps even a novel. He had written nothing on the trip, however, and almost nothing in the years that followed, except for the required articles he handed in to the editor of his newspaper. Ethan was thankful he could produce material in order to earn a living. But he hadn't been able to write anything else.

The trip after college had started his long bout of writer's block. The trip also happened right after Sara said no to his proposal. Memories of that journey still haunted him.

Hopefully this trip would be different.

So much was different now, although writing continued to be a problem. At the same time, writing wasn't his top priority anymore. What he needed to figure out was what he was going to do with his life. At thirty years of age, Ethan was basically starting over again. It frightened him.

What if I do find Sara? he wondered. *What will I tell her? That I have no job and I can't write anymore? That I have no idea what I'm supposed to do with my life?*

He didn't care. All he wanted was to look into those healing eyes one more time and hear the truth once and for all. Why had she stopped loving him? That's all he wanted to know.

He drove on toward North Carolina with only a vague idea of what would happen next. For now, it seemed like the only logical thing to do. He needed to get away from Chicago, yet he wasn't ready to go to Europe and be bound to his uncle indefinitely. He definitely needed to see Sara.

Please let me find some answers, Ethan thought.

Now I understand the things
you once described for me.

Hilltops

SARA was on the third playing of her favorite Enya CD as she took the exit that would take her to Hartside. The uplifting voice and soothing music helped to dispel the cloud that rested over Sara's mood. She had already been driving in her convertible for four hours; she figured she had a couple more to go.

What am I doing? Sara wasn't exactly sure. Maybe she just needed some time and space away from everyone and everything. But going to Hartside to try and find it? No, there was more to this trip.

Maybe he's there. But that was silly. Of course Ethan wouldn't be in Hartside. But still Sara longed to see those beautiful hills one more time in order to think about what she was doing. It was only July, but she knew that December would be there in a few blinks of an eye. And if she wasn't 100 percent sure about marrying Bruce, she didn't want to lead him on.

Weeks after Bruce's proposal, Sara still struggled with doubts. This trip would give her the answers she needed.

She hoped.

Enya was singing, "This is where I should be now," and Sara felt that the words confirmed the feelings in her heart. This is what she should be doing. Unplanned and spontaneous—so what? Ethan would have been proud.

Sara didn't feel guilty. She hadn't lied to her parents or to Bruce. She simply hadn't told them where she was going. In fact, only her friend Elyse knew where she was at the moment. But she would call her parents tonight and tell them the truth. And the truth was simple: She wanted to go back to Hartside. To take a mini-vacation and enjoy her summer break. She didn't plan on being away for long—maybe just a couple of nights.

A week ago she had even discussed with her parents and Bruce the possibility of her taking a trip like this by herself. The general consensus was that they would all take a trip somewhere this summer. But Sara had nixed that idea without a further thought.. She didn't want to go "somewhere." She wanted to go back to Hartside. And she couldn't bear the thought of going back there with her parents or, even worse, with Bruce.

Sara hadn't mentioned Hartside to her parents then. Her mother would have seen through her intentions. Her mother would have remembered the boy who once sent dozens of letters with a Hartside return address written on the envelope.

Like the highway that cut through rolling hills on each side, recollections of her past seemed to roll on and on. Light plumes of memory drifted across her mind. As she neared the mountain getaway, those reflections became clearer.

She was remembering the week she had spent with Ethan and his mother in Hartside after college. The week when Sara had realized she was truly falling in love with him, when he had told her for the first time that he loved her.

It had been only months before Ethan's mother passed away. Things had been so different then. For a while after that trip, Sara had even started to believe that Ethan was changing. He continued to raise questions with her in his letters, mentioned that he was going to Hartside Bible Church with his mother, and even admitted he had actually prayed for his mother's health. Sara continued to write to Ethan about how much she loved her Savior and what her faith meant to her. And Ethan seemed to begin to understand. At least Sara had thought so.

But then his mother died.

And everything changed.

It all seemed just like yesterday. With the music softly playing and the midday highway mostly empty, Sara continued to remember all the circumstances that led to their final farewell. Ultimately, she knew this was why she was going back to Hartside. To remember.

And what if I saw him today? Sara asked herself. *What would I tell him? What would I say if he asked how passionate my love for the Lord is now? Would I be as bold and brave in my response as I once was?*

The very thought brought a dread over Sara. She searched her motives and her feelings and tried to pray but felt the distance again. Maybe she was disobeying God by not putting enough trust in him. Maybe his will was so obvious and she was running in the opposite direction.

Sara thought of the passages in the book of Psalms she had read this morning:

"O Lord, you have examined my heart and know everything about me."

What do you see inside?

"O Lord, God of my salvation, I have cried out to you day and night. Now hear my prayer; listen to my cry."

Have you listened, Father? Have you heard me at all?

"Give thanks to the Lord, for he is good!"

I can't give him thanks. I am unable to. I know I should praise him in all things, but I just can't. I feel overwhelmed.

"For I am overwhelmed, and you alone know the way I should turn."

But it's so hard to keep heading in the right direction, Lord. I've had my faults and failures, but I've always trusted you like a child, Lord. All my life I've trusted and loved you, and yet why can't I have this one thing?

The Psalms continued to echo through Sara's thoughts. The words of David were always antidotes to sorrow, uplifting praises during life's heartaches. She knew the verses by heart and carried them close to her soul. But now she wasn't sure if they were more comforting or scolding.

"Have mercy on me, O God, because of your unfailing love."

I pray to see you again,
perhaps for just a moment.

Miracles

THE MOUNTAINS felt like home to Ethan. He always felt safe in their rugged sanctuary. While he had spent many months in them over the years, they stood out for two memorable periods in his life: the time after his father left them, when he and his mother spent an entire summer in Hartside; and the time after his mother passed away, when Ethan had retreated to the solitude of the cabin. Where Sara had visited briefly . . . and left for good.

The latter had happened eight summers ago. *Can Mom be gone that long?* Ethan wondered as he sat on a rocking chair on the cabin deck. Eight years.

What have I done in those eight years? Ethan thought. *Would Mom be proud?*

He didn't know. He didn't think she would have been proud. And this was the most haunting and hurting realization of his life. His mother had always wanted the best for him, and, growing up, Ethan had expected the best of himself. Dreams of being a writer, of finding the perfect place to live, of marrying the right woman—these had been normal for him when his mother was still alive. But everything had died when she did.

Everything except his love for Sara.

Ethan thought about writing to her again. Why couldn't he just give up and move on like any rational human being? When she didn't answer his last letter, surely he should have gotten the picture. For some reason, Sara was not a part of his life anymore. When she said good-bye all those years ago on the mountain, she really must have meant good-bye.

What will I say to her if I find her? Ethan wondered. He had never officially met her parents, so he would have to do some explaining to them. They might not be friendly, or they might not want to tell him where she lived.

But still he needed to know. He needed to be sure. *Just one more good-bye,* he thought. *One more good-bye is all I need.*

The midday sun warmed him as he sat there on the deck. The air was still and silent—almost too silent. Ethan stood up and stretched, then headed down the steps to the driveway. He would go into the town of Hartside to have some lunch. It might be good to go out in public and be around some other people.

⚜

It was around two in the afternoon when it happened.

He had just finished lunch at the downtown diner and was sitting in his car, wondering what to do next. The two-door Honda was nestled among a line of cars parked along the sidewalk. He was debating about whether to drive around or go back to the cabin when he saw her—and froze.

Could it be? No, surely not.

The woman walked casually by his car and along the small main street, stopping in front of the tiny bridal shop called Cherished Memories. He sat transfixed in his car seat and just watched her as she disappeared inside the store.

It was remarkable. She was stunning; he would have gawked at her regardless of whom she looked like. But the resemblance made everything in him stop, including his heartbeat.

Time and painful memories were getting to him. He knew they were. They had to be. The woman looked like an older and more beautiful Sara Anthony.

Impossible.

Never did he once consider that it might indeed be her. Things like that only happened in the movies. This was reality—dull, boring, normal reality. Painful reality. This wasn't the Jimmy Stewart movie in which

George Bailey wakes up and realizes the whole town has just saved his life by giving him a boatload of money on Christmas Eve.

It can't be that wonderful of a life. No way.

The woman had short, black hair with long bangs that fell into her face. Her outfit was dressy casual—khaki pants and a dark shirt with a khaki vest. He couldn't see her eyes because of her black sunglasses, but still, the resemblance was incredible. The high cheekbones, the graceful walk, the way her hand brushed the hair out of her face.

You're seeing things now, Ethan told himself. *The cabin and this town are getting to you.*

For a few minutes he sat with his mouth half open and his eyes riveted on the door to Cherished Memories. Then he shook his head and looked around, trying to make sense of what had just happened. Nothing came to him.

He waited. His heart ached, and his stomach felt like it might either explode or implode. His brain thought a million different thoughts.

What if? What if it was her—sweet and precious and wonderful Sara Anthony? Would she look like that now, so sophisticated and grown up? This woman was almost intimidating; she couldn't be the same bashful girl I met years ago. Could she have grown up to be such an amazing-looking woman?

Cherished Memories. It was the same store they had browsed through years earlier, during that wonderful week she had stayed with him and his mother.

So what now? What was this woman who looked like Sara doing in that store? The woman emerged from the bridal shop forty minutes later. In the instant before she put on the sunglasses, her eyes gave him the answer.

It *was* her. It had to be her. Sara Anthony was standing there only fifty yards away from him. The love of his life was there, right there, right in front of him.

All the memories and the driving and the hopes and desires—and there she was, just walking past him on a normal street.

Wake up, George Bailey. It sure is a wonderful life.

He watched the woman walk to a shiny, late-model convertible, maneuver into the front seat, and drive off. And without thinking, not even sure what to think, Ethan followed her.

For thirty minutes he followed her around the town. It was as if he was following himself a day ago, when he had just driven up and down the streets, looking around. He felt like an idiot, following this woman. If it indeed was Sara, why didn't he just stop her? Perhaps run to her car and declare his love to her right away? He could easily flag her down and talk. So why didn't he?

He told himself he wasn't sure this was her. But even if it was, what then? What about his last letter, about everything?

Doubt plagued him. Once again, he was a fifth grader, too shy to talk to a pretty classmate, too embarrassed and insecure to see her response. But he knew this was Sara. It had to be. So why was she in town? Did she live here? No, of course not. Her car had Georgia license plates on it.

So why was she visiting the bridal store?

This was crazy. Insane. Ridiculous. Ethan shouted out thoughts to himself. "I'm nuts," he yelled out loud, trying to see if this was indeed a dream. It wasn't.

So what now? Only hours earlier he had been hoping, searching for some sort of direction as to what he should do about Sara. Now there she was in front of him, and he still didn't know what to do.

Her convertible ended up at a bed-and-breakfast on the outskirts of town. Ethan watched Sara get out and go inside, her short hair bouncing as she walked. He couldn't believe he was actually watching the striking figure in person rather than looking at a worn and outdated photo.

He started to pull over as he passed the bed-and-breakfast.

Go see her. Go see her now. Go to her, fool.

Yet he drove off back toward the center of town. He parked and walked over to Cherished Memories. He could feel his heart pounding and his breath quivering unsteadily.

Inside the quaint store, things hadn't changed much from what he remembered. Peaceful music played, the scent of roses hovered in the air, and everything was white and pink. Rows of dresses lined the walls of the small shop. The older woman at the counter might have been there years ago when they visited; Ethan wasn't sure.

"Good afternoon," she said with a smile.

"Uh, hi there. I was wondering. I saw an old friend in here earlier——or someone I think is an old friend. And I was wondering if you might have gotten her name."

The older woman looked puzzled. *Well, that's it,* Ethan told himself. *I really have gone lovesick and insane. I'm seeing visions now.*

"Lots of ladies come in. Could you describe her?"

So Ethan described the love of his life. "She's fairly short, nicely dressed, dark hair, wearing a khaki vest—"

"Oh yes, the elegant young lady. Very attractive."

"Yes."

"Well, let's see here. She didn't tell me her name, I don't think. I asked if she was visiting, and she said yes. I think she said she was from . . . let's see . . ."

Ethan didn't breathe for a second or a minute or an eternity as he waited to hear. The woman behind the counter remembered.

"She was from Atlanta. Or the area around Atlanta— that's right. You'd be surprised how many Atlanta folks we get way up here."

Ethan gulped in a breath of air and felt woozy. "Did she say anything else?" Ethan asked. "That she's married or anything like that?"

The older woman gave Ethan a puzzled look. "Are you from around here?"

"Well, yes and no. I mean, my uncle has a place up in the hills. Peter Madden."

"Oh, Pete? Yes, I think I remember him. So you're his nephew?"

"Uh, yes."

"I think I might have met your mother years ago."

"Maybe. Her name was Marietta."

"That's right," the older woman said, a smile on her face. "How's she doing these days?"

"She, uh, everything's fine." Ethan didn't want to go into details about his personal life, especially not now.

"The woman we were talking about, the one from Atlanta," Ethan said. "Did she mention anything about being married?"

"Well, actually, she said her wedding date is December 26. Odd date, wouldn't you say?"

He let out a surprised gasp. The woman from Atlanta part was fine, was good, was wonderful. But what was this part about marriage on December 26?

"Wedding date of . . . to whom? Can I, do you have the, uh, name?"

The woman looked at him for a second. "Are you okay, Son?"

"Yeah, sure, just real—I don't know—excited. I guess. A name or anything? Do you have one?"

"No. I'm sorry. She didn't talk too much. She bought a picture frame, I believe, and a card."

"A picture frame and a card?" Ethan asked, shocked and delirious.

"Say, you look pale, Son."

And Ethan said no more. He forgot to even thank the older woman as he opened the door and stumbled outside into the hot and crumbling world.

December 26? The day after Christmas?

Ho, ho, ho.

Ethan stood on the sidewalk and stared at the Cherished Memories sign. *Cherished memories,* he thought. *Maybe that's all I'll ever be able to have with Sara.*

All this way, all these years, all the love, all the dreams, all the hopes and desires . . . for what? For this little piece of wonderful information— that Sara Anthony is going to marry somebody else a day after Christmas.

The sun made Ethan want to faint. The only other time he had felt this horrible was after seeing his mother close her eyes for one final time.

But then, at least, he had been able to brace himself for impact, like a passenger on a 747 plummeting to earth yet able to buckle in the seat belt and prepare for the crash.

This had been too sudden. This time he had been blindsided.

It's all over, Ethan said to himself as he got back in his car and wondered what to do now.

HARTSIDE   N.C.

There are so many things
I want to tell you..

HARTSIDE NC

Decisions

SARA HADN'T EATEN anything for a day and a half. She didn't consider herself to be fasting; food simply wasn't on her mind.

She had a decision to make. Actually, in her heart she knew she had already decided.

But having made the decision didn't take away the sense of disappointment she felt.

She knew she had been foolish to think something might happen simply because she was in Hartside. She had told herself that if something didn't intervene, some miracle or some kind of obstruction, she would go through with the wedding. And there had been no miracle that she could see—no clear word.

Yet here she was, in a guest room all alone, still thinking about Ethan. So maybe there had been an intervention after all. Maybe this sense of sad clarity about what she needed to do next was God's answer to her prayers.

But it wasn't exactly the answer she had hoped for.

She found herself wishing once again that Ethan had not stopped writing her. He had always been so good about keeping in touch and letting her know how he was doing. She had never understood why it suddenly stopped.

But maybe that had been her fault. Maybe her response to his proposal had been the final thing. Maybe her no had been the end.

When she first came to town a couple of days ago, Sara had driven out to the log cabin where she had first met Ethan. It had only proved to be a haunting reminder of the last time she'd seen him. The place looked empty and abandoned, the same way her heart felt when she saw it. She had only stayed around there for a few minutes. The place held too many painful reminders of the past.

Now, in the stillness of her guest room, Sara found her thoughts straying back to that cabin—and that last day they had shared together.

It had been the winter after his mother died. She had driven up to the cabin to see Ethan, who was still staying there. At the time, she wasn't sure what would happen. She only knew that their relationship over the years had intensified. What had begun as a summer romance had built into an enduring friendship then blossomed into real love.

But what would come next? Marriage? Of course, she had dreamed of marrying Ethan. But that was out of the question.

Marietta Ware had been right. She shouldn't go into a marriage knowing that the one thing they disagreed on happened to be the most important basis for a life together: God. She didn't want to spend her years with the man she loved trying to convince him about Jesus Christ and his never-failing love. She couldn't do that to herself—or to Ethan.

When she visited him on the mountain after Marietta's death, Sara had wondered whether Ethan's heart had changed. She had hoped this would be the case, but her hopes were not to be realized.

She had shown up at the cabin with a furious mountain storm on her heels. And immediately she had sensed that another storm had settled in Ethan's heart.

Although Ethan had welcomed her warmly enough, the change in him had been obvious. She hadn't seen or talked with him at length since his mother's funeral, and her first glimpse of him troubled her.

He had grown a beard and looked quite thin. He was still handsome; Ethan Ware would always look handsome. But he didn't look healthy or happy.

"I'm glad you came," Ethan told her, giving her a big hug. Then he broke down and cried in her arms.

And in the course of the few hours Sara spent with him, she learned much more about his past summer than he had written her—about his aimless wanderings through several western states, about his inability to write, about his pain and defiance. He said he believed in God now, but he also hated the God who killed his mother. His words startled Sara and pierced her heart.

"Please, Ethan, don't say that," she said, but he refused to stay quiet.

He blamed God for everything bad in his life—his parents' split, his mother's death, Sara's reluctance to be with him, his own miserable existence, his inability to write. He told her how unhappy he was, how miserable life was without her.

"It's not me that you need, Ethan," Sara told him. "It's Christ and his love."

But he couldn't hear her. Or he wouldn't hear her. They talked for hours while the storm outside the cabin worsened. Finally, Sara knew she needed to leave.

But before she did, out on the deck in the deepening gloom, a desperate and breaking man proposed to her. He begged her not to leave, begged her to marry him, insisted they could work things out.

And Sara had no choice. She had to say no, aware that this no was perhaps a final one. It was the hardest thing she had ever done.

But before she left, they made their promises to one another.

Promises.

She could still hear Ethan's choked voice saying the words that still hung heavy to her heart. "I promise you with everything I have and everything I am that my love for you will never die." And her solemn response. "I'm going to make a promise to you. I'm never giving up on you. Every night I'm going to pray that you find your place in this world, that you find hope." A place in this world.

Hope.

Promises offered up before good-byes.

But what had happened to those promises? She had kept hers. Had Ethan kept his?

Look at the irony, Sara told herself. *You kept both promises. You continued to pray for him, and you continued to love him. And why did I say no? Would I still say no? Would I still turn him away?*

"Love the Lord your God with all your heart, all your soul, all your strength, and all your mind."

I do, Lord. I love you so much. And I want my husband to love you as much, or even more. How could I possibly be with someone who doesn't even claim to know your name?

It should be so simple. But her feelings weren't simple. And no matter how many years passed, Sara was unsure if she would ever get over those deep-rooted emotions. Yet she knew the decision she had made back then and the decision she was making now were the right ones.

She began to pray. She asked God for peace, asked to be shown the way. And gradually she felt the peace settle in her heart. In this small Appalachian town so far away from home, peace came.

She had to be doing the right thing. She must.

She prayed for Ethan, for his soul, for his life. She finally accepted that what they had had was over now. Finished. And the finality of that acceptance filled her with a deep sense of sadness. Perhaps she should have realized that months, years ago. But those promises they made had haunted her.

Promises.

She had kept her promise. If only Ethan could know.

She thought of her life back home in Georgia. Of her parents. Of Bruce. She prayed for them, too, and for the courage to do what she had to do next.

Maybe Ethan wouldn't know that she had kept that promise, but Bruce and her parents would.

HARTSIDE N.C.

I won't dare ask again,
but I still wonder
what you will say.

Farewells

THE SUN creaking in on Ethan through the side window of his car woke him up. His back ached and his right arm that had been used as a pillow felt numb and lifeless. As he wiggled his arm to get the feeling into it again, he realized that he had fallen asleep watching the bed-and-breakfast where Sara Anthony was staying.

Yes, now I'm really going places in the world, he thought. *If she saw me now she'd think I was some wacko stalker.*

He still had not been able to go inside and knock on Sara's door. All night he had tried to get up the nerve to do it. But he couldn't. Now, early this morning, he still couldn't.

How could he do that to her? She didn't deserve that. And he didn't deserve her. He never had deserved her—her love, her steadfastness, her commitment. He couldn't just crash into her world now and destroy all her plans.

She had obviously made her decision. He couldn't try to change it.

Still, he needed to be sure. He needed and wanted to see her one more time, just once more. The certainty of her decision would help him bring closure to an unrealized dream. He could take this memory with him to wherever he might go. Wherever life, however hollow it might seem now, might lead him.

The morning was just beginning. He would wait—just as he had waited years ago for her to come to him.

⚜

Months after his mother's death, the sting of losing her had still felt fresh and sharp. As weeks dragged into months, he had gradually grown more despondent about life. First, he had taken the trip west, attempting to put the pain behind him, only to end up feeling more lost. Then he had stayed in his uncle's cabin and done nothing for days and weeks. It was only after a desperate plea to Sara that he got a chance to see her again.

That was when he proposed to her.

He should have never thought he deserved a girl like her. He didn't. But she wanted to be with him, even though she ultimately said no. Another no—and for the same reason she had always said no to him. God.

Ethan remembered cursing God many days and nights, blaming him for every horrible thing that had happened to him. Part of him had always believed in God's existence. It was the idea of a loving God that he had problems with.

As far as he was able to see, God had brought nothing but pain and loss into his life. God didn't love him—couldn't love him. And so he hurled curses and blame up into skies that seemed empty and cold.

So when Sara left him after he proposed—well, that had been just another reason to blame God. And it had been so easy to do. It was easy to curse someone who didn't give you what you wanted, to point a finger at someone in a distant heaven and place the blame.

That had been the beginning of all the events that followed, all the changes.

But, even though he had shared this with Sara, why hadn't she responded?

⚜

Half a day passed. It was coming down to one more good-bye. One final farewell. Ethan followed Sara back to town, back to fate and destiny and happily ever after and the end of all his hopes.

It was nearly noon. He had been sitting in his car for what—twenty-four hours? Almost. He felt dirty and greasy and his breath was probably horrible and if she saw him now she would surely run away from him. The years had only enhanced her beauty, made her look sleeker and stronger. And he looked, well, pitiful and desperate. Probably even insane.

Who cares? a voice told him. *Go see her; don't let her go. Don't, Ethan. Don't let this opportunity pass. You'll never have another chance like this.*

The voice lingered.

Sara's white convertible turned onto the main street and drove past his own car. The top was down, and Ethan watched her carefully as she passed. Her silky black bangs were blowing in the breeze. She had no idea he was so close.

Now, Ethan. Do something now. Don't let her go. Not again. Not like this.

But he couldn't say or do anything. He couldn't bring himself to speak or yell or move. She belonged to another. She loved someone else. He had never had any place in her life—not then, and not now.

He never would.

Honk the horn, the voice continued to yell. *Follow her! Come on, do something!*

But the convertible just drove down the street and out of sight. Ethan sat in his hot car and felt his stomach muscles tighten and his jaw clench and his hands grip the steering wheel.

He braced himself for an impact. An impact harder than any he had ever experienced. Lost love. The finality of it would hit him soon enough.

This was it. His moment. His moment to chase after her, to snatch her up and drive off into the sunset with her.

But Ethan knew life didn't always serve up happy endings. Sara deserved happiness. She deserved a joyous ending, a wonderful life. And all he would do was upset her, make her worry. He couldn't do that. He wouldn't.

"I love you, Sara," his breaking voice said out loud, as though she might hear and turn around.

She will never hear, Ethan thought. This was why he had come back—to find out the truth. And this was the truth: He loved a woman he knew he couldn't have—a woman who loved another man.

He started the car and began the drive—he didn't know where. He just
wanted to get far away from Hartside and from North Carolina and from
the memory of Sara. He wanted to go home. But where was his home? He
didn't have one.

He had thought—and hoped—that his place was still at her side. He
had been wrong.

"Good-bye, Sara."

PART FOUR

Am I simply being foolish
to think so much about you?

Confessions

SARA HELD Bruce's hand as he stared off into the lake in front of them. They had been sitting on the bench for a long hour.

"And the trip—did you see Ethan?"

"No," Sara replied. "He wasn't there."

"I just don't get this. One minute things are set in stone, and the next you're driving off to North Carolina to find an old boyfriend. And then you come back to tell me we're not getting married."

"I told you why, Bruce. I don't know what more to say except how sorry I am."

Sara had told Bruce everything. Everything. Now, there was a concept. This was a first for them—another reason she had decided to break off the engagement to Bruce.

I want the man I marry to be someone I can tell everything to, Sara had reasoned. *I want to be sure it's the right decision. I want to go into the marriage without any doubts. Sure, there might be fears, but no doubts. No doubts whatsoever of my love.*

Sara had told Bruce exactly that. Her feelings didn't match his. Her love for him—was it a genuine love? She didn't know. And until she did, she couldn't go through with the wedding.

For the last hour they had been talking. She had apologized as she gave him back his ring. He didn't cry or yell; instead, he tried to reason and bargain with her. He looked more puzzled than distraught.

"Please just keep the ring," he told her. "And think it over."

"I've already kept one ring, Bruce. I can't keep another."

"But —you need to think this through."

"I have thought things through, Bruce. That's why I went to North Carolina."

"To find a guy you had a crush on when you were a kid?" Bruce said, desperation slipping into his voice.

"You don't understand," Sara said, taking her hand away from his and shaking her head.

"Sara, look, I love you. I want to marry you. I'll wait for you if that's what you want me to do. That's okay. It's just—I thought you were ready."

"Maybe at one point, I thought I was, too. I wanted to be ready. But I found out I'm not."

"But all of our talk about finding a house and starting a family . . ."

"Don't you see? I always thought I would have those things by the time I turned thirty. I got scared."

"And that's why you said yes? You didn't have any feelings for me at all?"

"No, that's not true. Bruce, I really like being with you, and I think you'll make some woman a great husband. It's just—I'm not that woman."

"I think you are."

Sara took his hand again and looked out over the lake. Ducks swam around in groups. A small boy was throwing out bread crumbs in their general direction, quickly drawing a feathered following. The sky was a perfect blue, and the late July afternoon was unusually cool for summertime in Georgia.

Sara sought for the right words to say. "Did you ever have a dream when you were a kid?" Sara asked him.

"Sure. Starting my business, being successful—that sort of thing."

"My dream was to find someone who made me laugh, who loved me unconditionally, who was everything I'd never be. But I always ended up meeting guys who let me down. Then I met Ethan unexpectedly, and he was the somebody I'd dreamed of. He continued to write to me and stay in touch even as I dated other guys and lived far away. He never gave up on me. And years ago I realized I had fallen in love with him."

"But you don't even know where this Ethan guy is. It's been so many years. How do you know he hasn't given up on you?"

"I don't. But that doesn't really change things between you and me."

"But you want to marry this guy, right? If you saw him, you'd say yes and live happily ever after?"

"No. The things that kept us apart are still real. But I feel the same love I did years ago when he proposed to me. I can't explain that. I thought it would have faded. I didn't realize that the love I had for Ethan never left me."

"I can't believe this."

"Bruce, I'm sorry. I don't mean to hurt you. I just couldn't go on like this. I couldn't hide this from you—not something this important. And I couldn't go through with marrying you when I felt this way about someone else."

"This is just totally unlike you, Sara. I'm just surprised."

"Falling for a guy like Ethan was unlike me, too."

There was an awkward silence. Sara once again apologized to Bruce.

"What did your parents say?" Bruce asked.

"I haven't told them yet."

Bruce smiled for the first time that afternoon—a wan, regretful smile.

"Your mom isn't exactly going to be happy."

"I know."

They talked for another half hour; then they walked away from the lake and back to Bruce's car. He stopped her before they drove away.

"Sara, I know I might have pushed a little too hard for this marriage. And I know I'm not like this Ethan guy—I mean, I can't write poetry and romantic love letters and stuff like that. I'm just—well, what you see is what you get. But I want you to know I still love you—and I'm not going anywhere. When you're through waiting for someone who's never going to show up, I'll be waiting."

"Bruce——"

"I'm serious. You don't have to keep my ring. But if you have second thoughts in a week, or a month, I'll still be here. And you don't have to say that I'm the greatest love of your life or anything like that. Just say you'll be my wife, and that'll be enough for me."

"Please——"

"That's all. I won't say any more."

⚜

The evening's conversation would be even more intense and emotional. Sara was eating dinner at her parents' house. After they finished the meal, she asked if they could talk.

"You didn't touch your food, Sara," her mother said. "Are you all right?"

"Yes."

"How's Bruce? Are things okay with you two?"

Instantly her mother had picked up on what was going on. And instantly her mother's own fears had become apparent. Something wrong with Sara? Something wrong with the blessed marriage-to-be?

"That's what I want to talk with you two about. Bruce and me."

So for the second time that day, Sara told someone what she was feeling in her heart—that she couldn't go through with the marriage. Daniel Anthony listened with compassion and understanding on his face; Lila Anthony's usually composed expression turned to wide-eyed dismay.

"What are you talking about—you have feelings for someone else?" she said through clenched teeth.

"Mom, I still love Ethan Ware."

Lila looked at her husband, then back at Sara. "Ethan? The same Ethan from years ago?"

"Yes. The guy I met in North Carolina."

"Have you been seeing him? What? Did he contact you or something?"

"No. And if he had, so what?"

"It's just—I thought you were with Bruce."

"Mom. I know you two didn't want me seeing a guy like Ethan. I guess as the years passed, I thought my feelings for him would evaporate. But they haven't. I still love him. And I just think it would be wrong to go through with marrying Bruce when I feel this way about Ethan."

"Sara Anthony, what can you possibly be thinking?" Her even voice held an edge of hysteria.

"Lila—," Daniel said to his wife.

"No," she snapped. "This—this can't be happening. Why, we've been planning this wedding for more than a month now, and Sara can't be backing out just because of some ridiculous high school crush."

"Mom—"

"Lila, stop it."

The room erupted into a crushing silence.

"I'm sorry," Sara's mom said after a minute, her voice cracking. "I didn't mean that."

"You meant it. And I don't blame you for thinking it was a ridiculous crush. But it wasn't, Mom. It was more."

"Did you talk with Bruce?"

"Yes," Sara told her father. She detailed the conversation, told how Bruce had acted like a gentleman and still believed that Sara would come back to him.

"I don't want to hurt him any more than I already have, Dad. But he isn't the one. I know it now. Maybe Ethan isn't, either. But I can't force myself to love someone."

"Sara, maybe you just need to sort things out."

"No, Mom. I have sorted them out—that's how I came to this decision. Mom, I do want to get married. I want to have a family. But I just haven't found the one yet."

Her mother looked angry. "How do you know Bruce isn't the one?"

"Because I can't bring myself to feel for Bruce anything like I felt for Ethan. The feelings simply don't compare."

"But Sara, you haven't heard from Ethan Ware in years. What good is dreaming about something that won't happen?"

"You don't know it won't happen," Daniel said calmly.

"Well, I just don't want you to get hurt," Lila said to her daughter.

"Mom, please trust me. I know what I'm doing. I'm not waiting on Ethan. But I know—I just know Bruce isn't the one."

Finally Lila stood up stiffly and excused herself. Sara could see the unshed tears sparkling in her mother's eyes.

Alone with her father, Sara began to cry as well. Daniel came over and sat beside Sara on the couch. "So you really love this Ethan character, huh?" he asked as he put his arm around her.

Sara nodded.

"Don't give up on him, then. You know, I loved your mom for a long time in high school before she finally gave in and decided to go out with me."

"Things are a little different with Ethan and me," Sara said, managing a smile.

"I know. But God works in amazing ways. Allowing a bore like me to end up with a dynamo like your mother—now that's a miracle."

"You're not a bore, Dad."

"Well, your mother and I are certainly opposites; we always have been. Maybe that was the problem with Bruce and you. The two of you were too similar."

"I didn't want to hurt him, Dad. I didn't want to hurt anyone."

"You made the right choice, Sara. It's better you realized this now than a year from now. So no more tears, okay?"

"Okay."

He gave her shoulders a quick, tender squeeze, then pushed himself to his feet. "Now, if you'll excuse me, I think I'll go find your mother. I have a feeling she can use a good laugh. And I can always do that when she's upset, you know? One look at this mug, and she'll be smiling." He said it with an exaggerated wiggle of his eyebrows that made Sara smile, too.

"Good luck, Dad," she said as he left the room. Then she sat quietly for a minute before lowering her head into her hands and praying. *Lord, please let me know if I've made the right decision . . . or the hugest mistake of my life. Show me, Lord. Please show me.*

So I'll just say good-bye again.

Bridges

"WANT ANY MORE?"

Wiping the sweat off his forehead, Ethan looked over at the long-haired man who was offering the canteen and shook his head. "I'm good. Thanks."

Ethan sat on the edge of a low-incline roof, resting and enjoying the perfect July day. Jeff Richmond, whom Ethan had met only a week earlier, sat next to him and took a breather himself.

"Probably didn't think that meeting a neighbor would result in a bout of manual labor, huh?" Jeff asked, the wide grin on his face showing through his thick black beard.

"Actually, I was wondering about the last time I worked so hard. Kinda sad to admit I can't remember."

Jeff laughed. "Well, all I can say is I appreciate the help. And I know Mister and Miz Forrest will be grateful."

Ethan nodded. "Actually I'm having a good time. Like I told you earlier, it wasn't like my Thursday was packed with lots to do."

Since nine o'clock that morning, Ethan and Jeff and some other younger guys had used shovels and pitchforks to rip the shingles off the roof of the fifty-year-old cabin. The following day they would be putting up new tiles. Charlie and Rowena Forrest, the elderly couple who owned the cabin, had been living with a leaky roof since spring, but soon they would be enjoying drier quarters.

Enjoying the tranquility of the remote location, Ethan found it surprising that he was here. Not only on a rooftop working harder than he had in years, but still in North Carolina. Still staying at his uncle's cabin, only ten minutes away. Still walking the dirt roads of the rolling hills he was growing to love more than ever before. Still here long enough to meet neighbors like Jeff Richmond.

Ethan had seen Jeff on one of his afternoon walks. The good-natured man a few years older than Ethan had talked to him for over an hour, then invited him to dinner. After that, the two had seen each other every day, and Jeff had grown comfortable enough in their friendship to ask Ethan about this work project.

I was supposed to be in Germany. I was supposed to be working alongside Uncle Pete. But he was still in North Carolina, biding his time. *What am I waiting for? What do I really think is going to happen?*

"So, any more thoughts about that trip you're supposed to make?" said Jeff, reading Ethan's mind. "I hope this little job hasn't delayed anything."

"No," Ethan replied. "I wasn't really going anywhere. For a while I was thinking—I was convinced—that I knew what I was going to do. And if things didn't work out, then that was a sign that the trip was a go. But these days—well, I'm kind of thinking I should stay here."

"You're kidding! You mean, not go to Germany at all?"

"Is that crazy?"

"Well, I don't know," Jeff replied in his twangy mountain drawl. "I guess most folks'd jump at the chance to go to Europe and all that. But not me. I've lived around here most of my life, and it's been pretty good for me. I figure it doesn't matter where you live. It's what you end up doing."

"How long have you been helping out people like the Forrests? You do a lot of projects like this?"

"Guess so. No big deal, really. I've worked for the hardware store in town most of my life—that's because my daddy owns it. And he helps out on supplies and stuff for projects like this. Mostly I do things like this in the summer before winter comes and you can't do anything."

"I think it's admirable—helping people like that."

"The Forrests here—he's about eighty and she might be the same. They're right healthy for their ages, but it's been a while since he could get up here on the roof. I figure that's why God made us younger guys strong—so we can help out with some of the physical stuff older folks can't do. It's not so much admirable. It's just doing what you can."

"Well, let's just say I haven't always gone out of my way to do what I can," Ethan replied.

Jeff pushed himself to his feet, balancing carefully on the cabin roof. "You could've told me no. You even had an excuse. Germany. To be honest, when you first told me about that, I thought you were making it up."

"I sometimes wish I was."

"You got somebody waiting for you in Germany?"

"No, that's the thing. I was hoping someone was waiting for me here in the States. Someone really special to me. Turns out I was too late."

"Sorry to hear about it."

Ethan stood and picked up his shovel. "People move on, you know. I guess we all have to. Maybe I should, too. It'll be hard to be around here this winter."

"What's happening in winter?"

"That someone I was talking about is getting married."

"Oh," Jeff said, nodding and putting on his gloves. "Well, you know what they say. Hard labor is good for heartache."

"They say that?"

"No. But it sounds good, huh?"

Hard labor is good for heartache. "Yeah, it does."

Ethan began ripping more chunks of tile off the rooftop, deliberately pushing thoughts of Germany and winter weddings and Sara out of his mind.

It was the start of a new beginning. A moving on. A bridge had been crossed, and he stood on the other side, not wanting to look back.

Turn around, Ethan, a voice whispered. *Turn around just one more time. Just one more.* Ethan ripped up another row of shingles and hurled them off the roof. *Nope,* he told himself, *it's time to move on.*

But something pulled at his shoulder and begged him to not give up. He shrugged off the thought and dug into the roof again. *I'm moving on. This is it. Don't give up yet. Turn around. Go back over the bridge and make one more valiant attempt.*

That's what I did coming back here. I made one valiant attempt.

It just wasn't valiant enough.

Remember these words.

Discoveries

IT'S A BRILLIANT SUMMER DAY at *Hope Springs camp in Hartside, North Carolina. Ethan leads Sara through a golden field, holding her hand. Bands of horses race by them, hooves pounding, but when they turn to watch, the animals are gone. She and Ethan feel like children but they aren't; they're adults.*

Ethan sits down in the middle of the field, and Sara sinks down beside him. She looks at him and wonders why he has been so silent so long. It's not like Ethan to be silent.

"What are you thinking?" she asks.

They had been laughing earlier. Ethan still knows how to say things, crazy and bizarre things, that make her laugh. Sometimes she would laugh so hard that her side ached. Now, only minutes later, Ethan is serious.

"I'm thinking of you," his voice says as he looks into her eyes.

"I hope they're good thoughts," she replies.

"It's strange, you and I. I mean, how I can care so much about one person, yet realize that we can't be together?"

Sara doesn't say anything. She only stares at the handsome man beside her. He still resembles the kid she met years ago, but he's bearded now and thin. Terribly thin. His eyes are so sad.

"I remember growing up," he continues, "and always meeting new people and fascinating people and people I knew I could never get to know. Girls. So many girls. And for one reason or another, I always knew I would never get to know them. They were too stuck up or too shy or whatever. But you—"

"What?" Sara asks.

"You opened yourself up to me so many years ago. I got to see a side of you that made you even more charming, even more beautiful, than I ever thought or dreamed someone could be. And through the years of writing and all that, I grew to cherish that love. I grew to cherish you."

"Ethan," she begins, but he waves her off.

"Please. Let me finish. This might be the last time I ever get to say words to you."

"But you're here, beside me. What do you mean?"

"You know what I mean. I can never have you. We'll never spend a day together in a field alone without a care in the world."

"But we're in a field now," Sara protests.

But they aren't. They're in a hospital room, sitting on the edge of a bed. Someone else is in the room, but she cannot see who it is.

"I'll never be able to wake you up and kiss you on your cheek." Ethan is still talking, as if the scene had never changed. "I'll never be able to know what it's like to see you every Saturday morning, sipping your coffee and relaxing."

"Why can't you, Ethan?" She feels as wistful as he looks.

"Because you gave up on me, Sara. You gave up."

"Oh no I didn't. You don't understand."

Suddenly panicked, she reaches out her hand to him, but he's not there. He's standing on the deck of the cabin, balanced against the rail, leaning backward. She tries to walk toward him, but her feet feel frozen to the deck. His voice still echoes in her ears. "I'll hear your name two or four or ten years down the road and maybe I'll even see you. I'll still have these feelings. But I'll never be with you. . . ."

"Ethan, I want you to—"

"good-bye."

Sara finds herself alone in the hospital-room bed, under stark fluorescent light and echoing silence. She feels the protest welling up in her like the cry of a little girl lost.

"But I don't want to say good-bye. . . ."

Sara awoke before being able to. She tried to fall back asleep in order to capture the dream again, thinking somehow that she could put everything right if she could just go back.

But it was no use. She was wide-awake. The dream was gone.

She sat up in bed, hugging her knees in the cold room. She could still feel the sadness, the emptiness of that dreamed good-bye. But with it was an eerie calm, a strange sense that somehow, in spite of what had happened, all was well.

That was when it occurred to her that dreaming about a man she might never marry was still better than marrying a man she never dreamed about.

She rested her head on her knees as the dream began to fade away into daylight.

⚓

The chill of winter normally made summer and all its pleasant memories easy to forget. But Sara found it hard, even now—five days before Christmas and six days before what would have been her wedding day—to shake the memories of previous summers and to erase the pain of this past summer. She had felt a little better ever since school started; her kindergarten class of twenty-two kids was one of the best she'd ever taught. During the days, if she tried, she could lose herself in the world of fingerpaint and ABCs and put behind her the two chances at love she believed had passed her by.

She had no regrets. She still believed she had made the right decision about Bruce.

The memory of Ethan was fading a little. Now she could go a day without thinking of him. During the summer it had been so hard, especially after reading his letters and looking at the photos and other keepsakes. But months ago, after leaving Hartside and breaking up with Bruce, she had told herself no more. The box with all its precious, meaningful contents was back in the bottom of her closet, untouched.

Yet thoughts of him still haunted her unguarded moments. Even when she deliberately forced herself to move on, to stop dwelling on something that would not happen, she would wake up as she had this morning after dreaming of him.

Why can't I just forget him?

It wasn't as if anything had changed. There had been no word—not a letter or a phone call or anything. She had no way of knowing where he was—or even if he was alive.

But it's okay, she said to herself. *It just wasn't meant to be. I put it in God's hands and this is what he wants. Yet I still want to see Ethan. Just one more time. Just to find out what happened . . .*

In an empty house on a rainy Monday morning—the first day of her Christmas vacation—Sara found that she couldn't shake these thoughts. She found herself thinking about Ethan and her dream, of his smile and his blue eyes. Of his infectious grin and the way he always made her laugh. She had always loved that about him.

She could surely use a good laugh now.

She thought of going to see her parents. Dad was working, and Mom had probably gone off to do some morning errands. Sara wondered when her relationship with her mother would improve. They were talking, and things on the surface seemed fine, but she knew her mother too well to trust the way things seemed. Sara's mother had been devastated by the breakup, and the only way she had been able to cope was by staying busy. Things like reorganizing the church soup kitchen and volunteering for the symphony guild and even trying out new hobbies like teddy-bear collecting.

Sara recalled one of her mother's latest purchases—a Paddington bear—and thought, *What's she doing with all of these bears? Trying to find the right one to marry me?*

The flip calendar on a side table reminded Sara of how close she had come to marrying the wrong one.

Thank you, Lord, she prayed again, a prayer she had grown used to praying.

Since breaking up with Bruce, she had seen him only a handful of times. Almost every time, he had tried to bargain with her, giving her reason after reason why she should marry him. He hadn't even seemed to care that Sara still loved Ethan. Her resistence had only seemed to harden his resolve.

Then, the last time she had spoken with Bruce, though, he had made it clear that his patience was wearing thin. "I'm older than you, Sara," he had said. "I can't wait around all my life."

Since then, Sara had seen him talking seriously with one of the younger women at their church. It didn't bother Sara at all. It simply confirmed her conviction that she wasn't ready to get married.

Not to Bruce, anyway. Sara stuffed that thought. She wasn't ready to get married. Period.

⚜

Hours later, after a light brunch of a toasted, buttered bagel and coffee, Sara drove out to see her mother. It was close to one o'clock, and Lila was still out. Sara let herself in with the key, made herself a cup of instant hot chocolate to chase away the damp chill, and went to the front to bring in the mail. Sara always enjoyed getting the first look at the variety of catalogs and magazines her mother received. Lila Anthony probably had about a dozen subscriptions to magazines like *Better Homes and Gardens* and *Southern Living*. Flipping through one of those would help Sara pass the time until her mother got home.

The handful of mail looked too large to examine there in the entranceway, so she carried it over to the little table against the wall. Idly she sorted through it. Bills, junk mail, a magazine for teddy-bear collectors (what next?), and a letter in a long envelope.

She laughed when she saw the bear magazine, then stopped when she saw the letter. It had her name and her parents' address on it.

A chill went through her as she looked at the return address. The letter was from Hartside, North Carolina. From the place in the hills.

The last place she ever saw Ethan Ware.

She opened the envelope and unfolded the letter. The handwriting was familiar. Even after so many years, it looked the same. She glanced at the bottom and saw the name: Ethan.

She inhaled sharply. When she felt the tears begin to flow, she folded the letter up again. Looking around, making sure that nobody was near, Sara carried the letter into the family room. She needed to sit in case she fainted or passed out. Her hands shook as she opened the letter again. With the back of one hand she wiped the tears away.

How long has it been, Ethan? Why all of a sudden are you writing? Why now?
Sara wanted to read the letter but also feared to, wondering what he
might possibly say. Ethan, the man she had turned away but never given
up on. Ethan, her first love, perhaps her only real love.

She took the words in carefully. It had been so very long.

My Dearest Sara,

*For many months I have fought the urge to write you. But as I look on
the calendar, I know it is almost time for your wedding. Today is December 14, so it is only twelve days away. Twelve days. The pit of my stomach
still aches from knowing this, from knowing you're twelve days away from
saying "I do" and spending the rest of your life with somebody else.*

*Somebody else—two words I have told myself over and over yet neither
believe nor want to believe. I always believed you would be marrying me.
Part of me foolishly still does.*

*You are surely wondering how I know. But before I explain, I need to
ask why you never responded to my letter—the one I sent you last spring.
Months ago I found out the truth—that you had fallen in love with somebody else—and that explained a lot. But the things I told you in that letter, the things I expressed to you in that letter—well, I always thought
that you would be happy about that and write me back, even if you didn't
love me the way you used to. I imagined so many times the words you
might send. But no word from you ever came.*

*Perhaps you didn't want to write, or you couldn't write, or you didn't
know what to say. I wish you could tell me. But now it is too late. I understand that. You have your life to live, and I understand that, too. But I
need to tell you some things, some more things that my last letter didn't
say.*

*You know I still love you with every inch of my heart and my soul.
I began loving you under a star-filled sky one night as a teenager when
I didn't realize how big the world could be and how impossible some
dreams would be to achieve. My dreams—you know them all, Sara.
You know each and every one because I've shared them with you and
because you are in every one of them.*

Over the years I have spent so much time simply dreaming. Dreaming about spending time with you and dreaming about what it would be like if our love was to work out. I've been good at dreaming—you know that. I guess perhaps my greatest and grandest dream of them all was that, in the end, I would be at your side. I would hold your hand and walk out of that church into a crowd of smiling and happy faces, and I would know that finally, finally, Sara Anthony belonged to me.

I will never stop dreaming this, nor will I ever stop loving you, Sara. You were the love of my life. You gave me a part of yourself I don't think I can ever return. And, most important, you pointed me toward something more important than any of my dreams. You showed me where to find the answers to all those questions I had. You allowed me to find something, to be given something I can never fully thank you for.

But I don't want to go into that again. Surely my last letter said it all. But know that everything I said is still true. I still believe in you and in us.

In case you're wondering how I found out about the wedding, this summer I went to Hartside and I saw you there and found out about your plans. Why our paths crossed then was, well, beyond me. I don't even understand why I didn't speak to you then. But I am learning that I don't always have to understand—that's where faith comes into the picture. Didn't you say that once?

Anyway, I saw you and wanted to say something and take you in my arms—oh, Sara, how I longed to just simply look into those shining eyes and see you smile and hear your wonderful laugh. But I let you go. I watched you drive away.

So why I was in Hartside doesn't really matter. I found what I was looking for—the truth. And the truth hurt.

I am writing to you days before I board a plane for Europe. I'm moving to Germany to work for my uncle—you know, the one who owns the cabin. Much has happened to me in these past few months. So much—oh, I wish I could tell you it all. I will be gone for a couple of years or maybe even more. Remember my dream of traveling to Europe? Well, at least that will be coming true.

Oh, yes—one more thing I wanted to tell you: The words have come back to me. Remember, in my letter, I said they had left me? Well, seeing you in Hartside seems to have brought them back. So I am writing again.

I have written so much lately, it's like the words were stored up all this time.

Sara, you always have been and will continue to be my inspiration. After five months or so I just finished writing a novel. Well, a novella, really. It's about a young man searching for his lost love. He never finds her — but that's how classics end, right? Tragic? I guess we're destined to be a classic.

I wanted to say good-bye again. I've spent a lifetime telling others good-bye, half a lifetime telling you good-bye. Wishing you were by my side, but always realizing you couldn't be. Now, as I leave to be away for a long time, and as you prepare to be married, I say what could be a final good-bye.

Know this: Know that my promise still remains. I haven't stopped loving you, Sara. I will always love you. You will be in my heart wherever I go.

Thank you, Sara. Thank you for everything. I love you.

Ethan

For half an hour Sara sat still, reading the letter again and again and looking out the windows to the backyard and wondering why this letter had reached her and questioning everything about her life and fearing her own thoughts. The tears flowed, as so many had in the last few months. Sara touched them and then laughed when she realized they weren't tears of sadness.

She felt elated.

She read the letter again. It was true. He had kept his promise—he still cared for her, perhaps more now than ever before. How could that be? She didn't know, but she didn't need to know why. The only thing that mattered was that he still loved her. He still loved her.

And she knew she still loved him. She loved him beyond a doubt.

Yet he was leaving to go to Europe—for a couple of years, he had said. He believed she was still getting married.

Wasn't this where they had left things off years ago? He loved her so much, and she loved him so much. And they couldn't be together. So in a sense, nothing had changed.

Or had it?

What was that letter he kept mentioning? The "last letter." She hadn't received a letter from him in years. He had said he sent a letter in the springtime. She searched her memory for anything she might have received then. She was sure she had received no letter last spring.

If indeed he had written it—and of course he had; why would he lie?—what had he said? Would that letter have changed things?

She reread the new letter and realized that now, for better or worse, her life was going to change. It had to change. She needed to know if there would be—if there could be—a future with Ethan.

She thought for a minute on what to do.

She prayed for answers. "Father, please help me to know where to even begin with this. I feel helpless here."

Thoughts attacked her. Call him. But that was impossible. He had sent this letter from the cabin in the mountains, and the cabin had no phone. Besides, he had probably already left for Europe.

Try the Chicago number.

Better yet, go find him.

But that was foolish. Go where? She couldn't. She shouldn't. But she had to do something.

Still sitting on the couch, her eyes all teary and her face pale in shock, Sara heard the front door open.

"Sara?" her mother's voice called.

The footsteps came in, then stopped. Her mother looked at her with a smile frozen in horror, as if somebody had died. "Honey, what is wrong?" Her mother rushed to her side and sat next to her.

Sara shook her head and smiled, wiping away tears from her eyes.

"What happened?" her mom asked.

Sara picked up the letter and waved it. "I got this letter, Mom. It came in your mail addressed to me."

And as her mom looked in disbelief at the envelope, Sara suddenly felt a cold chill of understanding. Her mom didn't look surprised or bewildered; she looked angry.

"Mom—"

"Sara, he shouldn't be writing to you. Not after all that's happened."

"What are you talking about?"

"You said yourself that you had made the decision to move on—right, Sara?"

"What's that have to do with anything?"

"I just think it's unfair for this young man to continue to write to you and upset you."

"Mom, I'm not upset about the letter. It's the best thing that's happened to me all year." Sara thought for a minute, looked at the letter, then back at her mother. "Did Ethan send any other letters this year to this address? Mom?"

The initial silence answered her question. Sara stood up and backed away from her mother as the awful truth continued to wash over her. "Mom, answer me."

Lila Anthony looked grave and speechless. Brief tears filled her eyes, but she quickly wiped them away. She attempted a nervous smile. "Sara—"

"Mom, answer me now! Did you take a letter that was sent to me? Did you? Did you steal a letter from me and lie about it? Mom!"

"Yes, yes, I'm sorry, but, you don't understand—"

"What? What don't I understand? How you could have lied to me for so long?"

Sara could feel the anger building inside of her. She knew that if she stayed in this family room much longer she would say hateful things to her mother. She fought to control herself.

"I'm sorry," her mother was saying, "but—"

"But what?" Sara screamed.

"It was Bruce. He told me about his plans to propose to you this past spring. And I was so excited about that and for you. And then this letter came one day. It was from that Ethan, and—well, I always had a feeling about you and that boy. I was afraid if you started writing him again, that would just ruin everything. And well . . . I just took it."

"What? Mom! What were you thinking?"

"I don't know. I thought—I don't know what I thought. But he was never right for you. You said that yourself, Sara. You said you could never be with him."

"And that was my decision. Not yours. Not anybody's."

"I just thought—"

"You didn't think, Mom. You lied to me, and you stole what was mine. Where's the letter now? What did you do with it?"

Her mother's tears began coming again. She choked out her reply. "I threw it out. I'm so sorry."

Sara fought the tears and fought her anger. She needed to leave, to get out of this house and to be able to think and breathe. She headed toward the entryway to collect her purse and wrap. But she couldn't stop herself from saying more. "How could you do something like that to me? How?"

"Honey, I told you. Things between you and Bruce were going so well, and I thought the last thing you needed was to be confused. I didn't want you to be hurt any more than you already had been."

"What do you call this, Mom? You don't think this hurts me?"

"I'm sorry, Sara. I don't know what else to say."

Sara stared down at her mother. "You know, I've never understood what your problem was with me loving Ethan. You never liked me getting those letters, Mom. Never."

"Honey, I just didn't think he was the right one for you."

"But how do you know that? You never even met him. Besides, isn't that a decision you should leave up to me—especially now? Mom, I'm thirty years old. I can make up my own mind."

Lila Anthony remained silent on the couch, her face white and her eyes red.

Sara got her purse and put on her coat. Before leaving, she faced her mother.

"Ethan might not be the right one for me, Mom. But that's something I have to find out. You guys were so set on Bruce being the right one, but he wasn't. I just wish you'd stay out of my life when it comes to stuff like this."

Sara left her parents' house and got in her car and just drove. A cold rain splatted on the soft roof of her convertible, and she drove and cried and glanced at the letter on the front seat beside her. She knew she had a lot of decisions to make.

The only peace that filled her came later, after she had read Ethan's letter yet again.

You helped change my life.

Remembrances

ETHAN WALKED up to the small gravestone and laid a creamy white rose on the frozen blades of grass. The weather had turned bitterly cold, but so far no snow had fallen. Ethan wondered if the North Carolina mountains would get their usual helping of snow by Christmastime.

It had taken him a long time to get the nerve to come back to the cemetery close to the little church in Hartside, although he had passed it many times during the months he'd spent at the cabin. Now that he was here, all he could picture was the smiling face of his mother.

"Where are you?" he said aloud.

He wondered if her spirit was floating above him as he looked at her name on the stone. Or perhaps she stood beside him, holding his hand, telling him everything would be all right.

Will everything really be all right, Mom? he wondered. *Is everything going to turn out okay?*

In another day, Ethan would be on his way to Europe. This would be the last time he would visit his mother's grave for a while. *I hope I'm making the right decision.*

Ethan couldn't help believing that somewhere either close or far away, his mother could see him. That she knew about everything—how his life had changed, how he still loved a woman who was so close to getting married, how he had come once again to the mountains she had always loved. He wondered what she would tell him now. Probably something about how God has a purpose and everything works out for those who love him.

Her faith had never faltered, even through her illness. If only her son could be so strong.

Ethan knelt on one knee.

"Mom, I miss you," he said. "I wish you were still here. There are so many things I need help with, that I need to know about. I want to make up for lost time."

Images of his mother over the years passed through his mind. How can anyone ever replace the love they have for their mother? How can anyone ever try to fill the void a mother leaves behind?

He remembered one of his mother's last requests—to be buried in this cemetery next to Hartside Bible Church. Ethan still remembered almost every minute of the small funeral service. He had not been back here since then.

He stood and looked at the small church a short walk away. "God, I wish I understood why everyone I care about always leaves me," Ethan said. "I just want to know why. Can I know this one thing? Can I?"

The silent wind chilled him as Ethan walked back to his car. Perhaps some questions in life would simply never be answered.

HARTSIDE, NC

I will never forget about you.

Prayers

"HEAR MY PRAYER, heavenly Father. Please help me to know your will. I don't understand anything anymore—not my own heart, not my own actions. Everything I feel seems to contradict everything I do. Please help me know what to do, Lord. I want to do the right thing. I want to do what you want me to do."

Sara wiped the tears away from her eyes and looked up at the huge, glorious cross on the wall behind the church pulpit. She felt comfortable praying here in the empty sanctuary of her large church. This was the same church she would have been married in, the same church where she would have told Bruce how much she loved him and how she planned on spending the rest of her life with him.

Now she wondered if she would ever tell someone "I do." "Lord, please help me. Please give me peace. Please let me know what to do."

She knew what she wanted to do. Go find Ethan, tell him he's wrong about the wedding, tell him she still loved him, tell him everything could work out all right.

But would they be back at square one? Would he tell her once again that he still had no use for her God, the same God she prayed to now? that he hated God and blamed him for all his problems? What if it still boiled down to that one fact?

I won't cast you aside, Lord. You've allowed me to come this far. You've allowed this to happen. I won't dishonor your name.

Couldn't she make one exception? Couldn't she be with Ethan and hope that he would change one day?

What about Marietta Ware? a voice reminded her. *Remember what happened to her?*

But Sara needed to see Ethan. It had been so long. She needed closure. She needed to know what his earlier letter had said.

Sara thought of her mother again. The anger still boiled deep inside of her. Could she forgive her mother for hiding such an important letter from her? Would she ever know what that one letter her mother threw out had said?

"Lord, I know you promise us many things. You promised that you would send your own Son to die on a cross for all of us. You promise to take care of your children. I know you never fail to keep any of your promises. Yet why can't I have faith in that? Why can't I have any sort of strength now?

"Please, Lord, give me strength. Give me hope. Help me to forgive my mother when that's the very last thing I want to do. Give me strength, Lord. Give me your strength."

She looked up again at the cross.

"And Lord, if it be your will—only if it is your will—please let me find him one last time. I know it is selfish of me to ask. Maybe it would be better never to see him again. But please, Lord, please let me talk to Ethan one last time. I just need to know. I want to know if there is any hope of anything changing.

"More than anything, Lord, I want him to know you."

⚜

The doorbell brought Sara out of her trance as she sat in front of the television watching an uninteresting sitcom. So far, it had not even made her smile. She looked at the digital clock on the VCR and knew it had to be her mother. No one else would stop by at nine-thirty at night to say hi.

Maybe it's Ethan. The thought popped into her mind before she could stop it. She just shook her head and looked out the window next to the front door. Lila Anthony was standing out there in the cold. Sara opened the door and let her mother in without saying anything.

"Brrr, it's getting colder outside," her mother said as if the argument earlier that day hadn't happened. Lila took off her coat. "Sara, can we talk?"

"I'm not in the mood."

"I need to explain some things to you."

"There's nothing to explain." Sara sat back down on the couch and acted as if she were watching the program. Her mother sat next to her. In her hands was an envelope.

"Sara, please. I'm sorry. I'm so sorry, honey. I didn't think any of this would happen. I was just trying to look out for you—"

"I told you, I don't need you looking out for me."

"I know. That's what your father said, too. He was pretty upset with me."

"I don't understand why you would do something like this," Sara said.

"Here. Just look at these. I'm not saying what I did wasn't wrong. I want you to know why I did it."

Sara took the two black-and-white photographs and examined them. She recognized her mother with her glossy dark hair and wide expressive eyes. But in the photo her mother was much younger—her hair long and straight, her face rounder and smooth. She had to be in her late teenage years.

"Who's this?" Sara asked. "It doesn't look like Dad."

In each photo, a boy Sara didn't recognize stood next to her mother. In one, he wore a football uniform and held on to his helmet with one hand and Lila's hand with the other. In the second photo, he had his arm draped around Lila. It was obvious he was quite tall and well built.

"That's Paul Thomas, the young man I was going to marry when I was a senior in high school."

Sara looked again at the photos. "What? You never told me about him."

"I was in love with Paul from years earlier, but he never noticed me until I was a senior. He was a football hero and all the girls loved him. He just happened to be crazy for me—once he noticed me, that is."

"Wait a minute," Sara said. "You started dating Dad shortly after high school, right?"

"Yes. Actually, right around the time of graduation."

"But you were going to marry this guy? Seriously?"

"Oh yes. He even proposed to me."

"Really? Why didn't you ever tell me about him?"

Lila forced a bittersweet smile to her face. Sara could still see the young beauty from years ago in the face she looked at now.

"He was part of me that I buried a long time ago, Sara. Paul Thomas was everything I had ever wanted. He was reckless and wild. He drank too much at parties and was always with some new girlfriend."

"Everything you ever wanted? Yeah, right."

"I'm serious. He was. He was good-looking and exciting, and I loved being around him. I figured I could marry him, and we would live happily ever after."

"What happened?"

"I found out he was sleeping with my best friend. He proposed to me before the end of our senior year, and then he broke my heart."

Sara looked at her mother and couldn't believe the words she was hearing.

"And Dad?"

"Your father was heaven-sent. He had always loved me, but it was after I broke up with Paul that I discovered just how much he cared. He was so tender and so patient. He helped me get over Paul, to realize Paul was all wrong for me. I finally realized that I was in love with your father."

The photos in Sara's hands seemed unreal. "Why didn't you ever tell me?"

"Paul died a few years after we graduated from high school. I had already married your father and had never heard from him again. I heard one day that he had been killed in a car accident. They said he had been driving drunk, and I wasn't really surprised. But a part of me died, too. I still loved him, Sara. I couldn't believe it, and I never would have admitted it to anyone. But I did still love him."

"I'm sorry, Mom."

Lila took her daughter's hand. "Sara, I never meant to hurt you. I have only wanted the best for you. From the very first time I heard you describe this Ethan Ware, all I could think about was Paul Thomas and how much he had hurt me. I didn't want that to happen to you."

"But Ethan's not like that, Mom."

"Maybe not. I don't know Ethan—you do. And besides, you're right—you're an adult. I just—I didn't want your heart broken. I always thought you'd find someone stable and successful like Bruce and you'd be happy."

"You and Dad are happy, right?" Sara asked.

The fine wrinkles under her mother's eyes moved as she smiled and nodded. "Of course we are. I've never once doubted he was the right one."

"I never thought there was anyone else besides Ethan. I just thought he'd forgotten about me."

"Sara, please forgive your meddling mother. I'm sorry for lying to you."

For the first time in years, Sara felt like a child again as she hugged her mother. They talked with each other for another two hours about love, loss, and life in general.

It was her mother's final comment that stuck with Sara. "Take your father's advice, Sara. Don't let anything interfere with your dreams. If you still love this Ethan, then do something about it."

I will always thank you.

Questions

A PLEASANT AND WARMING FIRE crackled and lit the otherwise dark room. Ethan could hear the wind outside wailing into the night, confirming the newscaster's prediction about the winter storm. It had started two days ago, and it would still be pounding the North Carolina mountains for at least the next few days. Snow had already blanketed his car and the deck outside—so this Christmas Eve and tomorrow's Christmas Day would indeed be a white Christmas.

A lonely Christmas, too, Ethan noted. He would have been in Germany now, celebrating with his uncle's family. But flights out of the nearest airport in Asheville had been cancelled, and driving the distance to a larger airport was out of the question in this storm. His roofing buddy, Jeff, and his wife were out of town, visiting Jeff's sister in High Point. Even the Forrests, the elderly couple Ethan had come to know after fixing their roof, were away visiting relatives. So Ethan was alone.

He hadn't even bought a Christmas tree, but that was okay. Christmas wasn't about gifts and trees and all that other stuff anyway. He didn't need them to celebrate Christmas. And though it would have been nice to be with some family or friends, he could see that perhaps it was good to be alone. He had been alone for so long, and now he was about to leave and start a new life. Starting over was easier when you didn't have many attachments.

December 24. The date couldn't help but bring up thoughts of Sara. A day and a half from now, she would be getting married. It still amazed him that she had never responded to his letter from the spring. He wondered if she would reply to his latest letter.

Even if she didn't, Ethan was glad he had written them. And glad he had come to the mountains and ended up staying for so long. The last few months had left him refreshed and encouraged. He had been able to stay at his uncle's cabin, paying only for food, electricity, and water. He had made a little money doing odd jobs with Jeff, who had become a close friend. In his spare time, he wrote.

This was what life would be like if he was a full-time writer. What a great life that would be, too. Especially if he had someone to share that dream with.

Perhaps one day he would. But for now, he was alone in that dream— and he was surprised to find out that was all right.

In a sense, this past fall in the mountains had truly set him free. He was able to take walks in the high North Carolina hills with a notebook in hand and the entire universe seemingly at a standstill. Here, life didn't pass him by in a rush and a curse; here, one could breathe in life and the beauty of the earth. There were so many things he had grown up not appreciating— the blazing reds and sparkling golds of the autumn foliage, the nip in the air as winter approached, the comfort of a mug of canned soup sipped by the fire.

He found himself smiling every time he wielded the can opener, remembering the months when that had been all his mother could afford. Then, he had complained bitterly. Now, he relished the warmth of the memory.

That was something that had changed about him, he reflected. Now he appreciated so much more. For a while, he had almost given up on life. Now he was discovering, to his joy, that he valued life dearly.

Seeing Sara this past summer had been everything he wished it hadn't been. For weeks afterward, he had fought with himself about calling or writing or going to see her. He had kept on giving up on her, giving up on himself. But over time a strange thing happened. He had found his voice again. He had began to write—and now the words overflowed. Something was there. Something incredible. So he wrote and wrote and found that the same passion and the same yearning that had moved him as a young man was still very much there. If anything, it was stronger than it had ever been.

He had spent days reading and writing—enjoying the beauty around him and wandering the mountain roads looking for awe-inspiring views. His journals had filled with poetry and thoughts and love notes to Sara and dreams and desires. And then he had begun the novel, which only recently he had finished.

Perhaps this was the first big step in his life as a writer. He could already see the blurbs in the English-lit texts. Ethan Ware, after a difficult childhood full of loss and trauma, still loves his one and only childhood sweetheart, Sara. He discovers she is marrying another, so he goes to the log cabin to get away and in the course of the time there he begins to write—a little at first, then more and more, until he has penned his own Great American Novel. He goes to Europe and works some more on his writing, adding depth and resonance to his already distinctive voice. He gets his first book published, and, while it is not a huge success, it does start the career of perhaps the greatest living writer since Ernest Hemingway.

I'm crazy, Ethan thought. *That's what Sara would tell me if she knew I was thinking like that. Crazy.* But she'd smile when she said it.

And the dedication page of his first novel, the first of many great works, would simply state the following:

"To Sara. The promise remains."

If he ever did publish anything, the dedication would read exactly like that. His promise still endured—even now, after realizing she was gone.

Ethan thought of his dreams and realized that for a while, they had left him. But he had been given the gift of his dreams again. He could dream as high as the heavens above. And if his great dream of a life with Sara Anthony was lost, there was still time for other dreams. Perhaps he would write and be famous, or perhaps he would remain an unknown dreamer all his life. And he was fine with that. He was willing to take what life brought him.

On this Christmas Eve, he sat reading a timeless classic, a book he had ignored during most of his youth. Now he simply sat back and thought about life. He remembered and felt a peace inside—a peace that felt soothing even though he had lost a love he would never forget.

He thought of his mother tonight and wished she were there to see him. He thought she would be happy—proud of the changes that had taken place in him. Perhaps she was looking down at him and smiling. She would always be with him, no matter where he went or what he did. She had guided him in the right direction, just as Sara had. The two most important women in his life had helped shape and direct him more than either knew.

But one day they would know. And one day they would receive their reward.

This Christmas Eve, as so many other families and friends and loved ones celebrated together, Ethan watched the fire burn low and thought once more of Sara. He missed her. And he still loved her. And he wondered if he would ever see her again.

The fire snapped back at him, and the winds outside hummed. Another noise, distant and strange, sounded. Something outside with the storm, that was all.

"Please let me see her again," he whispered, drifting in and out of sleep.

When the banging knock sounded, he thought a tree had fallen against the front door. But it wasn't a crash, because it continued, again and again. *Knock, knock, knock.*

Dressed in plaid pajama bottoms and an old but comfortable Washington Redskins sweatshirt, his hair long and falling in his eyes, the month-old thickness of beard on his face, Ethan stumbled to the door, wondering who it could be. Hopefully it wasn't some psycho looking for trouble on Christmas Eve.

The knocking continued.

He opened the door to the fury of wind and snow and saw outside a small figure bundled up with a hood and overcoat and boots. He could only see her dark, questioning eyes, but instantly he knew who it was.

Sara had found him.

HARTSIDE N.C.

Thank you for not giving up on me.

$\mathscr{P}$romises

ETHAN'S LETTER had started everything. But in the end, it had been the comment by Sara's mother that propelled Sara into action. "Take your father's advice, Sara. Don't let anything interfere with your dreams. If you still love this Ethan, then do something about it."

Sara still could not believe those words had come from her mother's lips. But they had, and they were all Sara needed to go and try to find Ethan, to at least see him one final time.

Sara called and tried to find a phone number for him. His Chicago number had been cut off. Trying to find a number for his uncle's residence in Germany was impossible. So she called other places, to no avail. Finally she decided to try her last hope—going to the little cabin in the mountains. That was where the letter had been sent from, so he obviously had been there not long ago. Probably he was long gone, but she had to try.

So Sara left on the morning of December 24, two days before a cancelled wedding date Ethan still thought existed. Her parents were not happy about her leaving a day before Christmas, and they were concerned about the most recent weather reports, but they understood she had to go.

Before she left, her father handed her a hastily wrapped Christmas present. "You can open the rest when you get back home," he said.

Sara opened the package and found a compass and a candy bar. "The compass is to help you find where you're going, and the Snickers is in case you get lost."

He smiled and kissed her on the cheek. Her mother was restraining herself, holding back both words and tears, but she managed a taut smile as well.

Sara hugged her mother. "Thank you, Mom."

That was all that needed to be said. They both understood what the thank-you was for. It had taken a lot out of Lila Anthony to give her daughter permission to follow a dream.

It didn't take long for Sara's convertible to make its way from Herrington Lane to Interstate 85. The radio made occasional references to the winter storm moving into the Smokies from the west, but she was pretty sure she could get through before conditions got really bad.

She had to get there.

During the entire trip in her car, she prayed. "Please, Lord, show me what to do. For months you've known my questions, my soul-searching. I believe this is what I need to do, what I have to do, but I need you to show me what your will is. Let me find Ethan—or at least find the truth. I need to know if there is hope for the two of us. But whatever happens between us, please let Ethan find your truth, Lord. That is what I have always prayed, and I know that you always have a plan and a purpose. I hope and pray that there is a plan and a purpose for Ethan and me."

Again and again, Sara found herself praying for guidance and direction and peace. And the trip went smoothly—up the interstate toward Greenville, South Carolina, and then back west toward Asheville, through the brightly decorated downtown, and then along the smaller highway that led into Hartside. But she got lost in the snow-covered hills as the storm she'd driven into halfway across North Carolina turned into a full-scale blizzard. She drove for two hours in the dark, suffocating snow, trying to find Chestwood Lane. She cried and tried to get a grip on herself. For a while she questioned the decision to come here. Not only was it foolish; it was dangerous.

Thank goodness she brought a cell phone as well as the candy bar. But whether her digital phone would find service this far out was an open question.

Suddenly it was there—Chestwood Lane. She felt like a small child finding her lost sled in a snowpile. Her car plowed through the thickening snow until she made it up the steep driveway.

It was already evening and the cabin, what little she could see of it in the cloudy storm, appeared dark. If she had come here for nothing—if he was gone and nobody was inside—she would not only feel stupid but be in a lot of trouble.

She would also be devastated.

Sara opened the car door and instantly felt the stinging bite of the storm. She was cold and stiff from the drive, and her feet slipped on the icy driveway as she started toward the house. She noticed something in the driveway covered with a thick blanket of snow—could it be a car? Ethan's car? Her heart beat faster as she approached the door. Closer to the small, lifeless cabin, Sara noticed no signs of habitation. The windows were coated with snow, the deck unshoveled, no footprints anywhere. The tang of woodsmoke in the air could easily come from one of the other cabins nearby.

Her heart sank to think she might have missed him. Nevertheless, she knocked and knocked on the heavy wooden door, hoping against hope somebody, anybody was there.

And then in a glorious answer to one of her many prayers, the door opened. Before her in the doorway stood the man of her dreams.

A stunned and weary Ethan Ware looked back at her in shock. For a minute, he didn't say anything and didn't move. He just stared blankly at her as if he was waking up from a long sleep. "Sara?" he finally asked, ushering her inside.

And before he could say anything else, before she could take off her coat or pull down her hood, Sara embraced the man she so dearly needed to see and hold. He hugged her back and they stood that way at the open doorway, with puffs of snow drifting inside.

They didn't care. For the moment, after so many years and so many words and so many memories and so many miles, they had found each other.

❧

Sara sat on one of the two couches slanted in front of the fireplace. Ethan haphazardly threw some more big chunks of wood on the fire, apologizing for his lack of grace in maintaining the flames. Sara took off her coat and shivered, cold even in her jeans and sweater. Her frozen feet began to tingle as they warmed by the fire. She snuggled down into the big blanket Ethan had given her.

For a few minutes neither of them said much. Sara was cold and frightened and out of breath, so Ethan focused on getting her warm and relaxed. Outside the winds picked up and the snow continued to fall. His words came out awkward and forced, sounding strange in his ears.

Fixing her some hot tea took several minutes. He handed her the mug, then said, "Excuse me for a second."

He came back in jeans with his hair pushed back, a little neater. He sat on the couch across from her and smiled.

Sipping her tea and feeling warm and fairly sensible now, Sara looked hard at him. He was older, of course, and the beard wasn't a new thing. His blondish brown hair had grown long in front—the bangs fell down on his forehead—yet the back had been kept fairly short. He looked slim but healthy, his blue eyes glowing in the firelight. She stared and remembered— his eyes looked more captivating than she recalled. Something was different. The sadness that used to surround them no longer seemed to be there.

For a couple of minutes they only smiled at one another.

"I can't believe you're here," Ethan said.

"I can't either." Sara released a nervous laugh.

"Remember the last time you were here?" Ethan asked, smiling at her. "Seems like storms follow you."

"I was so afraid I wasn't going to find the cabin, that you weren't going to be here, that——" And the control she thought she had regained with the warmth and hot tea and the safety vanished. She began crying again.

Instantly Ethan was at her side, kneeling on the floor but not touching her. "It's okay. You're here. You made it. It's all right."

"Oh, Ethan, I don't know what to think or feel anymore. I just— don't—know." She continued to cry.

Ethan looked up at her and smiled. "You are so beautiful—you know that?"

"No, I'm not. I probably look terrible. I've been crying for the last day it seems. Make that the last six months."

Ethan looked at her and didn't say anything. He looked surprised by her comment. But then he smiled again and pointed to himself.

"I hope you know I sure wasn't expecting any company. Look at me. I'm like Grizzly Adams walking around here. My hair looks like it's out of some horror movie."

Sara looked at him and laughed. It felt good to hear jokes again. "It's good to see you," she said softly.

"I'd say the same thing, but that's quite an understatement," Ethan said, still kneeling beside her.

The fire and one other light were the only illumination in the room. Sara didn't mind. She only needed enough to look into Ethan's eyes.

"I got your letter a few days ago," Sara said. "I've tried to call, to get hold of you. I thought you had gone to Europe or somewhere and, well, I just panicked."

Ethan looked up, his face questioning. "Panicked?"

"Yes, I-I need to explain something to you. I need to tell you what happened."

"What do you mean? About getting engaged? I know about that."

Sara shook her head. "Ethan, I . . . I'm not engaged. Not anymore."

"You got married early?"

Sara couldn't help but smile as she answered his desperate reply. "I called it off."

The look on Ethan's face evolved in an everlasting minute. He looked elated and stunned and horrified all in one. He tried to say something but couldn't.

"I had to find you."

"When did you—you know?" Ethan asked.

"Back in July. After my trip to Hartside to find you."

"But you never found me."

"I know."

"Then why—"

She held up a hand to stop his words. "Let me explain. Please." Sara proceeded to tell him her story, to tell him words she knew he needed to hear.

She talked about Bruce, who he was and why she had started dating him. About being a schoolteacher and realizing she was thirty years old and not married, about her need to get on with her life. About Bruce's proposal and her halfhearted acceptance and about thinking she could learn to love Bruce, even though she still had all these feelings for Ethan.

As she spoke, Ethan's eyes began to fill with tears.

Sara continued, telling how she had returned to Hartside searching for an answer and realized she could not marry Bruce. She kept describing how she couldn't believe that he had not written or let her know how he was doing. She believed he had given up on her.

She saw the objection cross his face as she said it, and she held up a finger to silence him. Then she went on to tell about the past week, starting with the letter she had received and then the discovery that her mother had discarded the previous one.

"She what?" Ethan asked, stunned.

"My mom, she—I know, it's horrible. I'm so sorry. She didn't know what she was doing. I mean, she did, but now she's sorry. She is very sorry."

"The letter, my letter? She threw it away? Why?"

"She knew Bruce was going to propose to me. And she thinks Bruce is wonderful—he is, actually—and she wanted me to marry him. So then the letter came, and she just sort of panicked and hid it. Then she threw it out."

Ethan's face showed anger first, and Sara felt afraid he might say something bitter or cutting. But then his face changed. He glanced at the fire and then back at Sara. He burst out laughing. "You've got to be kidding."

"What?" Sara said, wiping tears out of her eyes.

"No, this is good. Actually, I think it's the best thing I've heard in a long time."

"What?" she repeated.

"Your mom. What she did, it was horrible, but—wow, am I relieved."

"You're relieved?" Sara asked. Now she was utterly confused.

"Yes. Tell me. Did your mom read the letter?"

"No, she just threw it out. I'm sorry."

Ethan stood up, moving over by the fire. He took the poker and stirred the coals. He was almost too excited to sit still. "No, no. It wasn't your fault. It wasn't at all your fault. That makes sense, I think. It's great." He laughed.

"What? What's so funny?"

"So you came up here on Christmas Eve to tell me all this?"

"Yes," Sara said. "And to find out about us. About you and me, I mean."

Ethan nodded and sat back down, this time beside her.

"The last time you were up at this cabin, all those years ago, you told me how sorry you were that we couldn't be together. You said you still loved me, but we couldn't be together. Has that changed?"

Sara wondered for a second. "No. I mean, the love and everything is still there, if that's what you mean. But, as far as the other—"

Ethan smiled and stood back up. "I've always dreamed of this. I've dreamed it for so long. I just didn't believe it could happen."

Then he disappeared. Sara felt unsure what his giddiness was about. She wanted to know about the letter, about whether there was any hope for them to be together.

Ethan came back with a piece of lined paper, crumpled and well worn. He sat back down beside her and smiled.

"You know, I've read this thing to myself a million times, I think, ever since I sent it. I just couldn't believe that you never responded or never said anything to me about it. I just couldn't understand why. But now—well, here you are."

"Is it a copy of the letter?" Sara asked.

"It was my first draft," he answered. "You know how we writers are, making sure we write the exact thing and get it right. So this one probably isn't as polished as the one I sent you, but all the thoughts are there."

"So can I read it?" Sara asked.

"Let me read it to you. I always wanted to tell this to you in person, but I hadn't seen you in so long that I wasn't sure how you felt about me."

So Ethan began to read the letter, sitting next to Sara in front of the roaring fireplace. Sara stared into his eyes, focusing on every word he uttered.

"My dearest Sara. Where can I begin? It has been a long time, too long, since you last heard from me. I am sorry for that, and I apologize for not writing to you sooner. Many things have happened to me and most of them, I believe, are because of you. For this I want to thank you.

"I also want you to know that I still think about you all the time. Every sunrise blossoms with the memory of you. All I have to do to see you again is close my eyes, and you're there. As much as I have traveled, trying to figure out why I can't write and why I can't even think straight, there has been one thing I can say with absolute confidence: I love you. I still dream of being with you.

"After my mom passed away, my whole world ended. I think you knew that. And you were there, as always, and I thought that if I could have you, if you could be mine, life would be okay again and I could get through anything. I believed I could find peace in you, the girl with a smile that could melt the coldest of hearts. So that day when you said good-bye to me at my uncle's little cabin, I felt I had experienced another death.

"I lost hope in everything. In every dream I ever had. In everything I had ever believed in. My writing stopped. My passion for life stopped. Everything stopped. And yet, I still continued to love you. You were all I could think of.

"I lost myself there for a while, wandering here and there and searching for something. But during that lost time I reread all your letters and tried to figure out what it was about this love of yours. Why was it different than mine? You loved me, yet you couldn't be with me—how absurd was that? But of course you had explained it before. You could not give yourself to somebody who didn't hold the same beliefs as you, couldn't share the same faith that kept you going. You couldn't do that to me or to yourself. You were unable to make that commitment—and you were right.

"Yet, at the same time, you loved me enough to never give up on me. I noticed in your letters the Bible quotes you would write and all the things you would say about them, and I usually passed them off as simply cute—like you. I understand now that you were trying to explain eternal things to me. I just never really listened."

Ethan stopped and looked up at Sara. "Are you okay? Do you really want to hear this?"

"No, no, I'm fine." Sara wiped her eyes and smiled. "Please, go on. I can't believe I almost never heard this."

"I always did want to read this to you myself," Ethan said. "Okay, where was I? Yeah, I just never listened.

"But then I started to listen, because there was nothing else to listen to. I had lost my family and you and my writing and everything that was important to me. So I started searching for something—I didn't even know what. I told myself that if believing in this God of yours could bring you back, I would do it. I would simply believe. But of course it wasn't as easy as that.

"I still had that little Bible you sent to me years ago. Remember? So I read it and read it and began to search myself and began actually to try to pray. And then I came across 1 Corinthians 13. The love chapter. I read it and reread it and reread it.

"I especially love the verse that says, 'There are three things that will endure—faith, hope, and love—and the greatest of these is love.' That's beautiful. I mean, it's not only great writing, which I can appreciate, but it says something beautiful about love.

"So I read more, trying to figure out why you loved me and yet didn't want to be with me. I read Matthew, Mark, Luke, and John. Verses stood out—like this one: 'Then Jesus told him, "You believe because you have seen me. Blessed are those who haven't seen me and believe anyway."'

"And then I came across that verse, the famous verse I have heard all my life but never understood: 'For God so loved the world that he gave his only Son, so that everyone who believes in him will not perish but have eternal life.'

"And I began to cry after reading that. I was at the lowest point I had ever reached. I felt totally alone, and I finally realized that nothing or no one could fill that emptiness. Only Christ could, this Jesus Christ I had heard about from my mom and from friends and from you—from sweet little Sara Anthony. From my love.

"So I finally prayed to Jesus not to help me find you but to help me find him. To forgive me for all my wretched sins and to give me some sort of peace. I needed help—not because I was so love stricken, but because I was lost and needed to open up to the truth I had been hearing all my life.

"And then, just like that, Christ answered. He gave me this peace—it's hard to describe, but I know it's real. I guess you know what I mean.

"Sara, do you remember the promises we made so long ago? I promised I would never stop loving you, and you promised you would never stop praying for me. Well, I guess you kept your promise, because those prayers were answered, Sara. My mom's prayers were answered, too, bless her heart. I want—I need—you to know this.

"There aren't enough words to describe my love for you. But I can understand if what you felt and the love we shared has passed by. No matter what, I want you to know that your love has meant more to me this way than it ever would if you had stayed by my side. You loved me enough to say no to me, and your love gave me a chance to find Christ's love. Now I think I can actually begin to understand that love, the love God has for us.

"I still have so much to learn. There is still so much to comprehend. But as John said in his last words in his book, 'I suppose that if all the other things Jesus did were written down, the whole world could not contain the books.'

"I believe this is so very true. Perhaps one day my insignificant words could somehow, in some way, describe this amazing thing that Jesus did for me. Rescuing me from a lost life full of unhappiness. Filling me with hope and with a life. Giving me his promise of eternal life. He didn't have to pick me, Sara. But he used you to lead me to him. I thank him for that.

"I know the future is in God's hands, and I feel okay about that. I used to want to bargain with life, but I know I can't do that anymore. I'm curious, though. What about our promises? Have you forgotten? I'm not sure I'll ever know. But if I don't hear from you ever—here on earth, I mean—then I know I will still see you in the future. I will see you and let you see the love you have allowed me to know. God's love.

"Thank you, Sara. Thank you for so much. Now I understand the things you once described for me. I pray to see you again, perhaps just for a moment. There are so many things I want to tell you.

"I won't dare ask again, but I still wonder what you will say when you read this. Am I simply being foolish to think so much about you? I don't know. So I'll just say good-bye again. But you need to remember these

words. You need to know this, how much you helped change my life. I
will never forget about you; I will always thank you. Thank you for not
giving up on me.

"Sincerely, The starry-eyed dreamer you met years ago and never gave
up on. Ethan."

Ethan put down the letter and smiled. He looked over at Sara, reached
out a hand, and gently wiped away her tears.

"Well, that was it," he said.

Sara sat speechless, overcome by a joy that sent a thousand days and
hours and lifetimes of worry away from her. She looked into the bright
blue eyes of the man sitting next to her and realized it now, realized why
something really was different about him. The boy she had fallen in love
with had been a starry-eyed dreamer, a hopeless romantic, and the love of
her life. She had loved the fun in his voice, the sparkle in his eyes. But he
had grown cynical and skeptical about his own life, and a sadness had settled over him, a sadness she could even feel in his laughter. This sadness
had only increased over the years, especially with the death of his mother.

Now that sadness had been replaced with a newfound love and a newfound faith. A faith in Christ. The sparkle had returned.

Sara threw her arms around Ethan and wept on his shoulder. This all
felt like some wonderful dream—some incredible, awe-inspiring dream
she could not have even imagined.

"I can't believe this," Sara said in Ethan's ear.

"It's true. It's all true. Everything."

"Ethan, I love you so much."

They continued to hold one another as the golden fire leaped in the
background and the gentle shadows danced on the walls.

God grants to all of us moments in time like this, Sara thought. *Moments that
we do not deserve, but moments we are given anyway.* This was one of the many
gifts God had given to Sara and to Ethan. One of the countless many.

*Thank you, Father. Thank you for letting me find him again. And thank you for
letting him find you.*

"Hold on," Sara said to Ethan. She stood up and went to her coat, which
lay on the kitchen table only a few feet away from them.

"What?"

"I've got something to give to you," Sara said. She fished out a small object and carried it back to the couch. She slipped it in his hand as he had done so many years earlier to her. "Perhaps the timing on this wasn't exactly right," Sara said.

Ethan opened his hand and looked down at the small box. He grinned, and his hands shook. "You kept it?" he asked.

"Of course I did. Just like I kept my promise."

"Did you ever—"

"No," Sara answered back, knowing his question. She had never once opened it, not even to peek inside. She knew what was in there. She had never wanted to look at it, not without having Ethan at her side, not without the ability to tell him yes.

Ethan didn't hesitate. He opened the box and looked at the simple gold band with the tiny diamond. Then he got on one knee in front of her.

"I couldn't think of a better time to ask you, Ms. Sara Anthony, than on the eve of Christ's birthday."

Sara looked at the glistening ring she had waited and prayed for so long to see, to accept, to wear. Now. Finally, now. Thank God she had waited for his timing to be more than perfect.

"You waited for me, Sara," Ethan continued. "You waited and you kept your promise. And as crazy as I've been, I kept my promise, too—I've never stopped loving you. And now I think that I'm either going to run outside in the freezing cold and wake up and realize this is a dream or else do what I should have done years ago. The right way."

Ethan took Sara's trembling left hand in his own unsteady one. "Sara, will you do me the incredible honor of accepting my crazy and long-awaited and dearly meant proposal of marriage? Will you marry me?"

And Sara nodded, speechless. Love. Dear love. Dear heavenly love. She had waited and believed and now, could it be real? Could he really be standing in front of her slipping that beautiful diamond ring on her finger? Could he really be there, kissing her hand and holding it to his face to wipe away his own tears?

Could this be true, Lord? Please tell me it is.

"I do, I do—oh, I do," she said.

And then she held him once again in her arms. Outside, a storm howled, and the rest of the world seemed remote and cold and brutal and unrelenting. But inside the light was soft and warm and infinitely safe. The two of them had found each other. The promise had indeed remained, after all these years.

When Sara finally spoke again, she said these words to Ethan. "Thank you," she whispered.

He chuckled, not understanding her words. "Why thank me?"

"For never giving up on me, even after all these years and even after finding out I was engaged. Thank you."

"I would have always loved you, Sara. Even if you got married and went off and spent a lifetime with somebody else you dearly loved. God allowed you to come across my path. He allowed you to inspire me. And he helped you point me in the right direction. How could I not love you, no matter what?"

Ethan pushed himself to his feet, then sat down next to her. She nestled up close beside him.

"The storm looks bad, doesn't it," she said, looking through the frosted window at the cold and dark world. "And it's only going to get worse, I think."

The man she loved, the man who had waited so long for her and had found his way in this cold and dark world, reflected on her words.

"We'll make it," Ethan replied. "By God's grace, we'll make it. We've come this far, right?"

The fire continued to burn and the winds continued to howl and the snow continued to fall.

And the promises two young and loving individuals had made to one another on another storm-filled day still held true. As would the promises of the one who had brought them together, for an eternity.

Sincerely, The starry-eyed dreamer
you met years ago and never gave up on.

THE END

the Watermark

A NOVELLA BY

TRAVIS THRASHER

To my parents,

for never giving up on me.

And to Sharon,

for somehow loving me.

Acknowledgments

With special thanks to the following:

Ron Beers, for your constant generosity.

Anne Christian Buchanan, a remarkable editor I am fortunate to work with.

Francine Rivers, for your encouragement and godly example.

All the people who gave me insight and encouragement in this project—
Anne Goldsmith, Ken Petersen, Becky Nesbitt, Jan Stob, and Danielle Crilly.

And to M. Zaglifa, whom I had the great fortune to meet the night of
18 May 1993.

WATERMARK:

A mark impressed on paper that is visible

only when the paper is held up to the light

"Grief can't be dissolved like rain washing dust off a roof. Sorrow knows no washing away, no easing . . . no end of time."

Francine Rivers, The Last Sin Eater

The son said to him,
"Father, I have sinned against heaven and in your sight, and am no longer worthy to be called your son."

Luke 15:21

Prologue

I WISH I COULD SAY that before you stands a new man. A changed man. A man transformed by God's grace.

I would like to show then-and-now snapshots, pictures of my miraculous example of healing and heart renewal. I would love to quote the good old songs and verses I heard when I was growing up, about how once I was blind and now I see and all that other stuff.

I wish I could say all this and more, but I can't.

I can say only three simple words: *God saved me.*

I call them simple because I know that for God, it was. I wasn't some magnificent sinner who presented the Lord with a grand challenge. I wasn't someone destined before the beginning of human history to make that much of an impact. I wasn't some Saul who needed to be blinded by the light in order to see, who needed a name change because of the amazing transformation in his life. God simply decided that I would spend eternity with him and a lot more important people in heaven.

Why? I wish I knew. Perhaps that's why I'm writing this—to try to figure out why. He saved a wretch like me. There's another one of those old verses—but one that means so much.

Still, I can't lie and say I feel like a whole new creation or I'm going to

be asked to sign up for the next Billy Graham crusade to tell my testimony. I've only told my story to a few people. I'm not good at public
speaking anyway, and I have no idea how to really communicate God's
grace. I'd probably fail, just like I have so many times since committing
my life to the Lord that long-ago day in fourth grade.

I think if God allowed me to live one hundred years, I still wouldn't
be proud of my story. Not a day will go by that I will ever forget how I
failed so many people.

How I failed the same Lord who saved me.

But the amazing thing is this: the Lord has never failed me. I stand
amazed that he still listens to me. And I know he does. Even now, as I
write these words, I know he's hearing them. Even though so many other
things are so much more important than my little life, I know God cares
about me.

I'm probably sounding like one of those Sunday school songs again.
Think I'm going to start singing now?

Jesus loves me, this I know.

I know because he took a little kid into his arms and helped him believe. He made him see how he had died exactly for that kid.

For the Bible tells me so.

It told me a lot more, too, though I closed my heart to its counsel. I
grew up and fell further and further away from him. But that didn't mean
what he said wasn't true.

Little ones to him belong.

I was one of them, too, but I insisted on running away. For many
years, I was a confused and lost child.

They are weak but he is strong.

Only someone so strong and so loving and so incredibly God could allow me to come back to him. Or even more amazing, could seek me out
and draw me back—simply because I was marked as his.

Yes, Jesus loves me.

And maybe in this, my story—my fateful account of how I came back
to him—I'll be able to give you a glimpse of why I know it's true.

PART ONE

an undeniable past

Dear Amy,

I'm not even sure why I am writing.

Today as I walked across the campus grounds I saw someone who looked like you. She passed me on a sidewalk with a smile that didn't notice me. I almost stopped her to say something. But of course, I knew it wasn't you.

All day long I wondered what I would say if I could actually see you or talk to you. I've wondered this for months, years. Perhaps that is why I'm still writing you, even after all this time.

What would I say if I could meet you face-to-face?

I guess above everything else, I would say I'm sorry. I would ask for your forgiveness.

I would ask for one word from you. Any word.

Maybe I'm writing in hope of one.

Sheridan Blake

One

I SAT ON A WOBBLY BARSTOOL in my apartment waiting for
the answering machine to haunt me again. The message played, the words
already memorized. It was the first time I had actually heard the man's
voice. After so many years, he had decided to contact me in person.

I knew he still hated me.

Pressing the delete button on that voice felt almost as good as locking
my apartment door and escaping into the October night.

The dark swallowed me as I walked down an alley to the main street a
block away. I felt more at ease knowing I was completely alone, unable to
be located by ghosts from my past. Yet a voice in my head reminded me I
wasn't truly alone. A thousand shadowy memories stuck to my every
move. I could never outrun them, no matter how hard I tried.

Chicago nightlife ignored me. I hadn't planned on going out alone
again on a Friday. I had told myself I might actually connect with my
roommate wherever he ended up, or I might call one of the three guys
I was on a first-name basis with at school. But the four-sentence message
on my answering machine had changed it all. I needed to go out and forget
about that message.

The night felt cool and damp from the earlier rain. I hiked the

twenty-minute distance across busy Chicago side streets to Covenant
College and passed under the arches of the arts building on campus.
Passing through its front doors always reminded me of entering a
church, though it had been years since I had actually set foot in one.

In the auditorium, I sat alone in my usual row of seats. I was half an
hour early, but I didn't mind. I would soon be surrounded by students
five, six, and seven years younger than me. Funny how relaxed I felt in a
room full of people when I knew they didn't expect me to talk with them.

I tried to forget about the message on my machine. But the words continued to play over and over again in my head until a stranger interrupted
them.

"Do you know what time it is?"

I glanced up at the figure who had walked to the center of the row of
seats in front of me to ask an obvious question. I pointed toward the clock
visible on the wall to our right.

"Is that right?" the woman said.

"I think so."

"Okay. Thanks."

The Asian girl with long, black hair pulled back and slim glasses perched
on her nose sat down almost directly in front of me. I felt annoyed, the same
way I would if someone were to sit by me on an empty plane.

"Do you know what they're playing?" she asked me after a few minutes
had passed.

"They never tell you."

"Really? I thought they advertised the movies in the school paper."

"That I wouldn't know," I replied, my tone laced with indifference.

"I've never come to one of these things. Usually I'm out on Friday
nights."

She smiled and I nodded, deliberately not looking into her eyes. I ne-
glected to tell her I hadn't missed one since the semester started.

I didn't say anything for a while. The young woman in front of me
continued to look around as if she was waiting for someone. The silence
made her wiggle uncomfortably in her seat. The only thing uncomfortable for me was noticing her every move and wondering if she was going
to turn around again. The nice thing about this particular auditorium was

its big movie screen. Every Friday night there would be a double feature of films tied together by a theme or an actor. So many students came that it had become easy to blend in and get lost in the crowd. Perhaps this was one of the reasons I enjoyed coming.

Students began filing in. I saw it was still almost fifteen minutes until the first movie. Last Friday the whole place had been packed.

"Excuse me. I know this is going to sound strange, but do you have a brother?" the dark-eyed stranger in front of me asked after turning around again.

"No."

She apologized with a radiant smile. "Oh, I just could have sworn— well, nothing. Sorry."

"I have an older sister," I found myself offering.

"No," she said, "this was a guy."

"Okay."

"In a class I had years ago."

"No brother. Sorry." That was all I could think of to say.

I searched my memory vaults but couldn't remember ever meeting any tall, slender Asian girl in any of my classes. I was certain I would have remembered her.

A group of students captured the young woman's attention—obviously, the people she was waiting for. They filled her row and began talking nonstop. I couldn't help overhearing their conversation. It was nothing worth noting, except for the fact that they all paid attention to the woman who had been talking to me. A wiry guy with frosted hair and an oversized soccer shirt sat beside her, chatting and whispering and making her laugh. He had an obnoxious laugh I instantly disliked.

Minutes before the first movie, I wondered if the woman was going to turn around again and say something. Yet why would she? And more important, why did I care?

The lights dimmed. So, I assumed, had any more chances of communication with her.

As the opening credits began to roll for one of my favorite movies, the young woman turned around again.

To smile.

⚜

The movies that night turned out to be *The Shawshank Redemption* and *The Fugitive*. The theme must have been injustice and escape. One guy was in prison and one on the run, but both were desperately clinging to hope.

Had someone known I was coming?

Most of the people around me cleared out before I left the auditorium. The dark-haired woman I still didn't recognize had looked back at me one more time as the second movie's ending credits showed. I saw the brightness in those dark, narrow eyes and knew I could not have seen her before. Surely I would have remembered her. I walked slowly back to my apartment, thinking of the young woman I just had the chance to meet and failed to connect with. Yet was it really a failure? Wasn't that my intention, especially with these Friday night movies—to lose myself in the big screen, to know I could avoid for several hours having to reveal anything about myself to anybody?

Maybe you need to stop living your life through actors on the big screen and simply start living a normal life again.

I knew this. And yet, another voice inside told me that the young woman probably hadn't given me another two seconds' worth of thought after asking me those simple questions. I didn't blame her.

An unseen mist fell outside, and I was soaked by the time I opened the door to my apartment to my old dog's familiar, tail-wagging greeting. Barney wandered over to smell the new and exciting scents on my legs.

I lived with my roommate, Erik Morrison, on the North Side of Chicago, only a short distance from Covenant College. Having lived with Erik since the end of summer, I knew he wouldn't be home—not at such an early hour as half-past midnight.

Maybe it was the combination of the movies and dreary weather and almost meeting a girl I couldn't stop thinking about and probably would never see again. It was that and a lot more, I knew, that made me feel so lonely.

Most of all, it was the reminder of the answering-machine message I had received only hours ago:

"Sheridan Blake. This is Mike Larsen, and I've been trying to find your number for a while. We need to talk. Please call me at 312-794-5348."

The man's gruff voice. The sharp, harsh tone. The unmistakable words.

I had been gone so long. Seven years. Seven long years spent living with my parents only an hour away in the suburbs, but far enough to make Chicago and Covenant feel like a world and a lifetime away. I never thought I would return, but now that I had, I was feeling overwhelmed.

Minutes later, as I slipped underneath comforting covers, the silence of my apartment allowed my mind to wander past the walled barriers I had erected many years ago. They drifted into areas I hadn't visited for a while.

Such as God.

The thing was, I knew God was there—watching, waiting. Part of me had always known it. Yet I couldn't say a word to him. I knew of his forgiveness, of his atonement for sins, of his amazing grace. Yet somehow it just didn't seem to apply to me. What I had done still seemed too close, too real, too unchangeable.

It had been years, and yet it felt like it all could have happened yesterday.

Talk to me.

And what if I did? another voice answered back in my mind. What if I did finally open the window and begin trying to pray? What could I say? Where would I begin? How could I even try, after so many years?

The words would fail me. I believed this.

I thought of the smile I had been privileged to see earlier that night and wondered when—or if—I would ever have such a carefree grin. I used to carry one around like a puppy, filling those around me with the same enthusiasm my smile showed off. The sort of smile the woman at the movie had displayed.

I could use a friend like her, I thought.

I'm not sure why of all nights I then chose to do the thing I had not done in ages. But I clenched my hands together and breathed in deeply and managed to say two words that had not come out in the last few years. In the last seven years.

"Help me."

Dear Amy,

I write again, hoping you understand these long-overdue words.

These days, I find myself wandering toward the past even as I plan for the future. I knew it would be a big step, coming back to the city and going back to Covenant. I am so often reminded of it all. Reminded of you.

I carry your picture with me still—I clipped it from the newspaper. A pretty blonde laughing at the camera. A smile so bright it's painful to look at. But I do look. I force myself to look. I deserve these memories.

I only wonder when they'll subside.

Sheridan Blake

Two

MY ROOMMATE reminded me of myself at his age. That was a bad thing.

Hours after the two prison movies and my feeble attempt at a prayer, I awoke at two-thirty in the morning—or at night, depending on who you talked with—and found Erik passed out in the dry bathtub. Clothes and all. I wondered if he had mistaken the tub for his bed. I spent ten minutes waking him up so I could lead him into his bed. He reeked of beer and smoke. I knew the scents well.

I slipped Erik's cover over him and made sure he was okay. My biggest fear in putting him to bed—and so far I'd done it several times—was that I'd find him dead the next morning from being strangled in his own sheets or, even worse, suffocating on his vomit. It's sick to say, but these things have happened to just as many college kids as rock stars and actors.

But Erik didn't seem to be in any distress. He slept like a baby. I found myself envying him.

I couldn't get back to sleep. Instead, I wondered how long Erik would continue his endless partying and when—or if—he would ever grow up and give it up. Would he be like me, learning the hard way? Would a God-sent two-by-four have to hit him several times over the head before he learned?

Had *I* learned?

And what was I doing to help him, anyway? What kind of influence was I? Sure, I didn't drink or smoke or curse in front of Erik, but I had never explained the reasons why. Maybe uttered an occasional "you might want to slow down" or something like that. But I hadn't said anything else. How could I?

I was a lot of things, but I wasn't a hypocrite.

Still, maybe there was something I could say to this young guy who reminded me so much of me. I hadn't really known him that long. He had answered my ad on the campus bulletin board back in May, when the Covenant school year was ending. I'd put a simple blurb about my desire to have a roommate:

> Senior guy at Covenant needs roommate for next semester.
> 2-bedroom apart. 15 min. from campus.

I had gotten several calls about the ad. But Erik's had been by far the most memorable. I'll always remember it.

"Yeah, are you the guy looking for a roommate next year?"

"Yes," I told the deep, laid-back voice.

"Yeah, well, I'm going to be a senior. Actually it'll be my fifth year at Covenant. I'm a communications major."

"Mine is music."

"That mean you're gonna practice a tuba at the apartment or something?"

"No, just the piano—and I do almost all my practicing at the college."

"Do you go to bed early?"

"Actually, no," I told him.

"Well, look, I'm wanting an apartment where I can come and go, you know. Not an animal house or anything, but I go out a lot. Covenant has lots of rules about these things, so it can be tricky living on campus."

"I know," I said with a smile.

"You don't mind a guy going out every now and then?"

"No." I didn't.

Erik had eventually showed up and I instantly liked him. He wasn't much of a talker, but he had a certain relaxed confidence as he checked the apartment out. He was dark haired, with a short spiked haircut, and he wore baggy cargo pants and what looked like a used gas-station-attendant shirt with the name *Bob* embroidered on the front. He didn't work at a gas station, though. He actually worked at a fitting place in his spare time: a Tower record and book store.

What really clicked between Erik and me was music—when he came into my room and found my compact disc collection. I'm one of those guys who eats and breathes music. Years ago, I thought I would be a concert pianist. More recently, I wanted to compose electronic music. Now my dreams of making it big in the field were long gone. But the love of music still remained with me, as Erik discovered during that first meeting.

"You have more CDs than I do," Erik had said as he picked up one of them and cursed—not a vicious, obscene curse, but the kind where I could tell he didn't even know he was doing it. The same way some people say *uh* all the time.

"Who is Tangerine Dream?" he asked me.

"An all-synthesizer group that's been around since the seventies."

"Like new wave or something like that?"

"No, it's instrumental music. They were experimental at first, but they ended up influencing a lot of today's music in both rock and the movies."

"You have like fifty of their CDs."

"I like their stuff. Most of it anyway."

The other apartment candidates I had talked to seemed responsible and levelheaded and studious—all the things I wasn't. Not that I was some kind of beer-guzzling, toga-wearing frat boy. Those days were long gone. But I could still never live with a college student who went to bed at ten and woke up at five and studied and knew exactly where he was going in life.

People like that scared me.

Now, months after choosing Erik and knowing it had been the right decision, I lay in bed wondering when and how I could ever talk to him about my life. I was a private person, an introvert, someone who rarely shared secrets and emotions. How could I even begin to talk to Erik about all the things that had happened to me?

⚜

I sat in front of the television the following Sunday morning around ten-thirty watching an NFL pregame show and feeling a little guilty. I knew where I should have been. I knew who I should have been listening to. The couch should have been a pew, and the voice of Terry Bradshaw should have been a pastor's. I knew it came down to a simple case of courage—and I just didn't have any.

So I just sat there, thinking of the girl I had seen Friday night and wondering what I would have told her about myself had I not blown the opportunity.

Let's see. Let's begin with the basics.

I was a twenty-eight-year-old senior, finishing up my last year of college after a seven-year hiatus—but still not quite clear on what I was going to do next. I was living with a twenty-two-year-old kid who still had a lot of growing up to do before he graduated—in other words, someone a lot like me.

I also lived with my most loving and trusting best friend, a dog given to me on my sixteenth birthday. His name was Barney. I had wanted to name him Cujo or Butch or something that completely didn't fit him, but my parents had insisted he looked like a Barney—and he did. Not the kids' purple monster, though. My Barney was half sheltie and half Pomeranian, with golden brown fur and a never-ending smile. He was also about ninety in dog years, and an insulin-dependent diabetic.

That's right. I was the proud owner of a diabetic dog who got shots every morning and every evening. His sight was almost gone, and I don't think he had heard a thing in two years. Gone were the days when he'd bounce up and down like he was on a trampoline, finally stopping to be petted or given a treat. These days Barney would totter toward me with the excitement of a man rolling down the hallway of his nursing home in his wheelchair. But he still got around all right, most of the time—except when I first moved into an unfamiliar apartment and he spent the first month bumping into the occasional wall or piece of furniture.

Like any senior citizen, Barney required some special consideration. He was definitely not low-maintenance. But he had been with me since

I was a teenager and seen me through a lot, both good and bad. And I had learned there were few things more satisfying than knowing that a beautiful and loving friend waited at home for you, one who could never be disappointed or hold a grudge and who always seemed to light up whenever you stepped through the front door. The time spent taking care of Barney paled in comparison to the time he spent taking care of me.

Besides caring for Barney and going to school and living with Erik, I also gave piano lessons to kids in the suburbs. This was something I had done in my spare time while working a variety of odd jobs since I was out of college. I had recently quit my last part-time job, waiting tables at a fancy restaurant ten minutes away from my parents' house, and continued with the fifteen to twenty hours a week of helping younger kids live out their dreams (or their parents' dreams) of being the next Beethoven or Elton John.

And that was my life—on the surface, at least. I tended to view the surface part as okay. But things got stickier when you began to peel off the layers.

Erik entered the living room and almost tripped over the hairy lump lying oblivious on the carpet. Barney barely moved.

"Long night?"

Erik nodded and sat on the couch, staring at the television while trying to wake up.

"Remember much?" I asked him.

Erik thought for a second. "Last thing I remember was having Jell-O shots at a party I was at."

"You mistook the bathtub for your bed."

Erik looked at me and laughed. After a few minutes, he must have realized that I had helped him to bed.

"Thanks, man," he said in a hoarse voice.

I wanted to say more, but the phone rang. As always, we let it go. The answering machine clicked in on the fourth ring. Erik's music-filled message played. Then a rough, irritated voice spoke.

"Yeah, I'm calling for Sheridan Blake again. This is Mike Larsen. You know what this is about. It's time we finally meet. We need to talk."

Erik looked at me. "I think he called and left a message yesterday," he said.

"I was hoping he'd get the hint," I replied.

Erik nodded. He didn't ask anything more. That was one of the things I liked about the guy. He kept to himself. He wasn't asking me questions about the past, questions about who this man was and why I wasn't calling him back.

Maybe Erik knew I was still running.

OCTOBER 10

Dear Amy,

I would give anything—anything—to talk to you. To know what you're thinking.

Once again, I question why I'm writing. Surely it does no good. But for some reason, I feel I need to write you these letters. I feel better penning these words on this paper. Perhaps it's because I'm back at Covenant. Being here has brought back a cloud of memories I thought had been rained away years ago.

I feel like I've been running from that cloud for so long. No matter how far I go, the cloud still hovers above me. It's so high, so untouchable, so unmovable.

I wonder if I'll ever be able to watch it disappear, Amy. What I wouldn't give to watch it simply fade away.

Sheridan Blake

Three

I SAT ON CEMENT STEPS in an indoor arena overlooking a giant pool. Next to me sat a little blonde-haired girl who sipped from a cup of soda.

"How do they do that?" her soft, high voice asked me.

"They train them to do that," I told her in my best impersonation of an adult, unsure myself how the people at the Shedd Aquarium taught the dolphins to jump up and down and glide on their backs.

"This is my favorite part," she told me, pointing. "When the people swim with them. I wish I could do that."

I nodded and looked out through the glass structure of the aquarium toward the deep blue waters of Lake Michigan. Even though I had spent most of my life growing up close to Chicago, this was the first time I'd visited the aquarium. Nita and her mother, Gail Primrose, had invited me on this big-city outing with them. Nita had been my piano student for four years, and in that time I'd gradually developed a friendship with her family.

The graceful creatures wooed the crowd and Nita. She would clap and smile and look at me to acknowledge her enthusiasm. I clapped and smiled a lot, too, acting as if this was the best performance I had ever witnessed in my lifetime. It *was* pretty amazing. And seeing the cute ten-year-old's grin made a part of me feel whole again.

Gail Primrose walked up the aisle and sat next to her daughter. "Here you go," the petite woman said as she handed Nita a sweatshirt. "A memento of the aquarium."

"Thanks, Mom," Nita said, still focused on the performance below.

"I would have gotten you something, Sheridan, but I wasn't sure about your taste. Would you like a T-shirt or something?"

"Oh, that's okay—I'm kinda overstocked on T-shirts these days. But thanks. This is great."

"We're so glad you got to come with Nita and me. Aren't we, honey?"

"Yeah," Nita replied.

Gail looked over at me above her daughter's head. "You really have been a blessing to Nita these past few years, Sheridan."

"She's very talented," I said.

"Dennis and I especially appreciate your continuing to teach her now that you're downtown at school."

"It's no problem. Really. I go home anyway to do my laundry."

"Still, I know you don't have to do it."

I smiled. "Nita's soon going to be too good for me to teach."

"Yeah, right," Nita replied.

"But until then," I told her, "you're stuck with me."

When the climax of the dolphin extravaganza ended and the mass of people began to leave to continue exploring the rest of the Chicago attraction, I asked Nita what she thought of the show.

"I loved it. Can we stay for another one?"

"We're going to go to Michigan Avenue now, sweetie," Gail said.

"Please?"

"We'll come back here sometime. And we'll invite Sheridan again."

"I'm up for it," I said in all sincerity. "It's a great way to spend an afternoon. I'll just have to make sure I don't have class."

"I think it's wonderful that you're finishing up at Covenant."

I nodded at Mrs. Primrose. She and her husband, Dennis, were longtime friends of my parents and lived only twenty minutes from them, in the suburb of West Chicago. Both of them knew why I had quit Covenant seven years ago.

"It's been interesting having to study again," I said.

"I have to study all the time," Nita said.

"That's right. And you'd better practice, too, before next week."

She made a face at me, then treated me to a dazzling smile. "I'm really glad you came with us today, Mr. Blake."

I had all my students call me Mr. Blake, even though I didn't feel like a mister. Nita had been with me for four years now, ever since she entered first grade. She had progressed so quickly that I realized my time with her was drawing to an end. She would soon be moving on to someone far better and wiser on the piano.

I hated to think about telling Nita good-bye. Most of my students came and went, and I had to accept this. Since I didn't have a degree and had never really played professionally, I didn't have the credentials to hold them for long—especially the talented ones. But I wanted to continue to teach Nita as long as I could. Every session with her reminded me of my childhood, of those days when I would play the piano for hours, always working to be better, always dreaming of what tomorrow would bring. Nita was like that too. She not only had talent, but she also remembered everything she was taught and practiced diligently to put it to use.

As Nita, Gail, and I followed others out of the large, humid arena, I saw a figure to my left who looked familiar. Startling eyes, shimmering and almond-shaped, a rich velvet brown in color—the sight of them almost knocked me over. I didn't recognize them at first without the glasses.

They instantly recognized me as a finger pointed my way. "Hey, movie guy," she said with a pleasantly surprised look on her face.

Movie guy?

"Hello, again," I said.

It was the Wednesday after the movie night. I had wondered if I would run into the woman on campus at any point, doubtful if I would say anything to her if I did. The thought of meeting her again at the Shedd Aquarium had never crossed my mind.

The tall guy with the frosted hair was with her. "How's it going?" he said, more as a passing statement than a genuine inquiry.

I nodded to him, knowing there was nothing more to say to either of them.

"So I run into you at the movies *and* the aquarium," the long-haired woman said to me, smiling and being friendly. "What next—the zoo?"

"Maybe." I still couldn't believe I had run into her here.

"I like the zoo," Nita said.

"And who is this?" the woman asked, curiosity filling her face.

"I'm Nita."

Gail was already walking down the stairs and didn't hear our introductions.

The woman from the movie looked at me and expected something more, but I didn't offer anything up. I felt uncomfortable, especially with the soccer stud at her side.

"Did you like the show, Nita?" the woman asked.

Nita went into a three-minute-long detail of her feelings about the show.

"Okay, Nita. We have to go now. Have a nice afternoon," I finally said as I led Nita away.

"You too," the woman answered. "Maybe I'll see you again."

She smiled a friendly grin that made me do the same. I wanted to say half a million things but instead walked away from the couple.

Actually, I wasn't sure if I even wanted to see her again. There wasn't any reason to see her again. I didn't know her name, had seen her twice with the tall guy at her side, and knew she had seen me alone on a Friday night and apparently babysitting a kid on another afternoon.

"That lady's beautiful," Nita told me as we walked toward her mother, who was waiting for us at the exit doors. "Is she a friend of yours?"

"Not exactly," I said, nodding in agreement with her first statement.

How could I have missed such beauty the other night? What was I thinking?

"Do you like her?"

"I don't even know her," I replied, doubting I would have a chance to talk to her a third time, already knowing the first impressions had been made.

"They were on a date, right?"

I nodded. Enough said.

⚜

Two days later, I sat in an empty row of the Covenant arts building, trying to act nonchalant and appear like I wasn't looking for anyone. I wasn't— not really. Yet I had still arrived thirty minutes early.

I had asked Erik if he wanted to break his usual Friday night barhopping tradition to come watch a couple of movies with me. He had said maybe, which both of us knew meant no.

Well, I'd tried. I knew there was more I needed to do, more I needed to say to him. I just needed time.

And courage.

Twenty minutes before the movies started, a tall, dark-haired girl walked down the aisle on my left side, arm in arm with what appeared to be her date for the evening. I wasn't sure, but it looked like the Asian girl I had met here before.

A wave of disappointment flowed through me. *Stop being foolish,* I told myself.

Meanwhile, someone had slipped up on my right side. "Excuse me, is this seat taken?"

I turned and faced the same person I had imagined to be rows in front of me with some muscle man in a leather jacket by her side. For a second I was surprised and said nothing; then I realized she was asking about the spot a seat away from mine.

"No."

Amazing how a week ago, I had been bothered by her presence. Now I was almost relieved to see her again.

"You sure?" she asked.

"Go ahead."

"My friends are going to be late, as usual," she announced as she sat down.

I nodded and noticed I was sitting in one of the only open rows in the place. "Mine are coming in a bus," I said, trying to be funny.

"Really?"

"No, just kidding." My sense of humor was a little rusty.

"So, we meet again," she said.

"Amazing," I replied.

"I'm beginning to think you're following me."

I soaked up the full smile she gave me. "Hey, I was here first."

"Oh, that's right. Well, maybe I'm following you."

"I'm a little worried, now that you mention it."

"So did you enjoy the Shedd Aquarium?" she asked me.

"Sure. And you?"

"Oh, it's great. I've been there before, though. Matt hadn't, and he wanted to go."

I nodded and said nothing. Matt. That was soccer boy's name—Matt. I bet he was one of those guys who could dribble a soccer ball fifty times on his legs.

"I guess I should be polite and introduce myself," she said. "I'm Genevie Liu."

"Sheridan Blake."

"I like that name."

"Thanks. My parents must have too."

"Are you a student at Covenant? I don't think I've ever seen you."

"Just my brother, right?" I asked, offering a slight grin.

"That was years ago."

"I'm finishing up my senior year. I took a break from college."

"From Covenant?"

"Yes."

"So it *was* you," Genevie exclaimed.

"What do you mean?"

"Did you ever take a philosophy course with Dr. Rich? The short, bearded guy?"

"You ask a lot of questions."

"I'm an inquisitive sort of person," she said with a grin.

"Actually, I think I did take that course."

"I was in your class. I *knew* that was you."

"Probably was. Sorry—I never did get into that class much. In fact, I don't think I attended it much either."

"That was my freshman year at Covenant. I came from out of state."

"So you graduated a few years ago?"

"Yes. I still work at the college, in admissions. I'm finishing my master's work this semester."

I wanted to ask more, but several people arrived and sat with her. She casually shifted over one seat, sitting next to me. I was surprised but refrained from showing it. She introduced me to the group, including Matt. I was especially thrilled to make his acquaintance again.

Before the movies started, Genevie whispered a question at me. "So why did you quit school?"

"Another question, huh?"

"Just curious."

"I had some growing up to do," I told her.

"We all have growing up to do," she replied. "If you ask me, I never want to grow up."

I raised my eyebrows and said nothing more. Even though I looked straight ahead, I couldn't get the image of Genevie's deep brown eyes out of my head.

⚜

"I had a farm in Africa," the accented voice of Meryl Streep began as the film *Out of Africa* began to roll.

The connecting theme between the two movies that night was Robert Redford, who starred in each of them. I had seen both movies before but enjoyed watching them again.

"I've never seen this one," Genevie whispered to me as the opening credits flashed across the screen.

"Come on," I whispered back in complete disbelief.

"Seriously."

"What island did you grow up on? This is one of the all-time classics."

"Actually, they didn't have movies where I grew up."

She looked serious and I instantly apologized, afraid I had insulted her heritage. "So where did you grow up?" I asked.

"California," she said, then giggled and kept watching the screen.

During the movie we continued making small comments to each other. I wondered what Matt was thinking, but he seemed to not notice or care about Genevie's talking to me. At one point he even got up and walked out. I wondered briefly if he was angry with her, then forgot about him completely as I lost myself in the movie.

There's a scene in the picture where the two main characters—Redford and Streep—fly in a small plane over the beautiful terrain of Africa. The cinematography hypnotized me, even after having seen it several times, and combined with the brilliant score by John Barry, the scene almost transcended the movie. It's one of those moments when a film becomes something more, a moment that lingers in the vast recesses of memory for many years. In a poignant moment during that flight, Streep takes Redford's hand.

I watched the familiar scene and realized that my mind was somewhere else. I was thinking of the woman I'd just met and how much I wanted to talk more to her. What I would have given to simply reach out and take her hand as well. It sounds silly. Writing it down, it sounds childish. But I needed a soul mate. Not a dog who couldn't hear his name when I called him or a roommate who went out drinking every weekend. I needed someone to talk to, to be with. Someone who could be a friend, or maybe even more.

Someone like the striking and pleasant woman who sat next to me.

I wondered if Genevie felt as strange as I did. There we were, sitting side by side, watching an extraordinary love story on the screen. And I didn't know a thing about her.

"How gorgeous," Genevie leaned over to whisper to me.

I glanced at her and nodded, agreeing with her as I studied her flawless complexion. Her skin looked smooth and babylike, her smile gentle yet subtly enticing, her eyes bright even in the semidarkness.

I adjusted my own eyes to the front of the room, yet focused not on the screen but on the ceiling above.

Barry's moving score soared, as did the plane. I followed them in my own thoughts, amazed that I could ride the wave of the music, analyze the orchestration, and be aware of the girl beside me, all at the same time.

During the intermission between the movies, Genevie turned and announced that she had to leave. "It was nice to see you again, Sheridan Blake."

"Same here."

"Maybe next time we can chat longer, in a less crowded place."

"Uh, yeah, sure. That'd be good." I felt like such an idiot. Had I really forgotten how to talk to a girl?

"You a coffee drinker?" she asked.

"Sure."

"The Barnes & Noble on Clark has a great café. I'm usually there most afternoons, studying and sipping coffee."

I nodded, not sure what to make of her comment. Her friends had already moved toward the aisle and seemed to be waiting for her.

"Well, then. Good night," she said, smiling gently as she stood and began to walk away.

I wanted to say something more but knew I couldn't.

At least turn around again. Let me see those eyes one more time.

Genevie didn't let me down.

OCTOBER 17

Dear Amy,

It's amazing what a simple smile can do to brighten up a day or even a week. Ever since I've come back to Covenant, I've been walking around avoiding almost everyone. Now I'm surprised to discover what a simple conversation with a friendly stranger can do.

I wonder if praying could make the same sort of difference.

They say God is all-knowing, all-loving, and all-powerful. What I don't know is why that same God would continue to choose to love me. Does he? Does he truly love me?

I know I should read the Bible, but to be honest, I'm afraid to find what it has to say. What will happen if I read it and only grow more cynical?

I know I need to move on. God, please help me move on.

Sheridan

Four

A WEEK HAD PASSED since I had heard from my phoning friend, Mike Larsen. Erik had obliged my request to let the machine screen all of our calls. He hadn't pressured me as to why. Not yet.

My fears were heightened one weeknight in mid-October, when we got a knock on our apartment door. I pictured Larsen tip-tapping on our door with a baseball bat, which he would proceed to use over my head.

Erik got up off the couch to get the door. The knocking was unusual, since most visitors rang our buzzer from a monitor outside the locked front door.

"Expecting visitors?" I asked Erik.

"No," he replied. "I'm going out pretty soon."

"That's a surprise."

"Maybe Psycho is wanting to borrow some sugar," Erik said with a laugh.

Erik and I had nicknamed many of the inhabitants who lived around us. Erik had come up with Psycho for the guy down the hall because he looked like Anthony Perkins from the original Alfred Hitchcock movie. Sort of acted like him, too.

Erik opened the door and found three strangers in their twenties, two guys and a girl. They asked if they could come in.

"Well, sure," Erik said, giving me an uh-oh look.

As the three wandered into our apartment, I noticed that one of them was carrying a Bible. I instantly felt the dread creep over me. The other guy carried a small notebook.

Red flags were beginning to go up all over the place.

The strangers introduced themselves. Two of them were students at Covenant and were trying to get to know their classmates who lived off campus. The third guy worked at the college in the student development office. They had just finished visiting some other students in our apartment building and had decided to stop by our place—they had gotten Erik's name and address from the college. None of the three seemed to have any idea I attended Covenant.

Did I really look that old?

"I'm Sheridan," I offered in my most casual and friendly of voices. "Senior graduating in music."

The guy holding a Bible was Mark Everly, dark haired and good-looking in a homecoming king sort of way. He was the one working in student development. He was friendly in a phony, forced way. I knew I shouldn't judge him, but I couldn't help it. I wondered what was coming with the Bible he held.

Actually, I knew what was coming.

After my introduction, Mark studied me for a couple of seconds, seemingly lost in thought. "Are you guys currently going to a church?" Mark asked us after we had conversed a few minutes about school and living off campus.

"No," Erik blurted out. He didn't seem too concerned about what they thought. He didn't try to hide the beer bottle in his hand either.

"I haven't found a place yet," I said. This was true. Of course, I wasn't looking either.

"Lissa and I go to the Bible Church on the corner of West and Randolph," Mark said. "Joel goes to Covenant Reformed."

"Yeah, I've heard of that."

"Are either of you involved in any sort of college group?"

"That'd be a big no again," Erik said.

"Not really," I said, not sure why I offered up a "not really."

We spoke of churches for a while. Mark was the main talker, always being friendly and suggesting places we could go, places they went, and reasons for visiting the college groups at their churches. Lissa added bits and pieces. The guy named Joel was obviously new at this and had no idea what to say, so he remained quiet and stared at all of us like he was studying some sort of science project.

Mark's laid-back manner made him easy enough to talk to, and after being around him for fifteen minutes I recognized him from my earlier years at Covenant. I couldn't place where, however. He seemed unfazed at Erik's mocking tone. And he continued to look me over as though something was on the tip of his tongue and he was holding it back.

"We also wanted to let you guys know that there are small groups that meet at school every Tuesday night. In the student center."

Erik laughed. "I've got my own small group. Meets on Tuesdays and Thursdays."

"Where's that?" Lissa, a short redheaded girl with a big grin, asked.

"Joey O'Douls," Erik replied.

Joey O'Douls was one of the local college hangouts located a few blocks away from our apartment.

The others understood Erik's remark, but nobody except Mark said anything—and what he said had nothing to do with Joey O'Douls. "You may want to check out one of our small groups." He spoke mainly to me. "It's a great way of meeting other people at school, especially when you live off campus."

I nodded, appearing interested.

"Any cute girls in them?"

"You might be surprised," Mark replied to my roommate.

"Oh, I bet I would." Erik laughed.

We had another few minutes of small talk before Mark had his revelation and exclaimed in surprise. "You're Sheridan Blake, right?"

I nodded.

"Wow," Mark replied. "You don't recognize me, do you?"

Everyone looked at me as I shook my head.

"I was your RA at the dorm your junior year. Mark Everly."

Bits and pieces of recollection came back to me. "Oh, yeah."

"Sheridan Blake," he said again, as though the name were legendary.

"You knew him years ago?" Erik asked, suddenly interested.

"Well, not all that well. But sure. I can't believe I didn't know you were back."

"I'm not advertising it," I said. "A lot of the people I knew are gone now."

"Still playing the piano?" Mark asked.

I nodded and forced a smile.

"And how are you doing with, uh, everything?"

Mark obviously knew my history. That made sense since he had probably been living on campus during the summer it happened. Thank God most of the student body had been gone.

"Fine. Trying to move on with life."

"A lot of people were praying for you." Mark stared at me, waiting for my response and confession.

I instantly felt a wave of cold anger grip me. "Oh, really? A lot being who?"

"Well, profs and faculty at Covenant."

"That's truly touching. But I guess not enough people were praying."

"I just meant—"

"Look, thanks for the visit," I said. "I think we're done here."

"I'm sorry, Sheridan. I didn't mean anything by that."

"Good night," I said as I opened the door to our apartment and showed them the way out.

As Mark passed by, he handed me a piece of paper with his number at the college on it. "I hope to see you guys around," he said, looking at me. "I'll be thinking of you."

I nodded and said nothing more.

The door shut and Erik returned to the couch, where he had been watching ESPN. "So you knew Mark?" he asked, picking up the remote control.

"I barely remember him. To me, those guys were all the same. Looking for a dozen ways to rat on fellow students who were just trying to have a good time."

"So now he's going around trying to make students feel guilty for not going to church." Erik grinned and cursed. Obviously the guilt treatment wasn't working on him. He added, "What was that stuff about people praying for you and everything?"

I looked at the beer bottle Erik was twisting open. "Oh, nothing. Just that I made a lot of mistakes when I was at Covenant. Before that, too. I never belonged here in the first place."

"Me neither," Erik said with a cutting laugh.

"Why'd you decide to go to Covenant?" I asked.

"My parents wanted me to. They're paying. Free ride. That sort of thing."

I nodded.

"And you? What about you?"

"I'm finishing off my time here. I figured I'd finish things where I started them. Besides, I'd lose a ton of credits if I transferred to another college."

"But why'd you start at Covenant in the first place?"

"Seemed like a nice enough place."

"Seemed like a nice enough place? Come on. Hawaii's a nice place, not Covenant."

I laughed in agreement. "Actually, to be honest, the reason's pretty lame."

"What? Parents paying for you too?"

"Well, yeah, but my reason's even lamer."

"What?" Erik asked as he took another swallow from his beer bottle.

"I followed a girl here."

"What? Who?"

"You don't know her."

Erik nodded. "Still seeing her?"

"No. Not for a long time now."

"Then you're right. Pretty lame reason."

I looked at the phone number Mark had left me. Mark Everly knew the whole story. He and how many others? And how many of those were still around?

"What happened to her?"

I almost jumped, did a double take. "What do you mean?"

"The girl you followed to Covenant. What happened?"

"Oh. Well, she had a life to live—a life that didn't involve Sheridan Blake. She made that clear the summer after my junior year. I vowed I'd never come back to this place."

"So why did you?"

I thought for a moment on the legitimate question. The honest answer hurt. "People change," I said.

"Have you?"

I faced my younger roommate. "I don't know, Erik. I really don't know."

Dear Amy,

I know there are so many things I should say to you. To say I hurt you and your family—that doesn't begin to express everything in my heart. I want you and your parents to know how truly sorry I am. I never thought things could work out like this.

I wish I could honestly say that what happened has changed me forever. And I guess some of the externals are different. But inside . . . I really don't know if I've changed or if I ever will.

This truth haunts me.

Sheridan

Five

I ENTERED the peaceful atmosphere of the bookstore and breathed in deeply. This was proving to be harder than I had initially thought it would be. I walked to the back of the store where the coffee shop was and where, true to her word, Genevie sat contentedly reading a book and sipping a drink. She wasn't surprised to see me.

"You're too late," she said.

"Excuse me?" I asked, taken off guard by her statement.

"I already have my coffee. You'll have to come back on another day to buy me one."

"I was hoping you were going to buy me one."

"Okay," she said, standing up without hesitation. "This time."

I let her buy me a vanilla latte. If I had thought this was going to be awkward, her affable response instantly made me feel at ease.

"You can buy next time," she said, handing me the tall cup.

"Thanks."

"I wasn't sure if you'd stop by. Ever come in here?"

"Sure. Sometimes. I was just passing by tonight."

She nodded and smiled.

I sat down at the table and picked up the book she had been reading. "*Advanced Techniques through the World of Play*. Looks like a fun read."

"I just finished my Nancy Drew book."

"Are you a teacher?"

"Actually, I'm studying to be a counselor for children."

"You look more like a counselor with your glasses on."

"Oops," she said, slipping them off. "I only use them when I read."

"Or watch movies."

She smiled. "Sometimes."

"They don't look bad on you."

"They just make me look like a counselor," she joked.

"Is that what your master's is in?"

She nodded. "Only one more semester left. I can't wait. It feels like I've been going to school all my life."

"I feel like I've been away from school for half of mine."

"Really? How so?"

"Just took some time off. That's all."

Genevie nodded and looked at me to see if I was going to say any more. I didn't.

"So did you go to the movies this past Friday?"

I nodded, knowing she hadn't. I had been looking for her.

We talked about the movies they had shown. I resisted the urge to tell her how little I had enjoyed them since she hadn't been sitting next to me.

"So no movies for you?" I asked her.

"No. Out with friends."

I wanted to ask which friends, which male friends in particular, but I resisted that urge too. I didn't want to be so obvious.

"So you remember being in my class?" I asked instead, changing the subject.

"Yes."

"Did we meet at all that year?"

"No. I was just a freshman. I lived on campus and studied all the time."

"Looks like you still do."

"Remember, only one more semester."

"So are you looking for jobs around this area?"

"Yes and no," she replied. "I've got opportunities around here and some other places."

"Where would you like to end up?"

"That's hard to say. I have a lot of friends here. But my family is mostly in California."

"You grew up there?"

She nodded. "My parents were originally from the Philippines, though."

"Have you ever been there?" I sipped my still-hot coffee.

"A couple of times. When I was little my parents took me to see where my grandparents lived. I would love to go back."

Genevie told me a little more about her family, her home in California, her first days in Chicago. She was refreshing to listen to; she spoke about herself and her family without any reservation or hesitation, as though her life was an open book.

"So, Mr. Sheridan Blake," she finally said, "I've been yapping about myself, but now it's your turn. Tell me about you. You go see movies on Friday nights. Go to an occasional show at the aquarium. Occasionally visit the bookstore."

"Exciting life, huh?"

"Sounds good so far."

"That's about the extent of the excitement, unfortunately."

"Oh, I don't believe that."

Her dark eyes locked onto mine. I smiled and muttered a few words, but they really didn't matter. I felt a peace inside of me. I felt happy for the moment. The coffee and the soothing background music and the quiet setting helped. But Genevie was the reason why.

I almost could forget about everything else. Almost.

"My life was a little more exciting in my first three years at Covenant," I told her. "A little too exciting."

"Exciting how?"

"Well, I was big into the party scene."

"You can have fun and excitement without all of that."

"Yeah, I just didn't know that at the time."

"So," she asked, "are you enjoying Covenant more this year?"

I laughed.

"What?"

"More than what?" I asked.

"More than when you were here before."

"I used to hate the school." I paused. "No offense."

"That's okay. I only work and live and take classes at Covenant."

"You like working at the college?"

"It's fine. I've been working in admissions for several years."

"Bet you're ready to move on."

"Yes. For the most part anyway. So why did you used to hate the college?"

"Oh, I don't know. I got in a lot of trouble my first few years. I'm surprised you didn't hear about me."

She didn't respond to that directly. "Can I ask a question?"

"You've been doing a good job at asking so far," I replied with a nod.

"If you got into a lot of trouble, why did you even *want* to go to Covenant in the first place? There are so many other places that don't have so many rules."

"I think I just had this conversation with my roommate not long ago."

"So what'd you say?"

I wondered if I should be honest. How honest could I be with Genevie? She didn't know anything about me except that I watched movies and seemed a bit introverted. And I had made her laugh a few times. That was it.

I wanted to start off on good ground. With a clean slate.

But you can't, and you know that, right?

"I knew some people here," I finally said. "I guess I followed them here."

"'Some people'? Who are 'some people'?"

"Different people."

"I bet it was a girl, right?"

I only smiled. Genevie looked as if she might continue to question me about this, but then decided not to. That's okay, her smile said. No pressure.

Over the next two hours, I learned many things about Genevie. Her parents had moved to Southern California from the Philippines right after their marriage. Since then they had divorced and she had lived with her father and his family most of her life in the San Francisco Bay area. She talked about both of her parents with love and respect but also with sadness. The divorce obviously had hurt her deeply.

She brought up her conversion to Christianity as easily as she might have been talking about a cup of coffee. She talked with an inner sense of strength and hope I hadn't been around in a long time. It didn't seem forced, nor did it seem trite or superficial.

"I became a Christian during my senior year of high school," Genevie said. "That's when I decided to go to a Christian college. There was a small Bible college back home I could have gone to, but Covenant was more the kind of place I wanted to be. Also, it got me away from my parents, who aren't Christians."

I nodded, unsure of what to say.

"It was strange, coming to a college where a lot of kids had been Christians all their lives. They'd been raised in Christian homes, and yet they didn't act or appear any different than any other kids I'd met in school. I was surprised and even shocked by that."

"Sometimes people can take things for granted when they're raised with them."

"Were you? Raised as a Christian, I mean."

"Yeah. Well, sort of. My parents go to church on and off, but it's more of a social thing. My sister was the one who really got serious about religion."

"How old is she?"

"She's thirty-one, three years older than me."

"Does she live near here?"

"No. She lives in Washington State. She's a lawyer, married a few years with no kids. My parents live here, though—out in the suburbs."

"So your sister was the good example?"

"Yeah. I actually became a Christian in fourth grade because of her."

The words came out of my mouth as a statement. A statement of truth. So easily. *I actually became a Christian in fourth grade.*

Of course, when I was growing up, most people probably didn't know this. Especially the older I got. Especially when I was in college doing my own thing. I didn't tell Genevie this part of my testimony. I was actually surprised at how casual and firm I was in my statement.

She tilted her head, a wistful expression on her face. "I've always thought how wonderful it would have been to grow up in church."

I nodded. I couldn't say anything more. I couldn't tell Genevie how growing up in my particular church had only helped turn my heart to stone. How I eventually had stopped going, and how I had tried running away.

How I was still running.

Genevie continued. "Church always makes me feel better, like I'm going to a place to renew my strength. What I would give to have had something like that when I was growing up."

And that was the way the conversation went. We shifted from topic to topic, each more interesting to me than the next. I wasn't sure where this was leading. All I knew was that she was personable and genuine and that it had been a long time since I'd engaged in this kind of conversation with anyone. Even the simplest details of her life seemed fascinating.

I wondered if she felt even remotely the same about me.

"So tell me what you do besides school," she said. "Do you work?"

"I teach kids piano on a part-time basis. Mostly grade-school kids. I used to teach more, but I just kept a handful since I have to drive out to their homes in the suburbs. I didn't want to abandon the students I'd been with for a while."

"Any really good ones?"

"Most are pretty good. I've got a little girl named Nita who is almost as good as I am. She's incredible."

"The little blonde-headed kid you were with at the aquarium?"

"That's right; you met her. She's really talented."

"How long have you played piano?"

"I don't know—most of my life. I grew up playing it. I can play the guitar and keyboards, but my parents wanted me to stick with the piano."

"So you're a music major?"

"Sure. Why? Does that surprise you?"

"No. You just don't look like the musical type."

"What type do I look like?"

Genevie appeared to be in deep thought. "Hmm. That's a good question."

"Maybe I should put on your glasses. Maybe I'll look like more of a musician."

"Good one," she replied. "Were you teaching after you quit college?"

"Yes, that and working other jobs. I was a waiter for a long time. Just what I wanted to do with my life—wait tables."

"So what do you want to do once you graduate? What do you do with a music degree?"

"I don't know. For a long time I didn't think I'd graduate at all. Regarding the music, I don't know. I wanted to be a composer, but I stopped writing music some time ago. Right now I'm studying music theory."

"Why'd you stop writing?"

"Not enough time and energy. That sort of thing."

But it wasn't that sort of thing *at all, was it?* Something inside of me died years ago. There was no way I could begin to tell this to Genevie.

We talked until I realized that the bookstore would be closing soon. I was amazed I had lost track of the time so easily. "You're very easy to talk with," I said as I stood up to go.

"Thanks. And remember—next time you buy."

"Next time?"

"Sure. If you're passing by this area, that is."

"You don't mind?" I asked. For some reason I was thinking of her soccer friend.

"If I mind, I'll tell you. Trust me on that."

She grinned, and I thanked her for the coffee again.

As I walked out, Genevie called out my name. "Excuse me, Mr. Blake?" I turned around.

"I'd really like to hear you play the piano sometime. Think you could come up with the time and energy to play something for me?"

I smiled, and for the first time since coming back to Covenant—since a long time before that, actually—I felt like my old self. "Maybe," I said. "And maybe, if you're lucky, I'll even compose something special for you."

NOVEMBER 4

Dear Amy,

*W*inter cold hasn't come yet. Odd how November can still feel like the end of summer. But I know the chill is on its way. It always comes eventually.

The semester and the year move on. And something is happening in me—a part of me is changing. Could it be that God waited all this time for everything to suddenly change? Or is it happening because I decided to go back to Covenant to finish what I started?

I often wonder how this year will end. For the first time in a long time, though, I find myself not dreading looking into the future.

Sheridan

Six

A TINY FIGURE seemed to tiptoe over a sea of black and white, each step precise and elegant, running and walking with confident grace. Nita's slender fingers moved up and down the keys with a natural flow that made the big instrument seem just an extension of her tiny body.

A wave of wonder washed over me along with the rippling music as I sat in the immense, ornately decorated living room of the Primrose mansion and listened to Nita play a Beethoven nocturne. I realized, not for the first time, that I had helped this young girl achieve something remarkable. And even though I knew that she would eventually move on, that I had done all I could with her, I was reminded of someone else when I witnessed her talent and determination.

Sheridan Blake.

"How was that?" a miniature voice asked.

"Excellent. Go ahead and play your final one."

She was ten years old and already had developed an impressive mastery of both technique and interpretation. The pieces came so naturally to her. I wondered what her future held. Would she be labeled as quickly as I had once been? Would people use the *prodigy* word as they had used it with me?

I forced myself to concentrate on Nita. When she finished her piece, I nodded. "For once I'd like to be able to say what a bad job you did," I told her. "It's getting just a little boring always having to tell you what good work you've done. But that really was great. I like what you're doing with the *allegro* section."

She grinned, still a little girl despite her incredible poise. "Thanks. I thought of that last week. I thought it sounded cool."

"I think you can play that piece better than I can."

"No I can't. I just practice longer."

I glanced on top of the piano at the large framed pictures of the Primrose family I had grown accustomed to seeing: Dennis and Gail in a tropical setting, a baby picture of Nita with her bold blue eyes, a family picture taken in front of a glowing fireplace, and a picture of a much younger Mrs. Primrose in her wedding dress.

"Mr. Blake?"

"Yes?" I responded.

"Do you ever write your own music?"

The question came from out of the blue.

"Why do you ask?"

"I was wondering. I asked my mom the other day. She said she thought you used to do a lot of other stuff besides teach piano. Have you ever wanted to be a singer or something like that?"

"I don't think I'll *ever* be a singer, Nita."

"But do you write music? Is that why you're going to college again?"

I rubbed my hands together. "No, not really. I never finished college. I was different than you. I never studied."

"But you practice the piano."

"That's different. I've always practiced the piano."

"So, what're you going to do after you finish college?" Nita asked.

"That's a good question. I don't know."

"Will you still be my teacher?"

"Well, I guess, if you want me to." I paused for a second and looked down at the sprinkling of freckles covering her nose. "You'll soon be teaching kids yourself. Or performing in concert halls."

"Why did you stop going to school?"

All these questions surprised me. I wasn't sure where they were coming from. "I needed a break from learning, I guess."

"Mom says it's harder to learn if you don't do it every day."

"That's right. It is. It's always harder to go back."

I thought of her original question: *Do you ever write your own music?*

Years ago, I had more hopes and aspirations, more music inside me than this ten-year-old could possibly dream of. They had all disappeared in one night. A bleak night that lingered, darkening my life for so many years.

Now maybe, just maybe, the shadows of that night were finally shrinking back enough for me to rediscover those dreams.

❦

After Nita's lesson I decided to stop by my parents' house before venturing back into the city. It was around five in the afternoon, and the only one at home was my mother, Helen Blake. I was glad to hear that Dad would be getting home late from the hospital.

"Pearl went home for the day," my mother said about our sixty-seven-year-old housekeeper who usually prepared dinner. "I told her Jim would be coming home late."

"I'll grab a sandwich."

My dinner consisted of a turkey and cheddar cheese sandwich and corn chips. I ate it at the kitchen table. My mother sat across from me, wrapping a birthday present for my Aunt Evelyn.

"Did you know that Josh and Jim are in training for the next Olympics?" Mom asked about my two younger cousins.

"Yeah. That's really great."

"They'll all be coming over for Christmas."

"Wonderful. I think I'll be ill that day."

"Oh, stop. You already avoid every family function you can."

"Maybe if I was going to the Olympics, I wouldn't."

"So tell me, are classes going well?" my mom asked, changing the subject.

"Yeah," I replied.

"Don't talk with your mouth full."

"You asked the question."

"How's your roommate?"

I took a sip of soda. "He's a nice guy. I told him I'd like to have him come over sometime."

"Anytime. Just give me proper notice so the place is clean."

"Mom, the place is *always* clean."

"No it's not. So how was your practice with Nita?"

"Fine."

"Gail said you guys had a fun time at the aquarium."

"They're a great family."

"Have you been practicing much at the college?"

I nodded my head. "As much as I'd normally practice. Hey, I was wondering about my keyboard. Is it still in my room?"

My mother looked at me with surprise on her face. It was the first time in years that I'd mentioned anything about my Korg keyboard system. "I haven't put it anywhere else. Why?"

"I might take it back to the apartment with me."

"Are you sure? It could be stolen. You know how expensive that was."

I chuckled and swallowed a bite of my sandwich. "I haven't played it in years—it's not exactly state-of-the-art anymore. You think it'd matter if it got stolen?"

"Of course it would."

"I still don't get why Dad always discouraged me from playing with it. You're the only reason I was even able to buy the thing in the first place."

"You know how your father is."

"Was he afraid I might actually try to pursue a career in synthesizer music?"

"Your father was just trying to protect you. That's all."

"Yeah. Well, he's done a mighty fine job doing that."

"Sheridan, please—"

"It's okay, Mom. He's not here. Don't worry. I can't get into an argument if he's not here."

"Sheridan, your father loves you and—"

"And shows it by bailing his son out of trouble. I know."

"Look, we've told you before—we just didn't know what to do. We did what we thought was right."

I wiped my mouth, surprised I was reliving the past this easily with my mother. "I know that," I said. "It's just—I still remember, when it was all said and done, sitting there in Dad's office. The Study. Sitting there in that 'visitor's' chair of his, feeling like a student in a principal's office. Sitting there crying and asking him to help me. And you know what he did?"

"Sheridan, please—"

"You know what he said? I'm baring my soul for the first and perhaps only time with Dad and he can only state how I need to grow up and abandon all these foolish notions like working with the synthesizer. As if that was my big problem."

"Your dad had a hard time coming to grips with all that happened."

"Denial isn't a river in Egypt," I said.

"That's funny," she replied, unamused.

I stood and threw away my paper plate. "I'm sorry for bringing all of this up."

My mother looked at me and smiled, looking so much younger than her age. "Let's go upstairs and get that keyboard of yours. I'll help you get it to your car."

⚜

That night, my conversations with both Nita and my mother echoed in my thoughts. Once again I was reminded of how far I'd let my musical ambitions slip away, and once again the realization hurt.

I wanted—I needed—to start over. Frankly, I didn't know where to begin.

Why don't you try praying?

I ignored the inner prompting like I used to ignore my mother when she suggested something I didn't want to do. How could I go before God and his throne after I had failed him time after time and done absolutely nothing worthy of his name? How could I dare say I was a Christian, one of his own, when all of my past actions for so many years had only indicated the opposite?

I sat in my bedroom, knowing that Barney was in his own little world and Erik was probably in the same, somewhere in the city. I was alone.

And yet, I wasn't. Despite my protests, I knew that.

I stood before God. He wasn't on his throne so high above that he couldn't see me. And standing there, connecting us, was his Son. I knew that too. I knew of salvation, and I believed that once you had it, you could not lose it. I knew of forgiveness, of how Christ atoned for all of our sins.

Why then was it so hard for me to talk to the same Christ who had died for me?

I walked over to my small bookcase, which was crammed with old textbooks and an assortment of paperback novels. On the bottom shelf I discovered an old Bible I'd used for classes, and I opened it. That had been so long ago. Years ago. Years of not listening, of not wanting to hear, of not caring.

Thumbing through the thin, rustling pages, I felt like an intruder. The words weren't for me. I knew them—I used to memorize verses, and I had studied them in Bible class. I knew the difference between right and wrong. I knew what I should and shouldn't be doing. Yet, for so many years I had chosen what *I* wanted to do, and those choices had been sinful. I had sinned without thought for the consequences.

Could a Christian, someone called by the Lord's name, fall so far away from him as to not care?

The passages I finally opened to spoke with simplicity and honesty. They held me accountable. They made the guilt foam over like frothy milk prepared for a latte.

I didn't need more guilt. I needed someone to take it away. I closed the Bible and wiped tears off my cheeks.

"Dear Father. My dear Lord. This sinner needs help. I need so much. Every time I look up to the heavens I feel nothing but shame. I only think of all the wrong I've done. In spite of everything I know about you, Lord, I'm stuck. Give me something, Lord. I don't know what, but I need something. I can't go on like this."

Silence. I looked at the Bible and opened it up again, this time to Psalm 102: "Hear my prayer, O Lord, and let my cry come to You. Do not hide Your face from me in the day of my trouble; incline Your ear to me; in the day that I call, answer me speedily."

The words came quick and fast, and I continued reading. Part of me noticed, with surprise, that the rest of me was unafraid.

"'Bless the Lord, O my soul; and all that is within me, bless His holy name,'" I read out loud from Psalm 103.

The words, the poetry of a man far greater than I could ever be, sang to me. I read for an hour, not realizing the passage of time.

When I closed the Bible, I realized that my simple prayer had just been answered.

It had been that easy, too.

What else could the Lord do? Could I ask him for more?

Could I possibly dare?

NOVEMBER 15

Dear Amy,

I've become friends with an incredible woman who somehow crossed my path. I can't believe I'm writing to you about her. But I have seen her a few times and have planned on actually going out with her in.the next week. I'm not sure if it's an official date. I simply asked if she wanted to go do something besides meet in the bookstore, where we've seen each other three times now.

She fills me with a hope I haven't had in years. Maybe I'll finally be able to move on with my life.

I still think of you every day, though. It's hard not to. I sometimes feel if I do begin to move on, if I actually find some happiness in my life, that I'll be doing something wrong. Yet whenever I'm around this woman, she fills me with so much joy I can't help myself.

It's probably really stupid to wonder whether you would approve. But somewhere deep inside me I do wonder. . . .

Sheridan

Seven

I WASN'T SURE what to call the upcoming night.

It wasn't an official date—even though I had asked Genevie out for an evening on the town. It had been an idea that just popped out the last time we had been talking in the bookstore, right after she told me she wasn't dating anyone.

"What about the soccer guy?"

"Matt?"

"Yes, Matt. I thought you two are—"

Genevie had laughed at that. "We're what? Going out?"

"Whatever you want to call it."

She continued laughing, as if the very idea was ludicrous. "We're good friends. I have lots of guy friends."

And I'm one of them.

"After I saw you two at the Shedd Aquarium, I just naturally thought you were a couple."

"He's too young," Genevie said. "Besides, I told him I might not be around here that long anyway."

"So that's deterring you from going out with guys?"

"I haven't been asked out by a guy for a long time."

This conversation took place at the end of our third bookstore chat that ended up closing the place down. I had felt more comfortable being myself, grinning more than I usually did, and probably revealing more about my feelings for her than I wanted to.

"So, then . . . let's go out," I had said.

"You mean, like on a date?"

"No, of course not," I replied quickly. "It doesn't have to be considered anything. Just one friend going out with another. Like going to the aquarium."

"I've already been to the aquarium," Genevie joked.

"Well, then, I'll surprise you with something else."

And so happened an unlikely date that wasn't even officially a date— though both of us knew better.

⚜

It had been more than seven years since I had gone out with a girl—and it felt like even longer. I only hoped that in an eager attempt to make up for lost time, I wouldn't blow my chances with Genevie and scare her away.

All I told Genevie beforehand was to dress up and be ready at a certain time.

"How dressy?" she had asked.

"Fancy. Nicer than church."

"What's that mean?"

"Good question. I haven't actually spent much time in churches lately."

"Somewhat formal?" she asked.

"Do you mind? We don't have to if you don't want."

"No, I like dressing up. It's just—I don't want you to go to any trouble."

Seven years. Seven long years.

"Don't worry."

Everything had been planned—as carefully as I had planned anything in recent years. My first date in over half a decade should have occurred without any problems. But sometimes no amount of planning can compensate for life's unfortunate mishaps.

The first bad sign was a phone call I didn't pick up right before I left my apartment. I almost did, thinking it might have been Genevie or Erik. It was neither.

"Blake, you there?" said the familiar voice on the machine. "Please pick up. PLEASE. I've gotta talk with you. All I'm asking for is a simple meeting. That's all. Please call me. I'm getting sick of leaving these messages."

The gruff, older voice of Mike Larsen left a number and hung up. The frustration in his tone sounded stronger than ever, as if each message angered him more. I erased the message without taking down the number, just as I always did.

What if he shows up during my date tonight?

It had been a while since his last call. I had hoped that he would eventually give up and leave things the way they were. But it sounded like he was far from doing that.

What good would it do to see him? What words could I possibly say that hadn't already been expressed in my letter years ago? Seeing me in person would only dredge up the past.

I put on a black sport coat that hadn't been worn in months, along with a medium blue shirt and coordinating yellow tie. I examined this ensemble in the mirror one last time and then left the apartment, ready for a memorable evening.

I had no idea how truly memorable it would be.

⚜

I've often dreamt of being the sort of debonair gentleman who would arrive at the doorway of his beautiful date and have exactly the right thing to say to capture the mood and her magnificence. Yet reality has often found me silent, fearful of not knowing exactly the right words to say.

And no matter how comfortable I had felt around Genevie before I arrived at her dorm, nothing could have ever prepared me for seeing her stride up to me in the first-floor lobby and smile.

Is this the same girl in glasses I first met in the theater not long ago?

To simply say Genevie Liu looked beautiful would miss the essence of the moment. I was standing there in the lobby and a totally unfamiliar woman greeted me. Her hair was pulled sleekly up and back, tucked and nestled perfectly so that only a few charcoal-black strands caressed her soft cheeks. She wore a long and fitted black dress, with slender heels on her feet that made her eyes inch up closer to mine.

"Is this too much?" she asked me.

Her high-boned cheeks were accentuated by full, round lips that parted into the hint of a smile. Her expressive eyes waited for my response.

I think I can't breathe anymore. What I said was, "You look very nice."

Moments afterward, I would hate myself for this four-word noose I had looped around my tongue. *Very nice* didn't begin to say it. It was like saying the *Titanic* had sprung a little leak—or the sun was just a little bright to stare directly into.

Sheridan Blake was still not debonair, nor would he ever be.

"I feel overdressed," Genevie said, pulling a soft gray wrap around her shoulders.

"You're not," I breathed. "Trust me. So, are you ready to go?"

Genevie nodded and we left. We almost made it to our destination.

In my car, the conversation seemed a bit awkward. I wasn't sure why. Maybe it was because Genevie didn't know where I was taking her, or maybe it was because we were so dressed up. Maybe it was because I hadn't felt this way since my high school prom. We talked like complete strangers, eventually landing on the topic of weather. I knew I had to put a stop to the unease.

"Are you okay?" I asked Genevie.

"Yes, why?"

"Do you realize we were just talking about what the weather is going to be like tomorrow?"

"Well, I was curious . . ."

"Weather is what strangers talk about."

"I'm sorry," Genevie said, with a tinge of nervousness in her voice that I had never heard.

"Remember, this is just another aquarium visit. I know we're dressed up, but I don't want to make this night weird or anything. I want you to be as comfortable as you are in the bookstore."

"I'm usually not wearing heels," Genevie replied.

"Well I just love wearing ties. And I wear one all the time, too," I said with a smirk.

"But it's not dressing up, really. I've actually only worn this dress once before. I'm glad to be wearing it. No, it's just—I don't know what my problem is tonight. I'm sorry."

"Sorry for what?"

"Sorry for acting goofy."

"You're acting fine. Just remember who you're with. You don't have to worry about what I'm thinking."

"What *are* you thinking?"

I was going to tell her I was thinking about how incredible she looked, and how long it had been since I had picked up a woman for a date, and how nervous and sick and awkward and strange I felt even if I didn't seem like it. I wanted to tell her how I'd been thinking of this night since the moment I asked her to go out, how I'd planned and prepared, and how everything was going to be perfect—

My cell phone rang. I carried a small one for emergencies.

"Sorry," I said as I searched the middle compartment that divided our seats. "I just brought it to look cool."

"Go ahead. You can answer it."

Erik was on the other end of the line. He sounded serious.

"What's up?" I asked him.

"Man, I don't mean to bother you, but your dog's acting kinda funky."

"Kinda funky? What's that mean?"

"I just got home. It looks like he got sick all over the place."

"Maybe he just ate something bad."

"I don't know. He's in the living room lying down and whimpering. He doesn't look too hot."

"Are you sure? Did you give him any water?"

"I tried to. He doesn't seem to be responding to anything. He's shaking, too. I don't know, man. I don't know anything about dogs. Should I give him a shot?"

"I already did. He's not due for another one today." I thought for a second. We were twenty minutes away from our destination. "He looks real bad?" I asked Erik.

"Yeah."

"How bad?"

"You know I wouldn't call you if he didn't. He won't get up. I even of-fered him one of those treats he loves. Acts like he doesn't know it's there."

I thought for a second as I glanced at the remarkable figure beside me.

"Do you want me to call someone?" Erik asked.

"No. Just hold on. I'll come and get him." I turned to Genevie, who was watching me with curious eyes. "You've never met my dog, have you?"

"Barney? The diabetic dog?"

"That's the one."

"No. You've told me all about him, though."

I turned down a side street and began heading away from Lake Michi-gan. "There's a slight problem," I said.

"What?"

"I think he's really sick."

"I'm sorry."

"Would you mind if we went back to—"

"No, please, hurry. Don't worry about me."

"I'm sorry," I said as I raced down the city streets.

"It's okay. Really."

"It's just, I've had this crazy dog since I was sixteen. My parents took care of him when I first went away to college, but for the past seven years it's been pretty much him and me."

"Sheridan, he's your dog. I'd be offended if you did anything other than go back home for him. Okay?" She gently squeezed my arm.

I looked at her and nodded. The clock on the dashboard said we had eighteen minutes to get to our original destination.

☙

By the time I arrived at my apartment and picked my poor little dog up and carried his shivering body out to the car, I knew we would miss our date. I didn't want to just put Barney in the backseat—I was afraid he'd fall off—so I placed him in my lap and drove with his head facing Genevie.

"You're going to be okay," Gen softly spoke as she rubbed Barney's head.

Barney kept shifting to make himself more comfortable, and I kept pulling him back from crawling into Genevie's lap.

"He's fine," she kept saying.

"I don't want you to get dog hair all over your dress."

"It's just a dress."

We were idling at a red light when Barney's little body suddenly jerked. He made coughing noises and tried to get up. All he could do was push his head over into Genevie's lap.

The light turned green, and I concentrated on the street again.

"Uh, Sheridan?" Genevie said.

"Yeah."

"I think Barney's sick."

I shot a look at Genevie in the darkness of my Honda Accord. "Yeah?"

"No, I mean, 'sick' sick. He just threw up in my lap."

"You gotta be kidding—oh, Gen—" I blurted out a few curse words.

"No need for that. Just keep driving—don't slow down."

"Barney! No, boy. Come here."

"It's fine. It wasn't much."

"I am so incredibly—"

"Sheridan, I said it's fine."

"Sorry."

"Do you have any napkins?"

"Yeah, the glove compartment. I think. Are there any—yeah, in there."

"See, no big deal," Gen said as if nothing had happened.

I was going to apologize again; then I saw the look of humor on Gen's face and burst out laughing myself.

⚜

Genevie and I looked like we had been planning to go to the opera, then accidentally taken a wrong turn and ended up in an animal hospital. The staff knew me well; when you have a diabetic dog, you tend to be a fixture at such a place. The all knew Barney and loved him. They'd find out what was wrong.

"How's your dress?" I asked Genevie.

"It's fine. Really. I got a wet paper towel, and it's as good as new."

We both looked at one another and laughed again.

I looked at my watch. "Well, we missed it."

"Missed what?"

"The boat."

"We were going on a boat?"

I nodded. "One of those dinner cruises that go out on Lake Michigan. Ever been on one?"

"No. I've always wanted to."

"Yeah, me too," I replied. "I still do."

"So the boat's left?"

"Yep. Seven-thirty." I looked around at the walls full of animal posters and how-to advice on taking care of animals. The area had a distinct animal smell—not horrible, but not exactly the sort you'd associate with a first date, official or unofficial.

"Well, aren't you glad you got dressed up to go to a vet?" I asked.

"It's not your fault."

"I know, but—"

"Look, they said it's good you brought Barney in. There's nothing else you could have done."

"I'm just glad this isn't technically a date," I said.

"Me too. Then I'd get *really* dressed up."

I looked at her dress again and apologized in the middle of laughing.

"Sheridan."

"What?"

"You've never seen me get angry, have you?"

"No. Do you get angry?"

"I will if you don't stop apologizing."

"Okay, okay."

We waited over an hour. Most of that time was spent telling childhood horror stories about throwing up. Genevie kept making me laugh with story after story. Even though I was disappointed about not making the dinner cruise, I felt as though I could have stayed in the animal hospital talking with her for hours. It was impossible to have a negative attitude being around her.

"Now you can see why I don't date," Gen remarked, causing both of us to burst out laughing again.

As we sat waiting on any news about Barney, a vet tech came in the lobby and asked us if we wanted to see some puppies. She took us to a room in the back, where she pointed to them in a cage. It was a litter of five-week-old sheltie puppies with their mother. Genevie instantly walked over and asked to hold one of the fuzzy creatures. Thoughts of her vomit-stained black dress or the missed ship seemed far from her mind. She gently took the ball of soft, light brown fur in her hands and held it close to her, softly brushing its head.

"Aren't you just precious?" she said, talking to the puppy. "Isn't it adorable?" she said to me.

I nodded and watched her holding this little puppy. I was moved by her tenderness. For a moment I forgot about everything that had happened and found myself lost in the fact that I was still with Genevie, still watching her smile and listening to her sweet voice. She looked like a runway model doing an advertisement for animal care.

"This has got to be the cutest puppy I've ever seen," Genevie said, her smile filling her whole face. "You didn't know I'm a dog person, did you?"

"Even if they throw up?" I asked with a smile.

"Sure. Look at him. Hey, little guy. I *adore* puppies. I've even been thinking about getting one, but I wasn't sure. This little guy here is such a sweetheart."

I opened my mouth to say something but nothing came out. I was stunned by how Genevie seemed to glow with excitement.

"Is this little guy for sale?" Genevie asked one of the young women behind the service desk.

"Well, actually, they all are. . . ."

⚜

Barney would have to spend the night at the hospital. The veterinarian told me that he had violently reacted to his insulin shot for some reason that they weren't sure of. We talked in specifics about what I needed to do once I took Barney back home. The vet also reaffirmed the decision to bring Barney in.

This made me feel better. That and the fact that Genevie left her name and number in hopes of having the little dog she had fallen in love with.

Sounds familiar.

It was after eight-thirty by the time we left the parking lot. We still had to eat, even though I realized I hadn't thought about food once during the entire evening. "Well, any ideas on where to go?" I asked her.

"Let's see. We're in Chicago. The night is young."

"And you have puke stains on your dress—plus a fair amount of puppy hair."

"Stop it. That puppy was so sweet."

"He certainly seemed to like you."

"Listen, are you real hungry?" Genevie suddenly changed the subject.

"Am I hungry? No, I guess not. Not really."

"Then I know a good place for us to go. And I know what we can do about dinner."

"Sounds good to me. My idea sank."

"It was a great idea. You were taking care of your dog."

"Stupid dog," I said, half joking.

"You love that stupid dog."

"I know. Erik's probably going to give me a hard time, though. He's always telling me how he'd never give a dog a shot every morning and night. He'd give the dog one *big* shot."

"That's horrible."

"That's Erik."

"Well, never mind that. Just go where I tell you to."

"Yes, ma'am."

"You'll like this. I promise."

"Do you take all your dates here?" I asked.

"This isn't a date."

"Oh, that's right."

"Anyway, it's good to have a backup plan. Just in case of animal emergencies."

I laughed and drove my Honda through the busy streets of Chicago, wondering where she was taking me.

⚜

An hour later, I stood next to Genevie as we looked down on Chicago from the heavens. Her smile was bewitching as she handed me our dinner.

"I hope you like either Twix or Milky Way," Gen said.

"I just *love* the cookie crunch of Twix," I said with a smirk. "I was just telling myself how I would kill for a Twix."

"Be quiet."

"Seriously, I do like them."

"It's not much, but—"

"It's fine. I'm not that hungry anyway."

We were standing on the observation deck of the Sears Tower, over-looking the night lights of the city. I felt as if Gen and I were in another universe, as if we had been granted a brief sojourn in a waiting station for the heavens. The world beneath us looked like a scene from a *Star Wars* movie, with thousands of blips of light stretching off in every direction except for the east, where the dark lake spread out silently. The city beneath us seemed to shimmer and move with activity and life. The magnificent view, the clear night that allowed us to see for miles in each direction, the lovely woman with me, and the fact that I had never once made it up to see the Sears Tower—all of this made the evening more ideal than any date I could have tried to plan.

Perhaps God is trying to tell you something.

Moments earlier, as we rode up in the elevator, Genevie had ex-claimed over the fact that I had never been up in the Sears Tower.

"Never?"

"Nope."

"And you've lived around here all your life?"

"Mostly," I said.

"When I came to Chicago, it was one of the first things I did."

"Take your date up to the Sears Tower?"

She nudged me. "This isn't a date, remember. And no. I came up here by myself."

"You're brave."

"I figured I had to see it sometime. The sooner the better."

"I always assumed I would. I just never got around to doing it."

"Well, you finally are tonight," Genevie had told me just as the elevator opened out onto the wide, glassed-in observation area. There weren't many people up there tonight, just a few couples who strolled around holding hands or cuddled up on a bench gazing out at the view.

"Do you want to sit on that bench over there?" I asked Genevie after we had made several circles around the room. "Your feet have to be killing you."

She glanced down ruefully at those beautiful pumps. "I'd love to sit."

I stared off into the city's nightscape and felt uncomfortable again, unsure what to say.

"What I want to know," Genevie began, eliminating any awkward silence, "is why Sheridan Blake doesn't have a girlfriend."

"Who says I don't?"

"You. Several times."

"Oh, that's right," I said.

"Well?"

"I could ask the same of you."

"I told you my reason. I don't know what I'll be doing in the next year. My life is at a point of transition."

"So guys stay away from you."

"Something like that," she replied with a smile. "Or maybe I stay away from them. But what about you?"

"I stay away from girls."

"And why is that?"

"My life is at a point of transition."

She laughed. "What transition would that be?"

"Finishing up school, trying to get a life, the basics. Yours?"

"Finishing up school, trying to get a life, the basics," Genevie gently mocked with a deep voice.

"Did you think you would be in Chicago this long?"

"Honestly? No. I always thought I would be here for only a few years. When I was little, I used to travel a lot with my parents—when they were together, that is. We would go on so many vacations together—even overseas, whenever they could scrape together the money."

"You remember those trips?"

She nodded. "Mostly. I loved flying. My parents always told me I was going to grow up to work for a travel magazine or something like that."

"So what happened with the dreams of traveling?"

"That little thing known as divorce," Genevie said. "My whole world changed. I ended up wanting to help hurting people like I used to be."

"I'm sorry—"

"It's okay. It's worked out for the best. And I still have those dreams, you know. Some days I dream of just leaving all of this behind and going off on some wild adventure overseas."

"So if you show up missing one day, I should go look for you in Fiji or somewhere like that."

Her smile warmed me. "Or Kauai. Or Australia."

"You're a brave woman."

"Why? You don't see yourself traveling much?"

I shook my head. "My home is here. I once attended a school out of state. For a year. I hated it."

"But you're sort of a loner, right?"

I nodded.

"So what prevents you from getting up and leaving it all behind? Your family? Friends?"

"Myself." I said nothing more.

Genevie squinted her dark eyes and appeared to be examining me.

"What?" I asked.

"You're hard to figure out. You know that?"

"Is that bad?"

"No. I kinda like that. The silent and mysterious type."

"Please," I replied.

We spoke about everything, from our childhoods to recent television movies we had seen. Once again, I found Genevie refreshing and easy to talk to. I hadn't known how badly I had needed someone to talk with until I found myself opening up to Genevie. It seemed like I had a dam full of silent memories and thoughts that had risen to the point of overflowing.

At one point I singled out one of the small illuminated dots on Lake Michigan. "That's where we should be now."

"No," she said softly. "This is where we should be."

Half an hour before we were to head back down to earth, to the ground level, Gen excused herself to use the ladies' room. I decided to venture into the small gift shop—where Genevie had bought our dinner—and found a small metal tin that bore a picture of the Sears Tower on it. The box held commemorative chocolates. Perhaps a small gift would help Genevie remember this night.

I was sitting on the bench looking out over Chicago's stunning nightlife when something even more gorgeous came into view. Gen walked toward me, her silky black hair falling down below her shoulders. She brushed it back with her hand as she sat next to me. "I wanted to put it down. Hope it's okay."

I nodded. "You know, I never—"

"What?"

"I never told you how incredible you look tonight."

"Yeah you did," Gen replied.

"I didn't say it with any justice. Gen, I think you're one of the most beautiful—"

She put a slender finger on my lips to stop my sentence.

"Thank you," she said.

For a moment, I let go of the Sheridan I had been for so long, the glum and hesitant stranger I wouldn't have recognized a decade ago. I moved closer to Gen and held her hand in mine. I wanted to say more, wanted to ask her permission to do what I wanted to do, then glanced at her striking look of contentment. I looked down at her lips and then back into her eyes for a brief second, before I closed my own and kissed her. Her lips opened gently, the kiss soft and sweet. I didn't know how long it lasted. Gen squeezed my hand as if to confirm our actions.

I opened my eyes and saw her smile.

"That was nice," she replied. "I was hoping you'd kiss me tonight."

"You were?"

Gen nodded and closed her eyes as I leaned over to kiss her again. The thousand-pound weight on my shoulders began to disintegrate. How could a simple kiss do such an amazing thing?

Gen's eyes opened, and as I glanced into them, I wondered if this was really happening. I still held her hand in mine, and I looked down as I rubbed it. I wanted to say something, but no words could convey how I felt.

"So, what's that in your hand?" Gen asked me.

"Oh, yeah. Here. I got you a little something."

When I gave it to her and told her my reason for getting it, she laughed at me. "I don't need anything to remember this night by. You think I'll forget so easily?" she said.

I took Gen's hand again and, without thinking, kissed it. She seemed pleasantly amused by my spontaneity. "It's just—I just want to thank you for bringing me up here," I said. "And for listening to me. I've probably talked way too much tonight."

"*You* talk too much?" She laughed.

"I usually don't talk much at all."

"So then what's making you? The view? The incredible candy bar?"

"I guess it's just you. The way you listen to everything I say. The way you never have a negative comment about *anything*. I don't know. I feel I can tell you almost anything."

"You do?"

"Sure."

Genevie held my hand in both of hers. "Then tell me this," she said softly. "What really made you quit school? Seems like it had to be something pretty big."

"Listen, I really don't want to think about the past. Not tonight. Not now. I don't want to ruin an incredible evening."

"But you said you could tell me anything."

"*Almost* anything," I replied. "And yes, I feel I can. When the time is right, I will."

"You promise?"

I thought about it. It was so much more serious than she realized. "How about I promise to take you on a cruise the next time we go out?" I asked her.

"You can take me on that cruise, but it doesn't have to be the next time we go out."

"Why not?"

"Those don't go out every night, do they?"

"No, you have to plan ahead for them—" I saw what she was saying, and once again I admired her directness. "Well then, maybe the next time we go out, we can actually have more than a Twix bar."

"Sounds good. You can pick the place."

We stood to walk toward the elevator, still holding hands, still looking out over the glittering lights. We could see everything for miles around us. But what would it be like if Genevie saw miles deep inside my heart? If she saw the secrets I carried there?

Maybe there would be a right time to let her see.

Maybe.

NOVEMBER 22

Dear Amy,

Thanksgiving approaches, and somehow I can actually say I have many things to be thankful for. I feel guilty writing that, guilty for finally feeling good about my life. But someone has shown me so many reasons to give thanks. And I do.

I know all my words, my apologies, have been years in coming. I hope it's not too late to express them now. I hope for so many things, realizing that many of them won't ever happen. That they can't happen.

I just hope your family will understand and accept my apologies one day. Is it too much to hope that they might even forgive me?

Sheridan

Eight

"YOU GOTTA BE KIDDING ME."

I looked over at Erik and laughed. We had just spent the last hour in my car blasting a variety of CDs as we sped above the speed limit from our apartment to my parents' house in St. Charles for Thanksgiving dinner. Erik had told me his parents were visiting relatives out of state for Thanksgiving, and he didn't want to go, so I had invited him over to my house. I hadn't told Erik what to expect. His surprise was amusing.

"Kinda small, isn't it?" I referred to my parents' house.

Erik's mouth was hanging open. "It's humongous. Are your parents loaded or something?"

"Is *humongous* a word?" I asked.

Erik cursed in astonishment.

"I *know* that's not a word," I said.

I drove up the sweeping circle driveway and parked on the side in front of the three-car garage. "I guess you can say my parents are well-off," I answered him.

As we walked toward the two-story, brick house—Erik called it a mansion—I thought of the word I had spoken: *well-off*. It depends on who you ask. Yes, we were well-off. And yes, we had problems just like every family had.

The familiar steps up to the porch, the massive door leading to the entry-way, the marble floor and the hovering chandelier inside—I rarely even noticed all of these things. But Erik continued to gape. He had never asked me about my family, so I had never told him. It had never been a big deal to me that I came from a wealthy family. It didn't always feel like an advantage.

Seeing Erik's eye-opener took me back to childhood. I had forgotten the sort of burden I carried around with me during those years.

⚜

Have you ever been in a class where one kid was, in Erik's appropriate word, *loaded?* Ever been friends with a kid who always seemed to pay for everyone else, who always had parties at his house, who always had the nicest clothes and even nicer toys? I was that kid, that friend.

I was the one born into a family with a father who had inherited mil-lions and made even more in his surgical practice, and with a mother who grew up with old money herself. No one ever used the word *multimillion-aire* in our house when I was growing up. I didn't even know what the word meant for a long time, and when I finally realized what it did mean, I thought nothing of it. It's hard to appreciate money when your family has so much of it. Come to think of it, it's hard to appreciate many things when you grow up in that sort of environment.

I never flaunted the fact that my father had money—or that he was a well-known surgeon. I always thought that was a boring profession. As a kid pushed to excel in my musical pursuits, I once wanted to be a concert pianist. The older I became, though, the more my interests shifted. At one point I wanted to be a rock star, living in squalor and trying to find gigs to support myself. Later, during my high school years, I seriously thought about being a composer, specializing in electronic arrangements, perhaps a composer of movie music.

All of this sounded romantic to me. To my dad, it sounded ludicrous. And to my mother, the music lover in our family—she could only go so far in supporting dreams that appeared preposterous to my father.

It seemed like my sister, Kiersten, was the lone child my father could be proud of. Only three years older than me, she was doing what she had always wanted to do: practicing law. I, on the other hand, had messed up royally, dropped out of school and now . . . gave piano lessons while finishing up my senior year. Hmm. You make the comparison. Imagine how my father felt.

Over the past few years, when I was struggling to support myself independently of my parents, I had been surprised to learn just how comfortable my "normal" life had been when I was growing up. I never had a summer job. Most of my summers were spent playing or going on family vacations or doing whatever I wanted. I had lots of time on my hands and plenty of weekly "allowance" to spend. I see this now as one of the biggest sources of my troubles.

Still, I couldn't blame my parents for the mistakes I had made. The only thing I could accuse them of was bailing me out of trouble and then trying to forget there was ever any trouble in the first place. During my most difficult years—especially the year after I quit college—my busy and well-to-do parents didn't know how to treat me or how to help me deal with my mistakes. So they more or less acted as if nothing had happened and continued to indulge me. In a way, I wish they hadn't. Money can solve a lot of problems, but not when your biggest problem happens to be a guilty conscience.

I guess I might have turned out worse, though, if I had grown up in poverty or with abusive parents. So I tried not to harbor ill feelings. As I said, my mistakes were mine and mine alone. My parents had certainly never forced me to go to parties, to befriend the people I did, to go down the dangerous path I was determined to take. They helped me get out of trouble and made it a little easier for me to run from my problems. At the same time, I was perfectly capable of running all by myself.

⚜

"Anybody home?" I called out in our echoing front foyer.

Pearl D'Arby bustled into the foyer, greeted both of us, then took our coats. As she walked away, I told Erik she was our housekeeper.

"Your housekeeper? Like they have on *The Brady Bunch* or something like that?"

I laughed again and couldn't think of anything witty to say before my mother swept into the foyer. As she made pleasant small talk with my roommate, I found myself surprised at how elegant my mother looked. That happened whenever I looked at her through the eyes of one of my friends. Still trim and classy looking, with a recent haircut that made her look maybe ten years younger than she was, Helen Blake had always been a sort of Christie Brinkley of mothers. When I was younger, guys would always comment on how great she looked—not in a leering way, but with a "your mother's *actually* good-looking!" gasp of astonishment.

"I'm glad you finally made it home," Mom told me with a small peck on my cheek. "Dinner will be in half an hour. Be sure to compliment Pearl on the meal; she's been in a tizzy about it all morning."

"Pearl does a lot of our cooking too," I told Erik, which prompted another look of astonishment.

"While we're waiting on dinner, you could show Erik around the house," my mom prompted.

I threw Erik a questioning look. "Want the grand tour?"

"Sure," he answered, his enthusiasm unusually high.

"Where's Dad?" I asked.

"He's in his office. Say hi to him. We were just talking to your sister."

"They're with Henry's family?"

"As usual," Mom replied.

Kiersten and her husband, Henry, usually spent Thanksgiving with his side of the family and Christmas with us.

I showed Erik around the house, from the upstairs bedrooms to the ground-level office where my dad sat behind his large desk playing on his computer. He was tall like me, with gray-white hair I knew I had helped to color. He wore a burgundy sweater vest with a crisply ironed, button-down shirt underneath. He spoke a few words to us and I knew that was all he had to say, so we moved on.

Erik loved the basement entertainment room, which had a built-in, wide-screen television in the wall and a stereo system with surround sound that played DVD movies. I had watched a lot of those in the past few years while I was living here. "This is incredible," he exclaimed, looking all around him.

We also had a game room in the basement, as well as another kitchen and three bedrooms.

"It's fun to watch movies down here," I told him. "We'll have to watch a couple tonight." I showed Erik what the DVD system sounded like as I played a snippet from a movie. "My parents just bought this one," I told him. "It's a great movie."

We stayed downstairs until my mom called us up for dinner. As I walked up the carpeted stairs and felt my stomach rumble at the aroma of the Thanksgiving dinner, I couldn't help wishing Genevie was here as well.

⚜

Thanksgiving consisted of the four of us. I had grown used to this over the years. My mother's side of the family lived in Maine, and we rarely saw them. My father's side lived in the northern suburbs of Chicago, and we would usually get together for a big family meal only at Christmas and an occasional birthday. We always headed out to see my grandmother on Thanksgiving evenings, usually going to an aunt's or uncle's home as well. For the main meal, however, it was usually just our small family.

That's why I had asked Erik to come. It would be easier having a guest to help relieve some of the tension that existed between my father and me.

My father, Jim Blake—professionally, he was Dr. James Blake—talked with Erik as if he were a potential business partner. "So, Erik, what's your major?"

"Communications," Erik replied between bites. He was wolfing down his food as though he had never eaten a meal like this in his life. Living off beer and bologna sandwiches will do that to you.

"And what are your plans for after college?"

"I don't know, to be honest. I'd like to get into journalism."

"Television or radio? Or newspapers?"

I knew what Erik was going to say next.

"I'm not really sure."

My mother slipped into the conversation and began talking about a Barbara Walters special she had seen. My mother was the diplomat of our family, the peacemaker and interpreter for my father. My father saw everything in black and white; everything related to a plan and a purpose.

He just couldn't understand people who didn't have a ten-point mission statement in their life.

This was one reason he couldn't understand his own son.

"So how are the classes going these days?" my father asked me.

"Pretty good."

"Sheridan spends most of his time buried in his books," Erik offered.

Both my parents looked at Erik as if he had told them I had learned to fly.

"Really?" Mom said, looking at me and then meeting my father's eyes.

"Oh, yeah," said Erik. "I keep telling him he needs to lighten up, go out a little more and enjoy life." Erik laughed as he stuffed himself full of more food. He didn't realize what he had just said and what it had done.

It had blown my parents away. I knew this simply by their silent and stunned expressions.

"Still giving piano lessons?" Dad finally asked.

I nodded, wanting to stay clear of this subject. My father had always thought my music was a "waste of time" and that I should be "working and investing in my future." The thing was—for a long time, music was my work and my future, and now it was my livelihood. Dad couldn't understand that. Even when he grudgingly agreed to my music major, he kept pushing me to "be open to other options."

"Any other job prospects come up?" he asked me.

Mom looked at him and gave him a squint of disapproval.

"No," I replied. "But with school and everything, I haven't really been looking."

"I still think you should take that internship I've been telling you about with RG Associates. Rick in our church keeps reminding me about it."

"Maybe after I graduate," I told Dad.

"So have you met any pretty young girls?" my mom asked me with a bright and composed smile, more to get off the "work" subject than out of curiosity.

Erik looked over the table at me and smiled. He didn't say anything.

"Actually, I did."

My mom looked surprised. "And who might that be?"

"Her name is Genevie. She's a Filipino girl I've been seeing some."

"Genevie. That's a pretty name."

"You guys would like her."

"You should have brought her for dinner," Mom said.

"We're just friends," I said, not wanting my parents to think I was getting serious with another girl.

They had always disapproved of my last girlfriend, especially when I decided to follow her to Covenant College.

"Well, you need to come home more or at least call and tell me about these things," Mom said.

"I was home just the other day," I mentioned.

"Just for a quick bite to eat."

"You need to at least let us know you're staying out of trouble," my dad blurted out.

Erik glanced over at me, and I could see the question in his dark eyes. I didn't say anything, and I remained quiet for most of the rest of the meal as my parents exchanged pleasantries with my roommate.

❦

In the afternoon, Erik and I rented a couple of DVD movies and watched them downstairs. As Erik sat on the soft leather couch drifting off to a turkey-induced snooze, I slipped away and went to my bedroom. It was exactly the way I had left it months ago—minus the keyboard I had extracted from the corner a few weeks before and a few small items I had picked up when I dropped by to see my parents.

I looked outside to the sprawling back lawn. Snow was falling—the first of the year.

Memories followed.

Perhaps it was because I was back home, in a house I could at least consider my home—the same house where I had first been forced to confront my mistakes and failures and where I had been left alone to fend for myself. Or perhaps it was the photos that were still tacked up to the corkboard on a wall—dozens of smiling and happy friends I hadn't spoken to in years. Maybe it was the assorted posters remaining on the walls, the trophies on my dresser. Even the framed pictures of my old girlfriend and me could be seen with one easy sweep of the room.

Why hadn't I taken all of these reminders down?

Because you want to be reminded. You need to be reminded.

I saw the stack of musical composition books in the corner of the room. I could almost feel the dust that had collected on them. Years. Years since I had turned on my keyboard, since I had played it, since I had composed anything at all.

How many musical works had I created? Hundreds perhaps. Each one capturing a dream once held. Dreams that were now long forgotten.

Stop feeling sorry for yourself, a voice reprimanded. *It's Thanksgiving, and once again you're in your room feeling sorry for yourself.*

I grabbed the cordless phone in my room and dialed one of the few numbers I knew by heart.

Please let her answer. Dear Father, please let her answer.

"Hello?"

"You're there?" I said in surprise.

"Happy turkey day to you, too."

"How are you?"

"I was just about to leave. Are you at your parents' house?"

"Yeah."

"Is Erik still with you?"

"Yeah. We were watching some movies downstairs."

"I should be there if you're watching movies."

"You could have come," I told her.

I had not asked her about spending Thanksgiving with me since she had already made plans with a friend and her friend's family. Plus, asking her over for Thanksgiving would have been pushing the "serious" button.

"How was the meal?" Gen asked me.

"Delicious. Great."

"I'm starving. I can't wait to have my dinner tonight."

We talked for a few minutes about Thanksgiving and food and what we liked and didn't like. It was small talk, but it was the kind of small talk I needed. It was nice that someone cared enough to ask what sort of things I liked and didn't like for a Thanksgiving meal.

Before I got off the phone with Gen, I told her something that had been on my mind for a while. "You remember the other night on our date—"

"The Barney date?"

"Yeah."

"How could I forget that night?" Genevie softly replied. "I still have that wonderful little tin."

"Well, it's Thanksgiving, and all I've been thinking is how blessed I was that I sat behind you one night at the movies."

She gave a small laugh. "And how I annoyed you?"

"You never annoyed me."

"Well, I could say the same thing."

"Gen, I'm serious. I—maybe it's easier for me to tell you this over the phone. I don't know. But the last few years, well, I haven't been a very thankful person. I know we should give thanks to God for everything. But I haven't wanted to and haven't been able to. Anyway, I just want you to know how thankful I am that you came into my life."

The line was silent for a few seconds before her soft reply, "I'm glad I did too."

I could picture her slight smile, her velvet brown eyes, her frank but gentle gaze. All I needed to do was close my eyes and see them. "I don't want to freak you out by saying any of this," I said.

"You aren't. Don't worry."

We exchanged a few more conversational pleasantries before I worked up the nerve to say what I wanted to say next. "Uh . . . remember when you asked me why I quit school?"

"Sure."

"Well, something really bad happened that summer. There was an accident."

"What kind of accident?"

"An . . . uh . . . auto accident." Even I could tell how lame that sounded, but I didn't know what else to say.

"Was anyone hurt?" Genevie asked me.

"Yes."

"Do you want to talk about it?"

"No. I mean, yes, at some point, but not now. Not over the phone."

"Okay."

"I don't know how to talk about it."

"You can tell me anything, Sheridan. I mean that."

"I just—I was a different person years ago. In a lot of different ways."

"So you've changed."

"But that's the thing. I have so much further to go."

"We all do, Sheridan."

I wanted to say more, but I held back. "I'm sorry for putting all this on you now. Can I see you this weekend?"

"Of course," she replied.

"Thanks for being there for me," I told her.

"I'm glad I was."

Thanks for being there. Period.

I told Genevie good-bye and sat in my room for a few more minutes.

Was it true that I could tell her anything? What would she do once she knew the truth?

Trust her.

My hands shook. How could I tell her? And when should I?

She deserves to know.

I looked at one of the framed photos on my dresser and saw a guy I didn't recognize. He was upbeat and glad to be away from two parents who didn't support and believe in his dreams. He stood with his arm around his girlfriend of three years, the same girlfriend he had followed to college and planned to marry one day.

That guy was forever gone. That couple, that boy, those moments, and those smiles.

I clasped my hands together.

"Dear Father, how long do I have to remember this? Can I ever forget, ever put it behind me? Will I be able to forget all the ways I hurt so many people, including you?"

The photos haunted me.

"Do you hear me, Lord? Can you search my motives and my heart? What do you see, Lord?"

The memories still burned inside of me.

"Lord, can I ever ask your forgiveness? Will I ever be able to accept it?"

THE WATERMARK

PART TWO

an uncertain present

Dear Amy,

As Christmas approaches, I can't help but think this might be one of the best Christmastimes ever. My friendship with Genevie has deepened. I believe she really cares for me. Someone has finally come along and pointed the way toward hope and happiness.

But this brings up a bit of a problem. You see, I think I need to tell Genevie about everything. I feel maybe it will work out if I don't hide things. At least, if I don't hide things about you.

The question, of course, is how—how do I even begin to tell Genevie about you?

I pray I can find the right words to say.

Sheridan

Nine

"OKAY. OPEN THEM."

Genevie's eyes flew open and instantly spotted the open cardboard box in the middle of my apartment living room. From out of the blanket wiggled a tiny sheltie I had just brought home.

"You didn't!" Genevie hugged me and then knelt down to examine the lively puppy.

"He was one of the last ones left," I told her.

"But, what about—I told you about the school's policy—"

"It's okay. We'll keep him here for now."

"Are you sure? You already have Barney."

I looked at Barney, who lay stretched out underneath the dining table. "Actually, it was Erik I had to persuade. I told him I'd do all the training and such—and the whole thing would be temporary until you finished school and bought that big mansion of yours."

Genevie picked up the light brown, squirming sheltie and kissed its head. "It's a boy?"

"Yep. You have to name him."

"Hey there, little guy. Aren't you just adorable? Yeah." Gen continued to speak as she thought of a name for the puppy. "How 'bout Ralph?" she finally said.

"Ralph?" I asked. "Well, sure. It's a—name."

"After all," she went on slyly, "that's what I'll always think about when I remember our first date."

I thought of Barney throwing up in Genevie's lap and laughed. "You're never going to let me live that down, are you?"

"Nah."

"That's the main thing you remember about that date?" I asked her with a smile.

"Let me think." She looked at the puppy, the little guy named Ralph, and talked to him. "Was there anything else about that night that stands out? Hmm . . ."

"Maybe I'll just take back little Ralphie."

"Wait, hold on. Come to think of it, there was that wonderful boat ride. Oh, wait—that had to be cancelled."

I chuckled. "You're ruthless."

She gave me a seductive grin she probably knew I couldn't resist and then kissed me gently on the cheek. "And you're a sweetheart. Thank you. Are you positive it's okay?"

"Positive. The only stipulation is that you have to come by more often to see him. And you have to help me train him, so he'll know to respond to you."

She looked at the puppy and then back at me. The enthusiasm in Genevie's face made all the work of getting Ralphie worth it.

⚜

A few days after surprising Genevie with the puppy, I surprised myself by accompanying her to church. Sitting in the pew, I took note of the beautiful weather on that Sunday. It was an exceptionally bright December morning, and the sun filtered into the sanctuary through the side windows and the skylights that opened up the ceiling above the pulpit.

I sat next to Genevie, and I listened to her pastor preach about God's grace. This was the first time I had been in a church in years. After everything that happened, I had felt I couldn't enter without getting struck by lightning. Not that I believed this would literally happen, but I felt that it would happen in my heart—that something would break and never be healed. That my guilt would be too overwhelming.

But Genevie had gotten me into the church just by asking. She hadn't asked me why I hadn't gone in a while, but had simply invited me to join her that morning. So I had.

Now I sat holding hands with her in the pew. Having her by my side helped. It had really been a long time.

I can't remember much of what the pastor said, and there wasn't any sort of altar call that would have made my inward change visible to the rest of the church. I doubt I would have gone down for an altar call anyway. But something happened to me during that service. The Scripture readings spoke to me. And I realized that they weren't harsh or mean or biting—they were *healing*.

Healing.

The songs—familiar hymns and familiar prayers—didn't seem redundant or foolish but felt somehow comforting. The sermon, like aloe lotion on a sunburn, felt soothing and cooling. But, of course, the burn was still there.

At the end of the service, I prayed a simple and silent prayer. *Lord, thank you for not giving up on me. Help me not to give up on you.*

And the service was done.

⚜

Afterwards, Genevie and I went out to a local family restaurant that served breakfast and lunch. Though it was lunchtime, we both ordered breakfast plates and coffee.

"So," she said, "what'd you think?"

I smiled at Genevie. "Actually, I sort of enjoyed it."

"Not that bad, huh? They have a really great Christmas Eve service if you want to go to it."

"I guess I wouldn't mind going again. Next Sunday even."

"Okay," she said, a bit surprised. "You could try out my small group, too."

"Isn't that all women?"

Genevie flashed me a grin that made me know she was kidding. "My point exactly. You'd be very popular."

"I'll stick to Sunday mornings for now. So, speaking of Christmas, you haven't told me what you are doing."

"Who says I'm doing anything?"

"It's Christmas," I replied. "You have to be doing something."

"Would you believe me if I said I wasn't?"

"Are you serious?"

"Actually, yes, I am."

"What—you're going to be alone on Christmas?"

She nodded and sipped her coffee. I had struck a chord with her, perhaps a dissonant one.

"Now wait a minute," I said. "I'm not going anywhere."

"Well—we haven't exactly made plans yet."

"I just assumed you were going back home to California."

"I told my parents I wasn't."

I stared at Genevie and waited for more, but she just let that statement hang. This came as a surprise. She had always been so open, I was surprised to see her holding back. "Can I ask why you aren't going home?"

She replied as if she had read my thoughts. "You know how you said that there were things that you wanted to tell me but couldn't just yet?"

I nodded as she continued.

"I think everyone has stuff like that. You know how I told you about how surprised I was at being in Chicago for so long? Well, it's been my own doing. I don't exactly love going home."

"Why not?"

She sighed. "There're a lot of memories back home. You know that both my parents are unbelievers. They're actually very strong anti-Christians. They were raised as Buddhists and didn't accept my conversion. I don't know if they ever will. My Christmas would be a lot better away from all of that."

"I'm sorry to bring it up."

"No, don't be sorry. It's okay. It's just—I love Christmas. It's such a wonderful time, celebrating the birth of Jesus and all. When I was growing up, we usually traveled on Christmas and treated it like it was any other normal day. That's why I avoid going home. It's kind of a lonely way to celebrate."

"Look, I thought you were probably going back home, but since you aren't—well, do you want to come to my parents' for Christmas?"

She looked at me with uncertainty.

"No pressure or anything," I continued. "I mean, I know meeting someone's parents is a big deal, especially at Christmas, and I don't want you to feel like—"

"I'd love to, Sheridan."

"Great," I said, a bit nervous about what she would think of my family. "And I'd love to go to that Christmas thing the church has."

"It's a Christmas Eve concert with choirs and an orchestra."

"Sure, whatever."

We both laughed and talked about Christmas and gifts and various things in the present. I actually liked the fact that there were places Genevie didn't want to go regarding her past; it made me feel a little better about my own secrets. I didn't press her. I knew that she would tell me eventually when the time was right.

I hoped I would feel confident enough to do the same.

DECEMBER 9

Dear Amy,

Over the past few weeks, I have found myself thinking about the future. That's a change. For so long I have tried not to think about the days ahead, just to live my life. But recently I've been realizing that the last seven years haven't been much of a life. I've been stuck, unable to move away from the past.

Could it be that now I'm finally moving on?

Sheridan

Ten

MY ROUTINE after my two late Wednesday afternoon lessons in the suburbs was either to swing by my parents' house and grab a bite to eat or to do the drive-through at a burger joint before heading back into the city on the expressway during the tail end of rush hour. There's nothing like trying to eat a cheeseburger and fries during stop-and-go traffic on the Eisenhower.

This particular evening, though, I decided to hurry back to my apartment in hopes of finding a halfway decent parking space on the surrounding side streets. Then, instead of heading to my apartment, I wandered down a couple of blocks to the nearby Wendy's.

Maybe I was avoiding Erik. In fact, I *knew* I was a little hesitant to see him. I no longer knew what to say to him or how to act around him. His life was becoming more and more out of control, and all I was doing was standing by and watching it. He was going down the same dangerous path I had once gone down, but I didn't have a clear-cut solution to give to him. I could tell him some basic stuff he already knew—how all that drinking wasn't good for him, how it could lead to all sorts of trouble, and on and on. But how could I tell him it was wrong to get drunk all the time? He would ask me if I ever had, and then I'd have to tell him. I'd have to tell him everything.

Then, of course, how in the world could he take me seriously after all that?

The restaurant was crowded and noisy, but I ignored the bustle as I sat there with my spicy chicken sandwich, fries, and milk shake. I barely noticed the balding, stocky man in faded jeans and a big sloppy sweatshirt who approached me.

"Blake?" the man demanded, startling me.

I looked at him, my body half in shock from having my name shouted in a crowded restaurant, and said nothing. Even though the man appeared to be in his late forties or early fifties, he had a boyish face, the sort that can never fully grow a beard. His eyes looked tired as they scanned my features, seeming to recognize me.

"You ever answer your phone messages?"

The voice registered, and instantly I knew I was facing Mike Larsen for the first time in my life. He was shorter than me, perhaps five-eight or five-ten, but stout, with a stomach that looked like it could comfortably hold several mugs' worth of heavy ale. His sparse brown hair seemed to be sticking out on one side of his head, just above his right ear, like he had slept on it. I wondered if he was drunk.

"You are Sheridan Blake, right?"

I froze, unsure what to say. Instead of saying anything, I looked down at my half-eaten fries and the large vanilla shake that had been the highlight of my meal so far.

"I'm Mike. Mike Larsen. I found your apartment. For someone who doesn't want to be bothered, you're pretty easy to locate."

His voice sounded burdened and anxious, although surprisingly not as irate as I had imagined it could have been. Maybe he was one of those soft-spoken types who let their fists express their anger. I looked at him again, still silent. I wasn't sure whether I was safe sitting in the corner of the restaurant.

"The Internet," he went on. "The address was easy to find."

Was he threatening me?

"I've seen you at the college, too. What made you come back?"

What business was it of his?

"For God's sake, would you say something?" His volume increased as the frustration filled his face.

"What do you want me to say, Mr. Larsen?"

He spit out an amazed chuckle and squinted his eyes in disbelief. "I just want to talk to you. There are things you need to know."

"Look, Mr. Larsen, I'm sorry for everything that happened. But I can't do anything to change the past."

"Yeah. Well, answering a simple phone call would be *something.*"

"I said everything I could in my letter years ago. I never heard a word from either you or your wife. What else can I say?"

"I can't speak for Amanda. We divorced."

I wanted to say I was sorry, but I think my silent, stunned expression said enough.

"But you just—can't you have the common *decency* to grant a simple request?" Larsen asked.

"I'm sorry. But I don't know what good calling you back would have done."

"It's called being courteous. Is that too much to ask?"

Larsen's face was turning red, and I was beginning to get really nervous. "Listen, Mr. Larsen, now is really not a good time."

"And when is? I've been trying to talk to you for months now!"

"Mr. Larsen, I could say I'm sorry a thousand times and—"

"Just wait and listen."

"I'm sorry. Please, I don't think this is—"

"Hold on. Wait."

As I stood to leave, the frustrated man looked at me as he moved his arm and then jerked his wrist quickly. I didn't see it coming because everything happened so quickly. At first I thought he was swinging a knife, that a blade was driving toward my exposed throat, that this was how all of it would end. I threw up my hands to protect myself.

Suddenly the remaining two-thirds of my shake splattered on my head and face and chest.

Mike looked at the cup in his hand with horror and then at my shocked, vanilla-splattered expression. "Listen, I'm—you just . . ." He took a deep, frustrated breath. "You just don't understand . . ." His sentence drifted off with him as he quickly exited the restaurant.

I wiped the sticky, cold goo from my face with a napkin. The few people around me looked on in curious delight and probably wondered if there was going to be any more action, if I was going to be a man and follow him outside to save face.

I could never save face, no matter what I said or did to Mike Larsen.

I felt the syrupy shake creeping down my neck as I headed to the bathroom with the angry echoes of Larsen's last words to me filling my head: *You just don't understand.*

⚜

When I got back to the apartment, I found Erik on the couch listening to U2's latest CD. Next to him in the middle of a big blanket slept little Ralph. Erik looked at me and said hello. "You're wet," he added.

"Slightly," I said, and left it at that.

I found Barney in my bedroom, lying on his side like a car-wreck victim. I tapped the floor several times and he jerked up, looking like a blind man who just woke up on the street after someone put change in his can. I always feared the day when I would tap and there would be no response. Thankful this wasn't the moment, I tapped a few more times, and he came to me. He could smell the shake and instantly began to lick my face and ears and neck where vanilla had dried.

I petted him for a few minutes, admiring the fact that regardless of who and what I was, this dog would always love me unconditionally. Perhaps that's why I didn't care how many shots I had to give him or how old he was. He never stopped loving me.

I never stopped loving you either, Sheridan.

I dismissed the thought and took a quick shower. In fresh clothes, I went to see what Erik had on his agenda.

"I don't know," he said. "My stomach's been kinda hurting lately."

"Maybe that's because your diet consists of beer and more beer."

He laughed. "Yeah, that can't be too healthy, huh?"

"So what are you doing for the holidays?" I asked him.

"I don't know. Maybe go back home for a few days and be with the family—if I can stand it. Hanging out around here mostly, I guess. Maybe going out."

"There's a service being held at Genevie's church on Christmas Eve."

"And you're going?"

"Sure. With Genevie."

"Sorry, I don't have a date for church. You find me one and I'll go."

"It's not so bad, you know."

"Probably not. My parents and family go to their church on Christmas Eve, too."

"Do you go with them?" I asked.

"No. And they end up lecturing me. That's why I wanted to go home with you for Thanksgiving. So they'd stop riding my tail about things."

"Then come with Gen and me to church. It would be good. Something different."

Erik looked at me suspiciously from the couch. "Who are you—and what have you done with Sheridan Blake?"

I shrugged. "Hey, look, it's just something different. I've been going with Genevie every once in a while. Actually, it's been all right."

"And why's that?"

"I don't know. Lots of reasons. I always leave feeling pretty good."

Erik stretched and grinned. "I feel good after I've had a six-pack."

I didn't know where to go with this. I had my faults, but I certainly wasn't hypocritical enough to push the man into going to church. "Just think about it. Gen likes you."

"She doesn't even know me," Erik replied.

"Sure she does. She likes being around you and me. We make her laugh."

"How so?"

"Maybe it's just *you* that makes her laugh. Maybe it's the patch of fuzz on your chin."

"Hey, I just started growing it. It's quite popular with the ladies."

"It looks like the plague broke out under your chin." I continued to jest with Erik. "Yeah, girls really like that blotchy thing."

"Just because *you* don't have face hair doesn't mean you have to go knocking mine."

"It looks like you taped some of Ralphie's fur to your face."

"At least I didn't have Barney puke on my date."

"Yeah, that's because you last went on a date in—oh, when was that? Eighth grade?"

"Funny," Erik replied. "Very funny."

"Truth hurts."

We continued bantering with one another the way we had grown accustomed to doing. For some strange reason, the closer guys seem to become, the easier it is to verbally joust in a good-natured way. This was my way of communicating with Erik. Eventually, the climate would be comfortable enough for each of us to say anything we wanted to the other.

As Erik played with Ralph, I began sorting through Erik's variety of discs.

"Oh, by the way," my roommate told me, "that Mike Larsen dude called again and left a weird message."

"When?"

"After you came home. When you were in the shower."

"What'd he say?"

"Listen to it."

My gut clenched as I crossed over to the answering machine and played the message. The voice sounded tired.

"Seven years," it said. "Seven long years. I just wanted to talk to you, Blake. Why couldn't you understand that? Why'd you have to make things so difficult? Oh, well . . ." Then the message trailed off.

I erased it quickly.

"What was that all about?"

"It's about past mistakes I can't seem to get away from."

He gave me a curious look. "What sort?"

"Mistakes anybody could make. The kind you wonder if you'll ever be able to forget."

"From your college days years ago?"

I nodded.

"So why all the secrecy about it? What's the big deal?"

"You know when you go to a party and do or say something really stupid—like get in a fight with someone or say something horrible about your best friend? And then you wake up the next day and wish it had never happened? That's sorta what it's like. A memory of something bad that you'd rather forget than relive."

Erik shrugged. "So you apologize and move on."

"Apologizing's the easy part."

"Yeah, but—"

"It's just not that easy," I interrupted.

"Okay, then, I won't ask anymore." Erik turned his back to me as he walked over to the television to switch on his PlayStation game system. His words were nonchalant, but I could tell he was peeved.

"That's why church helps, you know," I said, hating the preachiness in my own words even as I said them. "Church and Gen. I pretty much need them at this point in my life."

Erik's back was still to me and his voice was flat. "Yeah, man. Well, if you ever need me, you know where to find me."

DECEMBER 14

Dear Amy,

Everything in me wants to tell people like Gen and Erik the truth. But I'm afraid of their reactions, especially Gen's. And I'm also ashamed.

The other day I finally saw him for the first time—you know who I mean. After all this time, he decided he needed to talk with me. But we didn't get much talking done. He ended up throwing a milk shake in my face.

I know I probably should have done more than simply write that letter years ago. I should have actually faced them, said I was sorry. But I was afraid of what they would say, just as I fear what Genevie will say and do if I tell her the truth.

Even after all this time, I have so far left to go.

Sheridan

Eleven

I SEARCHED radio stations with my finger, my other hand on the steering wheel of my Honda. Eventually, I slipped in a disc by a relatively new electronic musician.

"What's this?" Genevie asked me in the darkness of the car.

"It's a new CD I just got called 'I Can't Take Any More All-Boy Bands.' "

"You know—the Beatles were once considered a boy band, too."

"Please," I said.

"I'm just kidding. Come on—lighten up. You're supposed to be in a good mood."

"I'm in a fine mood," I replied.

"You've been quiet ever since we left the church."

I drove down the expressway, almost unrecognizable with its open lanes on this Sunday night. Genevie slipped her hand in mine as we talked.

"Not any more than I usually am."

"I thought Nita did a wonderful job."

"I did, too."

"So what's wrong, Sheridan?"

"Nothing. Really."

"Oh, come on. Your star pupil played three pieces in front of her entire church. She really is incredible."

"I know."

"Was this the first time she played in a program?" Genevie asked.

"No. She did it last year, though I didn't come."

"Why not?"

"I didn't have anyone to go with." I squeezed her hand, hoping the lighter comment would disguise my somber mood.

We didn't say anything for a while. After ten minutes Genevie turned down the melancholy music. "Sometimes I really don't get your moods, Sheridan."

"What moods?"

"Like the one you're in right now."

"I'm just tired. I'm sorry."

"I don't want you to apologize. I want you to be happy. It's almost Christmas. There's so much to be thankful for."

"I know."

"You should be so proud of how well you've taught Nita."

"I am. It's just . . . sometimes watching her is like looking into a mirror to the past. I'm pretty envious of her."

"Why?" Genevie asked.

"She's got her whole life ahead of her."

"And you don't?"

"She's so young. And she'll be able to do so much."

"And you can't? Come on, Sheridan."

"I'm just being honest."

"And so am I."

"There was a time in my life when I had a lot of plans related to my playing the piano."

"So what happened to them?"

I let out a sigh. "Good question."

"Tell you what," Genevie said, unfazed by my pessimism. "I want you to come somewhere with me next week. Can you take an afternoon off?"

"Sure. Where?"

"You'll see. Just promise me you'll be open-minded. And in a good mood."

"I'm in a fine mood."

"Sheridan?"

"Okay. I promise."

⚜

Five days before Christmas, I honored my promise to Genevie by accompanying her along the crowded stores on Michigan Avenue. My classes were finished and the exams were completed. When she told me where we were going, I pictured an entire day of Christmas shopping with Genevie. While the thought of wandering around stores didn't particularly delight me, I didn't mind as long as I was with Gen. Hopefully I would get some ideas on what exactly to get her for Christmas.

The street was awash with streams of well-dressed men and women carrying loaded shopping bags. Everyone seemed busy and preoccupied and unaware of each other. The shops were crowded with long lines at the checkout counters and packed with browsers searching for the right gift. After a while, the whole scene overwhelmed me, even though I was at Genevie's side.

"Big shopper, huh?" Gen asked at one point that day, as I stared dully at a heaping display of clothes on a sales table.

"Can't get enough," I replied as she laughed.

It was close to four in the afternoon, and we were almost finished (I hoped) when we passed by a bakery. So far, I had bought one small gift for my mother while Genevie had a couple of bags full. She had bought a blanket at one store and a few small baby toys at another, only saying they were presents for people she knew.

"Let's go in here for a second," Gen said, motioning toward the bakery door.

"What? Aren't we eating in a couple hours?"

"I'm not hungry."

I followed her inside and watched Gen order an assortment of cookies and pastries. The bill came to around fifty dollars.

"What are you doing?" I asked her in bewilderment.

She smiled and handed me a couple of the bags to carry. "You'll see."

We walked down Michigan Avenue, our arms loaded down with shopping bags and parcels of sweet goodies.

"What's going on, Gen?"

"Follow me."

A couple of blocks off Michigan Avenue was a nondescript apartment building. Genevie walked up to the door and pressed one of the buttons to call someone.

A short, plump, redheaded woman answered the door. "Well, hey, Genevie."

"Hi, Lizzie. Merry Christmas." Genevie gave the woman her two bags from the bakery.

"What's this?"

"Something for the ladies. We've got a couple more."

I handed the bags to Lizzie, who gave me a big, gap-toothed smile.

"This is Sheridan," Gen said to Lizzie. I nodded in greeting.

"Hey, you-all didn't have to do this," the woman said.

"Course I didn't—I wanted to. Here—I got you a little something in this bag. And a few toys for the kids."

"Genevie, you shouldn't have—," the woman began, but Gen interrupted her protests.

"You're loaded down—you want us to help with those?"

"Oh, no, it's okay." She fidgeted with the bags until I politely took a couple back. "Well, all right, then."

Gen and I followed her through a door off the first-floor hallway. Her small apartment smelled like garlic and old socks. Stepping in the family room, I was surprised at the sparse furniture inside the apartment. The building looked a hundred years old.

"You're such a sweetie, you know that," Lizzie said to Genevie. "I'll let the women know that you brought some gifts by."

"And Sheridan," Genevie replied.

"Yes, certainly." Lizzie smiled big round cheeks and winked at me.

"Have a good Christmas," Gen said.

"You too. Are we still seeing you next week?"

"Of course."

"Bye then. You take care and keep warm."

Gen and I found our way out of the building and began walking back toward Michigan Avenue. She looked at me several times and smiled.

"So?" I asked her.

"What?"

"Are you going to tell me about that, or should I just guess?"

"Lizzie is the director at a shelter for women I visit sometimes. It's part of an outreach program at my church. Anyway, I've kind of kept in touch with Lizzie and her ladies."

"Homeless women?" I asked.

"No. Well, yes and no. Mainly it's young girls with children who have nowhere to go. Girls in tough situations. A lot of the time they've been abused."

"How many are there?"

"I don't know. Maybe a dozen or more. The number varies."

"And you come down here a lot?" I asked her.

"Fairly often, I guess. What? Why so surprised?"

"I'm not. I just didn't know that. I thought I knew everything about Genevie Liu."

Gen laughed. "You don't know the half of it."

"Will I get to?"

She turned her head and caught my eye. "Don't you think that's a funny thing for you to ask?"

There wasn't much for me to say to that, so I didn't say anything. We passed by frantic shoppers who looked weighed down by presents and debt.

"That was a great thing you just did," I finally said. "But why'd you want me to come?"

"To be a part of it. To share in the fun."

"I just carried the bags."

"Sure, but didn't you see Liz's expression? The appreciation? The kindness in her eyes?"

"Yes."

"And that's someone who could be pretty angry at the world, especially after the cards she's been dealt. Instead, she's gracious and humble and serves women in need."

"I'm assuming this isn't the first time you've done something like this?"

"It's not like I'm keeping count. I don't know. I *like* helping people when I can. Not that giving away desserts and toys is that big a deal."

"I think it is. I haven't exactly been looking for people in need that I could help, you know."

Gen looked up at me with her open gaze. "You don't have to look far. I think everyone needs help sooner or later in life. You just have to take the time to find them." She paused for a second. "And they have to be willing to accept it."

Dear Amy,

I am amazed that God allowed someone like Genevie Liu to come across my path. What did I ever do to deserve a woman like her? She fills me with enthusiasm and hope. I find myself changed when I am around her.

I never expected to come back to Covenant and fall in love. I thought I had control of my life. I thought I could come back and finish out school and have nothing eventful happen to me. Instead, I meet this magnificent and beautiful woman and fall in love with her.

Sheridan

Twelve

I SAT ALONE IN my apartment bedroom, my trembling hands resting on the white keys of my synthesizer keyboard. I had been in my room for fifteen minutes, wanting to finally turn on my keyboard again and play something—anything. Yet I had done nothing except look at the keyboard sitting on its small table and breathe in and out.

Why couldn't I play it anymore?

When I was growing up, playing music had always been my comfort, my solace. Music relaxed me and brought out the best in me. I used to be able to sit down at a piano or with my synthesizer and play for hours upon end. Sometimes I would work my way through complex pieces, immersed in the power of the music, and other times I'd make up my own music. I had composed many pieces and saved them on discs I could manipulate in my computer. The process of creating layer after layer of fresh and vibrant tunes always inspired me. Even when my parents discouraged me from pursuing electronic music, I still composed and continued to hope that I could do this for a living one day.

That hope evaporated after I quit school. And ever since, I had felt afraid of coming back to something that meant so much to me: At first, I couldn't do it because I was afraid of feeling anything human again.

Then, I gradually realized I had lost the ability to create. I could teach younger kids and show them what needed to be done—how to hold their hands and read music and strike the keys, but that was it. I had not composed anything for myself in years. I didn't know if I ever could again.

Now, two days before Christmas, I had decided to try, but nothing was happening. The keys remained still; the speaker resting on the floor next to the keyboard remained soundless. I had no idea how to start.

Finally I decided to at least play *something*. So I began. Just scales, up and down. Simple drills I taught beginning students.

Gradually, the scales became something else. Suddenly, music was pouring out of me. I played for an hour, first playing songs I knew by heart, making sure I remembered how to use the Korg keyboard as I changed the programmed sounds every few minutes from the simple sounds of a piano to the harmonies of a full orchestra. The familiar songs became improvised pieces, works I simply started playing with a naturalness I thought had been long forgotten.

And then I found myself in uncharted territory, feeling like a man drinking water for the first time after being lost in the desert, playing compositions I had no idea were resting inside of me. I felt glad no one was around; no one could hear me. I was alone and I was creating again. It felt good, like talking to a long-lost friend.

As my fingers continued to wander over the keys, Genevie's smile kept coming to my mind. Now I let my emotions flood over the keyboard. The music sounded vibrant and optimistic, much like the amazing woman I was thinking of as I played. Soon I felt a new melody emerging.

It had been years. Maybe I was finally moving on.

⚜

An hour later, on the cold streets of Chicago, carrying a small backpack and bundled up in a thick winter coat and gloves, I passed by shoppers with arms loaded down with bags of gifts. Everyone was buying and looking and browsing and picking things out. It was usually an inspiring sight, with all the Christmas colors and lights and the realization that Christmas was only two days away. Tonight, though, something about the crowded and busy streets depressed me.

What had Christmas become?

I remembered delivering the pastries to the apartment building with Genevie only a few days earlier and how good that had felt. How long had it been since I had been involved in simply giving to another human being and helping them?

Of course, my parents had taught me to give to charities and to the church on a regular basis and to be especially generous at Christmastime. In my father's eyes, giving was our duty and responsibility. But it had always seemed so impersonal, and so futile; I never believed that what I gave actually *helped* anybody.

As the years passed, I had gradually stopped giving. Maybe I was just selfish. But what I think actually happened was that I began to feel cynical about anything related to money. For so many years I had felt different than others simply because my family had more money than most. The older I became, the more I resented my family's wealth and tried to do anything I could not to stand out.

This sort of foolish thinking had gotten me nothing but trouble. Yet, walking down the streets and looking around, I realized I still had that cynicism clinging to me.

What was Christmas anyway? My recent experience was that it was a time off from school, a time when my family gathered together to give each other a boatload of gifts and then sit down and commit gluttony. In a nutshell, that's how my Christmas holidays in recent years could be summed up.

I had gone to church when I was younger and knew it meant something to me. My sister was always a positive influence, taking me to church with her. Yet the older I became, the more I found myself skipping the Christmas Eve services. Instead, I focused on the new video game or stereo system or whatever I hoped to discover the next morning when we opened presents.

The true meaning of Christmas, as I've heard so many say, was lost on me.

I spotted a scruffy woman ringing a bell and looking cold and tired. I smiled at her and passed by. Then I stopped, backtracked, and dropped a few bills into her box. She gave me a smile and a nod as she kept ringing her bell.

The true meaning of Christmas. It wasn't just about being charitable, but that certainly was part of it. Friends and family, loved ones—they were part of it too. And there was more.

I walked on, warmed by the simple interchange, but still a bit depressed by the bustle around me. All these people walking by me, shopping and spending money and maxing out their Visa cards and purchasing way too many presents. What did they know of Christmas? What did it mean to them? Family arguments? Spiked eggnog? Getting gifts that mostly would never be used? Eating a huge meal and then falling asleep on a couch in front of a football game?

What about the little baby who was born on this day almost two thousand years ago? Didn't he play into this somehow?

I remembered one Christmas Eve service when our entire congregation lit candles in the darkness of the sanctuary and sang "Joy to the World" as midnight approached. I was probably ten or eleven years old then. As the twenty-fourth turned into the twenty-fifth, the congregation became quiet as we were encouraged to offer silent prayers of thankfulness.

I can still remember how easily the prayer came to me then, how certain I was that God heard my words: "Lord, thank you for coming down and being born," I had prayed. "Thank you for doing something you didn't have to do. Thank you for giving the world hope and for giving me eternal life. Please never let me forget this."

It was surprising that in the midst of the busyness this memory from my childhood had resurfaced. And somehow in that memory I was given a vision of what I really wanted for this Christmas. I wanted it to be different. I knew it already would be with Genevie at my side. And perhaps that was why it could be. I knew she probably treated Christmas with the reverence it deserved. Maybe some of that could rub off on me.

On the streets, I could hear "We Three Kings" coming from speakers and wondered if most of the people even realized what three kings were being talked about. Did they know? How many times had they heard this song? How many times had I heard it?

This year, I told myself, *I'm going to listen.*

Dear Amy,

It's Christmas Eve morning as I write. I've been listening to a station that plays nonstop Christmas carols, and I've really been trying to listen to the words and hear and understand them. For so long Christmas has meant nothing more to me than receiving a ton of presents and eating way too much food. The last few Christmases have been nothing more than a time to look back on the year and see how little I've done. I want this year to be better, to be filled with more hope. So I'm listening.

The song that just finished was "O Holy Night." I wonder if my music could ever express something as beautiful as those lyrics: "A thrill of hope, the weary world rejoices, for yonder breaks a new and glorious morn."

Well, maybe this is a little too dramatic—but I really do feel that a new and glorious morn has broken for me. I really feel like a weary man finally rejoicing. I eagerly await tonight's dinner with Genevie and the thrill of hope awaiting me in the new year.

Sheridan

Thirteen

MINUTES BEFORE GENEVIE was supposed to arrive at my apartment, I wandered around my place cleaning up. Ralph was in the living room fidgeting and trying to get out of the little red sweater I had bought him as a joke for Genevie. The little sheltie looked adorably uncomfortable in the oversized outfit.

I was just making several scans of the apartment to make sure everything was neat and orderly and set up when I heard a knock on the door. I opened it. Genevie stood in the hallway, a smile on her lips.

For a second I couldn't think of anything to say. I didn't want to be obvious, but I'm sure I was. She looked incredible in sleek black boots and a dark red dress that fell just below her knees. Her gray coat hung over one arm, and her arms were full of packages.

"You look—" I sought the right word to say—"nice."

She grinned at my fumbled word choice.

"You didn't have to bring those," I said, referring to the presents in her hands.

"They're just some things I got for Barney and Ralphie."

It was close to five-thirty on Christmas Eve. After dinner and perhaps watching a movie, we would be going to the church service that started an hour before midnight. Then I would pick Genevie up tomorrow morning on campus, and we would both head to my parents' house for our Christmas celebration.

"I hope you weren't expecting anything for Christmas," I told Genevie.

"I don't need anything," she replied.

I looked into her shimmering eyes. "You know I'm just kidding."

"I wasn't."

I laughed and took the packages from her to place under the tree, then returned for her coat.

"Nice tree," Genevie commented once again. We had joked about it ever since I got the three-foot-tall live tree and set it up in my living room. Erik and I had decorated it with a hideous assortment of things from around the apartment—an old CD Erik had found in his car one day, caps to an assortment of beer bottles, a small fly swatter, soap on a rope (something Erik had bought at a dollar store), even ballpoint pens. We had started by hanging up a few ridiculous things with the box of hooks we had bought and then decided to do the whole thing in Sheridan-Erik chic.

"Erik loves it."

"Where's he again?" Gen asked.

"He's with his parents. They live in the south suburbs, about an hour away. He'll be back late."

"So it's just you and me?"

"Don't forget the dogs," I said.

"So where's my little guy?"

"Last time I saw him, he was pretty busy."

It took Gen a minute to find him. I had put him back in his large box with a blanket inside. Genevie lifted him up and laughed at the colorful sweater the puppy had partially chewed but failed to take off.

"Where'd you find this?"

"At a Christmas store on Michigan Avenue."

"And there's Barney, our guard dog."

Barney lay on his bed in the corner of the room, unaware of the visitor.

"You know, I even got him a present," Genevie told me.

"He'll appreciate it. Really."

Gen sat on one of the two matching couches in our living room. I had dipped into the large savings fund I had accumulated over the years to buy most of the furniture in the apartment. Since I had lived at home for free and worked various jobs, I had managed to save quite a bit of money. I was even able to pay for my final year at Covenant, something I did in spite of my parents' offers to do the same.

"Dinner smells good."

I laughed. "You know, I haven't done this in like—well, to be honest, I haven't done this ever."

"So I'm your Christmas dinner guinea pig?"

"Yep."

"Well, at least it smells delicious."

"Well, I shouldn't tell you this, but I found some special 'Christmas dinner' spray that comes in a can like Lysol. Spray a little of it around, and your place smells just like Ma's good ol' Christmas dinner. Unfortunately, I can't say the same about how my Christmas hot dogs will taste."

Gen crossed her legs and smiled. I started the Christmas music waiting in my five-disc CD changer. Several discs had been bought especially for this evening.

Gen sat on the couch, looking a bit unsure about what to say. This was unusual for her.

"Can I get you something to drink?" I asked. "Eggnog? Sparkling cider? Tea?"

"I'll try some eggnog."

"Don't worry—I bought it at Oberweis, so it should be halfway decent."

It took me a couple of minutes to find a nice glass to serve the eggnog in. I gave it to her. She smiled a formal grin and accepted it.

I sat down beside her with a glass of my own. "You know, Gen. Just because I'm making dinner for you doesn't mean this has to be awkward or anything."

She let go with a nervous laugh. "I know. I'm sorry. I am being kind of stiff, aren't I?"

"Well, you better watch out. I'll get Barney to throw up on you again."

"Hard to be stiff when you have a lapful of puke."

I laughed at Genevie's words—and at the memory.

Gen continued. "It's just—this is so new to me."

"You and me both. Think I cook Christmas dinner for every girl I meet?"

"I'm not sure," she joked. "Maybe you do."

"Remember, you're my guinea pig. This is all for my future in catering."

"I like the candles," she said. "Very nice touch."

I nodded, noting another Christmas first for me—candles bought for tonight, perched on various surfaces around the room, lit and softly glowing. Even with the lamps on, the candles added to Christmas ambience. At least I hoped they did.

Before heading for the kitchen to finish the dinner, I squeezed Genevie's hand. "You know what I first thought when we went on our first date? It was how incredibly beautiful you looked."

"Please—"

"No, I'm serious. Remember when I came to pick you up at your dorm room? I told myself you were about the most gorgeous girl I'd ever seen in my whole life. And I doubted that you could ever look more stunning than you did that night. I was mistaken."

"Your food's going to burn if you don't go back into the kitchen," Gen said, a tinge of unease in her voice. My compliments seemed to make her uncomfortable.

We ate by candlelight at the small table next to the kitchen. The walls were a little bare due to my recent removal of Erik's beer posters, but Genevie and I both liked the shadows flickering on the textured surface. I couldn't help feeling a bit awkward myself at the start of the dinner, since I wore a vest and dress shirt and slacks and because Genevie looked so stunning tonight, almost untouchable. But as soon as I began making fun of the food, we both seemed to relax and act like ourselves.

Actually, the dinner wasn't all that bad. The ham was all right, the gravy a bit goopy, the potatoes only a little salty, and the sweet potatoes tasted exactly the way they should have—an easy feat, since they came from a microwavable package. I couldn't ruin the "brown and serve" bread or the frozen yellow corn. All in all, I had to admit it was a decent first Christmas dinner.

Close to the end of the meal, she thanked me for the dinner. "You didn't have to do this, you know."

"I really wanted to."

"Thank you. I can't tell you how much this means."

"I can say the same about these past few months."

"They've been fun, haven't they?"

I nodded.

"Last Christmas, I was by myself for the most part."

"How often do you see your parents?" I asked her.

"Maybe once or twice a year. But Christmas is hard. It's just not the same when you have parents who are divorced and who don't believe in Christmas in the first place. It's been hard to see my father remarry, too. They have a two-year-old daughter."

"Really?" I replied, surprised by the fact that Gen had a sister. Or a stepsister.

"At first I didn't think I could ever accept my dad having another child with someone else. It's still hard to accept. But I think God has really worked in me to accept both my stepmom and my new sister."

"That would be tough."

"It has been. It continues to be. I have to constantly pray for patience and for peace, especially when I go back home."

I wasn't sure what I could possibly add to Gen's comment. She ended up asking me what I was doing at this time last year.

"I'd rather think of what I might be doing a year from now."

"Let's don't."

Genevie's stern words surprised me. "Why not?"

She shook her head and looked down at the table.

"What? What'd I say?"

"Nothing. It's nothing."

"Gen, what? Look at me. What'd I say?"

In the glow of the candlelight, I could see the glistening of tears in her dark brown eyes. She wiped them away and smiled. "I didn't want to bring this up tonight."

"What do you mean? Bring what up?"

"Well, I just got some news this week—I was offered a job at a counseling office I had applied to a while ago. Starting this spring."

"That's great, isn't it? That's what you've been looking for."

"Yeah, it is."

"I didn't even know—"

"I know. I'm sorry. I don't want to ruin tonight with all of this."

"You're not. You haven't ruined anything. This is great news."

"The office is in northern California, close to where my father lives."

The air went out of me with her words. I breathed in and nodded, understanding now why she was hesitant in talking about the job and why she had not told me.

"California? Wow."

"I haven't said anything in response yet. I just found out this week."

I nodded. "Does it sound like a good job?"

Tears dampened her eyes as she nodded. "A very good job."

I swallowed hard, then forced myself to smile. "Then we *should* be celebrating. That's really wonderful."

"It is?"

"Of course it is. You've been looking for something like this, right? Why wouldn't you be excited?"

I shouldn't have said that. I was provoking her, trying to get an answer. I knew what I wanted to hear. I was only unsure if I would actually hear it.

"I am. It's just . . . well, you know why, Sheridan."

"What? A great job. Going back to be around your family. You have every right to be excited."

She looked at me with kind yet sad eyes. Her raven hair was pulled back except for a few falling strands that dangled perfectly along her cheek. "But it seems like everything is going so well—with us, I mean—and now, well . . ."

She controlled her tears and wiped them away. I should have never forced her to admit anything.

"I'm sorry, Gen. Look, I understand. I mean, I think I do. Look, this isn't really good news for me, either. I don't want you moving halfway across the country, not after I just met you."

"I know."

"I guess I'm not sure where things stand between us right now. Not exactly."

"I don't either. I thought I was beginning to. And I just . . . well, I assumed this job in California wouldn't happen, that I wouldn't hear back from them. So now I don't know. . . . "

"Gen, I don't want to pressure you. That's the last thing I want to do with you. Like I said, these last few months have been incredible. But if I can only be around you for a few months . . . well . . . so be it."

"Is that all you want?"

"Are you kidding?" I laughed. "Look at this, Gen. You think I would do this for anyone?"

She smiled in answer.

"If some of my old buddies could see me now. Candles and music and all that. They'd flip. Though my mother would approve . . ."

"I admit, it's all pretty incredible."

"Well, then, why don't we just concentrate on tonight? Let's not talk about California and jobs and all that stuff." I took her hand. "We can talk about all that later."

"You do still have your presents to open."

"I'm expecting something big, you know," I said with forced levity.

"Just wait."

⚜

We opened presents around nine o'clock, after watching *It's a Wonderful Life* while we ate dessert. All during the movie, as Genevie snuggled against me on the couch with her boots off and a blanket over her and her head resting on my shoulder, I couldn't help wanting to kiss her. At the end of the film, as Genevie's eyes teared up with emotion, I kissed her gently on the cheek and told her again how beautiful she looked.

Then we gathered all the wrapped packages from under the tree and started to unwrap them.

The dogs came first, of course. Gen had bought Barney and Ralphie each a flavored bone to chew on, which they began doing with contented looks on their furry faces—until Ralph grew bored with his and decided to investigate Uncle Barney's.

After we separated the two animals, I opened my gifts from Genevie. The first turned out to be a wonderful book that featured interviews with various movie composers.

"Where'd you find this?"

"It's new," she said, her grin revealing her pleasure in my surprise. "Amazing the things you can find on the Internet."

"It's great."

The second gift was small, heavy, and square. I opened the box to find a silver model of a piano. The meaning was obvious, and I thanked her for it without saying too much. I didn't want to let her see me get too emotional.

The third gift was a leather journal with the following words inscribed on the cover: *Sheridan Blake's Musical Journal.*

"It's for writing music in," she told me. "Some of the pages have musical staffs, and some are plain. For the words . . ."

I held the journal and marveled at the thoughtfulness of her gifts. She knew me better than I thought she did—not only what I would like but also what I needed.

"These are . . . these are all very unexpected, Gen. Thank you."

She beamed. "I knew you'd like them."

"Okay," I said. "You have to open your gifts now."

"Oh, Sheridan, your dinner is enough of a present."

"I know. It was a culinary masterpiece. But go on, open them."

I had given her three things as well. One was a cassette with choice selections from all my favorite soundtracks.

"I'll love this," she said, turning it over.

"It's got a lot of music from movies we've seen together."

"Thank you. I can't wait to hear it."

"I chose music that reminded me of you. Music that seemed full of passion and life."

And love, a thought told me.

The second gift was a pendant I had found at a jeweler a while back— a ruby stone in a gold setting. I had made sure it didn't look ostentatious or too expensive, but it had been costly. I was glad to spend some of the money in my savings account on this gift for Genevie. She certainly deserved it.

"It's gorgeous. Sheridan, you shouldn't have."

"It's no big deal, really. I wasn't sure if you'd like it, but—"

"I love it."

It's almost as beautiful as you are, Gen.

She tried it on. She gave me a hug since we were sitting together on the couch. "What's this?" she asked of the small box.

"That's your third gift."

She opened it up. It was another cassette tape. On it was a single recording, a piece I had composed a couple of days ago. It was entitled "Genevie."

She read the word and then looked at me with curiosity.

"It's something I wrote the other day," I said.

"And you put it on this tape?"

"Yeah. It wasn't that difficult. I was playing around with my synthesizer for the first time in a while, and—well, that's what came out."

I looked at Gen's eyes and the tears came again. Her hands trembled, and she looked up at me with questioning, surrendering eyes. "Sheridan, I can't believe you wrote this for me—"

"It's nothing, really. I just—well, I hope you like it."

"Can I play it now?"

"No, please—"

"Oh, I want to."

"Please, I'd rather you didn't."

"Why?" Gen asked.

"I get uncomfortable seeing others react to my music. It's always been a very private thing for me."

"Okay. But I'm going to listen to it the second I get back to my room."

"That's fine. I hope you do."

Her gleaming eyes were only inches from my own. So was her smile, her upturned lips. And her trembling hands holding something that had obviously struck a chord within her.

The CD player in the background played "It Came upon the Midnight Clear." The candles in the room still glowed. The lights weren't as bright as they had been. Maybe that was my imagination, but I couldn't tell since I was looking into Genevie's eyes and nothing else really mattered.

"Thank you," Genevie told me as she placed the tape next to her.

I was going to say "you're welcome," but Genevie stopped me with a soft and gentle kiss. We stayed on the couch for a long time, the rest of the world seeming far away.

Then with her cheek against mine, she whispered words I will never forget. "Thank you for coming into my life when you did. I don't think you'll know how much I needed someone like you to be here."

The words felt like they could have been my own.

DECEMBER 26

Dear Amy,

This past week I've been able to forget about these letters I've been writing to you. I have actually been able to forget about the past. But as I come to the familiar lines on this paper, I once again am reminded.

I wonder what would have happened had I never encountered you. Where would I be? Would I be at this point now in my life?

Would I have ever met Genevie?

I can never go back and change the past. No matter how many letters I write, Amy. No matter how many times I try to say I'm sorry. But for the first time, I'm wondering if this was all in God's plan. I've despised people mouthing that phrase in the midst of tragedy. But maybe—maybe God can work miracles— even out of horrible mistakes.

Sheridan

Fourteen

AN HOUR BEFORE MIDNIGHT on Christmas Eve, in a hard pew of a warm church full of more than a thousand people, I found myself far away in another time and another place. I imagined what it must have been like for Joseph and Mary, two familiar characters who took on a whole new meaning when I actually thought of them as real people. As the pastor spoke, I imagined their joy at the birth of their baby. Their wonder at all the events that went with his birth—with perhaps some anxiety over what was to come.

I thought of my special evening with Genevie and wondered if I could give up something so dear to me for the sake of someone else. But wasn't this what Christ did? Didn't he step down from the glory of heaven to live on earth as a simple and mortal man? Didn't he walk away from God's beauty and adoration to save sinners he had every right *not* to save?

Would I have done something even remotely similar? Of course I wouldn't have.

Why did you, Lord? Why did you come? Why would you allow yourself to be away from the magnificence of your home to be put to death by a bunch of uncaring, unknowing mortals?

The birth was truly a miracle—not just because Mary was a virgin,

but because Jesus actually came. He had every right not to come, but he
did—for a world that still had no clue who he was.

*Do they have a clue even now, Lord? Do I have any clue? Will I ever possibly be-
gin to understand the sacrifice you made in coming here to save us?*

During the final song and prayer of the service, I felt a love toward the
Lord that I had not felt in years. Perhaps in a decade.

Would I ever be able to really feel the love I knew he had toward me?

⚜

Genevie stood at the front door of my parents' house, smiling nervously.
An hour earlier I had picked her up on campus, and we had driven to the
suburbs.

I raised my eyebrows and returned her gesture of slight alarm. "It'll
be fine. They're pretty harmless, you know."

The door opened on my mother and all her typical radiance, who
folded me in a warm hug.

"Mom, this is Genevie Liu."

"Well, hello, Genevie. It's certainly a pleasure to meet you. And it's
so good to see Barney again. But who might this be?"

"This is Ralphie, Gen's puppy," I told my mom. "We couldn't exactly
leave him alone all day."

"Sheridan bought him for me as a gift."

"Well, he's certainly cute."

"I'll stick him in my room for today. We brought his crate and everything. He'll be fine. He's *almost* house-trained."

"Sheridan's just joking," Genevie told her.

"I can grab some old blankets for him," my mom said.

"Your house is beautiful," Genevie said as she gave my mother her
leather coat and took off her cap, revealing a waterfall of shiny dark hair.

"Come on in, please. Are you two hungry?"

"No, we just stopped off at Taco Bell a couple of minutes ago."

"Well, that's okay, I guess, because—"

"Mom, I'm kidding."

She looked at me with startled eyes, then registered understanding and
forced a smile. I realized Mom wasn't used to my joking around, at least not

lately. After we took care of Ralphie, leaving him in his crate in a corner of my bedroom with Barney for company and some blankets for warmth, Mom led us through a large hallway toward the kitchen. I had grown accustomed to the surroundings of my home, but Genevie stopped and looked at the photos on the wall.

"Are these of you and your sister?"

"Yeah, that's us. Mom and Dad took a lot of photos of us when we were kids. This is the photo wall. Kinda embarrassing every time someone comes over and sees all of this."

"Is that you?" She pointed at the baby giggling into the camera.

"Yep."

"Look how blond your hair was. And those curls!"

"I think I should dye it back to that color. I always thought it fit me."

"These are great. You were a cute kid."

"Thanks. Yeah, things took a turn for the worse in my junior high years," I joked.

Genevie poked me in the ribs. "And this is your sister, right?"

I nodded.

"She lives in Washington?"

"Yeah," I replied. "She and her husband usually come for Christmas. But she just got pregnant after several miscarriages, and the doctor advised her not to fly. So they weren't able to come this year."

"You get along with her?" Genevie asked.

"Yeah, now that we're apart. When we were young I got on her nerves, but now we're pretty good friends."

"Do you keep in touch with her much?"

"No. Not as much as I should. I'm not good at long-distance relationships."

Genevie looked at me. I suddenly realized what I had said, but I didn't know how to take it back. I just stood there, feeling like a clod. She nodded and walked into the kitchen, deep in thought.

⚓

Christmas at the Blake home is never a simple and small affair. It's more like a month-long marathon full of carols and decorations and shopping and wrapping and candles and cookies and pecan pies and ham and turkey and presents that all culminates in a massive family gathering at our house on Christmas Day. It has been this way for many years—too many to remember the last time it was somewhere else. My parents hire lots of extra help and invite as many people in our family as possible. On this Christmas I knew there might be close to thirty-five people in the sweet-smelling abode where we had just arrived.

Fine for some people, but if anyone were to ask me, I'd tell them I enjoyed smaller gatherings, like the kind we had on Thanksgiving. I always felt like a stranger at one of these family functions—like my family had just written me off as the quiet and artsy musical type and declined to talk to me. It was my fault, to be honest, and I guess years ago I gave up trying to talk over certain louder and more extroverted personalities.

The thing with my parents was that they loved to host an event, but they disliked going somewhere else for one. This is why we stayed at home on Thanksgiving. They loved gathering at their own home so they could control everything—food choices, who came, what games were played, and on and on. Mom could be the perfect hostess, while my father could escape to his study if the company became too overwhelming.

I was sure this year would be more of the same.

Except I had Genevie at my side—and that made everything different.

⚜

Walking into the huge family room, which opened up into the oversized kitchen, I said hello to the usual suspects. Uncle Aaron, whom everyone called Uncle Buck because he looked and acted like John Candy in the movie by that title, was Dad's brother. His tiny wife, Evelyn, still managed to laugh at his jokes. Aaron and Evelyn's twins, Josh and Jim, were a few years younger than me—they were the ones training for the Olympics. Then there was my dad's mother, Grandma K as we all called her, who had been rather senile as long as I had known her and who scared me with her probing sinister stares and with questions like "Who in the blue blazes are you?" Aunt Kate, Dad's older sister, was the mother of Debbie, a tall, blonde cousin two years younger than me, who I always thought could have been a model but instead was a full-time mother of the three kids who were running and whooping through the rooms, dodging around small groups of other family and friends.

Uncle Buck gave me a big bear hug when he ran into me. He smelled like the assorted nuts he had been swiping from the fancy dish in the living room.

"And who's this lovely lady?" he belted out.

"Genevie Liu," she replied with no hint of nervousness. I was amazed. Uncle Buck tended to intimidate people, including me.

"Genevie, what's a pretty woman like yourself doing with this hea then of a boy?"

"Actually, he told me there would be an outstanding Christmas dinner here. I only came for the food."

Uncle Buck laughed as Gen smiled at me. "Good enough reason. That's why I come."

"Genevie is finishing up graduate work at Covenant," I told my uncle.

"That's where we met," she finished.

"That's right, Sher. You're back at college. How's it been, getting used to college life again? Same as before?"

"Not really," I replied, a nervous alarm going off inside me. "It's fine."

"I think it's great that you're finishing up school after everything that happened."

I nodded and smiled, looking for an escape route. "Thanks." Looking at Genevie, I could see the question mark on her face. "We should go see what's in the kitchen. I'm thirsty, aren't you?"

We got away from Uncle Buck for the moment. I had forgotten how many potential dangers there were in one of these family gatherings.

As it turned out, everything would be fine until halfway through dinner.

⚜

After Pearl and some of the extra help finished setting up the glorious display of food, twenty people sat around my parents' large dining-room table, which was extended as far as it could go for this occasion. Another group sat at a table in the kitchen, with a kids' table in the family room. After piling food from the buffet onto our plates, Genevie and I sat close to my parents. In the background, Christmas carols rang throughout the house from speakers that could be found in every room.

I managed to avoid the spotlight of conversation until we reached the end of our meal and plates began looking empty.

"So, Sheridan, how is school going?" Aunt Kate asked me.

"It's going well, thanks."

"So there wasn't any problem with letting you come back?" Uncle Buck asked.

I forced a smile and shook my head. "No problem."

"Well, I think it's splendid for you to finish out college at Covenant," Aunt Kate added.

"I don't think I could've gone back if it were me," my large and thoughtless uncle said.

"Well," I replied, trying to deflect him, "I knew I'd meet Genevie there. I was waiting to finally meet her."

Conversation then shifted onto Genevie, and she enchanted the entire room. She held everyone's attention with her animated and assertive charm, and with her dark features that seemed so out of place amidst my very Anglo-Saxon family. Genevie was so elegant and graceful and poised that I felt like a pauper next to her, like someone she had picked off the street and brought inside and sat down beside to eat dinner with. She made everyone laugh, knew all the right things to say, and probably left everyone thinking the same thing I was telling myself: *What's she doing with me?*

But during dessert and coffee, Gen slipped her hand into mine and grinned at me. "Thanks for inviting me," she whispered.

⚜

I slipped a new CD I had received as a Christmas present from my parents into the car stereo as I drove Gen and myself back to Chicago. In the backseat sat the two dogs—Ralphie in his crate and Barney curled on a blanket. Hopefully, since it was close to ten on Christmas night, Ralphie was comfortable and sleeping. Barney never seemed to have trouble sleeping anywhere.

"So what did you think? Honestly." I asked Gen after we had talked about the long day.

"I had a great time. You parents and relatives are great."

"You didn't care about them asking all those questions about you and your parents and all that stuff?"

"I didn't mind. I can't help the fact that my parents divorced. It was nothing I did. And I'm proud to be Filipino."

"I am proud of you, too. Yet I still don't think Grandma K realized we were dating. She asked me about three times who you were. Of course, she often asks the same thing about me."

Gen laughed and squeezed my hand as I drove. I was getting used to holding her hand.

"I didn't realize your family was so, well, how should I put it—"

"Loaded?" I suggested.

Gen laughed. "Well, to be honest, yes."

"I know. I was the adopted one. They don't love me or give me money."

"Come on," Gen said.

"I'm kidding. I know. I brought Erik home and he flipped out."

"I guess it just never occurred to me that your family was that well-off. I'm sorry to put it that way."

"It's fine," I replied.

"My parents did okay when I was little. I mean, we weren't rich, but there was enough for vacations and stuff. Then, after the divorce, money got really tight. Both my parents are doing a little better now. But I had to pay my own way to Covenant. I'm still paying off my college loans."

"You're going to hate me for this, but I was the exact opposite. My parents paid for me to go to college. They even offered to pay for this final year of college, but I figure a twenty-eight-year-old man ought to pay for his own schooling."

Genevie didn't say anything. I could tell she was looking at me and had something on her mind.

"What?" I asked.

"Then why did you quit between your junior and senior years? I almost had to quit for a semester to work, but I got a scholarship."

Even in the darkness of the car, with a soft melody playing in the background, with Genevie so close and so open and perhaps so ready to hear my story, I hesitated. "I told you, Gen. I had a lot of growing up to do."

"But what was your uncle talking about when he mentioned everything that had happened? Was he talking about the accident? The one you told me about?"

"Yes."

"Do you want to talk about it now?"

"I'd rather not."

"But why?"

"I promise we will, Gen. It's just . . . well, it's Christmas and I'd rather talk about today. And the future."

Gen let out a sigh. "It doesn't matter what happened, Sheridan. You can trust me, okay? I want you to know you can trust me with anything you tell me. It's not going to change anything between us."

I wished I was brave enough to believe her.

DECEMBER 30

Dear Amy,

How can I begin to talk about you to anyone? Where would I start? What would you have me say?

Sheridan

Fifteen

A NEW YEAR APPROACHED, and with it came expectations of change. I wanted and needed to change.

On the morning of December 30, I found myself lying in bed listening to music and thinking about Genevie. I was evaluating my life and I was hopeful about what I saw.

Over the past few months, I had slowly gotten into the habit of praying again. I could utter short, simple prayers. Yet I still felt like I was talking to someone on the other side of a door. God could hear me, and yet I couldn't manage to simply turn the knob and go through to him. Why? Why couldn't I simply step through the doorway and let him see me as I spoke to him?

I suspected that if Christ were to come back to earth and knock on my door at that moment—like I'd seen in that old Sunday school painting—I'd likely peer through the peephole and see him and then refuse to open the door. I'd be like the woman who refuses to have people come into her house simply because it is too messy. My spiritual house was still pretty much in disarray, and I knew that all I could do was lock the door and pretend not to be home.

Let me in, a voice in my heart kept whispering.

But if I did, what would he say? What would he do? I was like the doubting apostle Thomas. I was like the denying apostle Peter.

Do you love me? Sheridan Blake, do you love me?

I feared knowing what the answer would be.

⚜

Drifting in and out of sleep twenty minutes after midnight, I heard a brutal pounding at the door to my apartment. I got out of my bed, assuming it was Erik getting a jump start on his New Year's Eve festivities.

I opened the door and caught a glimpse of a man in a dark, oversized sweatshirt with a hood over his head. In my heart and in the brief second I saw the figure, I knew it had to be Mike Larsen standing in front of me. I say brief because it was just that—a short second of seeing him standing there, of seeing what looked like the high forehead of a balding man, and then of seeing something strike out at me and smash me in the nose.

It was his fist. After the first blow, which sent an amazingly quick stream of blood across my shirt, I fell to the carpeted hallway floor and began howling in pain. I felt another blow to my head, then another to my back, then another to my buttocks.

The beating felt like it lasted an hour, though surely it lasted only a few minutes. Everything happened so quickly that I could not do anything except feel the flashes of pain rush over me in a flood of hysteria. I heard a voice screaming and crying and shouting "Erik!" over and over. The voice sounded familiar and actually came from my own bloodied lips, though to my muddled mind it seemed to emerge from somewhere else. I lay on the floor curled up in a ball with my hands guarding my already beaten face. The punches and kicks still came, over and over. I screamed more and cried and coughed and protected my face and my burning nose.

The kicks slowed, interspersed with a few deep and low curses, and then everything stopped. I lay shivering, waiting for the next blow, but nothing came. Somehow I made it to my hands and knees and began crawling back into the white-tiled entryway of my apartment and then over the thick brown carpet toward the bathroom. I sucked in heaping, pathetic sobs. I eventually made it to the bathroom and leaned my head over the toilet bowl and hung my chin over the side.

Crimson droplets stained the white ceramic.

I fought to stand up. I leaned up against the sink and saw the red splattering trail follow me. Looking into the mirror, I saw a face swollen and bloody and in shock.

I fell back to the floor and stayed until Erik found me half an hour later. As I lay there, Barney wandered blindly over and began to lick my face.

⚜

Ten minutes after Erik arrived, I had to stop him from calling for help.

Erik had already helped clean my face up and walk me to the couch. He hurled questions at me I didn't hear or understand or maybe just didn't want to answer. I fought back tears as he wiped the blood off my eyes and nose. I couldn't smell any liquor on his breath, but then my nose was pretty well out of commission. He had just come back from a party, so I assumed he'd had a few. Thank goodness he was coherent enough to help me.

"Here, put this on that eye. It'll help. Sorry there's nothing better."

It was a cold beer bottle. What an ironic twist—this was what had gotten me into trouble in the first place. Now the cold glass felt soothing against my throbbing head.

"What happened, Sheridan? Who did this to you?"

"It's a long story."

"Didn't take long for you to get beaten to a pulp." Erik cursed. "Who was it? Anyone from school?"

My head felt swollen, and my eyesight kept fading in and out. "It was the same guy who's been calling me and leaving messages."

"That Mike guy?"

"Yeah."

"Are you sure?"

"Yes."

"Who is he, anyway?"

"Erik, not now."

"I gotta call the cops," he said, his hand reaching for the phone.

"No."

"They've got to know about this."

"No, they can't."

"But you know it's this Larsen guy, right?"

"Yes."

"You just got whaled on good, Sheridan. We've gotta do something."

"No, no cops."

"Look, I'll talk to them. It'll be fine."

"No!"

My scream made Erik put the phone down. "Listen, I gotta know what happened here," he said in desperation. "What'd you do to get the guy so mad?"

I didn't say anything. I couldn't. The chilled bottle felt good against my eye.

"Look, I want to help," Erik said. He cursed again, this time louder, as he looked me over. "You really got beat up bad."

"It's okay."

"You have to get to a hospital then. You might have a concussion or something." He paused. "Are you sure I shouldn't call the police?"

"Erik, please."

"You're *positive* it was this Larsen guy?"

"Yeah. I mean, it was so fast, but yeah. It had to be him—"

"Let's at least get you to a hospital, okay? That eye looks pretty bad."

I could only see out of my right eye; my left felt like it had Rocky-itis. *So this is what they mean by getting the tar beaten out of you.*

I finally agreed to go to the hospital. As Erik helped me up, he looked at the bloody mess of my shirt and the entryway floor to our apartment.

"I'm sorry I wasn't here, man," he told me.

"Don't be. This was a long time coming. And I brought it on myself."

Dear Amy,

If I could take on some of the pain I caused you and your family, would I? I wonder about that. I wonder how much I would accept. I guess I don't have such a great track record on stuff like that.

Sheridan

Sixteen

THERE'S AN OVERUSED EXPRESSION, maybe even a cliché, that says you see your life flash before your eyes before you die. I don't know if that happens, and I don't particularly want to find out anytime soon. What I do know is that in the three-, four-, or five-minute span of time that Mike Larsen was whaling on me with fists and boots, giving me a concussion and an almost-broken nose and a blackened and bruised eye, I saw all my twenty-eight years whizzing past.

The next day, after being held at the hospital overnight for observation, I continued to see it all. I saw everything. Just like yesterday. My whole life. Everything I did and didn't want to see.

Erik had stayed with me all night. He didn't have to do that. But this guy I knew only in a male-college-roommate sense had sat by my hospital bed and waited patiently to take me home. I still didn't think I could tell him why this had happened, but I thanked him more times than I probably needed to.

As we drove back home in the early morning of December 31, I watched snowflakes glide and fall and either melt on the windshield or be swept away by the wipers. Almost hypnotized by their quiet rhythm, I wondered what I would say to Genevie.

This was the only thing I cared about. I didn't care about how badly my head hurt or how much my nose throbbed. I didn't care that my back felt like someone had stuck a nail in the center of it. I didn't even care that nothing was going to happen to the man who had done all of this. I only cared that Genevie would see me in this state and rightly demand an explanation.

I could get by telling Erik nothing. Genevie was another story.

Snowflakes continued to fall—each one supposedly different, each one unique in its design and destination. Each one with its own story to tell.

What if I told Genevie my story? What would she say?

When I thought about it, I realized this was a good opportunity to tell her everything—maybe the best opportunity that would come along.

She will understand.

The storm outside seemed to build as we neared our apartment. I didn't want to go back there, but I had nowhere else to go. I couldn't go home. I didn't want to involve my parents in this anymore. They were already involved too much as it was.

God, why did this happen? Just when everything is going so well. What are you trying to tell me?

But I already knew that too, didn't I? Deep down, I knew the answers to the questions I was asking.

I looked at my hands. I held one in the other in silence. It reminded me of another time, another place.

Your life flashes before your eyes.

The snow continued to fall, and I kept wondering what I would tell Genevie. By the time we arrived at the apartment, I knew the words I had to say.

⚓

Actually, there were two words I needed to say to Genevie: *"I'm sorry."*

Genevie looked at me with complete bewilderment when I spoke them. It was a little after six o'clock that night. She faced me on the same couch where we had exchanged Christmas presents and thanked each other with kisses.

"I'm lost," she said. "I don't understand."

"I didn't expect any of this, Gen. None of this at all."

"You didn't expect what? Getting beaten up?"

"No. I mean, I didn't expect that, either, but I mean us. You and I."

"What does that have to do with this?"

"Everything," I said.

"Why can't you just tell me what happened? Who did this to you?"

I looked at my hands again. One in the other, my thumb pressing against the inner edges of my other hand's fingers. "Gen, there are things about me, things you don't know. About my past—"

"I don't know because you won't tell me. Why don't you think I'll understand?"

"Things are—"

"They're what?"

"Complicated."

Gen shook her head. "That's unfair, Sheridan. That's so unfair. I want to know what happened. One day we're talking about New Year's Eve plans, and the next, you show up looking like you stepped into some boxing ring. I don't get it."

"It's ghosts from the past."

She waited for more. She shook her head again in disbelief. "I need a little more than that, Sheridan. 'Ghosts from the past'? What's that supposed to mean?"

"The summer after my junior year—"

"Yes, I know. The accident. What exactly happened?" Gen demanded.

"I was driving. I hit someone."

"Who? What's that have to do with what happened to you yesterday?"

"It was the father."

"The father? The father of whom? Sheridan, what happened?"

I let out a deep breath. I couldn't go on. I couldn't finish the story. I couldn't let her know all of it. "I don't know how to tell you."

"All this time and you still can't tell me? Why not? I don't understand."

"I know. I need to figure out how to tell you."

"Didn't we just have this conversation?"

"Gen—" I reached my hand out toward her.

"No, don't. I don't want you to touch me." Gen stood up.

"Gen, please."

"I can't believe, after all this time, you still can't tell me about what happened."

"It's just—I really messed up, Gen."

"When? Seven years ago? You're still hiding from something that happened *seven years ago?*"

"I'm not hiding."

"You're certainly not moving on."

"Where are you going?"

"Out. Away. I need some air. Some space. Something."

"Gen, please—"

"Please what? Wait around for another month or year till you decide to open up to me if you feel like it? What's that going to take, Sheridan? Huh? Tell me."

"I don't know."

"Yeah, well, I don't know either."

"You don't know about what?"

"About us."

"Come on, Gen."

"No. I think I understand things a little better now. Those years you took off. You were hiding."

"Why are you being this way?"

"Why am *I* being this way?"

"You don't know everything that happened."

"Yeah, I guess I don't," Genevie replied, her narrow eyes distant and cold. "But I know I can't be around a guy—a grown man—who insists on staying stuck in the past. Whatever past that might be."

"It's not easy for me to open up," I said. "This is hard for me."

"Can't you open your eyes and see? This isn't just about you. This involves me too. Or at least it used to."

"What's that mean?"

"I don't think I want to see you anymore, Sheridan."

The words stunned me.

Genevie had the apartment door open and was looking back at me. "I'll figure out what to do with Ralph."

"Please don't go."

"You know, all I've ever wanted from you was honesty," she said to me. "All I've wanted was someone to be straightforward with me. And I've been really patient. And you know, I just don't think it's going to happen."

I wanted to tell Gen that from here on out I planned on being straightforward and honest with her. I *wanted* to tell her the truth. I *wanted* to finally tell her everything.

But the door slammed shut, as it rightfully should have, before I could be brave enough to do a thing.

PART THREE

an unexpected future

JANUARY 10

Dear Amy,

I thought I was moving on. But ever since Gen said she didn't want to see me anymore, I don't know what to think. Of course, it's all my fault; she's right for breaking up with me.

I guess I had more than enough opportunities to tell her everything that happened.

And now I might never get another chance.

Sheridan

Seventeen

"I'LL BE THERE IN FIFTEEN MINUTES," I told the distorted voice of Erik on the other end of the line as I clicked off the phone and went digging for my car keys in the front drawer of my desk.

A cassette tape caught my attention. I picked it up and looked at the case. "Genevie," the label read. Eighteen days after I had given it to her as a Christmas present, seeing the recording simply entitled "Genevie" hit me harder than Mike Larsen's fists and boots had.

I had not listened to the piece since making a duplicate tape for myself. But now, for some reason, I wanted to hear it again, to listen to the melodies I had composed. I wanted to see if it still moved me.

I slipped the cassette into the boom box that sat on top of my dresser, one I often played CDs in as I went to bed. The music began, and I could still remember how good composing it had felt. The melody started out slow and simple, just like our first meeting. I guess the whole composition, which ran about ten minutes long, was a kind of audio memory of my relationship with Genevie. It had a soft piano section in it, another using the Korg programming called Island Flutes, another with the resonance of a full orchestra.

This was one thing I could never understand about my father. Why had he encouraged me to play the piano but had always been dead set against my working with the synthesizer? A keyboard allowed a million sounds to be conjured up. A simple piece like the one I had written for Genevie sounded more interesting simply because of the various instrumentation it used.

I sat on my bed and listened to the song and thought of Genevie again. Her smile, her feistiness, and her sweet touch—all were gone. Once again, I had driven somebody I loved away from me.

"I don't want to see you anymore, Sheridan." Did she really mean this? With each passing day, I was starting to believe it.

As I turned off the stereo and headed outside, I wondered again what Genevie had ever seen in me. I tried to replay the steps from our first meeting in the fine arts auditorium to that first kiss on top of the Sears Tower. For me, she had been a streak of sunlight breaking through a storm-cloud-covered horizon. I should have known that the haze covering my life, covering my secrets, would eventually close in and send that beam of hope away.

Walking outside into another wintry evening, I thought of another good-bye I had uttered to a woman I once loved. It had been a day far removed from this evening, a glorious summer afternoon when the worries of the world shouldn't have mattered. But they *had* mattered. And there had been nothing I could do as she told me our relationship was over.

I made windows of visibility on the Honda's windshield as I scraped off snow with a bare hand. Inside the car, I turned up the CD player as loud as I could. I didn't want to think about what I was doing. The storm brewing inside me echoed the blustery weather outside the car, and both seemed to intensify as each day went by. Everything that had happened beforehand—everything with Genevie, with Christmas, with a thing called hope that was returning to me—had been canceled in a single and violent moment when Mike Larsen came to me.

And that was the way it should be. It had all been too good to be true.

God sent a messenger to give me what I deserved.

Now, besides still carrying around a black eye, I once again felt alone and silent.

I had tried numerous times to contact Genevie. She would not return my calls. Twice I had seen her on campus, surrounded by her friends, and she had walked the other way. I know I deserved this, too, but at the same time it seemed like all I had gained with Gen by my side had quickly slipped away.

Unable to pray, I had grown cynical again. Unable to erase the past and extinguish my guilt, I decided to try to find forgetfulness through an old, familiar habit. As the old saying goes, I was going to drown my sorrows.

I wasn't proud of this. Yet in my snow-cocooned car, the music deafening with its guitar and wailing lead vocal, I knew nobody knew. Nobody except God, the same God who already knew what was in my heart and soul—and apparently had given up on me.

My car slid over the barely paved backstreet of Chicago as I steered it toward Joey O'Douls bar. It had been a long time since I had stepped through the doors of what used to be my favorite college haunt. At one point in my life, I had thought I would never step through its doors again. But earlier this morning, I had mentioned to Erik that I might go to Joey's with him tonight. His stunned reply had consisted of one already known word: "Sure."

The traffic light three blocks down from the bar had always been badly timed, the red light seeming to last forever. As I waited for it to change, my thoughts kept straying back to Genevie and the first time I had seen her. I remembered the way she looked as she sat in front of me, watching a movie while she sneaked a few glances at the guy behind her. Somehow between that night and the new year, I had fallen in love with her. That love had not died.

So what are you doing here, Sheridan?

I had not talked to Genevie in eleven days. Those days and nights not only felt clouded and empty—they felt like a prison, a gulag of pain and guilt. I needed to contact her. I needed to finally be open with her and tell her everything—every single thing I could.

So where are you driving? Where are you going?

I thought of a line from the movie that played during our first meeting— *The Shawshank Redemption*. It was a quote from a letter at the end of the film: "It always comes down to just two choices. Get busy living—or get busy dying."

I knew what choice I had made. What path I had decided to travel down. As I approached the orange glow of the pub, that road seemed completely inviting. I could imagine the jokes, the camaraderie, the cold liquid sliding down my throat, the warm glow that would help me forget. . . .

Isn't that what you've tried doing for the last seven years? a voice asked me. *And where has that gotten you?*

Annoyed, I shook off the voice in my mind. I spotted a parking place and steered toward it. The bar lights beckoned. Then I remembered one of the last things Gen had said to me: *"Can't you open your eyes and see? This isn't just about you. This involves me too. Or at least it used to."*

Thinking of those words again did something to me. Perhaps I understood them for the first time. At any rate, instead of failing like I had countless other times, I did something unexpected.

I turned the car around.

The wheels slipped on the slick street, and the car rolled up to and smacked the curb. For a second the car stopped, waiting. Just like I did. More than anything, I wanted to go into that bar, to sit down with Erik and toss back a beer (or two or three), to laugh and let my life slip back into its comfortable, numbing rut. But this time I couldn't.

"This involves me too."

I just couldn't let her go that easily.

I pressed the gas and headed back to my own street as fast as I could. Minutes later I was standing in the middle of the Chicago side street while thick snowflakes fell around me. I looked up to the heavens and felt the flakes melt against my forehead and cheeks. "Please don't give up on me, Lord. Not yet. I've made it so far, Lord. I don't know what all I have to do. I just—I just don't think I can do it without Gen. Lord, I need her. I know I should have been brave enough with her. I know I should have trusted her. I know I should trust you. Lord, you gave me a second chance. And I'm trying. I know I need to try harder. But, please, Lord, let Gen give me another chance as well."

As I stepped back into my apartment, thankful that I had not entered through the door where Erik and disappointment awaited, I was aware that the Lord still waited on me.

Maybe, just maybe, Gen did too.

Dear Amy,

A year ago, I probably would have given up on Gen, just like I have given up on so many things. But this time I'm not giving up on her. I know she has every right—and reason—to stay clear of me. But if she does walk into my life again—if I have even the slightest bit of a chance—I know what I have to do.

Sheridan

Eighteen

AT THE END OF our one-hour lesson, Nita asked me what was wrong.

"What do you mean?"

"You seem really sad," the young girl said.

"I'm sorry. Things have been busy lately. You're playing very well, though. Have you talked to your parents about possibly finding another teacher?"

"I don't want another teacher."

"You're going to need one. You're getting too good for me."

"You're good too."

I laughed. "Thanks. But sooner or later I won't be able to give lessons anymore. So we should think about getting you started with someone who can really help you."

"Well, I don't think so," she said, then changed the subject. "Play something for me, Mr. Blake."

"Play what? Play this?" I gestured to the Chopin *Etude* lying open in front of us on the piano.

"No. Play one of the pieces you've written."

I shook my head. "Look, I've got to get going soon."

"Please. Just play me anything."

"I don't know—"

"Anything. Please, Mr. Blake?"

If it had been anyone else, I would have told her no and stayed firm on my decision. But Nita was special. This little girl had so much potential, and somehow, in some mysterious way, I had helped her begin to discover it. How could I do anything to discourage her? She wanted her teacher to play one of his songs. So I nervously obliged.

I recalled one of the last pieces I had composed on the keyboard and began to play. Midway through, Nita asked me what it was called.

"Hummingbird," I told her.

It wasn't anything too complicated, just a set of chords that grew into a simple, chromatic melody. But it sounded light and optimistic, hence its title. After a few minutes Nita began touching one key and then another, composing her own part to the song. The simple melody turned into something more moving, more powerful than I ever thought it could be. Nita invented new directions, a new melody, a different beat, a completely different song. I changed directions as she did, and soon we were jamming like a couple of jazz musicians who had played together for years. Occasionally we would land on something that didn't sound particularly correct, but then Nita or I would correct our chords and continue on with the song.

I was the one to stop us.

"That was really great," Nita said. "I liked that song."

"It got a lot better when you started playing."

"But I wouldn't have known where to even begin. You're really, really good, Mr. Blake."

"No, really—"

"I always want to make up pieces but I never know where to start. I can add to a song once I hear it, but I can never make one up myself."

"If you play from your heart, you'll be able to do it," I told Nita as I stood and prepared to leave. "If you keep working hard and don't give up, you can do anything."

"Just like you?"

I smiled into the young girl's eyes and simply nodded.

꙳

That night I dreamed of hummingbirds. Six of them, flying in front of me on a porch as they took turns sipping from a feeder.

I sat in a rocking chair on the porch, swaying back and forth. My hands looked tanned and wrinkled. I opened one hand and looked at it in amazement.

"Play me that song," a familiar voice asked me.

I looked to my right and saw Genevie. She looked . . . older, but more beautiful than I had ever seen her before. The years had been kind to her. Her pleasant and amiable disposition seemed to have blossomed in her sweet smile and her kind eyes.

"What song?" I asked her.

"The one you composed for me our first Christmas."

"Our *first* Christmas?" I asked. "There were more?"

"Stop being silly. Play it for me."

And then I found myself at a piano, softly stroking the keys with an ease I had not felt in years.

Genevie stood behind me and rubbed my back. "I love you," she told me.

"Gen, I need to tell you so much."

"It's okay. Just play for now. Do you remember when you used to close your bedroom door and play the keyboard for hours on end? Do you remember that?"

"I do, but—"

"Remember how you would make a mistake, and then you would just compose new music around the mistake and make it disappear?"

"But how do—"

"Just remember that no matter where life takes you, no matter what you've done, God can turn your mistakes into something beautiful. He can turn your dreams into something better than you ever dared imagine. Look at the two of us."

"But I . . . where are we?"

"Just keep playing."

I knew this was real. At least it felt real. Gen's touch felt warm and genuine. I could smell her next to me. Her words seemed to brush against my ear.

"You know what I always wanted?" she asked.

"What?"

"Someone to grow old with."

"And I'm that person?"

"You can be, Sheridan. You still can be."

Dear Amy,

*Dreams can be funny things. The other night I had one that I awoke from with
a certainty that I would see Gen again. I don't know when that will be, but I
know it has to be before she leaves for California. I won't let her board the plane
without hearing what I have to say.*

*I don't know what she will say to me. Perhaps she won't say anything. But I
know what I need to say to her.*

Sheridan

Nineteen

MY WINTER OF SECLUSION ended with a simple phone call. A simple phone call made late one night in March of my final college semester—the night my life would once again change and I would come face-to-face with the two loves of my life.

"Is this Sheridan?"

"Who's this?" I asked, fearing another phone call from Mike Larsen. Since the beating, I had not heard anything from him.

"Sheridan, this is Mark. Mark Everly. Remember a while ago, a few of us visited your apartment—"

"Yeah, hey," I said quickly, making it clear I wasn't in a chatty catch-up mood.

"Sheridan, something bad has happened."

"What?"

"It's your roommate, Erik. Well, I guess he's still your—"

"What about Erik?" I interrupted. "Where is he?" My mind was still trying to get around the fact that it was Mark calling me. How did he know where Erik was?

"He's in pretty bad shape," Mark said. "Look, I got a call from some-one at the party where he was. They found him passed out in a bedroom and called 911. They rushed him to the hospital."

"He's fine, right?"

"No."

"What did—did you call anyone else? His family?"

"Yes, well, I got in touch with his parents. They're on their way, but it'll take a little while. I'm at the hospital now."

"And Erik—"

"I don't know. They said he went into cardiac arrest."

"From what? How?"

"Like I said, I don't know. Do you know if he was on anything? Taking any sort of drugs?"

"No."

"Are you sure?"

"What hospital are you at?" I demanded, angry at the insinuation.

"Westside Hospital. Know where it is?"

It was the same place Erik had taken me.

"I'm coming down there now. Listen, do you think . . . did they find him in time?"

"We can only pray."

I grabbed my leather coat and rushed outside to the bitter cold night. It was shortly before midnight, and the frigid air felt impossible to inhale. In the shelter of my Honda, I felt numb and chilled. It took the car at least ten minutes to begin warming up.

Though it was March, winter still held its grip over Chicago. Scraps of snow, once beautifully soft and white, remained unmelted and dirty on portions of the ground. I drove down busy side streets and stopped at a red light. Its glow hypnotized me as I realized I was on my way to see one of the only friends I still had, one who had almost died tonight. What would happen to Erik? I didn't know. What had he taken—and why had he taken so much? Was he trying . . .

A car horn behind me made me slam on the gas and go. I was lost on these streets with no names on them. I had nothing to say or think—though the thoughts kept running through my head anyway.

I wasn't there for him.

"This isn't your fault," I told myself out loud, as if my actually saying it would make it true. I hadn't done anything. I hadn't made him go out and party himself into a hospital.

I could have said something. I could have said more.

At least I had turned around on another stormy night instead of falling back into my old habits. But that hadn't really helped Erik at all; if anything, it had made me pull away from him when he needed me. And looking back, I could see that Erik *had* needed me. Ever since the beating I took, he had seemed to blame himself, as if his not being there was the reason I got pummeled. *Did this have anything to do with tonight?*

I should have made more of an effort.

But an effort to do what? To tell Erik what a struggling and wandering Christian I was? Tell him how I confessed to believe in the Bible even though I didn't read it? How I believed that God heard and answered prayers except for those coming from my own mouth?

Stop it.

What would I have been able to say to Erik? What could I have done to prevent this night?

I did as much as I always have. Nothing.

The people on the sidewalks smiled as they walked, probably on their way to bars or clubs. These were people who weren't thinking about life and death and mortality and God and heaven and hell. They were people like Erik, just wanting to have a good time. People like I used to be.

I should have said more to him. I should have been there, at least.

I was terrified that once again I had blown a chance. What did Erik know about me anyway? Had I been an example to him? Had I showed any remote sign that I was living what I believed?

What do you believe, Sheridan?

Well, for a while I thought I had made progress, but that fell apart in a hurry. What if my past and my mistakes stayed with me forever?

Though your sins may be scarlet, I will make them white as snow.

Caught up in my inner dialogue, I wasn't ready to acknowledge the new Voice that had entered the conversation. I continued arguing with myself as I passed a mound of snow that had been scraped to the side of the street. Even in the dim light of streetlights and headlights, it looked dirty and gray.

That's me.

I reached the hospital and found the parking lot. Before getting out of the car, I fired off a message to the other side of that all-too-familiar door. "Please, Lord, help Erik be all right. Help him be okay. And help me, too."

⚜

The nurses wouldn't let anyone except immediate family see Erik. A lot of people, none of whom I knew, were walking around or sitting in the waiting area. I didn't say a word to anyone but remained an outsider, someone with seemingly no ties to anyone there.

Just like I had been with Erik.

I overheard people talking and made out that Erik was in a coma, that his heart had actually stopped at one point because of a combination of drugs he had taken earlier that night. Drugs? What kind of drugs? Had I known about any drugs Erik was on?

I realized that it shouldn't have been a surprise. Had I been that naive? Or so lost in my self-pity that I never noticed my own roommate had worse problems than I did?

I sat in my chair, drinking a cup of noxious hospital coffee, waiting for something. Not knowing what I was waiting for.

An man in his fifties with gray hair and a kind, sad-eyed face came over and sat beside me. "Excuse me. Are you Sheridan Blake?"

I nodded and said nothing.

"Sheridan, I'm Gerald Morrison, Erik's father."

"Hey, look, I'm so sorry about all this."

"I understand you weren't with him."

"No. I'm sorry."

"Don't be. This isn't your fault. Erik's made a lot of bad choices before, and this was obviously one of the worst. We just have to pray that his body will recover from what he's done to it."

I nodded and could feel my face flood with color. I spoke with the man for a while and realized that I was more distraught than he was. He had a strange peace about him. I couldn't figure out how he had it. He mentioned prayer a few more times and something about God's will. The references didn't seem phony or trite. He actually believed in the words he was saying.

After a few minutes, Mr. Morrison stood to return to his family. He thanked me for being there and for being Erik's friend. I nodded and got up and tried to find the nearest place to escape.

I felt like throwing up.

Instead, I found myself wandering into an empty chapel.

Inside the dimly lit room, with the door shut behind me, I sat on a chair that faced a podium with a picture of Christ on the wall behind it. It was one of those pieces of art showing Jesus with a flock of sheep and making him look like a loving friend. It was a painting and nothing more. The real Christ stood beside me, waiting for me to say something. Waiting for my apology. Waiting for me to open my mouth and ask for forgiveness. Waiting for me to come to him.

I've hurt so many people, Lord.

I thought of the horrible night in the summer after my junior year and felt tears in my eyes. I thought my heart had hardened so much that tears were no longer an option. I had not cried since that first night after I woke up and discovered all I had done. So many years without a single tear.

They came now, though. They streamed down my face. I looked at my hands as they gripped each other and saw the tears splashing down on them.

That's what you've been doing for the last ten years. Trying to hold yourself up. Trying to do it on your own. Trying to let your hands solve it all. Thinking that rubbing them together might rub away the sin and the hurt.

I had fooled myself, time and time again. And now everyone had left me—because I had forced them to. Every decent relationship that ever meant anything to me had ended up evaporating—not because of my failures, but because of my unbearable pride, my refusal to trust. So many, including Genevie. Now, I might even have helped Erik kill himself.

I have to change. Please God, help me.

I clasped my wet hands together and prayed out loud. I didn't care if someone came in. I didn't care what I looked like.

"Dear Father, please help me. Please forgive me. I don't know where to begin, but I'm scared. I'm so scared that I can't be forgiven. I'm scared that I was never one of your children to begin with. I know I can't ask for anything but . . . I need to. Please, God, forgive me. Be real to me. Please let these hands somehow be clean."

More tears fell. No one saw them. I hated crying them, but they fell down to the carpeted floor as I prayed. My nose was running now. I could hardly breathe. I kept on crying.

"I abandoned you, Lord. Even recently, I had hope given to me, but then I left you again. My faith is horribly weak, Lord. But I can't do this anymore. I can't live this way. I need to change. I need to change so I don't keep coming up short, wishing I could have done something, knowing I should have done something."

I looked up again, through bleary eyes, at the picture of Christ on the wall. Who knew if that was what he truly looked like, but the picture still felt right to me—a gentle shepherd taking care of his sheep, seeking out the lost ones. That was me. I was not only lost, but had been savagely wounded and left for dead by the cunning enemy. And I was too afraid to cry out for help. Part of me feared that the shepherd would abandon me, too.

Please don't leave me, Lord. Please forgive me and help me to get up.

But he wasn't just a good shepherd, of course. He was a prophet, a priest, and a king. Words I had grown up knowing and listening to but never understanding started running through my mind. He was a loving and giving person who never once turned his back on those in need. He was also the Savior of the earth. The one who gave himself to be crucified. Because of me . . .

Forgive me for hurting you.

For the nails I drove into your hands and your feet.

Forgive me for denying you.

For every single time I decided to do something I knew I shouldn't do. For giving up hope and for forgetting that you died for me.

Forgive me for failing to look at you, Lord.

My tears tasted salty as I remembered Christ's words while on the cross: *"Father, forgive them, for they do not know what they do."*

The very people who put him to death and spit in his face and despised and defied the Son of God—he said this about them. And about me.

I remembered a young boy who didn't know much about the world and about growing up and failing and forgetting. The young boy saw the world as a large and unknown and exciting place. And he put his heart and his soul into Christ's hands. He asked for forgiveness, for comfort, and he knew it could come. He believed with all his heart in Christ, the Son of God. That boy had accepted Christ on a long soul-searching night that ended with a simple prayer. Now so many years later, that same boy, grown older, was praying again: "Father, forgive me for all my many sins. I know you are my Lord and Savior, and I ask that you change me."

It had taken so long to utter such a simple, sweet prayer again. I thank God that he waited.

And that he heard me.

Somehow, for the first time in many years, I knew he had.

I exited the chapel, unsure of how long I had been sitting inside praying. It was late at night, and my head felt like it was bobbing on top of water. I went to check on Erik and, as I walked toward the waiting area, I caught sight of Genevie. She was looking at me with a hurting smile that in some mystical way seemed to resemble the portrait of Christ in the hospital chapel. She looked like a beautiful, dark-eyed angel.

"Sheridan, I'm so sorry—," she began as she stood up and let me come to her.

I buried myself in her arms.

Dear Amy,

I thank God for not giving up on me. He hasn't—as I'm sure you know. I only hope that others haven't given up on me as well.

Sheridan

Twenty

"I NEED TO TELL YOU what happened after my junior year of college," I said as I held a cup of coffee in my hands and looked into the rich chocolate eyes I hadn't seen in over two months.

"It's late, Sheridan. You don't have to do that now. It's okay."

"No, I need to. Now might not be the best time. I just—I don't know when I'll see you again. And you need to know this."

It was close to one in the morning. We had said little except for Genevie's explanation of hearing the news about Erik from a girl on her dorm floor who had been at the party. She had come immediately to the hospital. I hadn't asked her why, nor had I tried to explain my red and tear-filled eyes. I simply led her to the dimly lit and mostly empty cafeteria, where I knew I would tell her everything. Even if it didn't change anything between us, my explanation was long overdue.

"I've gone for seven years trying to keep this from as many people as possible, including God. I know I should have told you all about this a long time ago. Now there's nothing left for me to lose. I already feel like I've lost everything."

"Sheridan—"

"No, please, just hear me out, okay? Then say whatever you like, make whatever judgment you need to."

She nodded and let me continue. I was unsure how to begin.

"I've told you I was different in college, that I made some mistakes. That seems to put it way too lightly. I made *a lot* of mistakes leading up to my senior year of college. That summer—what happened that summer could never be called simply a mistake."

Genevie sat across from me, listening, not moving at all, her dark eyes solemn.

"I had a best friend named Chad. We had pretty much done everything together for three years. We were roommates our sophomore and junior years at Covenant, and we were going to get an apartment our senior year. That summer, both of us were bums who basically did nothing. Chad was living downtown with some older guys who had just graduated, and I spent a lot of time with them, doing nothing really except getting drunk and wasting my time away.

"One night, some weekday night when nothing was happening, Chad and I decided to drive to a local bar and play some pool and darts and have a few drinks. Nothing unusual. I think we went there around eight, which for us was pretty early. I remember playing darts for a couple of hours and talking with Chad and drinking a lot. And I mean a *lot*. My tolerance for booze back then was insane, Gen. I drank every day, and I usually got drunk every day too, and it took a lot of stuff to get me there. So this wasn't anything abnormal—this was my life back then. I'm not proud of it, but that's the way it was.

"Anyway, the place we went to was maybe fifteen or twenty minutes across town. As usual, I had driven us there. By the time we were leaving, I could barely stand. Chad ended up disappearing with some lady friend he had just met. I guess this ticked me off, since I promptly got in the car and sped off. I didn't think anything of driving home drunk—I'd done it hundreds of times before."

Gen looked at me with no expression, with no surprise or concern. She waited for more of the story.

"I told you there was an accident. You probably see this coming, don't you? Driving my car at maybe eleven or twelve at night—not extremely late for Chicago. I don't exactly remember the car ride, but I remember bits and pieces, like a dream you wake up from the next day with only flashes of recollection. All I know for sure is that I left the bar angry and plastered, and the next thing I remember I was in the hospital and someone else was dead."

I breathed in and took a sip of coffee, not quite believing I had said it. Then I continued.

"They told me after I woke up. I had a broken leg, and my face and arms were gashed up a bit. You know how they say someone has 'minor cuts and bruises'? That was me. I hadn't been wearing a seat belt. Yet I wasn't hurt that badly. My hands—my hands made it out in perfect shape. The only thing I ever really cared about—my hands.

"The other driver never had a chance."

Gen's beautiful eyes teared up when I said that, yet she said nothing. Not a word.

"What I had done—what it turned out I had done—was drive my car into another car at an intersection where she had a green light and I didn't. She was turning, and I just plowed through her. That's what they told me, anyway. I still don't remember anything about the accident. It was like one minute I got into the car and the next minute I was in the hospital and my entire life was over. I was still drunk too. I had to hear all this news and face my parents and many others all *while I was still drunk*. The other driver—a girl who wasn't even twenty—lasted until she got to the hospital."

"What was her name?"

"Amy. Amy Larsen."

"I'm so sorry, Sheridan." Gen held my hand. "It was a horrible accident."

I shook my head. "Don't you see? It wasn't an accident at all. It might as well have been murder. I got drunk and went out driving and someone ended up dead. That someone should have been me."

"It wasn't your—," she began, and apparently thought better of it. But I knew what she had been about to say.

"It was *all* my fault. I drove. *I* was the one who came up with the idea to go in the first place. It was *my* car. Everything about it was *my fault.*"

Her face never changed expression. "What happened? Were you arrested?"

"Yes. That's the worst part about the whole thing, I think. I was charged with reckless homicide. But because of my parents' money and clout and the expensive lawyer they got me, we managed to get the charge reduced. I had this spotless record, you see. I mean, a child prodigy gifted with playing the piano could never be put into jail, could he? It was horrible, the whole thing. It was almost like my lawyer made me into some hero who had had one mishap happen to him."

"So you never went to jail?"

"No. Just counseling for several years. Lost my license for about five. I was on probation for three years. Had a probation officer. But none of that felt like justice. I still feel guilty."

"But that was so long ago."

"I should have faced a family who lost their one and only daughter, a family who was already torn apart and only needed me to further mess up their lives. But I couldn't face them. I once wrote them a letter apologizing, asking if I could see them, but they sent it back to me. So I just went on with my life. I never even tried contacting them again.

"Remember the beating? Remember those bruises on my face from the fight I couldn't tell you about? This is why, Gen. I couldn't say anything because they came from Amy Larsen's father. After all this time, he tracked me down. And he had every right to do it. He has a right to beat me up again."

"Why didn't you tell me about all of this? Why didn't you tell me early on?"

I let out a cynical chuckle. "I didn't know how to tell you, Gen. I didn't know where to begin."

"Then why here, why now? Why after all this time?"

I ran my fingers through my hair, wondering briefly what I must look like. Probably bloodshot eyes, a runny nose, an unshaven beard, messed-up hair, pale and scarred skin, body too lean. Whatever could Gen be seeing?

"I kept telling myself that I would tell you, that you would understand. But after Mike Larsen beat me up—that made everything seem like it all happened yesterday. All my hope sort of flew away when I was lying there getting the tar beat out of me. I thought of you and about all the baggage I was bringing into this relationship and decided I couldn't do it. I didn't dare do this to you. Not when you were moving so soon and not after things were going so well with us."

"So why did you do it now?" Gen repeated, not in an angry tone but in more of a bewildered, curious voice.

"Because of Erik. I never told him, either. I kept telling myself that eventually I would tell him, that I would try to shed some insight on what had happened and maybe help him see where he might be heading. But I had no insight. I had made a huge, horrible mistake and yet could not admit it to anyone or ask anyone's forgiveness. So I was stuck with my secret, and now look what's happened." I paused for a second. "I'm sorry, Gen. For everything."

She just kept looking at me, her face impossible to read. "I guess I still don't understand why you thought you couldn't tell me."

"But don't you see?" I said. "It changes everything."

"How?"

I stared at her, not believing the words she said. "What do you mean?"

"How does this change anything? You're still the same guy I met in that theater that one night, right? The same one who got to know me and took me out and allowed me to have a wonderful night on top of the Sears Tower and who wrote me that incredible song."

"I'm also someone who did this—this horrible *thing* I can never take back. For years I've kept it stored away. I've been afraid to talk about it with anyone—even those who know what happened. The one and only love of my life—the girl I thought I was going to marry—left me because of this. And she loved me! How could I expect any different from someone like you—"

"I would hope you think a little better of me than that," Gen replied sharply. "I just wish you could have trusted me enough to tell me all of this months ago. It wouldn't have changed anything, except maybe allowing me to understand you a little better."

I couldn't believe the words I was hearing. I thought of the many so-called Christian friends I had known during college, the ones who I never heard from after the accident. I thought of my serious girlfriend back then, who had always done the right thing. Was leaving me the right thing, too? She could never be with someone like me—we had both known this. How could I expect to be with someone like Gen?

"I don't deserve you, Gen."

"I'm really getting tired of your saying things like that!" she snapped. "Please, just stop it. It's not a matter of deserving anybody."

I didn't really know how to answer that, so I didn't try. Instead, I made a stab at telling her what had happened to me back in the chapel. "The thing is, I've been afraid of asking for God's forgiveness. Afraid of thinking it could actually come."

"All you have to do is ask."

"I have. I just don't know if I deserve it."

Gen took my hand. "None of us *deserves* anything God gives us. But he's already given us so much. He gave us life, Sheridan. That time in fourth grade, the time you surrendered your life to him—you didn't *deserve* to be saved, but you were. And nothing can take that away from you."

"I haven't been what you'd call a Christian role model, especially not the last eight years or so."

"But don't you see? You've been given another chance. God gives us so many chances after we fail him—that is what forgiveness means. All that stuff we read in the Bible and hear in church about how our sins are washed away? I believe it's true. I wouldn't have any hope at all if I didn't."

"But how can you be taking all this so calmly? How can you be acting so—"

"So what?"

"So . . . loving?"

Gen squeezed my hand. "Because I do love you, Sheridan. In the short time I've gotten to know you, I believe I've come to love you in a way I can't fully understand—it's like a gift I've been given. You've got so much tenderness in you, and you're a lot stronger than you think. You might not think you've changed, but I think in many ways you're nothing like the guy you were when that accident happened."

"I've had a hard time moving on. It's like—I don't know how to describe it. It's like I've been stuck for a long time."

"Then get unstuck. Sheridan, I know I could never understand the pain you've gone through, and the guilt. But you *have* to look forward. You're different than you used to be. I know you are. I can sense it. God's still working with you, just like he's working with all of us. And I believe that God can use anything—even a horrible accident—for his glory."

"I just feel so—so messed up," I said. "My roommate might die to-night, you know. Everyone around me always ends up leaving me, and for good reason."

"Sheridan," she said, "look at me. Please."

I looked at her, unsure of what she was getting at.

"Look at me," she repeated. "I'm still here. Can't you see?"

I saw, but I still couldn't keep myself from asking, "But for how long?"

A slight smile tugged at the corner of her mouth, and she gave me the look of someone who was being patient with a stubborn small child. "Well, who knows, Sheridan. I just might end up leaving you. But guess what—God will never leave you. He is the one definite. He never leaves us. Never."

"I left him. Years ago I ran away."

"But he stayed with you. You're one of his children. He wasn't going to let you go. You tried running away, but bit by bit he's been drawing you back to him."

I knew she was right. I guess part of me had known it all along. But I wasn't quite ready to talk about it, so I changed the subject. "What can I possibly say to Erik?"

"Just be there for him when he wakes up. Be a friend, like he was a friend to you after you were beaten up. The words will come in time. You don't have to go out and try to save the world. Maybe all you need to do is show some love to a guy you can probably easily identify with."

I nodded. I couldn't believe that Gen was sitting there, across from me, after what I had put her through. "So where does that leave us?" I asked Genevie.

"I don't know."

"Gen, I love you."

"I know, Sheridan. But it's not that simple. Even tonight—this isn't enough."

"What do you mean?"

"Just admitting what you did doesn't change things. Self-pity and guilt don't equal repentance. You *have* to move on—not just for me, but for you. You have to deal with the consequences of what happened. There are things you have to do."

"What?" I asked, unsure where she was going with this.

"I can't tell you that, Sheridan. I just know that I can't be with someone who's all hung up on the past and refuses to do anything about it. It's not that I don't love you. I just can't live that way."

"I'm going to try."

"Then start tonight. Start by being there for Erik and being his friend. Tell him the things he needs to know. Open up to him. The rest of it will come to you in time."

"I can't believe you're here, being so kind to me—"

"Believe it," Gen interrupted. "Look, it's going to be a long night for you. I think it might be best for me to go."

I nodded, not wanting her to go. "Could we see each other tomorrow?" I asked. "Or maybe sometime this week?"

"Maybe. Why don't you call sometime?"

"You'll answer the phone this time?"

She grinned and nodded. We stood, and I hugged her again, this time a longer hug, a more hope-filled one. She smelled like strawberries, and I found myself wishing that spring could be upon us already.

Then I remembered: *She will be leaving in the spring.* "Thank you, Gen."

"Let me know if anything happens to Erik."

"I will. And I'll call you—"

"No," Gen interrupted, then paused and smiled. "I'll call you. I promise."

I nodded and walked her out to the opening glass doors of the hospital. Then I stood watching her tall figure disappear into the early morning darkness of a city over which she had cast such a huge light.

MARCH 12

Dear Amy,

I told Gen what happened and couldn't believe the compassion in her heart, the acceptance. I still can't believe it! It boggles my mind that my heavenly Father would allow someone like her to come into my life—that he would not only forgive me, but continue to bless me. But that's what's happening.

I don't know what the future holds. All I know is that I somehow found my way back into the arms of a heavenly Father who hadn't forgotten about me. I was the one who had forgotten about him. I don't know what he has planned for me. But I don't want to fail him again.

What that means right now is that I have some work to do. I have to try and face the past—to attempt to make amends for what I did to so many people.

For what I did to your family.

For what I did to you.

Sheridan

Twenty-one

I TRIED TO MAKE out the directions I had scribbled down an hour earlier after looking up the address on the Internet. I drove through the suburb of Palos Heights, trying to find the right street. Vangelis played on the car stereo, a soothing piece of background music I appreciated. Soon I found Lexington Street and turned onto it, driving slowly.

I reflected on the past month and a half. It's amazing how easily the blanket of despair can be lifted from your life. I had been walking around afraid to confess my mistakes and failures to anyone, especially to God, and then found myself opening up and receiving something I never really expected—forgiveness and hope.

Forgiveness and *hope*. Two words that sound good on my tongue.

It was a second beginning of sorts. I had started to change earlier in the fall, in part with the help of Genevie. But this time I was on my own. I was finally moving ahead on purpose, trying to make peace with my past while moving toward my future. For the first time in many years, I wasn't afraid.

It didn't hurt, of course, that April had finally arrived. That, in itself was a source of hope. I think sometimes that the only reason I can endure Chicagoland is that the springs are so glorious. I've always loved the spring, when the snow finally melts away and the grass turns green and the trees and flowers begin to bloom and the sky opens up in a panorama of azure beauty. When we finally remember what it's like not to trudge outdoors bundled up in sweaters and gloves, only to scrape away the icy covering that had encased our cars overnight. When we could walk outside in short sleeves and open the car's sunroof and drive down the road breathing the air and feeling new. Whole again. Like things were beginning all over again.

For me, that spring, that's exactly what was happening.

For one thing, the news about Erik was good; he'd suffered no lasting damage from his overdose. The doctor had confirmed that the mixture of drugs in his body had included something called paramethoxyamphetamine, or PMA, which is sometimes passed off as the popular hallucinogen known as MDMA or "ecstasy." This is why Erik had ended up in convulsions and almost died. He admitted that he had taken ecstasy before and thought it was fun and harmless. But the PMA he ingested at the party had been far from harmless. Erik was lucky to be alive.

When the doctors released him from the hospital, I had driven him back to our apartment—he had insisted that it be me and not his parents. The silence in the car provided a welcome blanket for my roommate's cold emptiness. I didn't say anything to him about my own story—not then. I would find the time for that later. I also wanted to be his friend, the same kind he had been to me.

All I had told him was one thing: "You've got a lot of people who care about you." I'm not sure if those words meant anything to him, but they were the sort I wish I had heard many years ago, after the accident, when I had felt so alone.

The house I was looking for on Lexington Street was not large, but it seemed to loom high above me as I pulled up to the curb in front of it. The walk toward the front door felt prolonged and eerie. I seemed to face the door for ten minutes after pressing the doorbell, which I could hear sounding deep within the house. Each second that passed felt like a second closer to my turning around and sprinting back down the walk to my waiting car. But finally the oak door opened, and a face I had tried to imagine for many years appeared behind the screen door.

"Yes?" the woman asked. She was in her fifties, with black curly hair. She obviously was not ready for company.

"Uh. Mrs. Larsen?"

"Yes."

"Is your husband at home?"

"He no longer lives here. We are divorced."

"Oh." I remembered he had told me that.

"May I help you?" she asked through the screen door.

"I'm Sheridan Blake."

She stared at me, and her mouth slightly opened.

"I wanted to come by and talk—"

"Talk about what?" she asked, her formerly pleasant face turning cold and losing all of its color.

"I know I can never begin to tell you how sorry I am."

"Please leave."

"Mrs. Larsen, I just want a few minutes. Please."

"*You* want a few minutes. I don't think you should be asking for anything."

"I want you to know how sorry I am. I know I can't understand—"

"No, you can't. You won't ever understand a thing."

"I know I can't. I should have come and done this years ago. I've been afraid to face you and your former husband. I've been a coward—"

"You were a coward to hide behind a lawyer all those years ago. You should have gone to jail."

"I can't argue with that. But all I can do now is ask for your forgiveness."

The woman's eyes narrowed, and I could tell she was clenching her jaw. "I can give you something," she spat. She shut the door.

I thought that was it, that she was through talking with me and that I had done as much as I could. But a moment later, the door opened again. She opened the screen door and handed me a three-by-five snapshot.

"That's the last picture ever taken of Amy. I have made duplicates so others can see what an insufferable, drunken fool can do in a second. I want you to take it. I want you to look at this every day for the rest of your life and know that you *killed* this beautiful girl. I want you to know the pain you've caused her family, pain you can't begin to *ever* understand."

"I'm sorry——" I began, tears clouding my guilty eyes.

"Just because you're sorry doesn't mean you're not guilty. I will never forgive you. Never."

This time the oak door slammed shut, and I was left there on the doorstep, holding the picture in my hand. It was the same picture I had cut out of a newspaper years ago, the same shot I had seen every day since the accident.

I turned around and walked back to my car, wishing this could have turned out differently, but knowing life doesn't always work like that. I walked past a row of maple trees that seemed to stand at attention like soldiers do right before they aim rifles at you and shoot.

I wanted to feel sorry for myself. But instead, I simply felt sorry. Nothing I could do would ever bring Amy back to her mom. And regardless of how many words I wanted to express to her, and how many words I dearly wanted to hear expressed back to me, I knew she had every right to say and do what she had. She could have spit on me, and I would have deserved it. But at least I had done what I needed to do.

I prayed a simple prayer as I started my Honda and began to drive away. "Lord, please let me find Mike Larsen now. Let me find the words to say to him. And please be with this woman I hurt so badly. Help her, if she doesn't know you, to find her way into your healing arms. Show her hope, the same way you showed it to me."

⚜

I could see her alone at a table, reading a textbook while sipping a cup of coffee. The café area in the Barnes & Noble felt unusually empty this evening. I stepped next to her and made a loud enough shuffle to not surprise her. "Excuse me. Is this seat taken?"

Gen looked up at me, her dark hair neat in its ponytail, and smiled. "I think that table over there looks fine."

"I'd actually like to sit at *this* table. I'm supposed to meet a beautiful woman at this exact table. I'm running a little late."

"Would you settle for little ol' me?"

"Yeah, I think so," I said as I sat down. "You look pretty good to me."

"I didn't know if you were going to come, so I already ordered a latte."

"You need to be taught patience."

"I do?" Gen asked with a laugh, closing her book and taking a sip from her cup. "Who has been harassing me for the last couple of weeks?"

"I'm sorry. I just know that time is winding down and you'll be moving soon."

"I have to finish this paper first before anything else happens."

"Are you sure you have time to—"

"Yes, I do. It's fine."

"Mind?" I asked, pointing to the coffee bar.

She shook her head no, of course not, and I went and ordered a large vanilla latte. I was nervous. It was the first time we had been together in public, except for church, since that conversation in the hospital the night Erik almost died. I had spoken with her numerous times on the phone—though it had taken her a while to call me, and another few days to call again. She had deliberately kept her distance, always being friendly and polite and herself but never seeming to be anything more than a friend. I didn't know where she stood on things—on us—and I didn't want to ask her. Not yet. I found myself content to hear her voice, to express to her things I hadn't managed to tell her before. I was elated to know she still had a place for me in her life, whatever it might be.

This meeting tonight at the bookstore had been her idea.

"So how are you doing?" she asked me when I sat down again. "How did it go?"

"Well . . . I did it. So I guess *that's* good."

She threw me a searching glance. "Are you all right?"

"Yeah," I said, a little surprised to realize it was true.

Genevie knew I had planned to visit the Larsen household, though I had forgotten to tell her about the divorce. Truth is, I had forgotten about it completely. The house was still listed under Mike and Amanda Larsen on the Web site I checked.

"So," she said, "were they there? What did they say?"

"The Larsens separated."

"Oh no."

"Mrs. Larsen was there."

"Did you talk with her?"

"She didn't want to talk."

"Really?" Gen asked.

"Yeah. I guess I really didn't think it'd be easy, not after all this time. But I had hoped for something. I don't know—anything."

"What'd she say?"

"That she held me responsible, that I killed her daughter, that I never got the punishment I deserved. Stuff that I couldn't reply to because I knew she was right. All I could say was 'I'm sorry.'"

Gen reached out and touched my hand. The gesture shocked me into silence. "That was a brave thing you did."

"No. It was just long overdue. On the way home all I could think about was how it will be with her husband. I don't even know where he is. He hasn't called me in a long time."

"I'm sure that once the time comes, it will go well."

She still held my hand and I couldn't help but look at her soft, slender hand in mine. She smiled and half ashamedly took it away. "I'm sorry. I shouldn't have done that," she said.

"No. It was all right. Really."

"No. I shouldn't have—"

"Why?" I asked her.

"I don't want to complicate things."

"How can you complicate things?"

"Sheridan."

"Gen, I need to know something." I couldn't help myself any longer. Seeing her brought back too many memories. Feeling her gentle touch made me need to ask her. "Where do we stand?"

"I honestly don't know."

"My feelings for you haven't changed."

"It's not that easy, Sheridan."

"What do you mean?"

"You know what I mean. It's not that easy."

"Is it because you're moving?" I asked.

"It's more than that. It's going to take me a while to fully trust you."

"But I told you everything."

"I know. It's just—I don't know. Please, let's not talk about that tonight."

I wanted to say more, but I suddenly realized how much I still loved her. I didn't want to pressure her. And for all the time in my life that I had wasted, a simple day or a month or a year didn't mean anything. Not anymore. "Okay," I said simply.

"So, are you coming to the service on Sunday?"

I looked across the table at the dark-skinned beauty smiling gently at me. Sometimes she still took my breath away. "Sure. You know, I'm thinking of asking Erik to come too."

"Think he will?"

"Maybe. I've mentioned it in passing, and I think he might if I give him a little push."

"Is he receptive at all?"

I shrugged. "I'll just tell him to come this one time. He owes me, so he will. It's a good service."

"The Easter service is wonderful. It'll be the last big service I'll attend at my church for a while."

"You're already counting the days until you leave?"

"It's only a couple of weeks."

"That soon, huh?" I was counting the days *and* the hours.

"I still wonder if I made the right decision."

"Gen, come on."

"I do."

"We talked about this. You did. You made the right decision."

"It's just such a big change. I don't know if I'm ready."

"I don't know much, Gen," I said. "I have no idea what's going to happen after I graduate. I got such a late start on my life, and I have no idea what's in the future. And yet the one thing I *do* know is that you're making the right choice. And that I'm not going to give up on us."

"That's two things."

"Well, maybe I know two things then."

"Didn't you once say you weren't good at long-distance relationships?"

"I said that?"

"At your parents' house on Christmas."

"Oh. I guess I did say that. I'm an idiot."

"You were being honest, though."

"I guess I was. But there are a lot of things I haven't been good at that I'm wanting to change. That could be one of them."

"Can it be that easy?"

"What do you mean?"

"Keeping in touch. I'm moving to California, Sheridan. It's a long way from Chicago."

"I know. A big change for Ralphie too. You know, Erik's going to be pretty sad when you leave. He's really attached to that puppy."

"So both of you guys will be in the dumps."

"Yeah, you're right," I said, nodding and holding my hand over my heart. "I'm attached to that little guy too."

Gen shot me a feisty look and then broke it with a laugh I knew I was really going to miss.

APRIL 18

Dear Amy,

The school year draws to a close, and so do my letters. I feel a weight has lifted off my shoulders even as I know I still have so far to go. For years I thought my horrible mistake required my silence. Now I know that silence has been one of my mistakes these past years—that and my fear that God could not forgive me. How could I be so arrogant as to think I was above God's forgiveness? And how could I not forgive myself if God could?

Looking at this stack of letters, I find myself thinking back to that day in the counselor's office a couple of years back. She told me to write letters to you, even if no one ever saw them. I scoffed at the idea, just like I scoffed at every single one of those counseling sessions. I was such a hardheaded, hard-hearted guy back then. I never listened to anything. But I guess I did listen a little. At least, I started writing to you, and I believe this has helped me in many ways. I thank you for that.

Genevie's departure nears, and I wonder how I will say good-bye. For so many years I have feared telling others good-bye, yet I don't fear saying that word to Gen.

That's because I truly believe we're not saying good-bye forever.

Sheridan

Twenty-two

ON EASTER SUNDAY, I sat with Gen on one side and Erik on the other. I would love to describe some memorable and moving service that culminated in an altar call that drove my roommate out of the pew and down the aisle and on his knees before a congregation singing "Just As I Am." I really would love to describe that. But that didn't happen. Nothing like that happened with Erik. At least not that I could see.

God is the only one who can see in our hearts, a voice told me. And he might have been working on Erik even then. I hope he was. I know he was working on someone else, someone who still needed a lot of divine labor. A concrete-encased heart was finally being chiseled at. An iced-over soul was finally beginning to thaw. The change was slow—slower than the coming of spring—but I could feel it coming.

That morning in church, I heard about the same Jesus I had heard about on Christmas Eve. The same Lord and Savior who had ministered to the poor and the prostitutes. The same prophet who had declared himself the Son of God, who would take on all our sins and die on a cross, the same cross I had helped erect. I saw him hanging there, a man of flesh and bone, dying, mocked by strangers, abandoned by his friends. Giving up his most precious gift—life itself—that we could find it.

He did this for you, Sheridan. He died for you.

In the pew, my heart and soul were stirred. Once again I felt the guilt wash over me like a cold engulfing river. But this time, in its wake, I felt the warm, comforting flow of mercy and forgiveness. I realized he had died not only to atone for my horrible crime, an offense in which I helped to kill a young woman I would never know, but also for every other sin I had committed and would commit in the future. And he had not stopped there. It would have all been a hopeless tale if not for the glorious Easter reality: He arose from the dead. He died, was buried, and then came out of the tomb. The images and stories were familiar but they were more than just images and stories—they were the truth.

Growing up, I had never fully lived out this belief. I had held it in my heart but never nurtured it, never acted upon it. It was easy to get lost in the modern world and fall into treating the Easter reality as simply another hope-filled fairy tale, but it was so much more. Now I knew I needed to do more than simply believe what Christ had done. I needed to stake my life on it.

Thank you, Lord, I prayed silently that Easter morning. *Thank you for conquering death—for giving me new life. And new hope.*

I wasn't a new creation. I was a work in progress. But the cross and the empty tomb were more than simple images. These things had happened. They had happened for a purpose.

But was there a purpose in Amy's death? It had to be more than simply bringing me back to you, Lord.

I wondered if I would ever know the answer. Perhaps not in my lifetime. Perhaps I'd have to wait and ask God in heaven. In the meantime, though, I had work to do.

What do you want of me, Lord? What does my future hold?

I held Gen's hand and wondered about us. On my right, out of the corner of my eye, I could see Erik's rigid figure. What did his future hold?

We sang "I Know That My Redeemer Lives." As we got up to leave, I saw an answer to one of my prayers—to one of my questions about what the future held, and what it was all for.

Mike Larsen stood in the middle of the aisle as people passed him, walking out of church. He stood, wanting me to see him, looking uncomfortable in a suit and a thin tie. I didn't hesitate. I started walking toward him.

Gen, right behind me, looked at Mike and then at me.

"Can you give me a few minutes?" I asked her. "I'll be there soon."

"Okay. Are you sure? I won't be long."

I nodded and walked over to face the father of the girl I had killed years ago.

"Well, Blake."

"Mr. Larsen." I didn't understand why he was here. I didn't know what he was going to do. But I knew I had to talk to him.

"Can I . . . uh . . . can we sit?"

I nodded and moved to an empty pew. There were only a few people left in the sanctuary, probably talking about the service and their plans for after church. I examined the slightly overweight, balding man with a profound sadness. Just as his wife had said, I could never comprehend the way I had wrecked this family's life. And I could never expect to be forgiven.

"You gotta know I've been following you," Mike said in his familiar rough voice. "That's why I knew you came here. So I came, too. I got some things I need to tell you. I thought that maybe here you couldn't duck me as easy."

I opened my mouth to say something, but he held up a hand. "I'm not good at this sort of thing. I know what you're probably thinking. But you need to hear me out on a few things. Please. That's all I want."

I nodded.

Mike Larsen took in a breath and looked around, nervous that someone was listening, his hands shaking as he clasped them together. "My daughter became a Christian a year before she was killed. Did you know that?"

"I read it in a paper."

"Yeah. That's all I heard during the funeral. About her being in heaven and all that. And all I knew was that I wanted to kill you and spit in the face of God. If there was a God, how dare he take the life of my little baby. How dare he! Hate was all piled up inside of me. I blamed the whole world for my problems. I blamed you. I think mostly I blamed God."

"I'm sorry—"

"Please . . . Sheridan . . . let me finish. I want to get this out, and I need to get it all out."

Again, I nodded.

"My wife and I never went to church. We never cared about any of that stuff. But a friend of Amy's took her to a youth group, and that did something to her. Changed her. You could see it in her eyes. I remember thinking during the funeral, *Will I ever see my baby again? What if heaven exists? What if I'm still mad at God? Will I be with my little girl? What right do I have to be with her, anyway?*

"I know now that Amy's death served a bigger purpose. I know this. And you need to know this. What you did was wrong. It was a felony that you walked away from. And I'll never feel right about Amy being gone. But about a year ago I found myself totally alone. My wife made me move out. Things weren't all that good between us before, but they really went down the toilet after Amy died. Anyway, I was finally alone, living in Chicago, and all I could think of was to try to find this God Amy had supposedly found. I wanted him. Maybe he even wanted me. I don't know. But last July, I dedicated my life to Christ and asked him to come into my heart and forgive me for my sins.

"I didn't do this because I wanted to see Amy again—even though I do want to. I did it 'cause I knew it was right. And my life has changed. My heart has changed, I should say. Things still need work. And I fail. I failed that time I saw you in Wendy's. I got a temper—I need to work on that. But that'll come in time. All you need to know is that some good came out of all that happened. You need to know this."

I nodded, almost overcome. I already knew that something good had come out of Amy's death, but this I never expected. I wanted to ask him how he could come to me after all this time and why he had beaten me up and if he was even going to mention it. I also wanted to tell him how deeply sorry I was—that I knew I could never give him back the daughter I took from him through a heartless and mindless act, and how I could never repay his kind words. I wanted to say so much. Instead, I simply sat weeping in the pew.

The father of the girl I had killed put a large hand on my shoulder and patted it before standing up. "I got a long ways to go before saying I'm not still mad at you," Mike said to me. "And there's no way I'll ever forget what you did. But if God can forgive a sinner like me—if he can forgive all us sinners who sent him to die for us—well then, I know I can and should forgive you. And I do."

Mike looked at me and forced a smile on his heartbroken face before walking away. I continued to sit there with tears running down my face, words failing me again as they had so often my entire life. But this time I honestly felt it was okay not to say anything, that this was the way Mike Larsen wanted it. His words, his pat on the shoulder, and his smile meant more than *any* number of words I could ever say to him in a million years.

Dear Amy,

My heart feels strong and alive for the first time in years. Maybe it's the beautiful spring that has finally come. More likely, it's the fact that I no longer carry a cache of secrets around with me. I feel lighter about everything. School is almost coming to an end, and so are many other things. But for once I'm not dreading the changes in store for me.

There is so much I need to do after I graduate. First of all, I need to make amends with some of the people I have hurt over the years. I need to repair my stale relationship with my parents. I need to tell my old buddies what has happened.

I might continue to teach piano while I look for a full-time job. And I know I want to continue with my music. What that means, I'm not sure. But I've been writing a lot of music these last few weeks.

I will soon be telling my best student good-bye, though. Her name is Nita. She's ten years old and very talented, and it's time for her to move on to someone who can take her to a new level. But I do think I made a positive impact in her life, and that feels good.

I still can't believe the meeting with your father and the words he said to me. I feel like they were a gift, something he opened and handed over to me, something that changed my life. I know I can never return his gesture and his kindness. But somehow I feel better knowing some good came out of all this pain.

Sheridan

Twenty-three

"HEY, WAIT A SECOND," Erik said.

"What? I have to go," I told my roommate. It was afternoon, and I was planning to pick Genevie up in a few minutes.

"I know. I just—I need to tell you something."

"What?" I didn't want to be rude, especially since Erik had graciously agreed to take the dogs out for me tonight.

"The thing with Mike Larsen. There's something you need to know."

"About what?"

I had recently told people like Genevie and Erik about the meeting with Mike Larsen and how incredible his revelation had been. When I told this to Erik and mentioned to him that nothing had ever been said about the beating I took that night in December, I could tell it bothered him. Now he told me why.

"Sheridan, it wasn't Mike Larsen who beat you up that night."

"What do you mean?" I asked.

"It was someone else—I still don't know who. Someone coming after me. A guy I'd bought drugs from. Things went bad a while back in December, and I refused to give these guys their money. The stuff they gave me was garbage, and I refused to pay for it. Then one night I get home and find you all bloody and black and blue."

"Are you sure? It wasn't Larsen at all?"

"Believe me, I'm sure."

"But I thought I saw him. His face."

"You said he was wearing a hood. Right?"

"Still . . ."

"Man, I'm sorry. That beating you took was meant for me. I paid those guys their money right afterward. I just didn't have any idea how to tell you."

"I would've understood," I told Erik.

"I know. But I don't. They mistook you for me—the guy who did it hadn't ever met me before. Things were really out of control back then. I think that's why things went so bad that one night—the night I almost ODed. I hated hiding that from you."

"It's okay, Erik. I know the feeling of hiding things from others. It wasn't your fault."

"It was."

"You weren't the one punching me," I replied. "Besides, I think in some way God used that to get my attention. He's tried in so many ways over the years. I'm just thankful he finally got through."

"Well, I know you've gotta go, but I'm sorry, man."

"Enough said," I replied. "Now listen, if Barney or Ralphie gets sick, don't call me. Take him to the vet yourself."

Erik laughed. "I can do that. For you."

⚜

Hours later, Genevie summed up the night in three simple words: "This is incredible."

"I told you that someday we would do this," I told her as warm air breezed over us. "I just didn't think it would take so long."

We sat on top of a charter boat named *SeaGar,* looking out at the sweeping night view of the Chicago skyline. It was nine o'clock, and we had perhaps another hour to go before the ship docked. And only one more night before Genevie left for California.

This time we had actually made it to the dock on time. I had opted not to go with one of the larger ships that held hundreds of people. The *SeaGar* was a small but classy ship, featuring a downstairs with two cabins, a galley with a bar and many seats, and an upper deck with cushioned seats encircling a wooden floor. Gen and I were one of five couples on the specially chartered evening voyage. Stirring music piped in as we drifted out over Lake Michigan—one of the pieces played was even by my favorite composer, John Barry.

Dinner consisted of chicken Veronique, wild rice, a spinach salad with walnuts, and an incredibly rich chocolate cheesecake Genevie especially enjoyed. We eventually ended up on the upper deck, looking out toward the city and the sparkling panorama.

"Sort of different from the Sears Tower view," I joked.

"Yeah, but just as beautiful—especially with the lights reflecting on the water," she answered; then she added after a moment or two, "I can't believe I'm leaving this behind."

"What if you told them you'd changed your mind?" I asked her, my smile contagious as I snuggled her up against me, one arm wrapped around her shoulder.

"I can't. I made a commitment. This is what I have to do."

"I know. It's just—it's so hard. Why couldn't I have met you earlier?"

"You weren't looking, right? You were in the suburbs, in your self-imposed exile."

"Good way to describe it. I guess you're right."

"I can be occasionally," Gen said with a smile as she reached down to take my hand.

"So can I ask again where we stand?" I asked, thinking this would be a good time, since Gen rested underneath one of my arms and held my other hand.

Gen let out a chuckle. "Do I really need to tell you?"

"Well, I'm just curious. I mean, tonight—and the last couple of weeks. I know we're friends—"

"Friends? And you think I go out on dinner cruises and cuddle up with *friends?*"

"I'm not sure." I grinned. "You always seemed real cozy with Matt. . . ."

"Stop," Gen said. "Why do you need things to be spelled out so clearly?"

"You were the one who once said you never wanted to see me again."

"At the time, I didn't want to. I didn't understand what you were holding back from me. I thought it had something to do with your old girlfriend."

"What do you mean?"

"Well, you've never mentioned her to me. Never told me about her. I always thought you still had feelings for her. You were going to marry her, right?"

"I thought I was."

"I couldn't figure out why you wouldn't open up with me, and I figured it had something to do with your ex."

"Lydia."

"Would you tell me what happened between you and her?" Gen asked.

"I told you the only reason I ever decided to go to Covenant was because of a girl I liked at the end of my senior year in high school. We were really serious. Lydia was nothing like me except that we both came from rich families. She was sort of like my parents, not really understanding my musical aspirations. She'd laugh when I told her I wanted to be a composer. But she also cared very much for me, and our personalities complimented each other."

"The accident changed things, right?"

I nodded. "It changed everything in my life. I don't know which was worse—having to deal with the family of the girl who died or having to face Lydia. The day after it happened, I knew before I even saw her that Lydia would break up with me."

"But how? Why did she leave you?"

"I had gotten into trouble at the college several other times. Mostly because of my drinking. There wasn't one exact reason why—I guess it had to do with the friends I hung around with and my general lack of motivation. Now that I look back, I think I was confused and frightened of what I was going to do once I graduated. I was angry that I had given up on my dreams. I blamed a lot of other people, but mostly I blamed myself."

"But if Lydia cared for you so much, why didn't she stay with you?"

"I guess I'd let her down too much. I had made so many promises that

I would stop partying. Obviously, I didn't. After Amy's death, I knew I couldn't expect Lydia to stay with me. Even when I told her how much I needed her. She told me I needed to get my life back in order—that I needed help. Actually, she was right. She just didn't stick around to see it happen."

Gen said nothing, but looked out over the water toward the bright Chicago skyline.

"The following year, after I had left school, she ended up dating one of my best friends and getting engaged to him."

"And how did that make you feel, Sheridan?"

"It's funny. When I heard the news, I figured it was another form of punishment from God. I was so wrapped up in self-pity that I couldn't see that Lydia wasn't punishing me at all. She was simply moving on with her life. She didn't deserve to wait years for me to come back around."

"Did she love you?"

"Yes, I know she did at one time."

"And what about you? Did you love her?"

"Good question. I don't know. Maybe if I had loved her, I would have tried harder. I don't know. I've always had this tendency to let down those I love. That is why, when I met you and got to know you, I was afraid to tell you about everything. It's not like I've always been God's gift to women."

"We all make mistakes, Sheridan."

"You could tell me about some of yours," I said with a smile, trying to lighten the conversation.

"I guess my biggest mistake was falling for the wrong guy."

"Well, obviously," I said. "I know that."

"I'm not talking about you, silly. In high school I was serious about a guy. Someone who treated me really badly. I didn't know any better."

"Why was he so bad?"

"He didn't respect women, especially not me. He was outspoken and insulting. He was the jock type, the kind who works out three hours a day and thinks he's God's gift to women."

"What were you doing with him?"

"I was stupid. Like I said, I fell for the wrong guy. He constantly tried to pressure me into having sex with him. I wasn't a Christian then, but still I knew that was a wrong thing for me to do. I eventually broke up with him, fearing his pressuring might result in something else."

"I'm sorry," I told her, my hand rubbing her arm and shoulder as she talked.

"You know, I still think about him from time to time. I still wonder where he is, what he's up to, what he looks like, and all that. Memories don't ever go away, and I believe that some feelings never completely go away either. We just grow older and distance ourselves from childhood loves."

"I wish I felt a little less old and a lot more distant from mine."

She didn't respond, just gazed at me in the dimmed light of the deck. In the semidarkness her eyes were dark, unfathomable. Finally she spoke almost in a whisper. "I think that was one reason I fell in love with you."

"Why?"

"Because you are so different from most of the guys I've known."

"Yeah, I think I'm allergic to fitness clubs," I joked.

"No. That's not what I mean. There's a depth to you, Sheridan. And a kindness. You've showed me sides to you that I thought I'd never see in any man, especially one I was attracted to."

"Was? So that's past tense, right?"

"How about 'one I *am* attracted to.' More now than ever before."

I shifted so I could kiss Genevie on the lips. The boat slowly made its way toward the shoreline, passing by Navy Pier with its crowd of people and music and lights and activity. I felt secluded and safe on the top deck of the boat, still holding Gen in my arms.

"Sheridan."

"What?" I replied.

"Would you ever consider leaving Chicago?"

"I've been here my whole life."

"You can't see yourself leaving?"

"For where?" I joked.

"For somewhere—I don't know—somewhere warmer, maybe. Perhaps on the West Coast, a land of fruits and nuts—"

"Hmm. Let me guess. Maybe somewhere like . . . California?"

"Now, there's a place."

"Gen, come on."

"What? What's wrong with at least asking?"

"Nothing. It's just—that's a pretty big step. I'm not the world's best in dealing with change."

Her shoulders fell just a little, but she kept her smile. "I figured I'd at least ask you once."

"There are so many things I still need to do around here. I'm going to be graduating this month. After that, who knows what's going to happen."

"But you're not bound to Chicago, are you?"

"I don't know. No, guess not. But still . . ."

"What?"

"I just—I just can't picture myself leaving Chicago. This is all I've ever known."

"There are a lot of job opportunities in California, especially for someone with your musical talents. Lots of movies being made. Lots of musicians out there, too."

"California's so far away."

"I never told you this, Sheridan, but for a long time, I prayed to God to bring someone into my life who would change the way I look at the world. Someone who would help me see God's grace in a better light. And he brought that someone."

"Oh, really," I found myself taunting playfully. "So who have you been seeing behind my back?"

She snorted, and the familiar fire was in her eyes. "You know, you don't give yourself credit for anything. You persecute yourself and put yourself down—and sometimes it gets a little tiresome. You know perfectly well I'm talking about you. What happened to those dreams that you used to have—those wild ambitions about music, about making a difference?"

"I changed."

"So don't you think you can change again? God continually changes us. He is always changing me. This last year has been incredible. I've seen how God has worked a miracle in your life by giving you hope again."

"But hopes and dreams are two different things," I replied.

"Are they?"

"Gen, I don't want to say good-bye to you. I want to ask you to wait for me. But there are so many things I still have to do around here. I'm just beginning to start living again."

"I'm in no rush for anything," she said.

"Still, I can't ask you."

"You don't need to ask anything," Gen replied. "It's not entirely up to you, you know."

I laughed and shook my head. "How did I get so lucky as to meet someone like you? to have you come across my path? to have you change my life?"

"I didn't do anything," she replied with sincere modesty.

I looked into the dark eyes that filled me with so much passion and hope. "You let me love you," I said.

Once again, I kissed her softly, forgetting about the boat and the luminescent skyline and the impending farewell. Gen was there by my side, in my arms, and there was nothing more I needed to tell her before I said good-bye.

⚓

The next morning I stood in the airport terminal, wishing for a better place to tell Genevie good-bye, but knowing it wouldn't change anything.

I knew I would forever remember the moment and the way she looked in those final moments. Cascading satin hair the color of midnight caressing her forehead and framing her face and falling down over her back. Long, oval, luscious brown eyes gleaming in the sun that streamed in through the windows. A sad smile. A tall body totally unself-conscious about its beauty and grace and command.

Thank you, Father, for letting me meet her. For letting me be able to tell her good-bye.

She waited for me to say something. I had talked to her about her morning bagel and coffee and about the in-flight movie possibilities and about our cruise the night before and about so many other meaningless things. I could take those words back and expound on how many ways

I loved her, but I would never be able to say anything remotely close to what I truly wanted to say.

"I don't want to leave," Gen eventually said.

"I don't want you to, either."

"If this was one of those Friday night movies, I'd either abandon the trip or you'd get a ticket and come with me."

"I wish it was. I wish we were flying over Africa right now, holding hands, knowing that nothing could ever keep us apart."

"Has this been a dream, Sheridan? Has all this been a temporary resting place before we get on with the rest of our lives?"

"I hope not."

"I don't want to go," Gen said again.

"You have to."

"I know."

"I'm never going to forget about you, Gen. And about the past year." I looked down at her, my arms still around her. "You're so beautiful, you know that?"

"No."

"I remember seeing you in that theater back in the fall. How we spoke briefly and how I couldn't stop thinking about you. I needed a friend so badly at that time. I never expected you'd be that friend. That you'd be so much more."

The loudspeaker had already begun droning out the usual boarding procedures—first-class passengers, people with small children, the very back rows. Now they were calling Genevie's row number.

"I have to go," she said, picking up the soft carrier with Ralphie in it. He would ride under her seat during the long flight.

"I don't know what I'll do without you," I told Gen.

"You'll find your way. You've come this far. I know you'll go further."

"Thank you, Gen."

"I'll be waiting for you, Sheridan Blake," Genevie said, a lost and lone tear sliding down her cheek.

I couldn't believe how easily the words came, how peacefully the sentence came out, how relieved I was to be able to utter it.

"Good-bye, Genevie Liu."

She was walking toward the gate, but she turned around once, smiling at me. It was the same smile she had turned toward a stranger in a movie theater many months ago, the same friendly, compassionate smile that showed just how caring a woman she was.

Then that smile was gone.

MAY 21

Dear Amy,

*T*oday I had my last session with Nita and said my good-byes to her and her family. I told them I would stay in touch, as I plan to do. But even as I played the piano with Nita for one last time, I realized it was time to go. I also realized that it was time to say good-bye to you as well. That is why this will be my final letter to you.

I still can't believe that I'm through with college, that this year has finally come to an end. Part of me never thought I'd make it to that glorious day when I received my college diploma. For so long that day frightened me, because I knew it would propel me into an unknown future. Now I look to the horizon and see all the possibilities awaiting me.

Before I move ahead toward those possibilities, though, I have to do one last thing. Make one final good-bye. It might be the hardest thing I ever do, but I need to do it before I begin to even think of moving on.

Thank you again for all you've meant to me.

Yours in Christ,

Sheridan Blake

Twenty-four

WEEKS AFTER GENEVIE told me good-bye, I could still hear one of the last things she said to me: *"You'll find your way. You've come this far. I know you'll go further."*

I didn't know how far I could go. But seven years to the day after it happened, on the monstrous anniversary of a pain-filled night that forever changed so many lives, I finally made that journey I should have made long ago.

It was a beautiful summer day with a clear canvas of blue sky stretching overhead. I found the site easily and approached it wearing dress slacks and a tie. Sweat ran down my back and neck. I carried a large bouquet of flowers in one hand and a backpack in the other.

Give me peace, Lord. That's all I ask.

I walked up to the grave site and set my backpack down beside the large stone. Fresh flowers had already been brought today. I laid mine down gently beside them and then bent on my knees to face the girl I had helped put into the ground.

Tears blurred my eyes as I wept into my hands. Once again, I felt ashamed and scared and guilty. Everything still felt like it had happened only yesterday.

Forgive me, Lord. Forgive me for not coming here sooner.

I looked down and made out the stone-etched writing:

AMY LARSEN, 1973–1992
A beloved daughter who gave hope to all she knew

Who gave hope to all she knew.

Hope.

The word haunted me. How long had I needed hope? How long had I been looking for it? How could I finally have found it through the death of a girl I killed?

Lord, there was a purpose in this, I prayed. *It wasn't just to change Mike Larsen's life, but to change mine too. And to give us all hope . . .*

For so long, I had run from the Lord. Yet, through a horrible mistake of mine, God had allowed me to come back to him. "Thank you, Lord," I prayed aloud. "Thank you for giving me renewed hope."

I see hope in the arms of a Lord who loved me. Of a Son who died for me. Of a Savior who rose again. For me, and for all.

"Thank you, Lord, for bringing me here," I said. "After all this time."

As I stood looking at the gravestone, something shiny caught my eye. Something was embedded in the dirt. I bent over to pull it up and discovered a little tin with a picture of the Sears Tower on it.

It was the souvenir metal case I had bought Genevie on the night of our first date.

What in the world?

My hands shook as I opened it. It had been outside for a while and was hard to pry apart. Finally the tin crackled open.

Inside lay a piece of folded paper enclosed in a zippered plastic bag. I opened it to discover a letter. Written to me.

My Dearest Sheridan,

I can only pray that this letter finds its way to you soon after graduation. I wish I could have been there by your side. Please know that in a way, I was.

I want you to know, too, that I believe everything that happened these past nine months was for a purpose. God had a purpose in our meeting and in everything that happened between us. Maybe we'll never know exactly what it was all for, but already I can see little inklings of God's plan.

I want to thank you for allowing me to be a part of your life. I know I will never forget getting to know you, witnessing your renewal of faith, discovering the man you really are. I feel that I've only seen the tip of the iceberg, too.

Do you remember what you told me once? You said God could never use someone like you for his glory, not after the mistakes you'd made. But you have to understand, Sheridan—it's not about you. It's about honoring a Lord that saved you. You've been given a very special gift— seeing how God could use your awful mistake to save a man's soul. Now you need to accept that gift and give God the glory for it.

God has plans for you. Know that, Sheridan Blake.

Have you ever heard of something called a watermark? It's one of those subtle marks on stationery that you can't see unless you hold it up to the light. For some reason, I think of that word when I think of you. For so long, you've been running from the light, Sheridan. But now your life has been held up to the light. And the mark that's always been there is now obvious to all who know you.

No matter what you've done, what mistakes you've made, what you can't go back and change, you still belong to Jesus, and he will never abandon you. He's marked you for life, and that mark will never leave you.

I still hold on to the belief that you can and will do so much more. Your life is before you, Sheridan. Don't let it pass before your eyes. Take a leap of faith and make the most out of everything that happened.

I love you. Thank you for letting me love you, and for loving me back.

Love,

Genevie

I stared at the letter to make sure it was real. It was. I read it again and as I did, I could see my hands start shaking.

All this time. This letter had been here all this time.

How did she know I'd come?

I smiled, then broke out into a chuckle.

I folded the letter back up and just stood there wiping tears from my eyes. Astonished, stunned, surprised, overjoyed—I felt all of this and more.

The letter had been the first I'd had from Genevie since her departure. We had talked over the phone numerous times, and Genevie had always seemed like her normal self. She had never pressured me, had never asked what my plans were for the future, had never seemed to want anything more than to reconnect with me and see how I was doing.

Never once had she mentioned this letter waiting for me here. When had she left it?

I slid the letter into my shirt pocket, then picked up the backpack I had brought and opened it. I pulled out a stack of folded letters bound together by a rubber band.

A year's worth of letters, written almost weekly to a girl I had killed.

"I know you've heard these words," I said. "I know the Lord has heard them too. They belong to you now."

I placed them in the small cavity in the earth where I had found the tin. I sprinkled dirt over the letters and then picked up the tin, placing it in my backpack. I needed to return it to its rightful owner.

I looked once more at Amy's tombstone.

"A beloved daughter who gave hope to all she knew."

"Thank you," I said.

I hoped Amy heard my simple words of appreciation as I walked back to my car without turning around.

I believe she did.

JULY 28

Dear Mr. Larsen,

I'm writing to thank you for searching me out and explaining to me what happened in your life. I know I will never be able to earn or deserve your forgiveness, but I thank you for it all the same.

There was so much I wanted to say that morning, but I was so moved by your words I couldn't say a thing. That's why I'm writing to you—to explain a little of what has been happening in my life.

First of all, let me say again how sorry I am about Amy. Writing it down seems so harsh, but I know I must—I am sorry for killing your daughter. I never meant for it to happen, but it did. My actions caused her death, and there is nothing I can do to bring her back or to erase the pain and suffering I've caused you and your family. All I can do is tell you how much I regret what I've done—and thank you for the forgiveness you expressed to me on Easter morning. I know you could only do it because God is with you, and I hope you continue to find peace with him.

As for me, I've finally come to understand that God forgives us for the mistakes we make, regardless of how wretched and wrong they are, as long as we face what we've done and turn back to him. That's what I've been trying to do in the past months. I've accepted his forgiveness, and he has filled me with hope once more. I don't deserve it. I am still so full of failures. But I see this as a new beginning. I wish it hadn't taken me so long to get back on the right track.

You need to know this: God has filled me with a peace I can't understand. He has given me hope that I've never had before. I would say he's given me a second chance, but he's given me so many chances that it's more like he's given me a second life. Now it's up to me to do something with it.

I never thought I would recover from the accident that took your daughter's life. When I finally returned to Covenant College, the memories of what had happened almost overwhelmed me. I decided to write weekly letters to Amy— letters to someone who would never read them. I wasn't even sure why. With the help of God and those letters and a woman I met, I managed to deal with my past. I know there's no way to really make up for what I did, but at last I know some sense of peace.

I once read a poem that said the following: "Mark well this road in life; it can never be traveled again. The imprints you've made are all that remain."

I look back and see very few meaningful imprints that I've made so far. I see a wealth of people who have come and gone in my life, but what do they remember about me? What sort of road did I travel with them?

I can't ever erase the memories. I can never travel down the path of my youth again. But I can move on in the right direction. Perhaps I'm ready to make some imprints of lasting value.

I write this letter in a plane bound for San Francisco and, I hope, for my future. For the first time ever, I feel all packed and ready for life. My dog—his name is Barney—is even on board the plane, probably completely unaware that he's currently flying over the Rocky Mountains. I'm going to a place where one of God's greatest answers to my prayers awaits. She doesn't know I'm coming, so I know I'll surprise her. I know she still loves me and still very much believes in me. I thank God for her.

I can't wait to see what she looks like when I finally get there. Maybe I'll knock at a door and greet her in the doorway at her office. Maybe I'll find her sipping coffee and reading in a bookstore. I savor the very thought of seeing her again.

As far as leaving Chicago behind, I think it's as good a time as any. My parents have seen the change in me in these past few months, and they believe something remarkable has happened. I have told them about my rekindled dreams for my music and how I feel moving will be the beginning of great things to come. My father will never understand these dreams, but I know he has always wanted the *best for me. So has my mom. And they both agree at the best thing going for me is the woman who helped give me back those dreams.*

I'm leaving behind a roommate. Perhaps you can keep him in your prayers. His name is Erik. He didn't graduate——he still has one semester to go. I told him he will be hearing from me. He still remains defiant in his attitude toward God. I figured that since I managed to do a good job writing letters to Amy over this past year, I would keep in contact with Erik. Maybe one of my letters will do some good. I hope so.

Mr. Larsen——your daughter's life did give to many unexpected hope. I know you know this, and I do too. I want you to know that I thank her. I thank her for helping me find my way back to the Lord. I hope I can somehow make some sort of amends for the tragedy that linked us together. I hope for my life to be a testimony to the same Lord who never abandoned me. And I hope that someday I can tell Amy in person how truly grateful I am for all that has happened in my life.

I hope.

Sheridan Blake

THE END

About the Author

Travis Thrasher was born in Knoxville, Tennessee, but spent much of his youth living with his family in Germany, Australia, Florida, New York State, and North Carolina. At an early age he dreamed of being a novelist and started to write fiction.

Travis moved to Illinois during his junior year of high school. He attended Trinity Christian College and graduated with a degree in Communications. For over twelve years, Travis has worked as Author Relations Manager at Tyndale House Publishers, serving as a liaison between the publishing house and Tyndale authors.

After writing eight full-length novels in a period of six years, Travis wrote a simple love story in the vein of Nicholas Sparks. *The Promise Remains* was his first published novel.

Whether writing love stories—like *The Watermark* and *Three Roads Home*—or suspense novels—like the *The Second Thief, Gun Lake, Admission,* or *Blinded*—Travis deals with the themes of second chances and redemption. With each book he writes, he strives to give readers something new and unexpected. His latest novel, *Isolation,* is a supernatural thriller that is his deepest work of fiction yet.

Travis enjoys speaking to crowds on the writing process and publishing industry, as well as encouraging prospective authors to get past their fears and simply write.

He and his family live in the western suburbs of Chicago. To find out more about Travis or his books, visit **www.TravisThrasher.com.**

OTHER TITLES BY TRAVIS THRASHER

THE SECOND THIEF

A suspenseful novel about a man who survives a plane crash and gets a second chance at life. As he runs from his present mistakes, he seeks to make amends for past ones and comes to grips with his own lack of faith.

THREE ROADS HOME

A collection of three novellas dealing with first love and second chances. Brimming with honesty and hope, these stories offer moving portraits of how people can grow in love through the storms of life.

GUN LAKE

The story of five escaped convicts and the people whose paths they cross. Weaving together twists of fate and fast-paced action, *Gun Lake* examines the consequences of sin and asks compelling questions: Where do you turn when there's no hope left? How do you leave past mistakes behind?

ADMISSION

A riveting tale of how buried mistakes can resurface at any time. Jake Rivers has moved on from his college days, but the memories of what he's tried to forget keep surfacing. Someone wants to keep him from discovering what really happened.

BLINDED

A story of one man's very own dark night of the soul. How much of Michael Grey's perfect life will he risk for the seductive smile of a stranger? Alone in New York on a business trip, Michael has a simple conversation and a short phone call that plunge him into a night out of his control.

ISOLATION

A missionary family on furlough moves into a North Carolina lodge. When a winter storm hits, it quickly becomes clear that spiritual warfare isn't just for the mission field. And crises of faith can happen to anyone. *Available 2007*

SKY BLUE

Colin Scott is a frustrated, burnt-out literary agent, tired of the authors he represents and the industry he works in. During a vacation with his wife, a tragedy happens that changes his life forever. *Available 2007*

have you visited
tyndalefiction.com
lately?

Only there can you find:

→ books hot off the press

→ first chapter excerpts

→ inside scoops on your
favorite authors

→ author interviews

→ contests

→ fun facts

→ and much more!

Sign up
for your **free**
newsletter!

Visit us today at: **tyndalefiction.com**

Tyndale fiction does more than entertain.

→ *It touches the heart.*

→ *It stirs the soul.*

→ *It changes lives.*

That's why Tyndale is so committed to being first in fiction!

TYNDALE
FICTION